HEAVY METAL

A GODDESSES RISING NOVEL

Also by Natalie J. Damschroder

Under the Moon

Heavy Metal

A Goddesses Rising Novel

Natalie J. Damschroder

Entangled Publishing, LLC
2614 South Timberline Road
Suite 109
Fort Collins, CO 80525
Visit our website at www.entangledpublishing.com.

Edited by Danielle Poiesz and Kerri-Leigh Grady
Cover design by Liz Pelletier

Ebook ISBN 978-1-62266-889-2
Print ISBN 978-1-62266-890-8

Manufactured in the United States of America

First Edition August 2013

This book is dedicated to my kids and all their cousins, in alphabetical order:

Alex, Austin, Ayden, Caleb, Cole, Dakota, Ella, Ezri, Gracie, Hailey, Hannah, Harley, Haylee, Isis, Jack, Jacob, Jake, Logan, McKenna, Michael, Miller, Ryan, and Tyler

You are all gods and goddesses. Use your power wisely.

CHAPTER ONE

"The Society for Goddess Education and Defense is your go-to resource for learning about your heritage, preparing for the onset of your abilities, and building supportive relationships with your fellow goddesses."

—Sam Remington, *promotional video, Society website*

Riley's sneakers crunched on gravel as she crossed the pitted lot in front of the squat, rundown bar just off a quiet road in Bridgeport, Connecticut. There was no sign over the door to tell her she was in the right place. Even if she was, her information wasn't necessarily reliable. But she'd reached her limit even before her car had been stolen, and now all she wanted was a moment to sit down and decide her next move. What it was would depend on who stood behind the bar when she went inside.

The door creaked when she pushed it open and thudded solidly behind her after she stepped through. She shoved her hands in the pockets of her denim jacket and glanced around. The room was dim, hazy even though smoking had been banned in bars and restaurants years ago. The tables and chairs were mismatched, some wood, some metal frames and vinyl seats, even a few molded plastic. Most were empty at this late hour. Riley had wanted to be here earlier, when it would be more crowded and she could linger unobserved, but the car thing had made that impossible.

She made her way past a couple leaning close over a two-top, ignoring their beers in favor of making kissy-faces. She settled with her back to a corner and studied the other people in the place. Stalling. Postponing the moment when she found Sam Remington, or didn't.

Three guys at the bar shouted at a replay of a European soccer match on the TV over their heads, groaning loudly when the goalkeeper made a diving save. At the other end of the battered expanse of oak, a grizzled old man held up two fingers at the bartender. He added some whiskey to the old guy's glass, and when he spoke, his deep, slightly rough voice reached Riley easily.

"That's your limit, Tedley."

"I can count," the old man groused, but he winked at the bartender and pulled a few crumpled bills from his pocket. A dimple flashed in the bartender's cheek before he turned to deposit the money in the till.

Riley sagged into her chair, her eyelids stinging. She'd found him. Maybe he could help her, maybe not. But for the first time in months—hell, in years—she had a move to make. Half an ounce of control, or at least the illusion of it.

Sam looked a little different from the video she'd watched, oh, fifty-five times on the website for the Society for Goddess Education and Defense. His dark hair was longer, for one. Shaggier. It looked just as silky, though, when he shoved one side behind an ear. And his T-shirt hugged his chest and biceps much more lovingly than the tidy button-down he'd worn in the video. She wouldn't have guessed he was so tall, either. At least six foot four. Her head would probably hit the center of his chest.

She swallowed and glanced away. The image that had flashed through her mind was definitely ill timed. No reason her head would ever have occasion to meet his chest. But if it did…

"What can I get you?"

Riley jerked her head up. In the few seconds she'd been fighting her thoughts, Sam had crossed the bar to her table. Why wasn't there a waitress working so he didn't have to leave the bar? Damn the assholes who'd taken her car and made her get here so late.

The soccer guys called goodbyes over their shoulders, and the couple followed them out. Sam waved and then rested his hands on his hips, waiting for her order. She cleared her throat, the sound loud in the now-quiet bar. The TV was off. Maybe she'd been lost in visualization longer than she'd thought. And there was that chest again, the hollow between his collarbones set off perfectly by the slight V-neck of his gray shirt.

"Uh, Coke, please."

"Pepsi okay?"

"Yes," she said even though she hated Pepsi, just so he'd walk away sooner. She needed time to think, to figure out how to approach him. She hadn't practiced anything before now, afraid to hope a vague Facebook reference could lead her to the right place. Traveling to Connecticut wasn't a big deal, since she'd been on the move for what seemed like forever, but she didn't want to expect too much and be flattened when she wound up in limbo once again.

So while Sam drew her soda from the tap, she tried to come up with an opening gambit. It wasn't easy with her brain so fogged from fatigue. She'd been sleeping in her car as she traveled, not having enough money for a motel anymore. She'd walked a few miles to get to the bar, too, and while she wasn't out of shape, it added to the toll of a stressful day after a very long string of stressful days. And it was well after one in the morning.

She took a deep breath and shook off the haze. She shouldn't lose this opportunity. What if she didn't get it again? So maybe just keep it simple. *Hi. What do you know about goddesses?*

No, that was stupid. She knew what he knew—it was all over the Society website. Brief mentions in news items and meeting agendas and press releases, plus that video about a new educational program, all added up to "this guy is connected." But he wasn't one of them. He couldn't be—he was male. That was the only reason she was here.

Maybe it would be best to blurt it all out. *I need your help. I'm all alone and crazy things are happening all around me, and everything I've been raised to believe has been flipped on its head. Goddesses don't exist, but if that's the truth, then I must be crazy.*

She snorted softly as Sam came around the bar with her soda in his hand. He'd shove her out the door and lock it behind her if that babble came out of her mouth.

He might do that anyway. The clock behind the bar said it was one-thirty, and Tedley shuffled across the uneven floorboards toward the exit. Surely Sam would want to lock up and go home.

"Night, Ted," he called. "See you tomorrow."

The old man waved a hand without looking up from his feet.

Riley straightened, feeling lighter. She didn't have to say anything now that she knew Sam would be here tomorrow. She could come back with a real plan beyond "see if he's there."

And then he was, just a scant couple of feet away. He towered over her, massive but not bulky, evoking a sense of protection rather than threat. A hint of something both warm and exotic drifted through the air. Riley inhaled, but the stronger scents of beer and peanuts made the more personal scent elusive. She suppressed a tiny shudder and tried to smile as he set a tall plastic cup on the table in front of her. Condensation soaked the thin coaster under it in seconds.

"You hungry?" He tossed a paper-wrapped straw beside the cup.

"What? Oh, no, thank you. I'm sure you're ready to close. I'll just drink this and get out of your way."

He shrugged one shoulder. Her attention caught on the play of muscles the movement caused, and her mouth went dry.

"Open till two, so if you want a snack, let me know."

He didn't linger, leaving it completely up to her. Riley's stomach growled, but he was far enough away—hopefully—not to hear it. She poked the straw into the drink and sucked half of it down, both to ease the growlies and to finish fast so she could leave. The man was making it hard to focus on anything but his exquisite form. Maybe she shouldn't come back tomorrow after all.

She hadn't anticipated this attraction, which made the whole thing a little nauseating. *Oh, please help me, Mr. Big Tall Man. I'm a damsel in distress! And want me, too!* It didn't help that he appeared to be about ten years older than her twenty-three. That put too much emphasis on the naïve, helpless girl image for her liking.

She'd just slurped to the bottom of the cup, rethinking her entire plan—such as it was—when the door opened again. Out of habit Riley shrank into the corner and shifted to put her profile to the door.

Sam, who was polishing glasses and setting them on a high shelf, cast her a thoughtful look before offering an easy smile to the newcomers. "Evening, folks. What can I get ya?"

"Three beers."

The small group didn't go to the bar or choose a table on the far side of the room, though they had a ton of privacy-laden options. Instead, they wove their way to a table only two away from hers, spun chairs around to straddle, and sat with deliberate movements. Two of them, one man and one woman, stared at Riley, both sets of eyes narrowed. The other guy went back to the bar to pay for the beers Sam had pulled from a cooler and set on the surface with a *clunk*. The pair sitting near her didn't even look away when their friend returned to the table.

Riley's heart leapt into a sprint, urging her to her feet. She hadn't recognized the man's voice, but something wasn't right. She firmed her jaw, determined not to look like she was running. And even though they'd already seen her face, she couldn't help dipping her head to let her hair fall forward, hiding it until she'd skirted the table next to theirs and reached the bar. Even then, when she dropped a ragged fiver from her pocket onto the battered wood, she couldn't raise her gaze above Sam's ribcage.

She kept her voice low. "Restroom?"

"Back hall."

"Thanks."

She felt Sam watching her until she'd rounded the corner. Some of the fear settled once she was out of sight.

She didn't know how they'd found her again. Hell, she didn't know how she knew they were the people who'd been harassing her, since she'd never seen them before. But after being hounded for months, no matter where she went, it didn't matter—she could *feel* them. Maybe she was wrong and they weren't connected to the phone calls and her lost job and eviction and everything else. They could just be random douche-bags, looking to mess with the only other woman in the place. But their glares had been more menacing than that, and leaving was the smartest move. First for her own safety, but also because causing problems in his establishment might set things off on the wrong foot with Sam.

She bypassed the ladies' room door and hurried through the emergency exit several feet past it. She didn't hesitate, despite the small sign that said an alarm would sound. Places like this didn't actually alarm their back exits. It was too much hassle for the staff who went out there to smoke or take out the trash, for one thing, and for another, there were always people like her coming through.

Once outside, she held her breath against the stink of the Dumpster beside her, a stink competing with old vomit and urine.

At least it was late April and not mid-summer, when heat would render the stench intolerable. Riley looked around to get her bearings in the darkness, longing for the safety of her beat-up old car. The parking lot and street were too open, too far out of the main city. They'd spot her immediately if she went that way on foot.

Back here wasn't much better. The building was separated from some kind of industrial compound by about twenty yards of weedy, empty lot. Powerful ten-story lights shone down on the area behind a high chain-link fence that disappeared into a tangle of underbrush and stunted trees. To her left, small, close-set homes were visible on the other side of a ravine running through the narrow strip of woods. There was more cover there, darkness under the trees. But no metal. Her fingers closed over her mother's pendant, barely enough of a source to make her fingers tingle. That wouldn't be enough to help her if she had to defend herself.

The fence beckoned, shiny and solid, as much as did the shelter of the scant woods and shadowy ravine. Hide or fight?

Hiding had gotten her nowhere. She went right.

She'd barely gained the top of the fence when she heard voices. Panic hit her again, logic fleeing and her will with it. She dropped to the ground and ran, knowing they'd see her movement, maybe hear her footsteps. It had rained earlier and the pavement was wet enough to amplify her footfalls, each one making a little splash.

Riley raced across the blacktop, eyes locked on the giant chutes and pipes looming way too far away. She should have stayed near the fence, but it was too big, would leave her with too little control and trap her more than help. Her breath came evenly, lungs conditioned from months of running, but she was slower than usual. Her heart thundered as she sensed her pursuers closing in on her. They caught up before she'd reached the center of the open area.

Whirling, she dodged the first swing. Her mind raced almost incoherently. They'd never come this close, never tried to hurt her directly. Why now? Why here? She darted between the two men, avoiding their reaching hands. But the woman's foot was too fast. It caught Riley's right ankle, sending her sprawling across the ground. Her palms scraped over the rough surface. She flipped onto her back, feet raised to fend them off, hands up to block her face. The urge to scream bubbled in her chest, but she swallowed it. No one would come either way.

"Don't give us trouble, Kordek." The taller of the men reached down as if to grab her sleeve and pull her up.

She swatted his hand aside and kicked out at his knee. He grunted and moved back a step, giving her enough time to jerk her legs under her and land in a crouch, balanced on the balls of her feet. She put her hands out and waited, trying to keep her breathing even. How did they know her last name?

The woman laughed as the stockier man stepped toward her.

"Come on with—*oof.*" He doubled over when Riley shot upward and drove her head into his groin. He tipped sideways and landed on the ground, his hands cupping the insulted area, barely able to wheeze his pain. The woman laughed again, this time at her partner. Riley scrambled all the way to her feet.

"What do you want with me?" she demanded. They didn't answer, and she backed up. The two not on the ground advanced. Her hands shook until she clenched them, chest heaving. She wasn't equipped for this. She needed metal, something portable to give her strength and hold them off. But they'd be on her before she could get to anything usable.

"Hey!"

The shout came from behind the pair, and they turned.

Riley ran.

• • •

Sam wasn't surprised when the young blonde didn't come back from the restroom. He'd noticed her tension as soon as the latecomers entered the bar. Well, noticed the change in her tension. She hadn't exactly been relaxed before that. She'd been checking him out from her well-chosen spot in the corner, but not in the way women in here usually checked him out, looking to get free drinks or something more carnal. She'd reminded him of the stray cat behind his house, wanting to approach but wary of his response. He'd offered a treat and then backed off, letting her take her time. She'd sucked down that pop so fast it should have been followed by an epic belch. He was sure she was about to leave without talking to him, but then the trio had come in and spooked her in a different way.

Sam kept polishing glasses and putting them on the shelf, watching the men argue with the woman too quietly for him to hear, even in the otherwise empty bar. He grabbed his keys and subtly locked the till. When the group split up, the woman and one of the men went out the front door, their buddy ambling toward the hall where the bathrooms were. Sam didn't hesitate. He ignored the baseball bat the owner kept under the bar—he wouldn't need it—and quickly locked the front door before following the single guy to the back. He took a quick second to check the bathrooms, in case he'd misread the situation and he was just taking a piss before joining his companions, but they were both empty. Sam pushed through the emergency exit and made sure it locked behind him.

His instincts had been dead on. All four people were spotlighted inside the plant's fence, the trio advancing on the lone young woman. Sam took off running along the fence line. Broken branches and trampled grass told him the others had already gone through this way, and sure enough, the rusty gate latch was broken. Sam wondered if they'd scouted the area before coming inside for their beer, or if they'd just gotten lucky. He knew the gate was here because he made a point of always knowing what was around him. Training and experience weren't easily forgotten.

He shoved the gate hard against the vines holding it in place and squeezed through the gap. When he was close enough, he shouted. Two of the attackers turned toward him. The other was curled on the ground, holding his dangly bits.

The woman took off across the compound.

Instead of chasing her, the guy still standing stepped toward Sam and swung. He ducked, then landed an uppercut on the guy's chin. Exhilaration rushed through him as his opponent staggered back. It had been a long, long time since he'd had a good old-fashioned confrontation. He couldn't hold back a quick grin, bouncing on the balls of his feet, hands loosely curled in front of his shoulders.

"That all ya got?" he taunted, hoping to distract the couple long enough for the young woman to get away.

The man launched himself at Sam with a growl, egged on by his partner's laugh. Sam didn't manage to dodge fast enough, and a blow vibrated his skull. He swung again through the pain, and the guy went down on one knee. Sam moved in to shove him flat on his stomach and almost made a fatal mistake—disregarding the woman, especially when her partner was losing.

Light glinted off the canister she swept into position only inches from his eyes. He knew he didn't have time to move or to squeeze them closed, but he tried. Just before his eyelids slammed together, he saw the blonde standing twenty feet away, a length of something shiny in her right hand, her left hand held toward them, palm out. Then there was a *whump*, and a puff of air stirred Sam's hair. The pepper spray he'd been waiting for never hit his eyes.

Raising one hand to block his face, Sam peeked through his fingers. The woman with the spray had disappeared. He spun to look for her and spotted her body lying limp ten feet behind him, sprawled at the foot of the chain-link fence surrounding the property.

"You—" He spun back toward the woman with the pipe just in time to see her heft it and make a pushing motion with her other hand. An invisible wave moved across the distance between her and the attacker now charging toward her. He flew backward and landed with a grunt, rolling over and over until he, too, came up against the fence, clothes twisted around his body.

A bunch of things became clear, and at the same time a million additional questions lined themselves up. The woman was a goddess, metal the source feeding her abilities. But she wasn't one Sam knew, which was odd. He hadn't been involved with the Society for a while, but she seemed like she was in her mid-twenties, and he'd have known if there was someone of that age registered with metal as her source. By the way she'd watched him when she first came into the bar, though, she knew who he was. But he couldn't begin to guess why she was here.

She'd lowered her hand, but even from this far away Sam could tell she was shaking. He walked over to her, keeping half his attention on the people on the ground. "You okay?"

She nodded without looking at him. "Thanks for helping me."

"Want me to call the police?" He slapped his pocket, annoyed to find it empty. He'd left his phone in the office because he was tired of ignoring calls, and even more tired of feeling guilty about it. "Do you have a phone?"

"No." She seemed to say it through gritted teeth. "Let them go. I can't deal with that, too."

"You sure? I can haul them back to the bar and call from there."

She finally met his gaze, her eyes crinkling with faint amusement. "You think so?"

"'Course," he scoffed at her doubt, mainly to hide his own. He only had two hands.

But she shook her head. "Maybe they'll think twice about trying to mug anyone after this."

Sam didn't think it was that simple, and he'd place bets she didn't, either. But it was two o'clock in the morning, and it was her choice.

The guy who'd already been on the ground when Sam arrived groaned and freed his hands from between his legs, struggling to get to his feet. Sam strode over and hauled him up by the shoulder of his jacket.

"Get your friends and get out of here."

He nodded, having to look up so far to see Sam's face that the skin at the back of his neck gathered into folds. When Sam released him, he limped to the other guy and helped him up, then the two scrambled over to the woman and dragged her to her feet. In moments they were gone, their shuffling, heavy gaits fading into the darkness.

The blonde stood next to Sam now, still clutching her pipe. "Where are they going?"

Sam frowned at her. "There's a gate down there. How did you get in?"

"I climbed over the fence."

Of course she did. Sam tilted his head to look at the top of it, sixteen feet up. Impressive.

"My name is Sam," he offered. If he'd guessed right, she already knew that, but he was curious how she'd respond.

She pivoted and faced him. Her shudders had slowed, but she still clutched the pipe as if someone would try to rip it out of her hand. "Riley."

"Are you okay?" he asked again.

She shook herself, snapping into alertness, her eyes focusing. "Yeah. Yes, I'm okay. They didn't hurt me." She winced and looked down at her palms. "Mostly."

Sam moved closer and took her hand in his. She'd scraped it raw. Patches bled and had smeared on the pipe.

"We need to take care of these. Come back into the bar with me."

She tilted her head and eyed the spot above his temple where he'd been hit hardest. It tugged when he shifted his eyebrows. The blow must have split the skin.

"You could use some first aid, yourself," she confirmed. "I'm sorry you got hurt on my behalf."

"You can make it up to me." They started walking toward the gate.

"I can try." She looked him over again, clearly checking for other injuries. "Lose any teeth?"

He ran his tongue over them. "Nope."

"Crack any bones?"

"Only the fingers that hit my hard head."

"Good." She heaved a sigh, and Sam heard a world of weariness in it, something even heavier than the late hour and the altercation warranted. "Thanks for coming out after me." She waited while Sam pushed the partially open gate against the underbrush holding it captive so they could squeeze through. Once he'd closed it and they'd continued on, she resumed talking, "Most bartenders wouldn't."

"I'm not an ordinary bartender." Judging by the way she glanced at him out of the corner of her eye, she caught the understatement. His curiosity rose even more.

A few moments later Sam led her back into the empty bar. She sat at a table while he retrieved a first aid kit, clean cloths, and bowl of water before joining her.

She sat quietly while he cleaned her hands and applied antibiotic ointment and bandages. As soon as he was done, she grabbed another cloth and dabbed at the various cuts and bruises on his face. She winced every time she touched him.

"It's okay. It doesn't hurt that bad," he lied, trying to make her feel better. But her concerned frown deepened.

"I didn't want you to get hurt for me."

"It wasn't up to you."

She seemed about to argue, but closed her mouth and smiled. The soft curve of her lips drew Sam's gaze, and for the first time, he saw her as something as simple as a woman. Her eyes were a deep green in the dim light, her skin creamy, and even after the running and the fear, she smelled of some flower that reminded him of his mother's garden.

And then she said, "You proved yourself a real champion."

Uneasiness curled through him, and Sam sat back. Riley dropped the bloodied cloth into the bowl of water, her expression closing off again.

"I think you'd better tell me why you're here."

Chapter Two

A goddess's support system begins with her family, but bonds of friendship and trust extend that support system into the goddess community. To facilitate these connections, dozens of local chapters of the Society across the country provide opportunities for networking, education, and socialization.

—The Society for Goddess Education and Defense, Quarterly Chapter Schedule

Riley swallowed hard. There'd been an edge in his voice she hadn't heard before. She'd thought calling him a champion was a compliment, but he apparently hadn't taken it that way. Now she had even less of an idea of what to say to him. But he'd asked a direct question, and she only had two choices. Answer him, or leave. And if she left, she would burn this bridge. No second chance—she'd never have the nerve.

"I don't even know where to start," she admitted, letting her bandaged hands fall limply into her lap.

He folded his arms and tilted his chair back on two legs. "How old are you?"

Riley frowned at the odd question, but hey, it was a place to start. "Twenty-three. Almost twenty-four."

"So you've only been a goddess for a couple of years."

The word chilled her, even as it drew a knee-jerk reaction based on years of conditioning. "Goddesses aren't real." She was almost surprised the words didn't come out in her mother's voice. "They're scam artists."

Sam didn't get annoyed or defend them, as she'd expected. He just nodded to acknowledge her statement. "Are you? A scam artist? Did those people pretend to attack you so you could draw me in and then steal from me or something?"

Heat crept up her cheeks. "No."

"So you did channel energy through that metal pipe and blow two people across open space."

How the hell did he make it sound logical instead of ridiculous? "I did."

"Do you know those people? Why are they after you?"

She lifted one shoulder. "I don't know who they are. I never saw them before." She paused, trying to pull together too many details, and Sam spoke before she could elaborate.

"So they're not the reason you're here."

"Not completely. They're part of it, I guess. I just don't know how everything connects." She pressed her fingers against her eyes. Now that the adrenaline was gone, everything was catching up to her again. She longed for a real bed and a soft pillow. With a deep breath, she tried to explain. "My life is kind of messed up. I don't know where this...power comes from. What's true and what's not. What's coincidence and what's—" She waved a hand toward the back of the building, indicated the altercation. "Deliberate. I was hoping you could help me, but I don't even know how. Besides, you know, beating up the bad guys." She twitched her lips, and Sam smiled back, reassuring her that he didn't think she was a nutcase. Not yet.

"Sounds like a long story." He stood and gathered the trash

and first aid supplies to carry behind the bar. "It's after two. Why don't we table this until the morning?"

She let out a short breath. It was going to be okay. "That sounds great." She stood and braced her hands on the rough tabletop as all remaining energy drained out through the soles of her feet and into the floorboards. She'd find somewhere to hunker down for the night—the woods across the road might work—and by the time they met tomorrow she'd have all her thoughts in order and know what to tell him and what she hoped he could tell her.

But Sam was too perceptive. "Do you have a place to stay?"

"Of course." The lie popped out before she weighed pride against practicality. Again, Sam read her too accurately.

"If you help me close up, you can crash at my place. It's a little house with a spare room over the garage," he added before she could even think about protesting. "Then we can talk in the morning."

Riley didn't want to impose that much on him, but she hadn't asked, he'd offered. And a room over a garage sounded like heaven compared to the cold ground. A bed and a pillow popped into her head again, and she could have whimpered. "Okay. Thanks." She almost offered to pay him, but remembered she had no way to do that. Besides, she had a feeling it would just annoy him.

They spent half an hour wiping tabletops, flipping chairs onto tables, and mopping before walking the six blocks to his little—and he wasn't kidding—house, where he left her in the one-room garage apartment with a towel, a T-shirt that would be gigantic on her but probably fit him skin-tight, and a promise of excellent coffee in the morning.

She slept better than she had in months. If she dreamed, she didn't remember. A few times a car passing or some other innocent noise woke her, but without the pulse-pounding anxiety she was used to.

Eventually, the room was light enough and her brain had recovered enough that she couldn't sleep anymore. She yawned and stretched but didn't jump out of bed. Sam had said he usually slept in because of his work schedule, which gave her time to consider how their conversation would go.

He'd already called her a goddess, a label she'd been too afraid to apply even after studying the Society website and checking out some of the Facebook profiles of women who did use the term. Goddesses weren't secret or anything. Some of them seemed to have businesses where they used their abilities in various ways. But it all sounded like psychics selling a bill of goods to the gullible, and Riley didn't know anyone who'd ever met a real one. They weren't connected in any way to her old life.

The Society website had a history section—that's how she knew the little she did. They claimed that the goddesses of ancient times were real, and their abilities—diluted by breeding and resource depletion—had been passed down through maternal lines. There were apparently a few hundred worldwide, about a hundred here in the United States.

So, if she were a goddess, what exactly did that mean?

She pulled herself out of bed. That was as good a place to start as any.

• • •

Sam cursed when his phone went off a little before eight. He refrained from throwing the thing across the room but stuffed it under the pillow he buried his face in. It stopped vibrating in his hand, and he drifted off, body and brain relaxing for only a moment before it went off again.

"Dammit!" He rolled over and glared at the screen. Nick. Of course. Sam had ignored his calls yesterday, so he was punishing him by waking him up too early today. The guy's tenacity was more ferocious than a pit bull's and would only get more aggravating.

He flipped open the phone and put it to his ear. "Yeah, Nick."

"Hey, Sammy."

He hated that name, but he didn't rise to the bait. "What's goin' on?"

"Quinn's finishing up some work in Boston. She said you're nearby, and we thought we'd drop by before we head back to Ohio."

Sam shoved his free hand into his hair and stared at the ceiling. "Not a good idea, man."

"Come on, dude, it's been three years."

That wasn't the point. Two years ago, Sam would have said no because he didn't want to see them together, the woman he'd loved and the man she'd chosen instead of Sam. A year ago, he'd have said no because he was still trying to find a new place after walking away from everything that was important to him. Now, he didn't want them to see how much of a struggle that had become. Back in Ohio, he'd managed a thriving bar *and* one of the most powerful goddesses of her generation. He couldn't stand to bring Quinn or Nick to the shithole of a bar he tended now, or have them, each in their own way, try to fix whatever was wrong with him.

"I talk to her all the time," he said.

"It's not enough," Nick argued. "She misses you. If you won't come at least for a visit, let us—"

"I've got something going here." He ripped the sheets off him and rolled out of bed. "It would be a waste of time for you guys." The tiles on the bathroom floor were freezing on his bare feet. "Just let me know when you're back east again and maybe we can go for dinner or something."

He barely listened to Nick trying to change his mind while he brushed his teeth, and then padded into the kitchen to start the excellent coffee he'd promised Riley. "Look, man, I've got to go. Busy day. Tell Quinn I said hey."

And with that stupid, not-fooling-anyone signoff, he hung up.

Damn the man for dredging all that up now. Sam leaned against the counter and watched the coffee maker hiss and burble, the first few drops hitting the bottom of the glass carafe. He'd actually been optimistic when he'd left Quinn. He'd worked for her for six years, managing her bar, Under the Moon, as well as the work she did as a goddess. It had fulfilled his early purpose, the one driven by his mother's death while he was in college. She'd been a goddess, too, pushing to help people beyond her own limits, and he'd always believed that was why she got sick and couldn't recover. He'd managed Quinn's limits for her, so she could help people without harming herself. She'd never promised him anything, but their relationship had been more than boss/employee. Unfortunately, not enough so. She'd been in love with Nick even longer than she'd been with Sam, and when the time came that she and Nick could be together, Sam had been the odd man out.

He'd worked for the Society until a year and a half ago, helping Quinn's sister Marley start up a new educational program after a leech had preyed on their community, stealing the abilities of several goddesses before they'd stopped him. Marley's job had been her punishment for her role in creating the leech by giving her boyfriend Anson the ability to take power in the first place.

After that, Sam had trained as a protector. The Protectorate was an autonomous organization as old as the Society, its purpose essentially to be bodyguards for vulnerable goddesses who were away from their power sources. The days of witch burnings and the like were long gone, but people still targeted goddesses for reasons both mundane and magical.

But Nick was the most respected and well known of the protectors, and Sam had felt like an interloper. Plus, it wasn't in his nature to stand around and wait for a threat. He wanted to use his mind as well as his body. The fact that he was doing neither at the moment didn't sit well with him, and he didn't care to expose his aimlessness to his old friends.

The coffee maker sighed that it was finished. Sam poured a cup and carried it out onto the tiny back deck overlooking enough of a slope to expose him to the morning sun. It cast a pink-gold glow with just a hint of warmth, and he focused on the birds chirping at each other in his neighbor's trees.

"*Mrrow*?" A dusty white cat glided up onto the deck beside him and rubbed against his ankles.

"Hey, there. Haven't seen you in a few days." He stroked her and scratched under the chin she tilted up for him. It was the stray he'd compared Riley to last night. It had taken months for her to come this close, but now she let him give her all the affection he wanted.

And all the food. She trotted to the Cool Whip container he used to feed her and looked up with another inquiring meow. He poured some kibble out of a box he kept in a storage bin and petted her a few more times while she ate.

The hair on the back of his neck prickled, and he looked up to find Riley standing on the landing outside the garage apartment, watching him. Her hair was in a damp twist over her shoulder, and she wore the same clothes as last night. Funny how he hadn't noticed the way the worn jeans hugged her hips and the plaid shirt nipped her waist. His hands would span that waist. And her breasts were the perfect...

What the hell? Maybe it was the angle that made everything look so good. Or the daylight. Things always looked different in daylight.

He stood and cleared his throat, uncomfortable at these thoughts so close to his memories of Quinn. "Morning," he called.

"Hi. I didn't think you'd be up yet. I came out to see how chilly it was."

He rubbed a hand over his bare chest, noticing the cool air for the first time. He'd forgotten he hadn't put on a shirt. "Coffee's ready, if you want some."

"Sure, I'll be right down." She disappeared inside.

Sam blew out a breath and pushed the sliding door to the kitchen open. He'd make pancakes and get Riley to open up about her problems, and then he'd send her to the Society—where she should have gone in the first place. And then maybe he'd figure out what the hell he was supposed to do with himself.

But first he'd put on a damned shirt.

. . .

Riley took a deep breath and let it out slowly. And then she did it again. She'd stepped outside after her shower thinking to check the temperature to determine how cold she'd be with her shirt still damp at the seams after washing it in the sink last night. She hadn't expected to see Sam standing out there, half naked, fairly magnificent, and petting a damned cat with more gentleness than those big hands should have been capable of. Now she was all flustered and flushed. And maybe some more F words.

So inappropriate.

She hurried to brush her teeth with her finger and some toothpaste she'd found in a drawer and ran her hands through her hair once more before checking that she'd left the room neat— bed made, towel hung, the T-shirt he'd loaned her folded on the bed. She hefted the metal pipe she'd carried from the bar, relishing the reassuring weight and what the cool smoothness represented. But Sam knew what she could do with it, and it seemed rude to bring an obvious weapon into the kitchen of a Good Samaritan. She'd take it with her, but leave it outside.

She took another deep breath and nodded sharply. Okay. She was ready for this.

She headed down the steps and followed the walkway to the deck. Sam had left the door slightly ajar. After leaning the pipe against the wall outside, she used her fingertips to nudge the door open some more.

"Come on in," Sam called. She stepped into a narrow kitchen

rendered even smaller by an old Formica table…and Sam's wide shoulders, now covered with a T-shirt.

Bummer.

The room was clean but old and worn, the linoleum curling along the edges, the walls a dingy tan that probably used to be white. The appliances might be older than she was, except for the fancy-looking coffee maker on the counter.

"How do you like your coffee?" He poured some into a gigantic, plain green mug.

"Black, please."

He set it on the table. "How are your hands?"

Riley sat and palmed the warm mug. "They're fine. Thank you." She indicated the healing cuts on his face. "Those okay?"

He gave her a dismissive look. "Oh, sure. Hungry?"

"Starving." She immediately felt uncomfortable. She meant it like anyone would at breakfast time, but given the circumstances, he might think she hadn't eaten in a while. *The burger I had for dinner didn't last* would sound defensive, so she held in her urge to say it. "I really owe you."

"Not yet, you don't." He pushed away from the counter and opened the fridge. "How do pancakes sound?"

"I don't want you to go to any trouble. Cereal would be fine." There was an open box of Cocoa Puffs sitting on the counter.

Sam shook the box and chucked it in the trash. "Empty. Sorry. You should have something heartier, anyway."

She laughed. He was kind of a mother, in a hot, manly way. "If you insist."

"I do." He bent and reached into the back of the refrigerator to pull out what looked like a whipped-cream canister, except taller and wider. "They'll only take a minute."

He took a flat pan out of the oven and set it on the stove, coating it with cooking spray as he turned on the gas. A few moments later, when the pan had warmed up, he shook the canister, aimed the nozzle, and squirted what looked like batter on the pan. The mix spread and bubbled.

"So," Sam said.

Riley braced herself.

"How did you find me?"

Embarrassment warmed her cheeks again. "I saw a video of you on the Society website. I thought maybe you could help me."

He raised his eyebrows. "That video didn't tell you where I was."

Why hadn't she anticipated that he'd ask that question? Her cheeks went even hotter. "I did some detective work." That sounded better than cyber-stalking. "Social media makes it pretty easy to find people through their contacts." She hoped he didn't ask more. From the little she gleaned from the Facebook comments, she wasn't the only one who found him…appealing.

Luckily, he left it at that, but with his next question, she almost wished he hadn't.

"Why me? Why not go directly to the Society? Especially if you're in danger. They can assign you a protector."

She wrapped her hands more tightly around her mug, not minding the sting of the heat against her raw skin. Her spirits sank a little. He'd been part of the educational program, so of course his first advice would be to talk to the Society. But because he was a guy and therefore *not* a goddess, she hadn't expected him to be indoctrinated in their propaganda.

She sipped her coffee for fortification, and because the mug was big enough to hide her face for a moment. "I'm not a member of the Society," she said after she'd swallowed.

He raised an eyebrow again but didn't look up from the stove, quickly flipping perfectly golden pancakes. "Why not?"

It was a long, confusing story that ended in *I have no idea*, but that made her sound weak. "Not every goddess is," she countered.

"Is your mother?"

Complicated pain squeezed her chest. "No. She wasn't."

"Wasn't." He looked sympathetic, obviously guessing the reason for the past tense.

That made it easier to continue. "My parents and younger sister were killed in a car accident at the start of my senior year of college. She was driving on her permit. They never figured out exactly what happened, but it was a two-car collision, four people dead."

Sam set the spatula down and took the single step toward the table to reach her. His warm hand covered hers, leaving the rest of her chilled. "I'm so sorry."

She shrugged one shoulder, only feeling half as cavalier as the gesture indicated. "I don't bother asking 'why me?' It's life."

"Still." He went back to the stove. "I've lost my family, too. Were they all you had?"

"My mother's family was already gone, and I haven't seen any of my father's since the funeral. I kind of fell off their radar."

He slid six pancakes from the skillet onto a plate and set it in front of her. "That had to be rough." He brought a butter dish to the table, grabbed a bottle of syrup from the fridge, and handed her a fork and knife before turning back to fix his own plate.

"It was." Riley's mouth watered. She doctored her pancakes with a little butter and syrup, cut one in half, and folded a piece into her mouth. Surprisingly delicious for pancakes from a squirt can.

Sam joined her at the table. "What happened after the accident?"

"I had enough money from the insurance policies to finish school. Sold the house, found a job in marketing." She paused. "I know I look like a vagabond." She gestured at her rumpled clothing. "But I had that job for three years. Somehow," she muttered.

"Somehow?"

She sighed and set her fork down, though she'd barely eaten anything. "About a year after my family died, something started happening. Something weird." She hesitated. Sam had seen what she could do, and he obviously believed in it. But a lifetime of skepticism, of listening to her family's disgust, was difficult to set aside. So was three years of feeling like a freak.

He waited for her to continue. When she didn't, he gave her a nudge. "Stuff like moving things around? Making things disappear or burn up?"

"Yeah. Essentially."

"You sound like it was a surprise, though. Your mother never told you that you were a goddess? Never showed you her abilities?"

"She didn't have any."

"You're sure?" When she nodded, he said, "Huh," and set his elbow on the table, hand covering his mouth and chin, to study her. "So you knew nothing before your abilities emerged?"

She shifted to prop her heels on the rungs of her chair, pulling her knees up and tightening her arms around herself. "Not really. It's complicated."

"Are you adopted?"

She shook her head. "Definitely not."

Sam set his fork on his already empty plate and leaned back, bracing his hands behind his head. Riley barely noticed the muscles rippling beneath his snug T-shirt. Okay, she definitely noticed. But she didn't dwell.

"So you lived your life not knowing you were a goddess. Your parents died before you turned twenty-one, when a goddess comes into her power. Your source is metal, obviously." He waited for her to nod. "So you probably found out accidentally."

She cringed at the memory. "It was silly, at first. I was walking down the street with a friend and kept bumping into parked cars. She laughed that it was like I was drunk, only it was eight in the morning and I hadn't had alcohol in days. But I wasn't off balance or anything—it was like the cars were pulling me toward them."

"Hmmmm." He looked thoughtful. "Every car?"

"No. Older models mostly. You know, big-car-old-people-club kinds."

Sam laughed, the sound vibrating deliciously. "What? Big car old people club?"

"Yeah, you know." She sketched a wide space with her hands. "Big boats that only old people drive. It's like they're a club."

He shook his head, still chuckling. "Okay. So, the ones that are made of steel instead of fiberglass."

"Right."

"Does it still pull you like that?"

She shook her head. "I don't know why."

He sat up, his voice taking on the educational tone from the video. "Goddesses have no sense of their source or how their abilities will manifest until they turn twenty-one. It can come on suddenly or subtly, and it changes as you adjust and adapt. What else happened?"

"I bent my pen. One of those Cross ones, the refillables? While I was writing with it, it got all misshapen. Then in a staff meeting, my boss said something nasty to me, I don't even remember what, except it embarrassed me and made me mad, and next thing I knew, his chair had dumped him on his ass."

"And that's when you knew you were making this stuff happen, that it wasn't just happening around you."

"Right." Riley was surprised at how easy it was to talk to Sam. He acted as if this was all normal stuff that happened to normal people. But when she thought about all the things she'd done since that day, the idea of describing them wore her out.

He read her mind. "Let's skip ahead. I bet you experimented and found that it was the metal itself that gave you power."

Riley hated that word. *Power.* She'd read comic books, enjoyed superhero movies as much as the next person. She knew what "power" meant, but for lack of a better description, she nodded.

"That's rare." Sam stood and moved the dishes to the sink, then grabbed the coffee pot and refilled both their mugs, though Riley hadn't drunk much of hers. "In the last three years, I've never seen or heard of anyone whose power source is metal. It's from the earth, sure, but it's processed. The only thing that comes close is a woman who uses oil and can get a little power from plastic. But we're talking only enough to snap a flame onto her fingers, not blow people across a lot."

She wondered if he judged her for that. The whole "power equals responsibility" thing. "I didn't mean to push them so hard," she said quietly. "It's difficult to regulate. Small pieces of metal, like jewelry, don't do much. I carry some metal nuts and washers and stuff in my pocket, just in case, but it takes something big like the pipe to be able to do anything significant. And when I'm scared or whatever, I guess I..." She trailed off, not sure how to describe it.

"You channel more energy than you mean to," Sam offered.

A knot of tension unraveled in Riley's gut. That made it sound at least understandable. Almost scientific. Maybe coming here had been the right thing after all.

"If you've had people after you, why don't you carry more metal?" Sam asked.

Riley fingered her mother's pendant and thought about the pipe on the deck outside. "I have some pieces in my car, but what am I supposed to do, drape myself in chains? Metal is heavy. And this is the first time they actually got that close. I've felt them watching, following, but there was no one to defend against until last night."

"Okay." Sam leaned forward, the front legs of his chair thumping to the floor. "Back to the Society. Was your grandmother a member?"

Riley snorted before she could stop herself. "My grandmother hated the Society."

"Why?"

She opened her mouth, but didn't know what to say. "I don't know," she admitted. "I always thought I did. I mean, it was just the way things were. My mother and grandmother would go off on rants about how evil the Society was, how they ruined good people. I didn't realize they never talked about specifics until this happened to me and I had no one to go to. I always thought they were scammed by someone claiming goddess abilities or something. But now that I know the power is actually real...I just don't know. They're not around to ask, and if they were still alive, they might not tell me, anyway." That was something she tried hard not to think about. They *were* all dead, so she'd never know if they'd have set aside their feelings and supported her, or if they'd have shunned her because she'd become the enemy.

"I'm sure we can figure it out," Sam said. "The Society records might shed some light. You really should have gone to them right away. They'd have helped you with all of this."

"No." That was the one thing she knew for certain. "I don't know why they hated goddesses so much, but the Society did something to them. There was a reason my family felt so strongly. I can't trust them. Or anyone, really."

"You trusted me."

She looked away. "I got desperate, and you seemed...nice. Plus, you're not a goddess. Or a god. Gods don't exist, right?" According to the Society website, any power *gods* originally had failed to be passed down, so Sam was an outsider. Maybe not exactly like her, but it made him more approachable than the Society itself.

"The people at the Society are nice, too. I promise. They can help you train, teach you about your origins and your abilities." Sam checked his watch. "They can also protect you from these people who are after you. Do you have any idea who they are?"

"No, but it's not just them, I don't think. There have been others in the last few months," she admitted. "For nearly a year now, I guess. I lost my job when someone told my boss I'd been doing drugs. I'd been acting strangely enough that he believed it. Then somehow these people tapped into my life. Phone messages disappeared, my mail was searched and some stuff stolen from the mailbox. Then I couldn't get another job. The electricity was shut off, so I assume they intercepted my payments. I handed my rent check directly to my landlord, but he claimed it bounced and evicted me." Laying it all out like that overwhelmed her again, bringing back the choking anxiety. She sat up straighter, trying to breathe against the constriction around her lungs.

Sam reached over and laid his hand on her arm, seeming not even to notice he was doing it. The touch was enough to slow her racing heart.

"But no one approached you while that was all going on?"

Riley slid her free hand under her thigh and curved her fingers around the sharp edge of the chair. "Not directly, but they kept getting closer. I closed all my bank accounts and used only cash, living in motels for a while. They kept finding me. I went to the police but everything was so vague, they blew me off. So I ran." She hated the admission and firmed her voice. She didn't want him to think she was weak, even if her actions made her seem that way. "I've been moving around for about six months, getting short-term jobs and trying to keep my head down, but they're tracking me somehow. I got desperate enough to look into the Society... because if my family was wrong about abilities being real, they could have been wrong about the other stuff too. Everything I read sounded like propaganda. Except for you. You were...different."

Sam blew out a breath. "Jesus, Riley. You should have come to us sooner."

Riley's feet thudded to the floor, and she flattened her hands on her thighs. "Aren't you listening? I came to you because you're not an 'us.'" That didn't make grammatical sense, but she knew he'd get her point.

Sam tossed up his hands. "What did you think you'd get from me? You need a protector. You need people who can teach you how to use your abilities properly. I can't do either."

"You did a pretty good job last night," she said softly. "You're exactly what I wanted. Someone who can tell me the truth but who won't have an agenda."

But Sam shook his head. "I'm sorry, Riley. You need more than me. I'll call the Society for you, and John, the head of the Protectorate. It's only about three hours up to Boston. You should head straight there. They *can* help you." He stretched to pull open a drawer under the counter and retrieved a pen and piece of paper. "I'll write the directions for you. Do you have GPS?"

Disappointed defiance drove her to say, "I don't have a car."

Sam looked up. "What?"

"It was stolen yesterday when I was inside paying for gas. The police said it's been happening a lot around here, so I don't think it's connected."

Sam whistled. "Life has really been kicking you in the teeth, hasn't it? Do they think they'll find your car?"

"They wouldn't commit, but they found the others. Joyriders, I guess. I'm supposed to check in with them today. My phone was in the car so they can't exactly contact me with updates."

He eyed her shirt, the same one she'd worn the night before. "I imagine all your stuff was in the car, too."

"What isn't in storage, yeah."

He wiggled the pencil, thinking. "All right. Since there's a chance they'll recover the car, you probably won't want to leave immediately. But here's the information you'll need when you do." He finished scribbling on the paper and handed it to her. Riley stuck it in her pocket, avoiding the temptation to crumple it into a ball.

"When you get to the Society, ask for Kirsten. She's the education coordinator. She and Alana, the executive director, can help you figure out your lineage and sign you up for classes, and John will assign you a protector. I'm going to see if he has someone in the area who can go up with you." He looked around as if searching for something. When his gaze landed on his phone on the counter, he stood to get it.

"Sam, wait." She stood, too, her sneaker squeaking on the linoleum. "I'm not going to Boston. I'm not letting some strange guy take me anywhere. And I'm sorry—you obviously trust these people, but I can't. Frankly, they sound like a cult."

Sam snorted. "I promise you, I'd never send you up there if I didn't honestly believe they could help you." He folded his arms and leaned against the counter. His expression went shrewd, which put Riley on alert. "You won't take my word at face value, I get that. But why take your family's instead? Especially when they withheld information from you, and you don't even know why they hated the Society so much. Don't you want to make up your own mind?"

Riley ground her teeth. Damn him for figuring out the right buttons to push. Of course she wanted to make up her own mind. But would the Society actually help her? "Every feud has two sides. How do I know they don't hate my family as much as my family hated them?"

"They might not know anything about your family," Sam countered. "You said your mother and grandmother had no abilities."

"They knew. Grandma complained about the way they treated her, and she told me I was lucky I never had to endure it."

Sam's lips compressed. "I don't know what went on. I can't promise anything. But there are different people running things now. There's no big list of people to shun posted on the wall."

Riley almost laughed, but remembering her grandmother's words dredged up another fear, one she'd always attributed to a child's imagination. Boogeymen and monsters under the bed. But her abilities were real, and… "You said that metal is a rare source."

Sam nodded. "Sources are usually more natural. Plants, crystals, water—there's a lot of water-based power. Rain, the ocean, rivers, even sometimes standing water, like puddles. The sun. The moon." A funny expression crossed his face, gone before she could identify it. "Metals exist in nature, but you're using processed metal. It's concentrated, so it gives you a lot more power. Without guidance and training, that can be dangerous."

"Yeah, so can experimentation. How do I know they won't lock me up to run tests on me? Maybe those people who came after me last night were sent by the Society."

Now Sam outright laughed. "That's not what the Society does, Riley. It's the Society for Goddess Education and Defense. Their purpose is to help you, not hurt you."

Riley folded her arms, mirroring his stance, and stared him down. "So why aren't you there anymore?"

His amusement disappeared and his face went blank.

A familiar chill returned, banishing the little bit of hope he'd generated. "See? You were helping with their 'education' program." She made air quotes and tucked her hands back into the crooks of her elbows. "So why'd you quit? You were a protector, too, weren't you?"

"Wow." Sam set his phone back on the counter and raised his eyebrows at her. "You did that much research on me?"

"Well, yeah." She couldn't meet his eyes. "I was trying to decide if I could—who I could trust. You seemed the least dangerous from the start, but I wanted to make sure. You left the job with the Society, *and* left the Protectorate, and now you're working in a *bar*. Why?"

Sam shook his head. "It has nothing to do with the organization and everything to do with me. Look, let me just call them. You can talk to them yourself. Make up your own mind."

She didn't know what else to do, and she couldn't argue with his logic anymore. She pursed her lips and met his gaze head on.

"Fine. All right."

But when he picked up the cheap little cell phone and flipped it open, her stomach churned and bile crept up the back of her throat. She stood on a precipice, and she knew the leap she was about to make would change her whole life.

CHAPTER THREE

Vulnerability is a counterpart to power. The stronger the goddess, the greater a target she becomes when the source of her abilities is inaccessible. Our mission is to ensure no goddess suffers at the hands of the greedy, ignorant, or malicious.

— ***The Protectorate**, Mission Manual*

Sam stared at the car, appalled. "This is yours?"

They stood in the impound lot, surrounded by sports cars and fifteen-year-old, stripped-down sedans interspersed with pimped-out drug-mobiles. After winning the battle to call the Society, Sam hadn't been able to reach anyone. It was too early for anyone to be at the office, and even John hadn't answered his phone, which was unusual. His message provided Nick's number for emergencies, so Sam had decided they could wait a few hours. As Riley had pointed out, he *was* trained as a protector.

Luckily, her call to the police had been more productive. They'd found her car overnight, just a few miles from where it had been stolen.

Riley opened the car's little trunk, looked satisfied, and closed it again. "Everything's here."

"You can tell that at a glance?"

"I don't have that much, and the big suitcase is locked." She opened the driver's door and slid in, one foot on the ground. "It all looks okay. Phone's here, too." She pocketed the battered, cheap, little flip phone—so similar to Sam's he couldn't help but notice. "Assholes spilled soda on the console, though." She glowered at it, but Sam still couldn't get past what she was driving.

"It's a Beetle."

"Yes, Sam, it's a Beetle."

"But it's not even the cool kind." It was only a few years old, but Riley had said she owned it outright. So she'd *picked* the damned thing.

"This coming from a guy who drives a Saturn." She laughed up at him, the sun shining on her face, making her eyes a clear, paler green. And somehow, all the strain and worry etched there had faded. Sam stood still, struck anew by the beauty he hadn't noticed the night before. Cleaned up, rested, and briefly free of tension, she was gorgeous in a wholesome, open way.

He shook himself. The last thing Riley needed right now was him hitting on her. "I don't drive a Saturn by choice," he argued. "My old car was an '84 Camaro."

She stood and rested her arms on top of the car door. The position emphasized the curve of her waist and swell of her breasts. What the hell was wrong with him? *Focus, Sam.*

"What happened to it?" she asked.

He shoved his hands into his pockets. "Uh, I rolled it. Back when—doesn't matter. It was totaled."

Riley looked curious, but Sam didn't explain. It was too long a story and wouldn't alleviate any of her fears.

He cleared his throat. "So, it all looks okay? Probably as the cops said, just joyriders."

Riley shrugged. "I guess. They couldn't have towed it here with an explosive wired to it, right?"

Sam chuckled. "I doubt it. Besides, if someone wanted to blow you up, there was more opportunity yesterday."

"Right." She picked at the rubber around the door. "So, now what?"

Now, Sam had a decision to make. The smart thing to do was to go to Boston with her. The harassment, the stalking, the level of ability it took to do things like make her rent check bounce—it all added up to something much bigger than the goons at the bar last night. She needed more than just a little advice and a map.

But he didn't want to go. The idea of taking charge, managing the situation, was like a comfortable old coat. Completely familiar and perfectly fitting. But he didn't want anything to do with goddess business anymore. He'd spent six years managing Quinn and her life, then almost three more helping Marley get straightened out and set up the educational program. The Protectorate was more of the same, and Sam had left because he didn't want to take care of people anymore.

And Riley had made it clear she didn't want anyone taking care of her. But she *needed* it. Sam knew the Society could help her, but he couldn't convince her of that by talking. Could he take her up there and leave her without getting sucked back in?

Movement to the left caught Sam's eye. When he turned to look, the lot was empty, but a scrape and metallic clink echoed lightly from the rows of cars. The hair on his arms and neck prickled.

"Shh," he said, though Riley hadn't said anything, only turned her head to follow his gaze, her whole body going tense so quickly he felt it from three feet away.

And there they were. Two of the people from last night, the woman and the guy Sam had fought.

"Fuck," Riley breathed, spotting them hunkered behind an old white Oldsmobile.

Sam grabbed her arm and tugged her toward the driver's seat. "Get in. Drive away. I'll—"

"No." She was sick of being on the defensive, sick of running, sick of letting everyone else make decisions for her. She pulled her arm out of Sam's grip and took off, his muttered curse and heavy footsteps following behind. He caught up as she reached the Oldsmobile and slammed her hand down on the trunk of the car. The couple lurking behind it rose, the woman grinning, the man trying to look intimidating.

But anger drove Riley this time, not fear, and she already had a weapon. This baby was over two decades old, and it was all steel.

The contact with the metal changed her, cleared her thinking. Her muscles tightened, filling with power. It was like sipping caffeine or stepping into the shower in the morning—that moment when alertness takes over—only magnified by a thousand.

Her left foot shot out, hooking behind the guy's right knee, and he sprawled onto the gravel. She set her foot on his abdomen and pushed just enough to hold him still. In the same movement, she caught the woman's arm before her punch connected with Riley's head. The woman's bright eyes widened when she was pulled against her will right up into Riley's face.

"Who are you, and what do you want with me?" she ground out.

The woman sneered. "Like we'd tell you."

Riley tightened her fingers. The woman yelped and twisted against the pressure of Riley's grip. "Who are you, and what do you want with me?" Riley repeated. Some of her anger settled and she became less focused, more aware. Sam stood behind her. He'd followed her but didn't interfere. He was just there if she needed him.

It was the first time she'd had someone in her corner since her parents died. For a few seconds, she wasn't sure if her gratitude made her feel stronger or weaker.

But now wasn't the time to contemplate it. Despite the pain and fear in her eyes, the woman sneered again. "We're pros. We don't talk."

Riley leaned her weight on the guy under her foot. She glanced down at him, not taking her eyes off the woman completely. "Hey, you, on the ground. I can move my heel a few inches south if it will be more comfortable."

He keened and pushed at her unmoving foot.

Riley smirked at the woman. "I think *he* might talk."

"I'll kill him first." The woman twisted again, hard, and pulled her foot back as if to kick the man in the head. The movement pulled Riley forward, almost lifting her hand off the car. She reacted instinctively, too powerfully, and yanked them both back so her hand stayed flat. She needed the contact, every cell of it.

And she'd just revealed her weakness to the enemy. The woman's sneer became more confident, but before she could act, Sam moved forward.

"Let's do this the easy way." He circled behind the duo and stuck his hand in the woman's back pocket for her wallet. "Sharla Cannalunis, Georgia," he read from her driver's license. "Mean anything?"

"Not yet." Riley had never been to Georgia and had never heard the name. She didn't have the skills to find more than Sharla's Facebook profile, but that wouldn't stop her from trying. "What else is in there?"

He flipped through a few bills, checked a couple of credit cards, and dug behind them to find some crumpled receipts. "Hokeland Motel and Exxon Mobil, both local. That's it."

"How about him?" Riley waited while Sam retrieved the guy's wallet. This one told them he was Vern Nurnan, also from Georgia. No credit cards, but a business card declared him an associate of a company called Millinger.

Sam dropped the wallets on the ground and dug in their

pockets again until he came up with one cell phone between them. He pushed a few buttons, then pulled out his own phone and stored some numbers into it. When he was done, he nodded at Riley. When she didn't move, he wrapped his fingers around her wrist until she released Sharla.

"I bet at least one of these numbers goes to their boss," he told her. "He won't be happy when we call him."

"Or she," Riley added, watching Sharla. She didn't react enough to indicate which was right.

Sam hauled Vern off the ground and gripped both of them by the scruffs of their necks. "Call the police," he told Riley.

"You don't want to do that," Vern said with certainty, and zero concern.

"Yeah, I think I do." Riley glanced at the guard shack at the lot's entrance. "In fact, the police are right there." But she didn't move, still reluctant to eliminate contact with the car's metal. She knew the power filling her would fade as soon as she did, leaving her shaky and weak.

"They'll ask why you didn't call them last night," Vern said in a very reasonable tone. "And we weren't doin' nothin' here. You attacked us. Threatened to do damage to some of my favorite personal parts."

Sharla snickered, earning a sour look from her partner that became smug when he turned back to Riley. "Look, call him over if you want. You can't connect us to anything that's happened to you before last night. Maybe we go to jail for half an hour before they realize they have no grounds to hold us. No biggie." He shrugged. "But you think your life's been difficult so far? Trust me, it can get a whole lot worse."

Riley backed away despite herself. "Weak threat when I don't know who's signing your paychecks."

Sharla leered up at Sam. "Our boss is well connected. He can get this guy arrested like that." She snapped her fingers. "I mean, look." She pried at his fingers on her neck. "I've got bruises, and they match his hands."

Sam didn't move, but Riley slumped against the car. She couldn't risk Sam getting in trouble, not when he'd tried so hard to help her. "Let them go."

"You sure?" When she nodded, Sam shoved them several feet up the aisle between rows of cars. They walked off, Sharla strutting and Vern moving with a bounce in his step that made Riley nearly regret the decision. Until she looked at Sam and remembered their threats. Not worth it.

Sam settled against the car next to her. "So we're back to the Society and the Protectorate option."

Riley suppressed a shudder. It was inevitable, she knew. She couldn't resist going to Boston anymore, but everything in her held back, and she returned to one of her arguments from earlier. "We still don't know if Sharla and Vern were sent by the Society."

Sam pressed fingers to his forehead, then dropped his hand. "If I can convince you they weren't, will you go to Boston?"

"I guess…"

"Then come on. Let's go to the library. You can follow me."

"The library?" She let him usher her into her car and automatically put on her seatbelt. "Why?"

He leaned into the open door, putting himself closer to her than he'd been since their mutual doctoring session the night before. A wave of awareness swept over her, and she slowly breathed in his warm, mellow scent, now spiced with laundry soap and aftershave. It took a few seconds to tune back in to his words.

"They have free WiFi. I can use my laptop to look up these numbers and the company Vern works for. *Then* we'll drive up to Boston."

He closed the door before Riley registered what he'd said. He wasn't sending her up there by herself. He was going with her.

• • •

Sam was glad they had to drive to the library in separate cars. Once he'd tuned into Riley as a woman rather than someone who needed his help, he couldn't shut it off. He wouldn't have advised confronting Sharla and Vern like that, but her fierce determination had been pretty hot.

He needed a distraction.

The drive would be long enough for him to call the Society again. He knew Riley didn't want him talking to them behind her back, but he could speak more freely if she wasn't listening. He stuck the earbud in his ear, connected it to the phone, and speed-dialed the main number. While it rang, he checked the rearview mirror. Riley was directly behind him.

A familiar voice came on the line. "S-G-E-P."

"Alana. I thought you got a new receptionist?"

"Hi, Sam!" The Society's executive director went from professional to pleased in two words. "Haven't heard from you in a while. The receptionist is out this morning. What can I do for you?"

If she hadn't sounded so welcoming when she'd heard his voice, the lack of small talk would have felt like punishment. He heard voices in the background and assumed she was busy.

"I need to talk to Kirsten, if she's available." She was the new head of the education department and would help register Riley and set her up for programs and training.

"Oh, didn't you hear? Kirsten is on maternity leave!"

"No. I didn't even know she was pregnant." He felt bad for not sending a gift. It was weird to be so out of touch, but he had no one to blame but himself for his sense of detachment.

"Marley took over again—temporary duty," Alana said. "I'll put you through."

Sam tapped his fingers impatiently while he waited for the call to transfer.

"Sam!"

Marley's greeting was several notches more enthused than Alana's. "Hi, Marley. How are you?"

"Excellent. It feels really good to be back here. How about you? I'd love to have you help out with a few classes."

He liked teaching, but that was the opposite of not getting sucked in. Saying no wouldn't be easy, though, if he went up to Boston with Riley. "We'll see. What do you have going on right now for newly empowered goddesses?"

"Why? Do you have one?" He heard shuffling papers followed by mouse clicks. "I didn't think anyone was turning twenty-one right now, and we haven't had anyone off the radar since we got the new database up and running."

Over time, the Society had gotten complacent about tracking births and empowerment, only recording them once reported by members. But when they'd set up the database, they'd found more pending goddesses than they'd known about through existing membership.

"I met a young woman, Riley Kordek, whose mother might have been dormant. She died right before Riley's powers manifested a couple of years ago. Can you check to see if she was ever registered?" He gave her the name Riley had provided earlier, both her maiden and married names.

Marley tapped on her keyboard, then said, "Nope. No record. No one by the name of Kordek at all, but there wouldn't be if that's her father's name."

"What about ancestors? They may have gone dormant a couple of generations back."

"I'll look. I might have to dig. A lot of the older stuff isn't in the database."

"I appreciate it." Sam changed lanes, making sure there was enough space for Riley to follow. "There was apparently some kind of rift between the family and the Society. Riley was raised not to trust you guys but doesn't really know why."

"I'll see what I can find. In the meantime, I can start her registration. What's her age and source?"

"She's almost twenty-four, and it's metal."

Marley whistled. "Wow. We've only had a couple other metal sources in the last century."

"That's what I thought."

"How does it manifest?"

"Channeling. She blew a couple of muggers about ten feet last night." He kept the explanation simple for now. Riley could tell her entire story to John when they got to Boston so he could assign her a protector.

"Muggers, huh?" Marley sounded skeptical, and Sam frowned.

"Why? Have other people been having problems?" It hadn't occurred to him that Riley might not be the only target.

"Not that I'm aware of," she said. "That's just too simple, given your track record."

"True enough," he said with a laugh.

"Anyway, we've got nothing going on right now. I have literature for her and she can go through the short-term mentorship program, but I don't have any other newbies to register for six months, so I can't set up a full class."

"All right. I'll talk to her about it, and we'll decide when we get up there."

He could hear her frowning when she spoke. "Up here? You're coming up to register her in person?"

"I'll explain when we get there."

"Okay, cool. It'll be good to see you."

"You, too. Hey," he hurried on. "Is John there? I tried to call him earlier and got voice mail."

"He and Jeannine had an offsite meeting this morning. He's here now, though. Hang on."

Sam pulled up to a red light and checked that Riley was still following. She was, but so was the car that had been behind her when they left the impound lot. It had a discreet rental agency sticker on the windshield.

"Hey, Sam! Just the man I wanted to talk to."

Surprised, Sam refocused on his call and the traffic in front of him. "I am?" He hadn't talked to John in months.

"Yeah, I want to get your take on something. Marley says you're coming up here?"

He rolled his eyes. "I don't know yet. What's going on?"

"I don't want to talk about it over the phone."

"Well, listen, I met a kind-of-new goddess down here in Connecticut, Riley Kordek. She's had some people following her and needs a protector. You have anyone nearby who can meet her and take her up to Boston to get registered with the Society?"

John chuckled. "Yeah. You."

"Ha ha. I mean a real protector."

"You are a real protector. I don't care if you haven't done it in a while. I wouldn't trust anyone more. 'Specially since I'm stretched thin right now. My closest guy is in D.C."

That wouldn't work. Sam checked the cars again. The same one was behind Riley. He took a right turn off the main route. Riley followed, and a few seconds later, so did the rental. Sam's heart rate picked up. No, they couldn't wait for someone to get up here from D.C.

"All right, I've got it covered. Hey, by the way, you ever hear of a company called Millinger?" The silence made his brow furrow. "John?"

"Where did you hear that name?"

"The people who attacked Riley."

Another delay before John responded, his tone so carefully dismissive Sam knew he was lying. "Never heard of 'em. So, get your ass up here *tout de suite*, yeah? Jeannine's dying to cook you dinner."

"Uh, yeah, probably be a few hours. Thanks, John." Sam hung

up quickly and yanked the earbud out of his ear. Dammit. Jeannine didn't *cook* for him—they didn't even like each other. So *get your ass up here* was about Riley, but about more than that, too, because his code meant he thought the phones were compromised. What the hell was going on?

Sam sped up, watching carefully for kids and cars in the residential neighborhood, and took the corner too fast. Riley didn't follow as quickly. She probably thought he was crazy, but add Vern and Sharla to the rental car and his cryptic conversation with John, and every protective instinct Sam had was on high alert.

Information was power, so Sam wasn't willing to cancel their trip to the library. He wanted to know what Millinger was before they got on the road. But what had been important was now urgent.

The rental didn't show up again for the rest of the ride. Either the driver knew he'd been made, or he hadn't been following them. No way Riley had lost him with the way she was driving. Sam took the last few turns toward the library and pulled into the parking lot with a screech.

Riley parked next to him and threw herself out of her car with a scowl. "What was that all about?" she demanded, but apparently noticed Sam scanning the lot and the street around them. She shifted closer to him and looked around too. "Were we followed?"

"Maybe. I don't know. But I talked to—" Crap. He wasn't going to admit that, but she turned betrayed eyes on him. Not angry ones. That would have been easier. "I'm sorry. I called the Society and the Protectorate to let them know we were coming. I don't know what's going on, but something is, and it sounds like it's bigger than only you."

Riley bit her lip and didn't move away when he instinctively smoothed his hand down her back. She glanced at the library, then back to the street. "I don't like not knowing anything."

"Neither do I. That's why we're here. Let's go inside." He

pulled his laptop bag out of the back seat, and they went in. Sam picked a large, empty table near the back and set up the computer with his back against the wall, giving him as clear a view as possible of the main entrance and putting space—and the table—between them should anyone come their way.

A few minutes later, Sam wished he'd considered more practically what huddling over a laptop in a quiet corner of the library meant. Or at least taken the surge of attraction he'd felt at the impound lot more seriously.

The wide wooden chairs at the library table should have provided a comfortable distance. But Riley had dragged her chair up against his, and as he struggled to remember the simple task of logging on to the free WiFi and connecting to the Internet, she positioned herself to see everything he did. Which meant thighs touching and her arm draped across the back of his chair. He sat up straight to maintain a buffer space, but every time she leaned to read something on the screen, her breasts brushed his upper arm. Despite the thickly woven cotton of his jacket sleeve, he could tell exactly how perfect they were, just the right level of firm softness.

He cleared his throat and shifted awkwardly, staring unseeing at the Millinger website. Lust had never been his driving force. When attraction wasn't fleeting, it heralded a connection beyond the superficial. So even though he'd just met Riley, he doubted this awareness of her would just disappear. Which put a new spin on his reluctance to take her to Boston.

Was he really afraid of falling into a role he didn't want anymore? Or was he actually afraid of getting romantically involved with another goddess when it had gone so wrong the first time?

It didn't help that Riley's voice turned husky when she tried to whisper, or that her long, wavy blond hair smelled like honeysuckle.

Honeysuckle. He didn't even know what the fuck honeysuckle smelled like.

Riley snorted derisively, snapping Sam out of his self-disgusted trance. "'We'll bring you to your brightest world'? What kind of vague crap is that? What are they supposed to do there?"

Sam shrugged to cover a subtle shift away from her. The half inch let him focus on the corporate website in front of him. "Consulting, I guess." He clicked a couple of links, but Millinger was very cagy about their business. The recruitment page sounded like a pyramid marketing scam, without making any real promises. That page linked to a word association quiz and a questionnaire inquiring about special skills.

"It sounds like they're looking for something, not offering something. Look at this." He waved a finger at the contact page. "Lots of pretty stock photography, but no photo of their building—or buildings, since they claim offices in twenty states." He opened a new tab and did a search for the state website for Georgia. "They list headquarters in Atlanta, so let's look for their registered business information."

He found it after a few minutes of clicking and typing—and getting drunk on Riley's faint sweetness.

"There it is." Millinger's tax certification status showed the business registration date…less than a year ago.

"How can a company be that big but only a year old?" Riley asked.

"Good question. Makes the whole thing suspicious."

Riley laughed, and the sound slid over Sam's nerve endings. "I don't know. I think the whole chasing-me-down thing is pretty suspicious already."

Sam managed a crooked smile. "This is a different kind of suspicious. Assuming Millinger is even connected. The company might not have anything to do with them following you." John had recognized the name, though, and it niggled at the back of Sam's brain, too. But he couldn't figure out why. Their public front was innocuous, but the face of evil often was.

He checked the data in a few other states where Millinger had locations and got the same registration date. He dug in his pocket for his phone and handed it to Riley. "Read those numbers to me, will you?"

She did, and Sam typed each one into a search engine. One was listed as belonging to Millinger, but the rest were either hotels or pizza delivery places, or came up unlisted.

"Those were all in towns I've stayed over the last few weeks," Riley murmured when he was done. She handed the phone back and leaned away, her elbow on the table, hand supporting her head. The distance didn't decrease their intimacy, though. If anything, now that she was looking straight at him, it had increased.

Sam concentrated on dialing the Millinger number. His big fingers hit the wrong tiny buttons, and he had to start over.

Riley gave a little sigh, her brow tightening. "I never saw anyone," she murmured. "They could be watching us right now."

Sam rubbed her knee in reassurance. Riley laid her free hand on top of his, and he regretted his impulsiveness. She was going to think he was making a move. He switched his phone to the other ear so he had an excuse for pulling his hand away, but the phantom imprint of her soft fingers remained.

After a few rings there was a faint click, and his phone beeped the disconnection. Sam looked at the screen. "Nothing. I think that's as far as we're going to get today." He shut down the laptop and stood to pack it up.

Riley sighed. "I'm going to the restroom. I'll meet you outside."

Sam watched her go, making sure none of the few people in sight followed her, then quickly finished packing and strode outside to wait. He sat on the low brick wall in front of the entrance and took a much-needed deep breath.

He hadn't been this attracted to a woman in years, and he didn't like how much it unsettled him. The last woman he'd been involved with was Quinn, and there'd been no uncertainty in that relationship, no sense of *don't go there*. Not until the end. Plus, he'd wallowed in his feelings for her for so long, he had no idea how to handle this now.

It's past time to move on. Just go for it, dude! Sam shook his head hard, trying to dislodge Nick's voice, but it wasn't wrong. He did have to move on. He was even *ready* to, at least to put the past behind him and stop letting it fester. But with Riley? She was six years younger than he was—except he was a big fat hypocrite using that as an excuse since Quinn was ten years older than *him*. But Riley was also vulnerable, and he was struggling with his aimless, flat existence. Not a good foundation for a new relationship. And what the hell did he know, maybe this growing attraction was just gratitude for giving him a purpose again, however much he tried to tell himself he didn't want it.

Maybe he needed to accept that helping people might be his thing, and he was never going to get away from it. But it was something else to turn it into another sexual relationship. There'd been too much damage from the last one, and he wasn't up for more. Not for him, and not for Riley. So he had to shut down this attraction.

What if you can't? They would drive to Boston in separate cars. Not ideal, especially if someone was following them, but he didn't want to strand her up there with no transportation. Once Marley took over education and John took over protection, Sam could remove himself from the picture.

He'd investigate this Millinger thing on his own. Something about it dug into him, hard. He was good at research and investigation, too. He rose and walked to his butt-ugly Saturn to toss the laptop case on the front seat, feeling lighter than when he'd come outside. Purpose didn't have to mean taking care of people.

He looked around the parking lot out of renewed habit, not expecting to see anything, but his eyes locked onto a familiar orange sticker on the windshield of a red sedan. The car that had been following them.

Sam knew it was pointless, but he stalked across the curved lot toward the vehicle backed up to the wall. Sure enough, he was only halfway there when the engine started and the driver pulled away. Sam froze, so surprised at what he saw that he failed to get the license plate number before the car bounced into the street and sped off down the road.

No fucking way. *Anson?*

Sam hadn't seen his old college roommate in three years, not since he'd been jailed for assault after leeching several goddesses of their powers—including Marley and almost Quinn, who'd taken it all away from him. Anson had been released a year ago, but they'd kept tabs on him during his probation, and he hadn't made any moves toward anyone. He'd stayed in…Georgia. Where Millinger's headquarters were.

Sam stood mired in worthless guilt as he stared after the car. Anson hadn't just been his college roommate. Everything he knew about goddesses, he'd learned from Sam. Maybe no one would have been hurt if the two of them had never met.

He suddenly realized how long Riley had been in the bathroom. Had someone gotten inside through another entrance and cornered her again? He dashed for the building, but the glass door opened and Riley came out.

"You okay?" Sam gripped her shoulders and studied her face. "Did something happen?"

"What? No!" She pulled away, tilting her head so her hair hid her face, but not before he saw her bright eyes and pale skin. "No," she said more calmly, walking toward her car. "No one came at me again. Sorry I took so long." Without another word, she climbed into her car, started it, and waited for him to take the lead.

Baffled, Sam shrugged and got into his own car, paralyzed by opposing forces—the pull to go back and fix whatever was wrong, and the figurative knife at his back, urging him to get her out of there. He should have made her ride with him. They could get separated too easily on the highway like this.

But he knew she'd never go for leaving her car behind, not when it was her only symbol of freedom and control and she'd just gotten it back. He'd have to keep a careful eye on her and make sure nothing happened.

Maybe he was wrong about Anson. The bright sky and tops of the nearby trees had been reflected in the driver's side window. Sam had only gotten a split-second glimpse of the guy behind the wheel, and people changed in three years.

But if he was right and that was who'd been following Riley?

Sam didn't have any other choice. She was his responsibility now.

Chapter Four

Once a young goddess has determined the source of her abilities, she is encouraged to experiment under safe, controlled conditions to determine the extent and range of those abilities. Privacy is also encouraged, to protect against the negative repercussions of public notice.

— **The Society for Goddess Education and Defense**, *New Member Brochure*

Riley cursed as she followed Sam onto the crowded interstate a few minutes later. She paid enough attention to barreling semis and flying Mercedes to avoid getting crushed, but half her mind was still back in the quiet library.

A few minutes into their Millinger search, she'd noticed tension in Sam's hands as he typed, and his tone had grown more clipped. She felt so stupid. Without intent, she'd pressed herself all over him. He probably thought every lean was a come-on, when she was only trying to see the screen better. When she shifted away in a hopefully not-too-obvious manner, he'd relaxed a little, confirming his discomfort. But what kind of discomfort was it?

Riley had been attracted to Sam since the moment she saw

him in the bar, a tower of steady strength. Rescuing her from Sharla and Vern and the other guy had turned up the volume, but she wasn't that shallow or out of touch with herself. She knew the difference between gratitude and chemistry. But maybe he thought she didn't and squirmed because he didn't want her attention.

There'd been a definite contrast between his reassuring manner this morning at breakfast and his abruptness when he packed up in the library. For a second, when he'd looked at her full-on before shutting down the laptop, Riley thought she saw a flare of interest, and heat had surged through her body. And then the tension returned. So maybe he *was* attracted to her but didn't want to be.

"Stop it," she scolded aloud. It would take three hours to get to Boston, and she would drive herself insane with all this. She liked Sam. He was sweet and courageous, not to mention friggin' hot, but she had way too much going on already. She was homeless, for one thing. Sam saw her as helpless, and that wasn't a good basis for a romantic relationship. So she'd force herself to forget all that, stop reverting to high school with all the he-likes-me, he-likes-me-not drama, and just concentrate on getting her life back.

She wasn't convinced that Sam's path—education and "defense" by the Society—was the right one, but he'd made good arguments. All her mother's and grandmother's ranting for all those years had become so much noise in her head now. Her insistence that the Society was dangerous and not to be trusted stemmed from a child's lack of understanding. Try as she might, she didn't remember any details that would explain why her family had felt that way. It was time to form her own opinions and make her own decisions.

Maybe her great-grandmother had been a goddess. A barely discernible image hazed through her mind of her mother's grandmother doing…something Riley had wanted to think was magic. G-Nana had died when Riley was four, so she knew she wouldn't remember any more than that, but maybe she'd still had her abilities. Why didn't her grandmother, then? Or her mother? And why had it suddenly reappeared in Riley herself?

The Society was as likely as anyone to have answers. What was the worst that could happen? They could refuse to give them to her. Laugh and turn her away. Throw stones and chase her out of town with a pitchfork.

But they could also welcome her. She could meet other people like her. Not real family, of course, but women who understood what it was like to be unique in the world. The information she'd read so far indicated some goddesses worked openly, using their abilities in their jobs. Others kept their heritage private, their talents for personal use.

Yeah, but none of them are like you. She swallowed bitterness. So far, her abilities only allowed her to harm people, whether unintentionally or out of self-defense. Sometimes even offense. She winced, remembering how she'd ground her foot into Vern's midsection. What good was that, unless she wanted to hire on with the mob?

There was so much else to deal with before she could worry about a career. She wasn't homeless and jobless because she was a goddess, though that little detail had helped things along. Getting some education and training might make her feel less lost, more capable of taking care of herself, but that was just a symptom. It would do nothing about the problem that was Millinger.

Millinger.

Usually, when Riley thought of the people who'd messed up her life, her shoulder muscles turned to rock and spawned sharp pains at the base of her skull. But a simple name changed all that. Instead of *being* a target, she *had* a target.

Taillights flashed in front of her and she slowed, keeping an eye on Sam's car as a couple of others quick-merged between them. Orange-and-white-striped barrels angled across the left lane ahead, funneling everyone to the right. Riley could almost hear the combined grumbling of all the drivers around her.

They crawled along for half a mile, and she studied the urban landscape out of habit, picking out metal items—lampposts and mailboxes and wrought-iron railings. House numbers and scaffolding, debris that might be metal but was probably plastic littering the side of the road. She wished she could come up with a practical way to carry more. The pipe rested half on the floor, half on the seat next to her. That was plenty of source material, but it weighed several pounds. What was she supposed to do? Hang it from a scabbard on her hip?

Squeaky brakes from the car in front of her alerted her that they were stopping again, and she glanced ahead to see what was going on. The overpass they were approaching was under construction. A crane in the grassy median slowly rotated, a dark green I-beam dangling from the crane arm as workers under the bridge used other equipment to haul it into place over the closed left lane.

That was a massive hunk of metal. How much power could she get from that? Enough to do superhero-type things? Like lift equipment off a pinned construction worker? She watched the I-beam swing over the road, ponderous and heavy, and imagined touching it, energy pouring into her, enough to fling an overturned bulldozer off its victim. In her mind, it tumbled end over end, crashing safely to the ground a dozen feet away.

Shouts jerked her out of her imagination. Tires squealed as someone slammed on the brakes, someone else hitting their horn as the I-beam swung wildly. Groaning metal echoed over everything. More shouts. Riley gaped, watching through her windshield as the I-beam tilted and began to slide in its harness. Men scattered on one side, others struggling to control it from the opposite.

A clang reverberated so deep and loud it vibrated Riley's car.

The I-beam had collided with some kind of forklift-like vehicle, and it tipped, in slow motion but still far too fast.

"Oh, my God." Riley clutched the wheel, frozen, staring at the hard hat and waving arm of the man now trapped under the forklift. What... Had she done that? Had her fantasies somehow pulled the I-beam toward her?

Doors opened, and people climbed out of their cars. A few pulled out phones, some assholes clearly taking photos or video, while others put the phones to their ears, probably calling 911. Riley numbly put the Beetle in park and shut off the ignition. Her legs shook as she opened the door and tried to stand. She wrapped her left arm over the top of the door to keep herself upright, her eyes locked on the man on the ground, his coworkers struggling to move the machine on top of him.

"Riley!"

A familiar shout a couple dozen feet away.

She tore her gaze away and found Sam, motioning for her. She couldn't move, couldn't comprehend what he wanted.

"Come on!" He waved again, then turned and ran toward the accident.

Something snapped in Riley's brain. She hadn't noticed that sound was muffled until she could suddenly hear again, excited chatter and revving engines and shouting voices. Colors went from tinted grays back to brilliant oranges and reds, gleaming blacks and blues. She took off, dashing around people but swerving close to their cars. Light flashed off chrome trim and wire antennas. Her fingers brushed metal as she went, something other than conscious recognition guiding her touch to the smallest bits of her source within reach.

Small infusions of strength fed her muscles, her pounding heart and aching lungs, and by the time she reached Sam's side, her shock had been displaced by determination.

"There." Sam turned his attention from the crowd to the

forklift. It lay on its side, canted where the body jutted out wider than the base, the man's entire lower half pinned near the spot where metal met concrete.

Riley nodded, recognizing the leverage point Sam indicated. "But they won't let me over there."

"I'll distract them." He didn't wait for her to respond, didn't ask if she was up for it, just assumed she was.

She firmed her jaw, clenched her fists, and strode after him. She damn well would be up for this. Especially if she'd caused it.

No. Guilt wouldn't help. She banished the idea and slipped between barrels. Under the shadow of the overpass, the moans and thumps of vehicles speeding above echoed around them, covering shouted orders among the crew. The crane operator and some of the workers had gotten the I-beam safely to bare ground, half on the grass, half on the cracked concrete of the road. All the workers gathered around the trapped man. A couple tried to wedge a long chunk of concrete under the forklift, but it wouldn't fit. Hands shoved at the tipped-over lift, but of course, no one was strong enough to budge it, and the positioning made it impossible to get enough people around it to combine their efforts.

Sam squeezed through the crowd, calling out instructions with enough authority that no one questioned him. Riley watched for a moment as they folded cloth to put under the guy's head, held a water bottle for him to drink from, and bent close to Sam when he asked the guy questions.

When everyone's attention was on Sam and the injured man, Riley hurried to the equipment. Her ridiculous, arrogant fantasy spun through her mind. She didn't know if she could even raise the small forklift.

Her bare hands landed on the cold metal, followed by the familiar sensation of everything about her body becoming *more*, and relief filled her. *Now to figure out the best way to do this.*

Leverage.

She turned her back to the machine and bent her knees, bracing herself against it and curling her hands around a lip above the gas cap. She closed her eyes, willing strength into her legs. For the first time, she concentrated on drawing energy from the metal. No, not from it. *Through* it. She could sense it, like flowing water except totally insubstantial, detected only in an eerie sense of movement out of the metal into her hands. She clenched her jaw, tightened her muscles, and heaved, shoving with her legs and pulling energy at the same time.

The forklift rose. Only a few inches, but Sam shouted something, other people yelled, something scraped across the ground, and the forklift became suddenly heavier. She strained not to let it drop and opened her eyes. Several feet of empty space between the machine and the crowd gave her permission to let go. But that would call attention to her, so she held on. Every muscle screamed so hard she almost gave voice to the pain, her mouth opening wide. But the sound only vibrated in her ears, externally silent. She slowly bent her legs and lowered the machine to the ground. As soon as she released it, she collapsed.

Riley gasped for breath, drawing up her knees and begging silently for the muscles in her legs to stop hurting so damned much. Suddenly, the screaming in her ears died into a low wail, and a paramedic truck bumped over the shoulder, approaching the scene. She laughed and lowered her forehead to her knees, tears stinging at the corners of her eyes as her body finally relaxed.

"Hey. You okay?"

She didn't need to lift her head to recognize Sam's voice or the heat and gentleness of his hand on her back. But she looked up, startled by the admiring glow in his golden-brown eyes, only inches from hers.

"Yeah," she managed, flushing. "Yeah, I'm okay."

"You were amazing." He glanced around. "We should get out

of here. Traffic's gonna be moving in a minute, and I don't think talking to the police is a good idea."

"Police?" She stood on unsteady legs, a wholly different kind of weakness than when she first got out of the car. Sure enough, the lights of three state police cars flashed across the faces of the watching crowd. "Crap. Did anyone notice?"

"Probably." Sam ushered her around a stack of some kind of rubber tubes that were tall enough to hide them. "But no one will believe their stories."

"Unless they got it on video," she muttered.

Sam didn't respond. His hand slid from her back down her arm. His fingers threaded with hers, and he tugged her to zigzag through the standing cars. Riley glanced over her shoulder once they were past the perimeter. A few cops waved at the traffic, ushering the first cars under the right side of the bridge, where they were supposed to go before the whole accident happened. Engines rumbled to life around them as people waited for traffic to clear.

"You okay to drive?" Sam stopped next to his car. He brushed Riley's hair back, tucking a few strands behind her ear, his expression now concerned. He kept casting quick glances at the cars and people around them. "Just to the next exit. It's not far. We'll stop at a restaurant or something."

Riley nodded and dragged herself away, trying not to shiver. They were in the middle of the highway. Even if Sharla and Vern or some other team had followed from Bridgeport, they wouldn't do anything with so many police around.

"I'll follow," she managed to croak, and pushed herself to a trot when cars rolled down the line. She got to her Beetle in time, ignoring the impatient honk from the guy in the car behind her.

She kept her mind carefully blank as she followed Sam to a diner near the highway, but it didn't stop nausea from digging in. She parked the car but gripped the wheel so tightly she couldn't let go. She sat there, shuddering, until Sam opened her door and gently uncurled her fingers.

"It's okay." He reached past her to turn off the ignition and pocketed her keys. "Are you hurt?"

"N-no." But the response was automatic. Sam lifted her knees and swung her around so her feet were out of the car. Crouching in front of her, bracketing her legs with his, he gently rolled her hands over. They were stained orange from the forklift's paint but not bruised or bleeding. They didn't even hurt, really. But her fingers curled over her palms, the tendons still contracted by the weight of the machine, compounded by her death grip during the drive.

Sam held one hand and pressed his other on top of it, flattening her fingers. His callused skin rasped against her still-tender palms, and her belly shivered. The tendons slowly stretched under the pressure, and Riley nodded. "That's good. Thanks."

Sam repeated the action with her other hand. "I should have done this before I made you drive here." His tone was annoyed, but the warmth of his hands seeped into Riley, settling the shudders and the chattering teeth. She resisted the urge to run her hands through his hair, so close now instead of two feet above her. Sam lifted his head suddenly, caught her looking, and she sucked in a breath at the impact of his eyes meeting hers. She'd never known a guy who wore his emotions so plainly. Now it was self-disgust and concern, but after a few seconds, his irises darkened from golden oak to brewed tea, and she read awareness and caring.

Oh, she was so going to fall for this guy.

She pulled her hands free and let them hang between her knees. "I'm okay." Except for the nausea. She thought of the road worker and had to swallow hard. "How's the guy? The one who was trapped? Did you see?"

Sam nodded but didn't move away. "He probably has a broken leg. Below the knee. That's where most of the pressure was. But he wasn't bleeding, and his upper body wasn't crushed. He'll be fine."

"Eventually," she mumbled. Knowing that didn't help.

"What's wrong?" Sam's hands landed on her knees. "You saved him. Or at least his leg. Don't you see how amazing that was? Not a lot of people, goddesses or not, could have done what you did." He smiled a little and stroked a finger across her cheek, evoking a shiver. "But you look miserable."

"What if—" God, she didn't want to say it, didn't want to see his admiration and pride turn to disappointment and disgust. But she had to talk about it. Had to know. So she could make a decision. "What if I *caused* it?"

"What?" It came out with a little laugh, but he immediately shook his head. "What are you talking about? No way you caused that."

"I might have. I—"

"No, hold on." He stood in one smooth motion and stepped back, drawing her up with him as he once again checked their surroundings. "Let's go inside and get some coffee. You look like you're freezing."

Coffee didn't warm a chill that wasn't physical, but Riley pressed the button on the handle to lock the car and went inside, this time going first and holding the door for Sam behind her, because she was tired of following.

"Seat yourselves, kids," the waitress called from behind a crowded counter. "Be right with you."

Riley chose a corner booth away from most of the diners in the half-full place, and sighed deeply as soon as she sat. Sam positioned himself so he could see the door behind her, but his attention was clearly on her.

"I was watching the beam," she told him right away. Getting it over with might not help, but it wouldn't hurt, either. "Thinking about touching…no," she corrected, remembering how it felt to use the metal in the forklift, "tapping that much metal. What I could do then. I actually thought about—" Shame cut off the words. Sam watched her with understanding eyes, and the nausea climbed up toward her throat.

She forced the words out fast. "I imagined saving someone trapped by equipment. And seconds later, the beam slid, knocked over the forklift, and gave me someone to save." She covered her face to hide both from the memory and Sam's expression, and maybe to keep her breakfast in.

"Sorry to make you wait," said a cheerful voice over Riley's head. "Coffee?" A beat, then, "Hon? You okay?"

Riley dropped her hands and nodded. "Yes, thanks. And coffee's good." She waited until the woman had poured and walked away without pressing them to order food.

As soon as the waitress was out of earshot, Sam grabbed Riley's hands and leaned over the table. "You didn't do it, Riley. I swear it."

"How do you know?" Tears welled, and she tried to tug her hands away, but he'd engulfed them fully in his. She didn't *want* him to let go, but didn't deserve how good they felt.

"Were you touching any metal?" he demanded.

She blinked at him. "No. I don't—no. Not directly."

"Have you ever done telekinesis—moved objects from a distance—when you *weren't* touching metal?"

Hope began to coat the nausea. She thought about things she'd done, testing the abilities once she understood what was happening, and slowly shook her head. Then stopped. "Wait. My boss's chair. The one that dumped him on his ass. The metal in the shaft snapped, and I wasn't touching it."

"Were you touching *other* metal?"

God, she didn't know. That was before she understood anything. She squeezed her eyes closed and thought about the conference room. Her own chair had been plush and padded, covered, so no, not even her legs were touching metal parts. She'd stopped using her nice metal pen once she melted it, of course, and the table was solid wood—no, wait. They'd gotten a new table for the executive conference room and moved the gigantic chrome and glass one into theirs. That was before she'd figured out what was going on, so she hadn't realized her arms were braced against the metal frame.

"There you go," Sam said when she told him. "Plus, I was watching when it happened." His voice was a low rumble, meant to be soothing, but it dug under her skin. "They hadn't secured the sling properly. It wasn't centered. So when they pulled it sideways, the weight shifted, and—"

"You're sure?" When he nodded, all the tension flowed out of her, leaving her as weak and trembly as she'd been when she first saw it all happen. "Thank you. I couldn't live with myself if I knew I'd done it."

Sam scowled at her but didn't say anything. He leaned back, and Riley grimaced at how dirty her hands were. She slid to the end of the booth. "I'll be right back."

Sam checked his watch and glanced outside, then looked around the diner. He had a direct line of sight to the restroom doors but shifted as if to follow when she stood.

Riley pressed her hand to his shoulder. "It's okay. I'm just washing up. I'll be quick, I promise."

Sam nodded, flipping open a menu and settling deeper into the cushioned seat, but she could tell he was still on alert. "I'll come after you this time."

Riley snorted. As if he hadn't come after her every other time, including at the library. If she'd been a few seconds slower, he'd probably have charged into the ladies' room.

She wasn't sure which of her responses to that was worse: the pleasure that he found her worth coming after, or the fear that eventually he would stop.

CHAPTER FIVE

Full potential is rarely realized without combined resources,
shared experience, and the right outlook. Achieve your destiny.
Expand your dreams. Become one of us.

— *Millinger.com*

Walking into the Society building after a year and a half didn't jolt Sam as much as he expected. The building's owners had done some work in the lobby, getting rid of chipped linoleum and painting the walls a faded tan color. A new directory had been mounted next to the elevator nook. *Society for Goddess Education and Defense* was in bold, blue lettering, larger than the other businesses in the list. They were the only company on the eighth floor now.

They rode the elevator silently. Sam resisted the urge to put his hand on Riley's back again. He kept finding excuses to touch her, but there wasn't anything he could do about the tension she must've been feeling. It would dissipate once she met these people and realized she could fit in here. He was sure of it.

The elevator dinged, and in the split second before the doors slid open, he wished *she* would put a hand on *his* back. His heart beat so fast his pulse seemed to vibrate in his neck. His apprehension was in direct opposition to the bland entryway inside the glass door—neutral carpet and visitor chairs, pastel watercolors on the walls, an unremarkable sign under a clock behind the reception desk.

A woman he didn't know sat at the front desk. She looked up when they walked in, her smile matching the décor.

"Can I help you?"

"Sam and Riley to see Alana and…Marley. They're expecting us."

The smile hardened. "You don't have an appointment."

Sam raised his eyebrows. "I don't need one." He'd given a lot to the Society with nothing in return. Helping take down the leech, build an educational program, and protect goddesses rated him better than *you don't have an appointment*.

Someone stepped out of an office down the hall and headed toward the break room.

"Alana!" Sam called.

She looked up with a grin and hurried toward them. "Sam!"

He held out his arms and accepted her hug, then stepped back to draw Riley closer to them. "Alana, this is Riley Kordek. Did Marley—"

"Yes, she told me all about you." Alana held out a hand to Riley, who shook it with only a slight hesitation. "Come on. I'll take you down to her office. You're lucky. Things are quiet around here right now."

They followed her down the hall. Alana swung through an open office door and moved to the side so Riley and Sam could squeeze in behind her.

"Marley, good. I was afraid you were on the phone."

Marley looked up, and Riley gasped, a small sound that Sam silently agreed with. Even after working with her for a year, seeing her like this startled him every time.

Marley flinched, even though she had to get the same reaction from everyone she met. She waved a hand at her eyes. "I know. Freaky, right? They used to be almost lavender. Quinn—my sister—calls them Easter-egg eyes." The description was a good one. The leeching had bleached most of the color, leaving purple specks that did remind Sam of candy eggs.

"What…happened?" Riley asked.

Marley managed a smile. "Long story. I'm sure I'll have time to tell you later. You're Riley?"

Alana nodded. "Yes, Riley Kordek—Marley Canton, our education coordinator."

"Temporary." Marley waved a hand around the small office, crowded with filing cabinets that ringed the walls, barely leaving room for her desk and one guest chair. "I'm sorry, I'd stand, but as you can see, there isn't really room for that."

"No problem." Riley tucked her hair behind one ear and folded her hands. "It's nice to meet you."

Sam watched Marley do a quick assessment of Riley and tried to see her through the other woman's eyes. For the first time since the attack, he saw the runaway who'd walked into the bar with her vulnerable core hidden under a tough veneer. He liked the shagginess of her blond hair, but suspected the other women thought she needed a haircut. Her teeth were straight, as if she'd had braces, but she didn't wear makeup. Not that she needed it, with lush lashes around her dark hazel eyes and a natural light pink tinge to her golden complexion.

He realized what he was doing and swung his attention to Marley, who was already watching him, a half smirk on her face. "Hey, Sam."

"Hi, Marley." He hunched his shoulders with his hands deep in his pockets, glad she hadn't gotten up to hug him. But she surprised him by rolling her eyes and turning her attention back to the others.

"Did she fill out the registration form yet?"

"No, can you go over that with her? And Sam, umm—" Alana turned back to him, obviously unsure what to do with him.

"I have to talk to John. He here?"

"Yep. In his office."

"Great." He smiled at Riley. "I'll be back. You're in good hands here."

Riley nodded and sat in the chair next to Marley's desk, her jaw tense and lifted slightly. Defensive, but she'd be okay.

Alana crossed the hall to the break room, and Sam went to the right to John's office. The man sat at his desk, a phone to his ear and a scowl on his face. "I don't care if it's three thousand miles, find a way to get there. You're closer than anyone else, and she needs you now… Fine. I'll tell her." He slammed the phone down, grumbling, and looked up when Sam rapped on the doorframe. His expression cleared and almost became a smile. "Sam! Get your ass in here!" He stood to clamp Sam's hand with his and motioned for him to sit. Sam closed the door behind him and sank onto one of the sturdy, padded wooden chairs.

John's office was bigger than Marley's, with fewer cabinets, and had the advantage of a big window on the back wall. The two chairs in front of the large, file-strewn desk were nicer than the single worn visitor chair Marley had. But Riley probably preferred that one, Sam thought, because it had a metal frame.

"What was that about?" he asked, indicating the phone.

John shook his head. "Goddess down south. Young, naïve. Asshole ex has been harassing her. Power source is live trees, and she rarely leaves her forest. But she went to a family wedding on the plains, and it looks like the ex followed her."

Sam nodded. "Out of her element, not enough access, perfect time to attack. You didn't have a protector scheduled to go with her?"

John gave him a "you know better" look. "She didn't tell us. Figured she wouldn't need it. Until he showed up, she tried to scare him away, and everything fizzled." He closed the file on top of the mess and shoved everything to the side. "The guy I'm sending is good, though." He launched into a story about his protector and the kid's two brothers, who'd signed up for training because they thought it would have the cachet of the Navy SEALs without the hard work. Their trainer had quickly disabused them of that but convinced them to stay anyway.

"Would you believe," John said, "Nick got those three shaped up and ready to work in less than a month?"

Of course Sam believed it. Nick Jarrett was a friggin' Mary Sue. He could do anything, protect anyone, had every skill a protector needed and then some. Forget about the time he almost died because he underestimated his enemy, or the time he let Quinn be bait for a guy who'd turned out to be more dangerous than any of them had presumed. Nick had his share of flaws, but the head of the Protectorate seemed to forget that.

"I'm not here to talk about Nick."

"'Course you're not." The older man stood. "Come on, let's go outside. Hate being cooped up in here."

Sam followed without protest. John had been in charge of the protectors for over twenty years, but only in the last three had he been so tied to the Society. Before, he'd had a role on the board and a loose working relationship, but he'd operated out of his own home base. He hadn't hesitated to volunteer for his new job, but it meant a lot more paperwork and a lot more indoor time. As far as Sam could tell, John hated the city.

They took the stairs instead of the elevator, and once outside, John lit up a cigarillo and strolled toward a park a block away. Sam shrugged off his jacket in the unseasonably warm late-afternoon sun.

"Much better," John sighed. "Air's not always too fresh, but it's better than in there. Less compromised, if you know what I mean."

"Ahhh…" Sam frowned, not sure he did. "Yeah."

John returned a greeting to a cart vendor on the corner before they crossed the street. "So you ran into Millinger, did you?"

"Worse. I saw Anson. I think," he corrected immediately. "In Connecticut. Someone was following Riley. I only got a glimpse of the driver, but he looked like him." He related everything that had happened and everything Riley had told him. "What's his status?" he asked John at the end.

"Don't know. We can't find him."

"What?" Sam stopped walking to stare at him. "How?"

John shrugged, the gesture deceptively casual. "His parole officer said he never missed a check-in. But he cleared parole last month and in the past week or so, he's managed to elude our guy. Can't catch him at home or at work. Which is…guess where?"

Sam didn't have to work hard to come up with that one. "Millinger," he ground out. "Why does it not surprise me that Anson is in the middle of something again?" They should have kept the asshole in jail, but it was pointless to gripe about that. The civilian authorities had had no reason not to release him. In their eyes, worse offenders had gotten off easier.

They reached the park, and John settled down on a bench that faced into the trees instead of onto the rush-hour traffic clogging the street.

"So what are your thoughts on this?" He squinted at Sam through his cigarillo smoke.

"They've been following Riley for months. They orchestrated things so she was alone and vulnerable, watched her, pushed her beyond her limits. Like they want to see what she can do."

"And?"

"Millinger has to be a front."

"For?"

Sam shook his head. "I don't know. But Riley can't be the only goddess they're looking for. She wasn't even registered."

John stubbed his butt out on the sidewalk and pocketed it. "I've had reports from some of my team about strangers sniffing around their assignments. Mostly, they approach when they're in power, so our guys aren't around." Protectors generally worked when a goddess's source wasn't available and she was, for whatever reason, vulnerable. For a while, a few years ago, they'd worked around the clock, but once the leech story had been contained and they'd determined the threat level was low, they'd backed off again.

"So your information is mostly secondhand," Sam said.

"At first, yeah, but bits and pieces add up to structure. I put out some feelers, found others who'd been approached but hadn't realized it at the time. Marley's mom, Tess, was one who called me directly."

That surprised Sam. Tess was also Quinn's birth mother, and she'd eschewed involvement with the Society most of her adulthood. "What did she say?"

"She got a customer in the greenhouse. Very debonair, she said, knowledgeable about his plants. Charming."

"So not like Vern and Sharla."

"Not much. But you know Fairfield. Lotsa money in that town."

"Right. And? What triggered her about this guy?"

"The questions he asked. About where she got her talent, and that he'd heard she also did plastic work."

Sam nodded. Tess's talents made her skilled at non-surgical physical changes like eliminating scars and fixing flaws.

"She pretended she didn't know what he meant," John went on, "because she always asks her clients to give her a heads up before they refer someone, and no one had told her about this guy. But he got pushy about it. So she called me, asked if I thought she needed a protector."

"Did you assign one?"

"We sent Quinn down. She was still here—you know you just

missed her? And Nick?"

"Ah, yeah. I know."

John laughed. "So she and Nick went down to visit. Stayed a few days, and then 'left,' but didn't really, and the guy didn't show up again. I'm thinking it was a fact-finding mission."

"So the question is what facts did they find, and why did they use such different methods for Riley?" His phone buzzed in his pocket, and he automatically reached for it.

"Depends on what they want. Maybe different things from different people," John speculated, "because some of the others weren't so slick. Made a few goddesses pretty nervous. Our assignments are up again, and we're stretched thin watching for threats and providing peace of mind." He watched Sam check the phone and pocket it again.

"How far have you gotten researching this?" Sam asked.

John's expression flattened. "Jeannine and I have been meeting with some people we think are related, but they're not very cooperative. We don't know who's behind it or what their goals are. They could be legit, fall into some gray area, or be planning something completely illegal. We have no—"

He was interrupted by Sam's phone going off again.

"Go ahead and answer it. I'll be over there." John motioned to a sausage cart across the grass and got up to head over.

Sam sighed and sprawled across the bench as he flipped open the phone. "Yeah, Nick, what?"

"It's time to come home, Sam. Quinn needs you."

Sam waited, but Nick didn't elaborate. "What, we cut to commercial break or something? What are you talking about?"

Nick sighed. "That was supposed to make you drop everything and come running."

Sam tossed up his free hand in exasperation. "You have never, in the entire time I've known you, wanted me to drop everything and come running. Most of the time, you wanted me to disappear."

"Yeah, well, you've proved yourself useful." Nick chuckled, but Sam could tell his heart wasn't in the joke.

He frowned, concerned. "What's going on?"

"Quinn's not doing well, Sam. I can't let her keep waiting you out."

"Not doing well how? And waiting me out for what?" He didn't have the patience for beating around the bush. He wanted to get back to the Society and see how Riley was doing.

"The power she's holding from the leechings. It's having an effect on her. She's trying to hide it, but she's weaker and tires more easily. She can't tell me how long she's slept."

"Shit." That more than anything told Sam Nick had reason to worry. Quinn's source was the moon, and that connection gave her the ability to tell how much time had passed, to the minute, even while she was sleeping. She acted like it was a parlor trick, but when Sam had been her manager, he'd used it to gauge her health and stress levels and keep her from overtaxing herself. The only other time she hadn't been able to tell, the situation had been serious.

But he didn't know what that had to do with him. "What can I do that you're not already doing?"

"She's ready to transfer the power back."

A burst of excitement sent Sam to his feet. "Really? She found a way? How?"

"We've been doing obscure research, and she's experimented a little. We think there's a way to transfer power back to Tanda and Chloe without doing anyone any harm."

"That's awesome." From the day she'd drained all the stolen power from Anson, Quinn had wanted to get rid of it. Sam hadn't expected it to be so difficult. "When are you going to do it?"

"As soon as you can get here."

Sam looked at his watch, then signaled to John before heading out of the park. He wanted to get back to Riley. "I can't. I've got something going on here that I can't break away from."

Nick heaved a heavy breath. "We can't do it without you, Sam."

"Why?"

"Quinn needs to explain it to you, she understands it better. But something about needing a filter."

Sam wanted to help. Anson's victims deserved to get their abilities back, and he didn't want Quinn to suffer. But he couldn't just walk away from Riley, not until he could fulfill his promise to her. Once she was settled at the Society and they'd made sure she was safe, then he could go.

John fell into step beside him, and he lengthened his stride, gaze locked on the Society building a few blocks away. "How long can we put it off?"

Nick's silence was laden with disappointment and frustration. "How much time do you need?"

"I don't know. I'll keep you posted."

"Yeah, do that. And in the meantime, I'll keep trying to keep Quinn alive." He hung up before Sam could find out if he meant it or was just being dramatic.

It didn't matter if Nick was exaggerating the threat. However urgent the situation in Ohio, it meant Sam needed to take care of the one in Boston as fast as possible.

• • •

Riley filled out the registration paperwork while Marley did whatever an education coordinator did, and then sat silently while Marley reviewed the packet.

After a few minutes of studying the first page well beyond what Riley thought it merited, Marley asked, "What did Sam want to talk to John about?"

Riley shrugged. "He didn't say."

Marley nodded and finally seemed to focus on the paper

in her hand. "Riley Kordek, twenty-three, orphan, yada yada," she mumbled, skimming. "No fixed address...that's unusual nowadays." She seemed to realize she'd been thinking out loud and raised her head. "In the early days of the Society, secrecy was paramount and goddesses often had to move a lot to avoid persecution. Sometimes they were labeled witches."

She waited until Riley nodded, clearly uncertain if she should offer the history lesson. But despite herself, Riley was fascinated.

"Things are a lot different now," Marley told her. "You can find small-mindedness and fear without looking too hard, but you can also find welcoming communities. And the more we help people, the more accepting they are."

She jotted a note on a pad and flipped to the second page, skimming again. Riley had written a little bit about how her power manifested and how she used it. She'd left off the part about the forklift, still freaked about the whole thing.

"So." Marley stuck the papers into a file folder and scribbled Riley's name on it. "Tell me about how you figured out metal was your source."

Riley shrugged and wiggled her hands under her legs, pressing them against the rough, nubby fabric of the chair. "I can't pinpoint it, really. Stuff just seemed to happen, and eventually I realized I could *make* it happen, and once I figured that out, I realized it was always when I was touching metal."

"Can you describe how you do it?" Marley wrote on the back of the registration form as Riley tried to express the sensation of making herself *more*. As she struggled to explain something so unique, Marley's writing got faster and harder. The pen dug into the paper, and her knuckles turned white. Like she was...mad?

Riley tapered off, but Marley didn't say anything. "Um...how does it work for other people?"

Marley heaved a big sigh and dropped the pen onto the pad. "It's different for everyone."

Riley waited. That was it? That was all she was going to say? She'd been sitting here like a little kid registering for school, fighting the sense of inferiority because Sam insisted these people could help her. And she got *different for everyone.*

"Is this a bad time or something? You don't seem very happy about doing this."

Marley's mouth fell open with a look of dismay. "Oh, Riley, I'm sorry. It's not like that at all." She sighed again and straightened her shoulders. "Every manifestation is similar, but every goddess describes it differently. Everyone accesses the energy in unique ways." She leaned her arms on the desk and focused on Riley. It was the first time she'd made real eye contact, and the strange paleness of her eyes jolted through Riley. It took a few seconds for her to catch back up to the conversation.

"My sister, Quinn—her power source is the full moon. When it's up, she says she has a constant awareness of it, like a sense that it's available, and she can reach out and use it."

"What's your source?" Riley asked. Ah, that was the problem. She could see it on Marley's face. Riley thought she wasn't going to answer, and when she did, her voice was much softer and less matter-of-fact than it had been seconds before.

"My source is…was…crystals. If I held the little ones—like you can get in a touristy store—I was filled with light. That enabled me to make an impact on the things around me. With bigger, purer crystals, I didn't need to touch them. I had a connection like a laser beam and could use them to open myself up to the energy."

A spurt of jealousy went through Riley. She ignored it, because Marley was talking in the past tense. "I have to be touching metal to use it."

Marley nodded and made another note. "You can probably do more, but you need training." She blew out a breath and shook her head. "I enjoy tailoring classes and mentorships to a goddess's abilities, but I wish I could do demonstrations."

Riley tried to let it go, she really did. But Marley was talking like Riley already knew the story, and she couldn't contain her curiosity. "You…can't do it anymore?" Marley looked ashamed, and Riley rushed to correct herself. "I'm sorry. I shouldn't have asked. That's prying—"

"No, it's okay. It's common knowledge. I assumed Sam had told you." She tilted her head and frowned a little. "What *did* Sam tell you?"

"About…you?" When Marley nodded, Riley shook her head. At the diner Sam had talked a little bit about the people she'd meet and how he knew them but not in a lot of detail. "He used to work for your sister, right?"

"Yeah. And me, for a little while, when I first started this program. I don't run it anymore. I'm just filling in while the new director is on maternity leave." She pressed her lips together. "I wish he had told you everything."

"You don't have to tell me if you don't want to." Riley had really mucked this up. "You're here to help me understand what I am, right? It's none of my business what happened to you."

"Unfortunately, it's everyone's business." She sighed and stood again. "Look, it's getting late. Do you have a place to stay tonight?"

Riley bit her lip. Where was Sam? He hadn't said what would happen next. Whether he was going to drop her here and move on, or what. She *wanted* to stay with him tonight, but A, that was presumptuous, and B, no way was she going to admit it. So she shook her head.

"Come on. You can stay with me. We'll get takeout and I'll tell you my sordid tale, and tomorrow we'll figure out what we can do for you. Okay?"

Riley didn't even get a chance to hesitate. The door behind her opened, and Sam filled the space, looking deliciously disheveled. He'd carried fresh air into the tiny office with him, as well as an air of distraction.

But his tense expression eased into a smile when he saw Riley.

"How's it going in here?"

"Fine. Everything okay?" She twisted more in her seat to study him. His brow had furrowed again almost immediately, his gaze focusing inward. At her question, it snapped to her and Marley again.

"Yeah. For now." He angled his chin toward the messenger bag Marley was stuffing. "You done for the day?"

"She's all registered." Marley switched off her computer monitor and slung the bag across her body. "She needs training, not that we have many people here right now to do that, and we can dig into the archives and see if we can find out anything about her family. I was just telling her she could stay with me tonight. I'm in the Society apartment." She raised an eyebrow at Sam. "Where are you staying?"

"Ahhh…" He looked from Riley to Marley and back. "She really needs a protector with her right now."

Marley smirked. "Okay, you can stay there, too. There's room."

"I wasn't—"

From the hall behind him, an older man's voice rumbled, "You should. I don't have anyone in town right now. Told you we were stretched thin."

Sam stepped back and introduced Riley to John.

He looked very much like she'd imagined. Older, maybe fifty or so, but as fit and tough-looking as he'd probably been twenty years ago. His hair was mostly gray, as was his five-o'clock shadow, and he clapped a proud hand on Sam's shoulder as he joined the little group.

"I heard Marley say something about training," he said. "What kind?"

Marley answered. "She needs to test her ability, see what works best to channel energy, do trials to see how it manifests. Determine her skill set."

"You'll need a goddess for some of that." John eyed Riley. "But I can do some preliminaries. Sam tells me you defended yourself pretty well against some attackers."

Riley nodded and shrugged. "If he says so."

"We'll start there tomorrow, then. You'll cover them tonight, right, Sam?" He slapped Sam on the back and strode away, whistling.

"Looks like I'm it." Sam raised his eyebrows at Marley.

"Good." Marley ushered them out of the office. "Chinese for dinner. I'm buying."

. . .

An hour later, Riley sat on a fat cushion next to the coffee table in Marley's living room, twirling lo mien noodles with a set of wooden chopsticks. Sam perched on the very rectangular couch, elbows on his knees, and dished himself sweet and sour chicken out of a cardboard container.

Marley had said on the way over that the little apartment furnished in worn castoffs wasn't technically hers. It was owned by the Society and used by goddesses in town for short visits. Marley had rented it while she was serving her time, so she still thought of it as hers even though she'd only be using it for a few more weeks. Riley was still trying to decide whether or not Marley had meant "serving time" tongue in cheek.

"Okay. My sordid tale." Marley dropped a handful of paper napkins on the cheap particleboard coffee table and sank onto her own cushion at the short end of the table. "Has Sam told you about the leech?"

Riley shook her head.

"Hadn't gotten around to it." Sam eyed Marley thoughtfully. "I thought you didn't like to talk about it."

Marley shrugged. "It doesn't bother me anymore. Much."

Sam didn't look like he believed her, and Riley wouldn't have, either. Marley's tone was too sharp, like she was trying too hard to act like it was no big deal.

"I can tell her," Sam offered. "It was my fault."

Marley snorted. "Hardly." She turned away from Sam and directed her next words to Riley. "To understand what happened to me, you have to understand us. Since your mother was dormant, how much do you know about goddesses?"

"Not much. Just what I could get from your website and the street." She cringed a little at the words that separated her from them. "I'm a complete newb." She picked up a piece of broccoli and watched it drip soy sauce so she didn't have to see Marley's expression.

"Well, you know how people talk about connected life force? An energy that's created by all the life on earth and stuff like that?"

"Sure."

"That's essentially true. Energy is the core of our existence. Science has proved that, even though it doesn't really deal with what most people call magic. And it's fed by a lot more than life force. Okay, here's an analogy." Marley's enthusiasm and warmth revved up, drawing Riley in. "You know how certain things conduct electricity better than others, and in different ways? Wires carry it into our homes, right? If lightning strikes a body of water, the electricity travels across it, but if power is generated in a power plant and directed through specific conductors, it comes into our homes and businesses to do different things. Run appliances, turn on lights, etc."

"I get it." The concept wasn't difficult. She applied Marley's analogy to what she'd done that afternoon with the forklift. "The source of the power is a conduit, connecting us to the main pool of energy. How we use it is based on how we're created or something. Like someone has a talent for painting or singing. I use mine as a force. You—" She cut herself off. She'd gotten carried away and forgotten the story they were leading up to.

Marley forced a smile. "My sister can heal, among other things. Some goddesses are more specialized than others, but most can do a broad range of things, only limited by what they try. We'll get you into some training and testing, see how broad your application is."

Riley nodded again and waited while Marley toyed with her fried rice, deep in thought.

"Have you ever been in love?" Marley finally asked, looking up at Riley.

Sam's dimples flashed in the back of her mind. Out of the corner of her eye, she saw his head lift slightly. She flushed. "Not really."

"I was. Big mistake. I guess he was using me, and he got what he wanted. I gave him the ability to draw power, and it turned him into a leech."

Riley raised her eyebrows. She had to sort through the details of that short sentence to decide what to ask first. She went with the part that seemed least personal to Marley. "We can do that? Give someone else the powers we have?"

Marley's shoulders dropped half an inch, and her hand relaxed on the chopsticks. "Only under very certain conditions. It takes a goddess with the capability and the son of a goddess with similar capabilities. But he's not a natural vessel with an energy source, so once he uses what he's initially given, it's gone. He has to constantly reacquire power in some way." She gave up the pretense of eating and dropped her chopsticks, slumping over her plate. "Anson was greedy. What I was willing to share wasn't enough. He used what I'd given him to drain another goddess of all of her power. That's permanent, and made him far stronger. In total, he drained four other goddesses. And then, when we tried to stop him, he drained me."

Riley wasn't sure what to say. Poor Marley, to be so utterly betrayed by someone she loved. But in the back of her mind, part of her was ranting, demanding to know if that was why Sharla and

Vern were after her. Funny how this power thing had caused her so many problems, but the realization that it could be taken from her turned her fingers to ice.

"Is that why your eyes…" she began tentatively.

"Yep." Marley brushed a hand over them before picking up the chopsticks again. "All of us have abnormally light eyes now. Freaky, huh?"

"What happened to the leech? Is he still out there?"

"Somewhere. Quinn, my sister, defeated him and sucked all the power back out of him." She dug in the takeout bag for a wax-paper-wrapped egg roll and a packet of duck sauce. "He was in jail for a little while, but the normal authorities didn't have much on him, so he's free again. But powerless."

Riley's appetite had left her. She drew a leg up and rested her chin on her knee. "What happened to the other leeched goddesses?"

Sam cleared his throat and poked at a piece of chicken. "One died of complications from diabetes last year, unrelated. The other three, Jennifer, Tanda, and Chloe, are okay. Normal. But—"

"But not really," Riley finished. "How could they be?"

The reality of their loss sat heavy in the silence for several moments.

"What about the power she pulled from him?" Riley asked when she couldn't hold her curiosity in any longer. "Is it gone?"

"No, Quinn has it." Marley's tone cooled but not toward Riley. More like she wanted to be done with the conversation. "She says she's working on a way to return the power to the leeched goddesses, but I'm a broken vessel, since I ignored all the fairy tales and warnings about bestowing power in the first place. I created the monster that did so much damage, so my punishment—besides my own leeching, which they deemed poetic justice—was to start the educational program that will hopefully prevent it from happening again. Among other things."

Sam shifted on the couch, stretching one long leg under the table and bouncing the other knee. "Anson's back," he said, his jaw flexing.

Marley gaped at him. "What?"

"I think I saw him in Connecticut. He was following you," he told Riley. "I wasn't sure, I only caught a glimpse, but the more we talk the less likely I think it is that one party has been harassing you and someone completely different is approaching other goddesses." He told them what he'd learned from John earlier that afternoon. "I have to figure out what he's up to."

Riley's head spun with everything she'd learned tonight. "Why do you have to do it? Isn't there some kind of authority in charge of that? The Protectorate?"

"We have a security team," Marley explained. "But they don't have to do much. We're a pretty quiet community. They weren't very useful last time."

"And the Protectorate doesn't investigate." Sam stood and carried his dishes and some of the food containers to the kitchen area. "But it's my responsibility anyway."

"Oh, it is not." Marley got up and followed him, and Riley scrambled to her feet, too.

"Anson was my college roommate," Sam told Riley. A weight seemed to have settled on him, but one too heavy for what he was saying.

"So?"

"Everything he learned about goddesses, he learned from me."

Marley made an exasperated sound. "That's not true. You didn't even know about leeching, and he made all his own choices. Like I did," she added, as if used to holding up her own culpability before anyone else could. "All that's over. He can't leech anymore, Quinn assured us of that. So why does this have to be on your shoulders?"

Sam leaned against the counter and folded his arms. "Quinn's sick."

Marley halted halfway through stacking dishes on the counter. "Oh."

Riley got the implication right away. "From the power she's holding?"

"That's what Nick says." He abruptly unfolded his arms and turned to run water in the sink, squirting a stream of dish soap into it. "Anyway, whatever Anson's up to, I want to get to the bottom of it before any of you get hurt."

Marley handed Riley a towel and dumped a handful of silverware into the hot, soapy water. "We also need to bring you up to speed," she told Riley. "The more you know about what you're capable of, the better you can defend yourself. So let's talk about your options."

They discussed them while they did the dishes and cleaned the rest of the kitchen. There weren't many. Most young goddesses had mothers and other relatives to help guide them, so their mentorship program was limited, and no other goddesses currently used metal. Classes on history and culture as well as safety and security weren't scheduled for months, and Riley had her doubts they'd provide anything immediately helpful, anyway. But she found Marley's stories interesting, and she was full of small details about the world Riley had just entered.

"I'm sorry," Marley said after Sam had excused himself and carried his laptop into a bedroom. "This probably isn't what Sam led you to expect."

"Are you kidding? This is more than I've had in nearly three years. Knowing *why* goes a long way toward restoring my sanity." She did a final swipe over the damp counter with a paper towel and nodded at Marley's offer of coffee. "I really appreciate everything you're doing."

Marley stuck a single-serve cup into the coffeemaker and added water to the reservoir. "I should be thanking you. You listened to my story without judgment, and you haven't made an excuse to run out of here. Why?"

"Why would I judge you?" Riley chose a hazelnut-flavored cup from the rotating stand on the counter. "It wasn't like you were being malicious. You were in love."

Marley laughed. "Maybe it's because you're so young. Most people think I should have known better."

For the first time in a long time, Riley had a sense of friendship with someone. So she didn't protest the "young" comment. It wasn't like Marley, in her early thirties, was old by any means, but Riley didn't feel what a normal twenty-three probably felt like. Even if she hadn't gone goddess, losing her family forced her to grow up in a hurry. Being stalked, having all the important things in her life taken away from her, and struggling to survive on her own for the past six months also gave her a less superficial perspective on life.

Then again, none of that experience was in romance. Maybe she did have a more naïve viewpoint about being in love. At the thought, she couldn't help but glance at the closed door hiding Sam from her.

They finished fixing their coffees and went back to the living room, where Marley talked as if she'd been alone for a decade. She asked Riley questions about her family and her life since they died, and in turn Riley learned all about the political structure of the Society, how much most people disliked Jeannine, the current president, and missed Barbara, the former president who'd all but disappeared into her townhouse, rumored to be in her last days.

"It's sad, but she's really old, so no one is really surprised."

Marley also talked about the inn she owned in Maine as well as her family, about how her parents had Quinn too young and gave her up for adoption, and how they hadn't met until Marley was thirty and even then only because Anson had targeted Quinn as his next victim. That was also how Marley met Sam, who was working for Quinn at the time, *wink-wink-nudge-nudge*, but Quinn was in love with her protector, Nick, and now they were together.

It was clear Marley was conflicted about her newfound family. She spoke about Quinn with respect, but Riley detected an undercurrent of a deeper despair or something equally painful, and she thought that was probably because of the power Quinn held, some of which used to be Marley's.

Riley reeled from the bombardment of information and couldn't help dwelling on the part about Quinn and Sam. The woman was apparently a hero, willing to make sacrifices for the people she cared about and even the greater community. Sometimes people like that were actually assholes, but what if she was as cool a person as she sounded? That was the last woman Sam had been involved with? Talk about a tough act to follow.

Marley cracked a yawn and uncurled herself from the sofa. "You've got to be wiped, after the long day you've had. Come on, I'll show you where everything is."

Once Riley was settled in bed a short time later, tired as she was, she couldn't sleep. The caffeine could be a culprit, but that was minor compared to everything she'd learned today. And she kept thinking about Sam and how preoccupied he'd been since his meeting with John. He'd been especially uncomfortable whenever Marley talked about Quinn. How sick was she?

She rolled over and punched the pillow into a fluffier ball. Her eyes wouldn't close, and her mind kept rolling things over in a big loop. The clock on the nightstand ticked over to midnight.

This was nuts. Lying here staring at glowing red numbers was not resting. She needed her mother's vanilla milk. That always worked when she was a kid and fretting about a test or just off her normal sleep cycle. The memory made her wish she were back there, when her biggest worry was not getting an A in geometry and she had no clue what was in store for her.

Would there be any vanilla in the kitchen? It wasn't a typical staple, and this apartment was meant for temporary living. But it did keep forever. Maybe someone had made cookies or something and left a bottle.

She threw off the covers and quietly opened her door. The place was dark except for a faint glow from a bathroom nightlight, and silence came from the other two bedrooms. Either Sam didn't snore, or he wasn't sleeping very deeply himself.

Three steps took her to the kitchen area. She snapped on the light over the stove and started checking cupboards, being careful not to the let the doors bang closed. Bingo! A small bottle of artificial vanilla extract sat next to a few spices and disposable salt and pepper shakers. Riley grinned and set it on the counter. "Please let there be milk," she whispered as she opened the fridge. *Yes.* A half-full quart sat on the nearly empty top shelf. She grabbed it and turned.

And almost slammed into Sam's chest. She gasped and leaped back, her free hand slapping to her chest in a classic gesture of shock.

"Jesus Christ, Sam!" she whispered fiercely. "What the hell?"

"Sorry." His voice was a low rumble, perfect for the intimacy of late night and darkness. He took the milk from her and closed the fridge door. "Couldn't sleep, huh?"

She made some kind of sound of agreement but couldn't manage more than that because Sam was wearing those sweats again and nothing else. And he was close, the narrow space between the stove and the breakfast bar behind them seeming so much smaller than when the three of them were doing dishes. Probably because then he'd been wearing a shirt. With long sleeves. Now she could see every groove of every curving muscle in his arms, the wide, hard expanse of his chest, and when he turned away to get a saucepan from a bottom cupboard, the amazing strength in his back and shoulders. Just enough of his heat reached her to make her aware of the chill in the apartment and imagine him folding her into his long arms, warming her head to toe.

Okay, she wasn't chilly anymore.

The pan clattered a little when he set it on the stove, and Riley winced. "Shh. Marley's sleeping."

"She wears earplugs."

Riley scowled, and Sam noticed. His dimple flashed. "When she first moved to Boston, she complained about the traffic noise at night. She's used to living in an old inn in the Maine woods."

She tried to toss off a casual shrug to pretend she hadn't suspected—or cared—that he knew for a more personal reason. Sam backed away when she moved to the stove and flicked on a burner.

"You want some vanilla milk?" she offered. "I'm assuming you can't sleep, either."

"No, too much going on." He leaned against the counter a couple of feet away and rubbed his hands over his face. "I'd love some. Never had vanilla milk. It works?"

She shrugged again and poured the milk into two mugs, then the pan. "There's tryptophan in the milk, just like in turkey, and that's what makes us sleepy after a turkey dinner. The warmth is soothing, and the vanilla just tastes good. I haven't had it in years, though. Something made me think of it tonight and it seemed worth trying."

Sam stood by silently while she added vanilla and sugar to the pan and stirred. Then there was nothing to do but wait. She stared awkwardly at the still milk and struggled for something to say. Sam was looking down at her, and between that and the growing need to flatten her hands on his chest, she couldn't think of a word.

"I heard you and Marley talking earlier." Sam unfolded his arms and braced his hands on the edge of the counter behind him.

Riley flushed, wondering if she'd said anything stupid or embarrassing. "I didn't realize we were that loud."

"You weren't. Tiny apartment. Flimsy walls."

She nodded and tore her gaze away from the stove. To look up at him hurt her neck, so she shifted to lean diagonally opposite him, putting a few feet between them. Sam's gaze skimmed down her body, and a new wave of heat followed. Her oversized T-shirt and cotton sleep pants weren't very sexy, but *something* put appreciation in his eyes.

He cleared his throat and turned to give the milk a stir before resettling into position. "Yeah, she told you about Quinn and me. I just wanted you to know that's long over."

Riley's mouth twitched into a smile before she controlled it. Her heart bounced. There was only one reason for him to tell her this. "Okay."

"She's still my best friend, and I'd do anything for her and Nick. But that's all there is."

"Okay," she said again, her pleasure fading when he lapsed back into concerned contemplation. "How sick is she?"

He sighed and pushed a hand through his shaggy hair, then leaned to glance down the hall as if to make sure Marley's door was still closed. "I didn't want to talk about it in front of Marley. Apparently, pretty sick. The power the leech took, it's energy from four different goddesses. She's not supposed to have it inside her like that, and I guess she's starting to suffer for it."

Riley didn't understand. The energy she drew on left her when she used it. "Why can't she expel it?"

"This is different." He shook his head, rubbing one hand over his chest. "It's more than just energy, it's…I don't know, potential? She can't get rid of it, not without sending it back where it came from."

"And she can't do that?"

He winced. "Nick says they've found a way, but they need me to help."

Riley felt a sinking disappointment. "Are you leaving, then?" A curl of steam rose over the pan, and she stepped forward to test the temperature, glad to be able to hide her expression from Sam. But his answer surprised her.

"No. Not now."

She looked up, and his eyes were intense on hers. She

swallowed. "Why?"

"Because I'm needed here. We need to figure out what Anson's doing. John said he works for Millinger, and there are other people from that company approaching goddesses."

"Attacking them?" It hadn't occurred to her that Vern and Sharla and all the other harassment might not have been personal.

But Sam shook his head again. "No. Some of them are uneasy about the whole thing, but no one's gone through what you have. Which makes me more concerned."

"Yeah. Me, too." She carefully poured the hot milk into the mugs. Being a target was bad enough, but for that to be part of some bigger plan added a new layer of nefariousness. "So what do we do?"

Sam accepted the cup and sipped, then smiled. "This is good." He turned serious again. "We train you. Help you get some control over your abilities and learn what you're capable of. Figure out what the deal was with your family, since that's the other main reason we came here. In the meantime, I'll do what I can to figure out what the hell Anson and Millinger are up to, so we can stop them."

Riley nodded. They drank in comfortable silence for a few minutes. Well, mostly comfortable. Every time he raised his mug, swallowed, licked his lips, something hungry got a grip inside her. She liked everything about him, from the shape of his mouth to the glide of his throat and the way his fingers wrapped almost all the way around his mug. Her body tingled, and she wished they'd met under different circumstances. When she wasn't a lonely, clueless woman in jeopardy looking for him to save her.

When her mug was empty, she placed it and the pan into the sink to wash in the morning. "I think I can sleep now," she lied.

"Me, too." Sam's arm stretched past her to set his mug next to hers, and he didn't ease back afterward. Riley stood still, breathing faster, hoping he wouldn't move away. Her nipples puckered against the soft fabric of her T-shirt. If he was looking, he had to notice. She soaked him in, just inches away, afraid to raise her head and find that she was delusional, that he was oblivious to her proximity and examining the dirt on top of the refrigerator or something.

But then his hand nudged her chin upward. The heat in his gaze made her breath catch. Her mouth parted and his eyes lowered to it, eyelids dropping seductively.

"Thanks for the milk," he murmured. His body tilted toward hers.

"You're welcome," she whispered, struggling to keep her eyes open, to keep her body from going completely soft in case this was all in her head and she was about to look very stupid.

But Sam slowly closed the distance between their mouths. A shiver went through Riley when they met, a gentle press, a perfect meeting with no awkwardness or misalignment. He smelled incredible, just himself this time, no city air or bar aromas mingling with pure Sam. Her hand came up to his chest, and his skin was hot despite the cool apartment. He made a small sound in the back of his throat, and then his hand pressed into the small of her back, pulling her closer. His mouth opened, parting her lips, and his tongue touched hers. Asking permission. She opened wider and he accepted the invitation with a sigh and a hint of hunger. His arms wrapped around her and his other hand cupped the back of her head. He surrounded her, and Riley melted with the realization that never in her entire life had she felt she belonged somewhere like she belonged here.

Sam slowly broke the kiss and loosened his hold. He wasn't breathing hard like she was, but unsteadily, and she could have sworn his hand shook when it swept her hair back over her shoulder. He smiled, a promise, and Riley smiled back.

He kissed her on the forehead and murmured, "Goodnight, Riley. Sleep tight," before sliding away. A moment later, his bedroom door clicked closed.

Hugging to herself the first sense of joy she'd had in a very long time, Riley went to her own room and fell asleep easily, a smile still on her face.

CHAPTER SIX

All goddesses have a unique range and combination of abilities,
generally with greater talent in one area and lesser ability in others.
Some of the most common abilities include: Telekinesis, ability to
heal, command over natural elements, transformative power over
perception…

—*The Society for Goddess Education and Defense,* Goddess
Source/Ability Catalog

"Wow," John said. "You're really sweating. Take a break."

Riley grabbed a towel from a short stack on a shelf and sank onto a roll of mats against the wall. The training center was one big room lined with crash pads. It took up half the seventh floor, and the rest was storage for another company. Sam sat in the corner with his laptop and cell phone, joining them every so often in a drill or chiming in with some advice or information, but otherwise ignoring them to focus on his research. Riley almost wished he weren't there at all. Testing was easier when no one else was watching, especially not a guy who'd kissed you the night before but then didn't act any different come morning.

Not that "testing" was a good word for what they were doing.

John wasn't a scientist. He was a fighter, something she should have thought of and been prepared for before she started this. He'd given her a tire iron and had her demonstrate what she could do with it. Not simply moving objects across the table or lifting something heavy, oh, no. He made Sam pretend to attack her, to give her impetus to throw him across the room. John wanted to see how much power she had to reverse momentum. When she'd described metal's effect on her body, he'd put her through some basic fighting maneuvers to test her strength, then acrobatics to check her agility. Never mind that she'd never flipped or cartwheeled in her life. At least, not since she was about ten.

But she could *do* it. He'd shown her an aerial and, after marveling that a guy nearly fifty was capable of doing a flip like that without using his hands for support—simultaneously pleasing and annoying him—she'd tried, and actually landed on her feet. Knocked the tire iron out of her hand doing it, and put a gouge in the floor—but already, she'd expanded her abilities.

The success gave her enough confidence to shed her self-consciousness as long as they were working, but when they stopped, her awareness zoomed right back in on Sam. He'd offered praise and suggestions and zero judgment, but there was still a new layer of awkwardness stemming from last night. She wanted to be impressive but was afraid she looked stupid with everything she did.

"Here."

Riley opened her eyes and took the bottle of water John handed down to her. "Thanks."

"You're looking good." He crouched next to her, his own bottle dangling from one hand. "You obviously have some force, both with channeling and with increasing your natural strength and agility. You're able to defend yourself, and that's important right now."

"Is that all I'm capable of?" She hoped she didn't sound

petulant. "It sounds like it has limited application. What about when I'm *not* being harassed by jerks?"

He smiled. "That's next. You ready?"

She drank a few more gulps of water. "Ready." She let him pull her to her feet and followed him to a card table he'd dragged to the middle of the room. She studied the items on its surface. A paper clip, a small screw, a book of matches, some coins, a crumpled ball of paper, a small book, and a letter opener. She sat in one molded plastic chair, and John swung his around to straddle it.

"What I want to see now is finesse," he said.

"You mean how little energy I need to draw?"

"Right. We know you can open up with contact to a large mass of metal. But how much do you need, and what can you do with it?"

"I can tell you now, it's not much." She glanced into Sam's corner, but he was engrossed in a phone conversation and staring at his laptop screen. "The last few months would have been much easier if draping my body in jewelry did the trick. All it does is make me a little less tired."

"You're still talking about blowing people across the room." He handed her the small screw, which she folded into her fist. "Can you move that piece of paper?"

Riley had been told she didn't need the gesture, but she was used to aiming so she held her free hand flat, fingers pointing toward the balled-up paper, and concentrated on flowing power through the screw, into her body, and out at the paper. A second later it flew off the table and smacked John in the shoulder.

"See? Glad I didn't choose something more solid."

"It's just paper," Riley countered. "I can't do that with something bigger." She tried with the book, a paperback, but the pages barely fluttered.

John tilted his chair to reach down and retrieve the paper. "It's okay. Whatever you can do, you can do. Some things take practice.

Some things you'll never be capable of." He set the paper back on the table. "Like I said, we're looking for control here, not strength. Try again, but just nudge it."

Riley nodded and concentrated. Again, the ball of paper flew. This time he caught it and set it on the table. "Draw back, only let a little power through."

She concentrated less hard, and this time the ball skittered a few inches and stopped. A grin spread over her face, banishing her frustration.

"Great. Now try the paper clip." She did, and the coins, and all of them worked as long as the object she tried to move stayed small and light. She still couldn't affect the book. Nor could she reverse the process—when she tried moving the paper toward her, it did nothing more than rock a little.

"What's it feel like?" John asked her.

Riley blew out a breath and shoved her bangs off her forehead. "It feels like my brain won't bend that way." She unfolded the hand clenching the screw. Red marks in her palm bracketed the metal. "Usually, I pull the energy through the metal into me, then push it out to do whatever I want to do."

"You've had this for three years," John pointed out. "What have you done with it?"

Her face flushed. "Not much. I mean, it took a while to figure out what was going on, and then I concentrated on *not* doing anything. I avoided metal, and when I couldn't, I kept it in." Holding the rushing sensation back hadn't been that difficult. At least, not when she wasn't afraid or angry. "The last six months, I've mostly been using it to keep people away from me. Everything I've done has been channeling outward."

John nodded. "So you've been directing the flow of energy in one direction, and this"—he nodded at the paper—"tries to reverse the flow midstream."

"Exactly."

He suggested imagery and steps to change what she was trying to do and still get the effect she was going for, but nothing worked. Riley got more and more frustrated, which seemed to dam everything up so she couldn't even direct the power out to the paper, never mind "tell" it to bring the paper toward her.

"One more thing," John said, glancing at his watch. "Then lunchtime."

Good. She was starving.

"I want you to set these matches on fire."

She stared at him. "The whole pack? At once?"

He made a face. "Okay, try one." He ripped one from the pack and stuck the end of it into the side of the paper clip, to protect his fingers, and held it out. "Try that. Hold the screw, and channel heat. Flame. Elements. Whatever."

"Very helpful," Riley muttered, but she tried. Nothing happened. When she held the letter opener, she could access enough energy to bend the match under the force of her attempt, and then twist the whole paperclip out of shape. But John said he didn't feel any warmth. She held the tire iron instead, with similar results despite the larger mass of metal.

"So what does all this mean?" Riley asked.

"It means you're average." He gathered up the things on the table.

Riley helped him, disgruntled. She didn't want to be a freak, but now that she knew she wasn't, she didn't want to be average, either. It was kind of a letdown after all the raving about her uniqueness.

"Average how?" she asked.

"Very few goddesses are like Quinn, able to heal and move stuff and sense things and alter perception and set fires. Most are concentrated in a couple of areas. Like her mother, Tess. She can grow the most gorgeous plants you ever saw, and she can make changes to living tissue. Remove scars, fix teeth, stuff like that."

Marley had told her a little about this already. "But she can't throw a person ten feet."

He chuckled. "No, I don't think she can." He hefted the table and moved it back to one side of the room. Riley got up and followed with the two chairs.

"So what would you call my thing?"

He shrugged. "No need to label it. Consider it a starting point. We can do other tests. Be careful what you try on your own, though, so you don't hurt anyone." He cocked his head as he looked at her, and she could almost see the thoughts spinning through his brain. "If you wanted, you could turn this into a lucrative bodyguard career, something like that. Or join the Protectorate. We haven't had a protector goddess in a long time. Not since I can remember."

Riley sighed. She'd barely adjusted to the idea that the Society wasn't a gang of con artists or something, and he wanted her to be a champion for them? "It's a lot to think about. But thanks."

"No problem."

They paused next to Sam, who didn't seem to realize they were there for a few seconds. But when he looked up, his gaze landed squarely on Riley, and he smiled enough to expose the dimples and make her insides swoop.

"All done?" he asked.

"For now," John said. "Marley set some time aside to dig with her through the archives, and I have meetings. You ready for lunch?"

Sam frowned at the computer. "I need a few more minutes. I'll lock up here."

John tossed him a set of keys and turned to Riley. "There's a shower upstairs if you want to use it before you cram yourself into Marley's office."

"Thanks," she said. "I will."

He left, and Riley hesitated. She didn't want to interrupt if Sam was deep into something, but he caught her hand when she started to move away. The contact somehow eliminated all her uncertainty, even when he closed the laptop and faced her with a very unhappy expression.

"You know what I told you yesterday about Quinn and the leeched power?"

She nodded, distracted by the way his fingers wrapped around her hand. His was so big, she wondered if he even noticed he was still holding hers, or that his thumb was stroking her palm. The sensation shivered its way up her arm and into her chest.

He sighed. "I have to go to Mississippi."

"What?" That wasn't what she'd expected him to say, especially after he told her last night that he was staying. "Now?"

He nodded, his mouth turning down and his eyes murky with worry. "Nick said Quinn's getting worse. She can't put off making the transfers, especially now that they apparently know what to do."

Riley frowned. "I can understand that, but why does it have to be you?"

He stood and released her to pack his laptop into its case. "Something about needing a filter to help separate the power. He didn't go into a lot of detail, just insisted it had to be me. Look." He set the case on the floor and faced her, his hands on her shoulders. "I don't want to leave here with the Millinger issue unfinished, but I've spent the last few hours researching and making calls, and I'm not getting anywhere. No one has any information. I can't reach anyone associated with Millinger at any of their claimed locations.

"On the plus side," he continued, not sounding all that positive, "no one has seen Anson anywhere near here. If you stick with John and stay around other people, you'll be safe until I get back."

Riley wasn't worried about her safety at the moment. She'd held her own against both John and Sam today, and she doubted anyone would approach her while she was around the Society. But she hated that Sam had to leave right now, when they were just getting started.

"How long do you think you'll be gone?"

He hefted the laptop case over his shoulder and walked out with her, flipping off the lights and locking the door with John's keys. "A couple of days at the most. I'll fly down tonight, meet up with them to do the transfer tomorrow, and fly back as soon as I can." They went into the stairwell and climbed toward the floor above. "I don't know yet how this all works, but I'll keep you posted."

"I hope it all goes well, and that Quinn's okay." Riley reached for the door at the landing, but again Sam's hand on hers stopped her.

"I'm sorry to do this now, when we haven't even had a chance to talk about last night."

Her heart fluttered, and she was sure it showed in her eyes when she looked up at him. "What is there to say?"

One side of his mouth twitched up. "It was that bad?"

She laughed. "Hardly. We just met, that's all." God, had it been barely two days ago? They'd packed what felt like a month's worth of living into such a short time. "I can't expect anything from you."

"Oh, yes, you can." He tugged her against him and cupped her face, his other hand hot on her back. Riley had time for a fleeting thought that she was a sweaty mess, but it vanished as soon as their mouths met. His lips were soft and smooth, but firm and talented as they swept across hers. He nipped at her bottom lip and she opened to him, accepting his tongue in a hungry dance.

Too soon, Sam cradled her head between his hands and released her mouth. His breath panted into hers, and he kept his eyes closed for several moments before he spoke.

"I really don't want to leave you."

Riley couldn't tell him not to, and she couldn't make herself say it was okay, so she stayed silent. The pads of Sam's fingers dragged across her scalp, igniting a cascade of shivers that forced her eyes closed. As soon as she did, he kissed her again, this one gentler.

"I'll call you," Sam said. "John will watch out for you, but please be careful."

"I will." The words came out rough. She cleared her throat. "Don't worry about me."

He chuckled. "I will."

Then, so quickly it felt gratifyingly like he was tearing himself away, he was gone.

CHAPTER SEVEN

The greatest of power is built not accompanied by fanfare and spotlights, but quietly, with a constant eye on long-term growth. Power and influence, invested properly, is its own return.

—Numina manifesto, *revised*

Riley felt better after she'd showered, but only physically. Knowing Sam was gone created a hole that was completely illogical, given how short a time he'd been in her life. But that life had irrevocably changed in the last few days, and he was an intrinsic part of the change. She missed him, and he'd been gone about half an hour.

She was about to leave the shower room when she heard raised voices and hesitated. John was in the hall talking to a woman Riley had briefly met this morning—Jeannine, the president of the board.

"This is the absolute worst time for us to lose you," she said.

"It's not like I'd be disappearing into the jungle. I'll be around. But you knew when I first came in here it was temporary. This isn't my thing, riding a desk."

"And you think Nick Jarrett is any better suited to it?" There was bitterness as well as argument in her voice.

"I think he'll be on the road a lot. But he's younger, smarter, less resistant to change. I'm not talking about doing this tomorrow." An edge had entered his voice. "Nick will come in to head recruitment, and I'll train him to replace me in a year or so."

Jeannine lowered her voice. "And what about Numina? I thought we agreed not to bring anyone else in on this until we had a better handle on what we're dealing with."

Numina? Riley had never heard the word, but the context gave it a sinister essence.

"The bigger it gets, the less comfortable I am keeping it to ourselves." John had lowered his voice, too, and the combination of what they were saying and the hushed-but-urgent way they were saying it sent shivers of apprehension through Riley. "Others will have to be involved before too long."

"Probably. But I won't let you walk away." Footsteps came closer. Riley hoped there wasn't steam seeping through the crack in the door.

The steps halted suddenly. "Make no mistake, Jeannine. You have no say in this. I may work in this building, but the Protectorate is and always will be a separate entity. I know you don't like that I'm not under your thumb, but I refuse to let you try to put me there, even now. If I want Nick to take over, Nick will take over."

Riley could almost feel the fury radiating through the hall. "It's not up to you, either. Nick has to agree. He might not."

"Then I'll find someone else. But you won't resist this."

"Whatever. Be ready in five minutes."

And with that, the woman stalked down the hall. Riley only had a glimpse of beige flashing past the skinny gap in the doorway. She waited, hearing nothing from John. He'd probably gone back into his office, which was in the opposite direction.

Riley bit her lip. She had only been part of the Society for a couple of days, but she already knew tension between it and the Protectorate was a bad thing. John was upset that they were keeping things from…whom? Everyone? It sounded like Numina was new to everyone, not just her. Old fears and suspicions reared up, and for a second she was ready to run again, but the feeling was short lived. Stronger was the urge to learn more, to join in the fight.

John and Jeannine knew more about what was going on than they'd told Sam. Whatever Numina was, it must connect to Millinger and Anson's plans.

Maybe Jeannine's secrecy should feed Riley's reservations about the Society, but everyone had been welcoming and helpful to her so far, and now she was torn between old fears and new loyalties. She couldn't just walk away and leave Sam and Marley and anyone else to be affected or harmed by this whole thing, especially when she seemed to be part of it. She had to do more.

Since she had no idea what, however, she'd start with the original plan and see what they could come up with in the archives about her family. Maybe tonight she'd be able to talk to Sam and tell him what she'd heard. He did say he'd call. She smiled at the thought.

Marley looked up from her computer when Riley reached her office. "Oh, crap, I lost track of time. Come on in. I just need to finish this e-mail real quick."

Riley pulled the guest chair around to sit next to Marley behind the desk. She had to lift the chair up and over, since there wasn't room to slide it past. "Thanks again for doing this. And for everything else."

"Don't be silly. I'm not doing much." She typed furiously for a couple of minutes, hit *send*, and pulled up another program.

"You're doing a lot." Riley was acutely aware of that and very grateful. "So what are we looking for?"

"Well, I already looked up your mother's maiden and married names in the database and searched the archives. There's no mention of her. What was your grandmother's name?"

Riley thought hard. "When you looked for my mother's last name, would my grandmother have come up in the search?"

"She should have, if she was part of the Society under that name. She didn't, though."

"So we have to look up my grandmother's maiden name. God, that's…" She put a hand over her eyes and went deep, struggling to remember a name she'd never had any reason to store. It popped into her head. "Freeman?" She looked up. "Yes! Nessie Freeman. I guess that would be short for Vanessa or something."

Marley typed in the name. "We've been digitizing old records for a few years. They go back centuries, so it's going to take us forever, but we've processed beyond a few decades, at least. It's not all organized, though. I have to dig in a few different places."

It took a while for Marley to search in the main archives database, then use the references to locate various files and the relevant documents within them. Finally, they had it all compiled for the three names the search had given them: Henrietta, Nessarina, and Beatrice Freeman. After clicking several documents open, Marley whistled. "Wow. There's a lot here. Mostly meeting attendance records, though. Let me print some of it." She clicked another link, and Riley skimmed the page with her. It looked like a genealogy breakdown.

"So Nessarina was my grandmother, and Henrietta was her mother, Beatrice her sister. I never knew about Beatrice. Not really." The page displayed a date of death before Riley was born. She remembered her grandmother mentioning a sister, now that she thought about it, but not very often.

Marley handed her a sheaf of pages. After shuffling them into what appeared to be chronological order, Riley read while Marley kept working on the computer.

Her great-grandmother, Henrietta, had been married to a man named Earl, owner of a company she recognized as part of a huge conglomerate now. He'd sold it before he died, apparently not willing to leave it to his daughters or their husbands. Back then, goddesses probably weren't as open about their existence or as interested in using their abilities commercially. Witch burning had peaked centuries before, but its effects had lasted a long time.

A membership roster listed rock and soil as the source for both Nessie and Beatrice, but Henrietta's listing was odd. Hers was wood, with a notation of "depleted" after it, and a date when Henrietta would have been… Riley did a quick calculation. About fifty years old. Five years before her husband died. She'd followed within a year.

"What does depleted mean?" she asked Marley.

"Depleted?" The color drained from Marley's face. "You mean like leeched?"

"Maybe." Riley grimaced. "Sorry."

"No, it's fine. What does it say?"

"Just a notation next to my great-grandmother's source. Wood. Both her daughters had rock and soil. Is it weird that neither one has their mother's source?"

Marley shrugged and took the page from her. "Weirder that they had the same one. There's no genetic component to source affinity. They might have misrepresented their powers to the Society—that could explain disassociation. Let me see if I can find something about the depletion."

Riley kept reading. Birth notices for her grandmother and great-aunt, then nothing until they each got married, one at age eighteen, the other at nineteen. Nessie hit twenty-one a year before Beatrice, and Henrietta reported their power sources within a month of their birthdays. But after that, letters repeatedly requested that both girls attend a Society meeting or come to Boston to demonstrate their abilities for the official record. The letters got more forceful until one said their continued membership in the Society was contingent upon such demonstration.

The last letter was short and to the point. It revoked both of their memberships.

Marley was right. Someone, whether Riley's grandmother and

great-aunt or their mother, had lied about their abilities. Maybe they'd hoped the Society would take them at their word, but they obviously hadn't. What had happened?

"No wonder my grandmother hated the Society," Riley said, staring at the revocation letter. The words looked stark black on white in a way the original typewritten page probably hadn't. "They kicked her out."

"Oh, my God." Marley hit a few keys and the printer hummed. "That's not all. You've got to read this."

Riley swapped pages with her and skimmed the old, cramped handwriting. She gasped and went back to start over, reading slowly. The words were stilted, the formal written language of several generations ago, and the paper had been old and worn when it was scanned. Fold creases made some lines hard to read, and a tear along one of them created a blank. But Riley got the gist. Whoever wrote this letter accused her great-grandmother, Henrietta, of letting her husband repeatedly drain her abilities for his own use.

"How is that possible?" Riley felt sick to her stomach. The old woman's description made it sound like abuse, but it wasn't any kind of abuse Riley had ever heard of. "Have you ever—"

Marley shook her head sadly. "It makes a lot of sense, though, you know?"

"How?" Riley cried, looking up from the page and setting it hard on the desk before she crumpled the paper further. "I don't understand any of this!"

Marley glanced at the half-closed hall door and kept her voice low. "Remember how Anson got started?"

It took Riley a few seconds to shift gears. She shook her head impatiently. "Something about giving him ability to draw power."

"Right. I bestowed some of my power on him. But it doesn't last." She leaned forward. "For us, as long as we have our source to channel the energy, we can access it. But when we take some of that capacity, some of what's inside us" —she clenched her fist around her shirt and pressed it into her breastbone— "and put it into a willing receptacle, they can use only the energy we give them. Then it's gone. I could have given Anson more, but it was limited and he was greedy. So he took it from other goddesses. *All* of it. It broke them, and changed him."

Riley blinked against tears of anger and shame that didn't belong to her, but to a woman she'd never met. "So you think my great-grandfather was a leech? But instead of attacking other goddesses, he just kept drawing on his wife's power? Depleting her to nothing? That's sick!"

Marley nodded. "I think he must have drained her very low before conception. Maybe kept her drained during the pregnancy. But that could explain why your grandmother and great-aunt didn't have the power they claimed. So then they didn't have it to pass on to your mother, either."

"That makes no sense," Riley argued. "How could I have it if my mother didn't?"

Marley shrugged. "I'm not a geneticist, and what we are defies science. But maybe you're a throwback in the purest sense? Like someone who becomes a piano prodigy 'just like Grandpa Joe' or something even though their parents have no musical talent."

Riley took a deep breath, uncertain why she was so angry about all of this. She'd never know if her great-grandfather had been greedy, if he'd forcibly taken what he wanted, or if Henrietta had given it willingly. With her grandmother and mother gone, she couldn't find out if Nessie and Beatrice had been born without power, or if he'd taken theirs, too. Had they understood why and how they'd been robbed of their legacies? Probably not, since Nessie, at least, had blamed the Society. And she'd passed on the hatred to her daughter.

A powerful longing for her mother overcame her. Her anger faded, and she understood it wasn't anger for Henrietta, but anger *at* her. She'd taken away something so vital and intrinsic from all of them, even Riley.

"Is there any more?" Her voice came out raspy and half its normal strength. She pushed the pages across the desktop.

Marley took them and stacked them neatly in a folder that she left on the desk, clearly available if Riley wanted it back. "No," she said gently. "That's it."

"How…I mean…" Riley cleared her throat. "Has anything like this happened before?"

"Not that I'm aware of. And I think they'd have told me. There are some members who would have been *very* happy to connect me with people like that. Or kick me out of the Society, if they knew it had been done before."

"Okay." Riley took a deep breath and tried to shake off the weight of this information. She checked the time. The offices would be closing soon. "We should get going."

Marley clicked to shut down the computer and hit the monitor's power button. "You okay?"

"Yeah. I just feel…adrift, I guess." She stood while Marley shoved some files into her messenger bag. "It's frustrating. I want to run to my mother and demand to know why she didn't tell me any of this. Why she let me find out the hard way. She probably had no idea it would happen, but this whole thing makes me feel even more distant from my family."

"I get that." The computer screen went dark. Marley switched off the wireless mouse and stood, stretching a little. "You said you have some cousins and stuff, right? Anyone you can talk to?"

"No, they're all on my dad's side." She went out into the hall and waited while Marley locked the door. "I don't want to talk about it anymore. There's no point. At least I understand things better than I did before."

She could blame the Society for not keeping track of her family, for assuming once the power was gone, it would never come back. But what good would that do? These women weren't the ones who'd made that decision. They weren't even aware of it. Riley just had to accept it for what it was.

"Where's John?" Marley stopped at his dark office. "I thought he said he'd take us back to the apartment."

Disgruntled and depressed, Riley resented feeling like a child who couldn't set foot outside without adult supervision. After training today, it seemed ridiculous to have to rely on a powerless man to protect her. And in the mood she was in, she dared anyone to try anything.

"It's only a few blocks," she said. "We can walk it okay." She wouldn't plow ahead unprepared, though. She needed metal, more than the handful of nuts and bolts in her pocket. She thought of the tire iron in the training room and decided to go get it. So what if she'd look foolish carrying it? It would probably ward off more than Millinger stalkers.

"Why don't you call John's cell?" she suggested. "I'll be right back." She hurried to the end of the beige-carpeted hallway to the stairwell, clattered down one flight, and pushed through the fire door into the big room now illuminated by two security lights on the wall. She grabbed the tire iron from its spot on the shelf and ran back to Marley, who was putting her phone away.

"He and Jeannine had another meeting on the other side of the city. He's *pissed*. He was supposed to be back here by now, but he's stuck on the highway. Overturned fuel truck. They're apparently turning cars around to go back to the last exit, but he figures he's got at least an hour before he gets back here."

Riley really didn't want to hang around, and part of her didn't want to see him after what she'd overheard today. "Did you tell him we'd be okay?"

"Yeah." Marley smiled. "He didn't like it, but he didn't have any other solution. He said to tell you to get the tire—Yeah, that." She laughed as Riley hefted it. "Okay, then. What do you want to eat?"

They discussed takeout options as they headed out into the waning twilight and walked toward the apartment.

"We have some chicken and pork in the freezer," Marley mused. "Do you eat meat?" They paused at an alley to make sure the way was clear. "I have a recipe I've been wanting to try, for this pork chop glaze."

Riley stopped walking. A stone had worked its way into her shoe, and she bent to slip it off and dump the stone. Marley didn't notice and stepped out to cross the alley. An engine roared, and Riley looked down the alley to see a motorcycle zooming straight at her roommate.

She didn't have time to think. She dropped her shoe and, with her left hand clenched hard around the tire iron, shot her other hand out. Power flooded her body and zipped through her. She realized then that the cyclist wasn't trying to hit Marley. He drove one-handed and seemed to be reaching for the satchel draped across her body.

Riley's surge hit him at the same time his hand curled around the strap. Marley spun, but the bike tilted when it hit the dip where alley met street. He fell sideways, and Marley shrieked and jumped back, tripping over the curb and landing hard on the sidewalk.

Tiny, hard fragments dug into her shoeless foot as Riley ran and awkwardly leapt over the cycle to land straddling the driver. He was young, his face shaved smooth, his brown hair trimmed short. He lay on his back, the shoulder of his long-sleeved shirt torn. Riley crouched and grabbed the shirt, pulling him up toward her. His eyes rolled, unfocused, as if he'd banged his helmetless head when he fell. One hand scrabbled at her fist.

"Who are you?" She brandished the tire iron, concentrating on drawing energy to boost her strength again, and shook the guy a little. All the anger at her family's lies manifested in a raging desperation for answers. "Who are you? Who do you work for?"

"Riley." Marley sounded confused. "He's a mugger."

He could be, but Riley didn't believe it. A mugger would have hidden his face and been on foot. Who mugged people on a motorcycle?

"Who?" she demanded again, and the guy reached for his back pocket. She released him to knock his hand out of the way and pulled out his wallet, flipping it open. On the left, in the plastic window, was his driver's license. The photo matched, but the edge of the window blocked his name. On the right, she spotted the top of a familiar-looking business card. Millinger's logo. She didn't recognize the name printed on it.

Marley murmured something behind her. Riley caught the words "security team" and realized she had called someone, probably John or a member of the Society board or Protectorate instead of the police.

Riley wasn't waiting for them. She dropped the wallet and grabbed his shirt again. "Tell me what Millinger wants with us."

"I don't know," the guy croaked out. He tilted his head back and looked pleadingly at Marley. She held her palm toward him, and he squirmed in panic, his heels digging into the asphalt. He twisted back to Riley. "Please, don't magic me."

"We don't do magic," she scoffed. "Just tell us."

"They told me to swipe the bag and bring the contents to the office, that's all."

"What's your job there?"

"I'm a consultant."

"Aren't you all." Riley shoved him away in disgust. "Who's your boss?"

"I don't know. I mean, I don't have one. I get my instructions from the owner."

"And he is?" She stood but didn't move away from him. "What's his name?"

"I don't know!" he insisted. He wiggled backward until she brandished her weapon. "Honest! I don't even know if it's a guy!"

"Why would you work in a job like that?" she asked.

"It pays a lot of money. But not enough for this!" He'd played her with his frightened weenie act, or just got desperate and then lucky. Either way, Riley wasn't ready for him to lash out. His fist struck her in the side of the head. Lights flashed, and she staggered back, gasping in pain when something, probably a foot, hit her wrist and made her drop the tire iron. Seconds later, the small bike roared to life. Riley's vision cleared in time to see the "mugger" skidding around the next corner and out of their sight.

Riley cursed loudly. Her head swam when she bent to pick up the tire iron. Only Marley's grip on her elbow kept her from toppling over.

"Are you okay?" Marley thumbed her phone again. "You need an ambulance."

"Don't bother. I'm fine." She rubbed her temple. "Who did you call?"

"John. He's alerting the security team. I should have called the police instead," she fretted.

"It's fine. Don't second guess yourself." Riley was going to have a headache, but her vision wasn't blurred and the lightheadedness had passed, so hopefully no concussion. "See if you can have them meet us at the apartment. I don't think we should hang around here."

They hurried down the street while Marley called again, John's anger coming through to Riley even though he didn't shout. They got safely into the apartment a few minutes later, and Riley immediately went to take a painkiller.

"You didn't know him, did you?" she asked when she came back to the living room. Marley shook her head. Her eyes were too wide, though, and her grip on the satchel too tight, despite being locked inside now.

"You know something, though," she encouraged. "He said something familiar to you. Was it Millinger? You know Millinger?"

She wasn't sure, but maybe they'd never said the company name in front of Marley.

Tears filled the other woman's eyes. She dropped the satchel on the coffee table, sat on the couch, and covered her face. "It's Anson."

Riley pulled her sleeves down over suddenly cold hands and wrapped her arms around herself. "You think that's who sent this guy?"

Marley shrugged a shoulder. "I don't know, but it's an awfully big coincidence."

"What is?"

"He was an orphan. His mother died in childbirth, and he said his grandmother let them put him in foster care but stayed in contact with him. I'm pretty sure her last name was Millinger."

Everything she'd been told about Anson paraded through Riley's head. He'd gone through a lot to get power the first time. How far would he go now?

Knowledge was supposed to make things easier. Take away the fear, give you something to fight. But the more she learned, the bigger the picture became, the more she hated sitting around waiting to be targeted again.

Joining the goddess world hadn't been all good, but she'd be damned if she let anyone take it away from her.

Riley stood and headed for the spare bedroom. "Pack a bag. We're going to Georgia."

"What?" Marley stopped in the doorway her eyes wide. "Now? The security team is coming!"

Riley tossed her bag onto the bed and shoved a stack of shirts into it. Over the past few months she had filed several police reports, learning quickly how little good it did. They were all overworked and had far more important things to worry about. Plus, this guy hadn't touched them, not until Riley had knocked him off his bike and threatened him. Vern's earlier threats echoed—a powerful person could turn this around on them. She could end up being arrested.

She grabbed a few more things from the dresser to stuff into the bag. "What's a security team going to do?"

"Protect us."

Riley shook her head. "All that does is give us a wall to hide behind while we wait for something else to happen. So I'm going to Atlanta."

"Why?" Marley challenged.

"Because that's where Millinger's headquarters is."

"What do you think you're going to do there?"

"Find out what the hell he wants. Are you coming?"

"Who, Anson?" Marley dropped back a step and shook her head. "I can't do that."

Riley zipped the bag's main section. "I'm tired of being a victim, Marley. My family, the Society, all these people who've been following me—this is my life, not theirs. I'm tired of running in the dark, and I won't keep sitting inside some office building surrounded by protectors. I have to end this."

Marley took a deep breath. "That sounds noble, but it's not me. I've rebuilt my life after what Anson took, and I have no interest in revisiting that hell."

Riley straightened and sighed. Marley had fought her battles already and earned her right to say no. She had to respect that. She carried her bag to the dresser to pack her toiletries in the side pocket. "I understand. It's fine. I can go alone."

"Is there *any* way I can stop you from charging down there? It's dangerous."

Riley had already done the calculations. "I'll drive straight down and get to Millinger on Sunday. No one should be there, and all I have to do is search the office for evidence of what they're trying to do. I promise I won't do anything stupid." Even if part of her wanted to confront Anson head on, she really did only need information. For now.

"You should have a protector with you, at least."

Riley only wanted Sam. He was trained as a protector, and he had as much stake in this as she did. But what he was doing was important, too, and the sooner he was done in Mississippi, the sooner he'd be back at her side. All the better if she had something to give them a direction to look in or an action to take when he was.

"I can't wait." She finished stuffing the little bottles into her bag and dropped it on the bed. "I know what I'm capable of now. Protectors don't cover goddesses in power, right?" Marley nodded reluctantly. "So I load up with metal. I have a pipe and a tire iron and some other things in the car." But nothing she could easily wear or carry. "I can take…I don't know, what do you have here?" She tried to think of something portable that wouldn't call a lot of attention. They went into the kitchen and she tested the utensils, but they didn't let her draw enough energy for what she might need. The pans were stainless steel and would be great if they weren't so impractical.

"I'll stop at a hardware store," Riley decided. "Can I borrow your laptop? I need to print off directions. My car doesn't have GPS."

A few minutes later she paused at the door, her hand on the knob. She looked back at Marley. "Are you sure you don't want to come with me?"

Marley bit her lip and shifted her weight from foot to foot. She glanced at the pipe and tire iron slung through the straps of Riley's bag, then at the wall between the living room and kitchen, lined with amethyst and other crystals. Finally, she shook her head. "No. I'd be worthless. I'll stay here and report to the security team, then see if I can learn any more about anything. Call me. And please, *please* be careful." She hugged Riley, who hugged her back with a surge of warmth.

"Thank you," Riley said. "For everything."

Then she was out the door and on her way to her car in the

parking garage, a little excited to have a mission. For the first time since she bounced off that big old Buick the day after her twenty-first birthday, Riley felt in control of something.

CHAPTER EIGHT

My foolishness should not have been rewarded, but my gratitude is endless. My debt will remain unpaid for the remainder of my life, but to become whole again, to embrace that which I lost through my own shortsightedness, has been the greatest joy of my life.

— *Meandress Chronicles, compilation of family diaries*

Sam spent his time on the plane and his layover in Chicago trying to nail down something, anything, on Millinger or Anson Tournado, but still came up agonizingly empty. He'd reactivated some old, not-entirely-legal methods of searching but still nothing. No financial records or leases or utilities in Anson's name, which might mean he was operating on a cash basis since getting out of jail, but could also mean he was using aliases or fronts to hide his activities should anyone go looking.

Vern Nurnan and Sharla Cannalunis turned up a little more, but none of it was helpful. Both had small-time criminal records, had bounced from job to job, and used their credit and debit cards for meaningless purchases. He couldn't find an employment record for Millinger, despite the business cards, but they had said *consultant*, so they probably weren't on any official payroll.

He'd texted Riley a couple of times and talked to her once. She'd sounded distracted and ended the call quickly, leaving him to wonder how upset she was, after all, that he'd left her. It made him more determined to get this done quickly and get back.

Once he'd landed in Jackson, Mississippi, and driven to the hotel where he was meeting Nick and Quinn, it was late, and he was exhausted and cranky after being folded into an economy seat for too many hours. He texted Nick his room number and got a response that they were still en route and would see him in the morning. It was too late to try to call Riley, but he fell asleep thinking of how he could make it up to her, and tested a few of those in his dreams.

He woke to Nick pounding on the motel room door at what seemed like only a couple of hours after he'd fallen asleep. He groggily dragged on jeans and manipulated the locks to let him in.

"What are you doing here so early?" he griped.

Nick looked way too chipper after driving twelve hours, but he was probably thrilled to be back on the road. He'd been stuck in one place for three years after fifteen as a protector, moving from one goddess assignment to the next.

He closed the door behind him and leaned against the wall. "Dude, it's almost noon. We've been waiting for you to drag your lazy ass out of bed and call us. You missed breakfast."

Sam rubbed his eyes and headed for the bathroom. "I'll be out in a minute." He left Nick sighing in mock annoyance and picking up the remote for the TV bolted to the wall.

Sam brushed his teeth and took a fast-and-dirty shower that managed to give him a measure of alertness. But he'd been so groggy he hadn't grabbed clean clothes. He wrapped in a threadbare towel and went back out into the room.

Nick was sitting on the end of the bed, boots planted flat on the floor in front of him. "So?"

"So, what?" Sam pulled clothes out of his duffel bag and started getting dressed.

"So, who's the chick?"

Sam narrowed his eyes at him for a second before yanking a Henley over his head. "What are you talking about?"

Nick flipped off the TV. "The reason you put me off the other day and are in such a hurry to get back to Boston."

"It's about a lot more than just a chick."

"Yeah, I talked to John." He stood and went to the chipboard dresser, flipping a few pages in the info book while he re-rolled the sleeve of the flannel shirt he wore over a T-shirt. "Believe me, I'm as eager to wipe Tournado off the face of the earth as you are. But you've got squat to go on, right?"

Sam grunted and sat to put on his socks and boots.

"So the only reason you'd be in a hurry to get back there must be this new goddess you've discovered."

"I didn't discover her." He didn't know why he was reluctant to tell Nick about Riley, except that he wasn't in the mood for brotherly ribbing or Nick's brand of smugness when he thought he knew it all, which was almost always. "She's vulnerable and a potential target of Anson's."

"And hot?" Nick waggled his eyebrows, and Sam couldn't help laughing.

"Yeah. But that's not why I like her," he defended. But when Nick hooked one finger into the side of the curtain and peeked out into the parking lot, and then scrubbed a hand in his shorter-than-usual spiky blond hair, Sam began to suspect there was something Nick wasn't saying. He wasn't normally this antsy.

"What's going on? Why were you in such an all-fired hurry to get me down here so quickly?"

Nick shot him a sideways look. "I told you. Quinn's sick. She's hurting."

And Nick would never let that go on a second longer than

necessary, Sam knew. "But there's something more than that." He thought about conversations he'd had with both of them over the last few months. "You're not very happy, are you?"

Nick's expression closed up, his eyes darkening. He'd hit a nerve. Sam knew Nick would die before ever admitting it to Quinn. But he also knew Nick. He waited him out, and after Nick tested the durability of the bar lock on the door and kicked the platform under the bed, he finally caved.

"I'm going crazy, man," he admitted. "I'm so freakin' bored, I catch myself hoping someone will attack her."

Sam laughed. "That would be entertainment, not action."

"Tell me about it. The woman needs *nothing*. She can flick her finger and knock a bad guy into next week. Her stamina is incredible, and she even pulls beer faster than anyone in the bar." He shook his head sadly. "I am definitely not needed."

Sam smirked. "Feeling a little inadequate?"

Nick jerked forward and poked his finger at Sam. "No. She doesn't need me for *that* stuff. She still needs me for—you know— other stuff."

Sam sobered. "So, tired of feeling unnecessary. Is that a deal breaker?"

"What do you mean, deal breaker?" Nick stared at him for a second. "You mean, am I done with Quinn?" His eyes blazed with a combination of love and torment. "Hell, no. I want to get married."

Sam was too startled to have anything but a genuine reaction, and that was to grin and start heading over to give Nick a congratulatory man-hug. But Nick warded him off with upraised hands.

"Don't congratulate me too soon. Quinn's balking until we get this transfer thing done. I think she's afraid I'll change my mind afterward, or that something will happen to her and she doesn't want to tie me or something." He threw up his hands and paced as much as the confined area would let him. "I don't know. We both avoided communicating for so many years, I'm not sure we have the skills."

Sam would have snickered at the macho protector talking about communication skills if the implication that Quinn might die hadn't struck him so hard.

"It's that serious?" he asked in a low voice.

Nick settled against the cinderblock wall and folded his arms. "Yeah, I'm afraid it is. And it happened fast. For all this time, she's handled the power fine. Most people would have gone overboard with it. Quinn's kept it low-key, not compromising her ethics or getting greedy. And she has complete control over using it."

There was an obvious *but* coming. Sam quirked an eyebrow.

Nick sighed. "The moon lust is gone, which hasn't been a bad thing, believe me. She's happy to have it all happen naturally. So she gets tired faster but recharges faster, with a short rest, and she hasn't needed to wait for full moon to have peak power."

"Has any of that changed?"

Nick shook his head. "It's just taken a toll. I thought at first it was guilt and sympathy for her friends, but it's deeper than that. She has nightmares. She said a couple of times she feels like something's pulling at her, almost like the power is trying to get back to its original owners, and that's gotten stronger."

Sam didn't like the images that evoked. "That's kind of weird, Nick."

"Of course it is, but hell, Sam, it's magic. As scientific as we try to get with it, we don't really understand how it works in anything more than a basic sense. All I know is that it's doing her harm." He took a deep breath. "Tanda and Chloe live on opposite coasts," he reminded him.

Horror dawned as Sam understood what Nick meant. "It's ripping her apart?"

"Maybe." He paced again. "I don't know. And I don't know if

she can transfer it, or if transferring it will make a difference. She could end up worse."

He glanced at Sam, then away. "Come on. Quinn's waiting. We might as well have the rest of this conversation together."

Sam followed him with a much greater sense of foreboding than he'd had when he left Boston.

. . .

Nick and Quinn had gotten a much nicer room than Sam had, in a newer section of the hotel. He'd been so tired the night before he hadn't even noticed there was a difference. He accepted a hug and a cup of coffee from Quinn, and the three of them settled in the comfortable sitting area to talk.

Quinn looked a little better than Sam had expected. Thinner than when he'd seen her last, and brittle in a way he'd never have described her or thought would even be possible. Her dark hair was shorter and had less body. But her color was good, and her eyes bright. Still, Nick hovered as if he thought she'd keel over, and Sam was surprised he'd left the room long enough to come get Sam.

"So tell me how this works," he said. "How is it different from the way Marley gave power to Anson?"

Quinn folded her legs, engulfed in loose yoga pants, up onto the love seat and leaned against Nick, cradling her coffee in both hands. "He'd never had any power to begin with. We know he was able to receive it because he's the son of a goddess, so there's a genetic factor there, and he wasn't altered before the power was bestowed. Tanda and Chloe had the ability, and it was ripped out of them." She sipped her coffee. "I tried to give Marley's back right after we caught Anson, and I couldn't. She was broken and couldn't accept it. I thought it was because of the way things had happened, but when I tried again with Chloe, it still didn't work. It's not a simple matter of reverse siphoning. I figured I have to fix the vessel before it can accept the power. That's not the hard part."

"The hard part is that the power of four goddesses is mixed together in you," Sam guessed.

"Right. Because it's all comingled, I need a secondary conduit to filter it through. Separate it. It has to be someone we can trust, but it can't be a goddess. Someone with no power, but who is blood relative to a goddess. That rules out a lot of people. It basically means—"

"The son of a goddess." Now he knew why they needed him in particular. He was the only one with the full combination of prerequisites.

He studied them, déjà vu hitting him despite the change in venue. Three years ago, they'd pow-wowed in Quinn's bar about a major threat and how to stop it. "This conversation sounds familiar."

Quinn took a shaky breath. "Yeah, it does. It's the same conditions that create a leech."

Fuck was pretty much the only response to that, so he let it go for now and asked, "How did you figure out how to do the transfers?"

Nick threw his feet up onto the coffee table and crossed his ankles. "We've been doing research since it happened. Some goddesses have family diaries and records of their entire ancestry. We just had to find the right one."

Quinn shoved Nick's feet down and rested her hand on a large, old book on the table. Its leather binding was worn at the edges, the black faded to a dirty gray. "It's happened at least once before, around a hundred years ago, and they were able to transfer the power back. Only one goddess got leeched, though. She gave some power to the man she worked for, and he leeched the rest from her. So that's different, obviously."

"How did she get it back?"

"Her mother retrieved the power from the leech. I don't know how she knew how. Maybe legends or stories told through the generations or something. Maybe she just tried, or guessed." She lifted the book and opened it to a bookmarked page. "Then she used her son, the leeched goddess's brother, as a conduit to filter his sister's power out of her own. He ended up with some residual power, enough to do what Nick calls magic tricks." She smiled at her fiancé with fondness and exasperation. He grinned unrepentantly. "It worked, and the goddess says here that she felt whole again."

"What does she say about her brother?"

Quinn closed the book and set it back down, looking troubled. "After he used the little bit of residual power, he's described as being 'taken with a sickness of the heart.' We don't know what that means or how long it lasted. I was able to find his death certificate, and he was eighty-three when he died in his sleep."

Sam thought about that. Sickness of the heart could mean anything. Love was the first thing that came to mind, but that could be him projecting. Lust was the next. He'd never talked to another goddess who had the moon lust Quinn used to suffer, the driving need for sex to help her recharge when she'd overused her power. That didn't mean they didn't have it. It was the kind of thing they'd keep private. A sister probably wouldn't know if her brother was whacking off all the time, just that he was being secretive and spending a lot of time alone. So it could be something like that.

"Maybe he didn't want the power," Quinn offered with a hint of anxiety when Sam didn't say anything. "Or he didn't know how to handle it, or was resistant to change or something."

Or maybe it was like an addiction. If he'd had a need to replenish it but didn't fulfill that need, Sam imagined the result could be something like a sickness of the heart.

What would happen when they did this three times? Jennifer, Chloe, and Tanda all had similar but different power sources—

flowing water like the Mississippi River, the ocean, and rain. If each left a residue in him, how much ability would come with it? And what would happen if he used it? He didn't want to become like Anson.

Not that he was worried he'd suddenly become a monster. Anson had planned everything, sought the power Marley gave him with the intention of stealing more. Reports on him after Quinn took it back indicated he'd been his normal, charming— and asshole—self.

"What are you thinking?" Quinn asked. Sam shook his head, and she didn't push. Instead, she picked up a notebook from the table and looked at it, though he was positive she'd memorized everything in it. "The trickiest thing is isolating which parts of the power belong to whom, and separating it for transfer. I've been practicing that."

"Seriously? You can feel it that way?"

She nodded. "I always could, to some degree. When I'm near the creek, for example, I can sense Jennifer's power. It rises up, almost has a taste in the back of my throat. It took some time to be able to deliberately sense it and pull it away from the rest."

"But I thought the power wasn't in you," Sam said. "Marley's instructors talk about the source allowing you to tap into worldwide living energy or whatever."

"Well, yeah, but I'm different." She grimaced as if she were being immodest. "It's not just that. It's almost like there's a repository inside of us that holds capacity. Like our brains hold brainpower and need oxygen to work right. The leech pulled out that capacity. The repository is still in there, in the goddess. So, if I can heal it and then isolate the capacity I have, I can transfer it back to them."

"Not all of them," Sam pointed out quietly.

Quinn shook her head. "No. Beth's energy is dissipating. That won't be a problem."

It took Sam a moment to remember that Beth was the goddess from South Carolina. "And Marley's?"

"No idea. I can't give it back." Her eyes were dark with pain and regret. "Marley damaged herself when she did the original bestowment, and when Anson leeched her, it made it permanent. I won't be able to heal her like I can do the others."

"How do you know that?" Sam pressed. When Quinn's eyes filled with tears, he cursed. "I'm sorry. Of course you wouldn't just assume you couldn't." He could count on one hand, without using any fingers, the number of times he'd seen Quinn cry.

"Every time I'm with her, I try," she admitted. "When I said I'd been experimenting...I thought if I could heal her, I could definitely heal the others. I found the damage, and it feels so different from Tanda and Chloe." She pressed the back of her hand to her mouth and sniffed, staring out the window. When she spoke again, her characteristic strength was back. Her gaze meeting Sam's was as steady as her voice now. "You know that bowl that was my mother's? The one with the lilies that my dad gave her for their twentieth anniversary?"

Sam pressed his lips together and nodded, wincing. He and Quinn had gotten careless in her apartment and knocked it off its shelf. It had fallen eight feet and hit the corner of the entertainment center. Some of the china had been literal dust.

"It would never have held water again. Marley's like that, but worse. More than just holding it, she won't be able to accept it. That part of her has been completely nullified."

He didn't like the sound of that, but he supposed that was a bridge they'd have to cross later. "So, where do I come in?" he asked. She shifted her position again, and this time Sam thought she looked uncomfortable, as if trying to ease pain.

"The power has been in me so long it's contaminated, in a way. If I transfer it to you, you act like a filter, disconnecting it from me so that when you then transfer it to the original goddess, it recognizes its origin and zooms right to it, without sticking to what it's mingled with for three years. In theory," she added. "Obviously."

Sam nodded, picturing the transfer. "So it's like separating a solution. I'm a strainer. Or a centrifuge."

"Something like that. The magical equivalent." She smiled.

Sam grabbed a pen and a blank legal pad off the table and started making his own notes. "Have you talked to Jennifer yet? Are we ready to do this today? What kind of prep do we have to do?"

"Yes, yes, and not much." Quinn flipped a few pages in her notebook. "I have everything written out, but it's really just making you two comfortable and then I do all the work. It shouldn't take long overall."

"Okay, good." Sam scribbled a few thoughts. "What about afterward? Any idea of the effects? How long will you need me to stick around?"

He sensed Quinn and Nick sharing a look, but his mind was already on Riley and how quickly he could get back to her. He'd call her on the way to Jennifer's to see how she was doing and let her know when he'd be there.

"Well, we want to give it a day to see how Jennifer takes it," Quinn said slowly. "And then we can go straight to Rhode Island."

Sam's head snapped up. Both of them were watching him warily. "What do you mean, straight to Rhode Island?"

"Once we start these," Nick said, "we have to get them all done. This is unprecedented, Sam. I told you, we don't know what it's going to do to Quinn as she takes this apart."

Sam shook his head and stood. "I told Riley I'd be back as soon as possible. I can't leave her alone with Anson and Millinger still a big unknown."

Fury tightened Nick's features, and he would have stood if

Quinn hadn't put her hand on his leg. Sam let his hands curl. Nick might want to clobber him for daring to refuse to follow their timeline, but Sam was no pushover, and Nick knew it.

Quinn looked at the books and papers on the table. "We can wait. It's already been three years…"

The note of despair in her voice made Sam falter, and it nearly did Nick in. His temples and jaw pulsed with the pressure of gritted teeth, and he evaded Quinn's hands this time to stand and face Sam.

"Dude, you're going to have to make a choice." His tone very clearly told Sam that there was only one choice to make. He sank back onto his chair and passed a hand over his face.

"I'm not going to make you wait, Quinn. But there's got to be a compromise. You're driving to Rhode Island?"

"Yeah," Nick said almost belligerently. "Quinn hasn't been doing well with flying, and—"

"And you know how much he hates airplanes." The note of despair was gone from Quinn's voice, and Sam knew she'd seen where he was going.

He spelled it out anyway. "I'll fly back to Boston, get Riley, and meet you at Chloe's." She wouldn't have gotten very far with her education and training, but that was going to have to be a secondary concern until he knew she'd be safe doing it. If he had to traipse all over the country on this transfer mission, he wanted her with him.

For more reasons than he was ready to reveal, though the way Nick and Quinn were looking at him right now, they already knew.

• • •

After too many hours and four hundred miles later, Riley followed late-morning traffic into Atlanta and found public parking near the downtown address of Millinger.

She slid the gearshift into park, climbed out into a gorgeously mild day, and stretched. Man, that felt good. She'd pushed hard, taking few breaks and downing a lot of energy shots. Traffic had been heavy enough through most of the drive that she'd kept her phone turned off. She would have a hard time ignoring it if it rang, and as much as she wanted to hear Sam's voice, she had a feeling she knew what he'd say about her trip. Better to wait until she was done.

A few people hustled up and down the sidewalk, but on a Sunday morning, this low-rise business district was eerily free of traffic and pedestrians.

Riley leaned back into the car and snagged the printout of downtown Atlanta. Squinting at the street signs on the traffic signal supports, she found her location on the map. Millinger was a couple of blocks away. She tilted her seat forward to reach into the back for the stuff she'd bought at a hardware store yesterday. Walking around carrying a big pipe was kind of stupid. She'd look like she was spoiling for a fight, or about to smash in her cheating boyfriend's windshield or something. The hammers had appealed to her, with their heavy, dense heads, but she wanted to be able to have her hands free. She ended up buying some lengths of mid-gauge chains and carabiner-style clips. She wrapped a chain a few times around each of her arms and clipped them in place, liking the sense of availability they gave her. They were heavy, though, and she didn't know if the extra effort to carry them would negate the energy she drew. Hopefully, she wouldn't need to find out.

After rummaging in her bag for a shirt with sleeves loose enough to cover the chains, she shoved her wallet into her back pocket, her keys into the front—more metal ready to grab if she needed it—and strode down the street. The sun glinted off skyscrapers and parked cars, and a light breeze sent a single french fry container dancing past. She smiled at a guy talking to the Bluetooth in his ear, but he never even glanced at her.

The narrow, old building Millinger was in had a taxi circle in front but no doorman. Riley headed purposefully for the entrance, pulled open the door, and cut straight across the lobby as if she'd been there before and knew exactly where she was going.

The lobby wasn't empty, which meant Riley didn't look suspicious. A guy stood looking out the front windows, probably waiting for someone, and a couple of women sat on a bench by a giant square pillar, drinking coffee and talking.

The bank of elevators was right where she expected, dead center lobby. She hit the *up* button and scanned the company listing on a large placard between the two sets of elevator doors. Millinger was on eight.

The elevator dinged. A group of men and women in suits stepped off, not even noticing Riley in their squabbling about jury selection processes. She stepped onto the car and waited. The doors stayed open. Her heart rate picked up. Seconds ticked in her head, sounding like minutes before the panels closed.

Slumping against the wall, she jabbed "eight," and the elevator began its ridiculously slow climb. Riley grimaced at her reflection in the mirrored walls. Over the past several months she'd grown used to not paying attention to her appearance. Her hair could look artfully tousled even when she'd slept in her car for two days, but her shirt was more wrinkled than she'd thought. Oh, well, it wasn't like she was here to make a good impression on anyone. She stopped fussing and watched the floor number fail to change. What would she find when she got to eight?

If she ever got to eight.

She realized that was the same floor the Society was on in its building back in Boston. Deliberate or coincidental? It would take a lot of effort to find an available office on the eighth floor, but from what Riley had heard, Anson was that obsessive.

The car groaned past six and headed toward seven. Marley had done some reconnaissance while Riley traveled, pretexting a call to the building management office. She'd pretended to be a client having trouble getting through on their phone system. According to building staff, Millinger didn't have open business hours. They'd advised her not to bother coming during the weekend because no one was likely to be there, which was exactly as Riley had hoped.

But she had her chains just in case they were wrong.

Finally, the elevator slid to a halt. She stepped out onto a serviceable, industrial-grade, dark blue carpet in a very basic hallway as a gleeful young woman passed her. Riley noted the satin-padded notebook she clutched—she must have been at the florist listed on the placard downstairs.

Riley looked to her right, and saw two doors on opposite sides of the hall, each with half-glass panels set in them. One had flowers painted on clear glass, and *Weddings by Marci* in gilt lettering in the center. The other had frosted glass with a guy's name and the letters *P.C.* after it, with no indication of what kind of professional he was.

She looked left, where there was a full-glass door with a matching glass window looking into the copy shop. At the far end of the corridor was a plain wooden door with a golden handle and *Millinger* mounted dead center. That was all. Shrugging, Riley headed toward it.

The door was locked. A good sign, but now what? She hadn't developed enough finesse in her training with John to slide a bolt or whatever that she couldn't see. She checked to make sure no one was in the hall and gripped the handle tight. All the metal she touched infused her with power. She closed her eyes and pushed down hard. There was a crunch, and the door opened. Tiny shards of wood littered the carpet, and the latch plate hung crooked in the jamb. The door wouldn't latch again, never mind lock, so they'd know someone had been here. She'd better find something to make this worthwhile, and find it fast.

There was no receptionist or cube farm inside. Just a wide entry at the top of a long hallway. A couple of standard waiting room chairs faced bare white walls, and a ficus at the corner needed dusting.

Riley could see two doorways on each side of the hall, staggered so neither was directly across from the others. But she couldn't see if the doors were open or had anything on them, like convenient nametags or department signs. She tried to picture the building from the outside, to gauge how big this set of offices might be. She wasn't very good at that, but by her best guess, not very big. Two small offices, probably, if each of those doors went into its own room, and then maybe a larger conference room or workroom or break area or something through the other doors.

She stood for a few minutes in case opening the door had set off an alarm, but all stayed silent, without even a clicking keyboard or music or voices. None of the doors opened, and no intercom or speaker was visible in the walls or ceiling. Nothing happened.

She concentrated on drawing energy through the chains around her forearms. They clanked softly when she moved. The familiar sense of strength infused her, slowly seeping up her arms and down into the rest of her body.

She moved down the hall, the carpet softening her footfalls. None of the doors were marked there either. Two were open, revealing a unisex bathroom and a combination workroom/ kitchen. The other two were locked.

She used less energy on the first handle than she had with the front door and managed to snap it open without doing as much damage. She closed the door behind her and dashed past the office's massive desk to the tall, gray filing cabinet next to the window. After jerking open the first drawer, she ran her hand over the files there, glimpsing some goddesses' names she recognized and plenty she didn't. She closed the drawer and opened the other three, all empty.

Back in the first drawer she flipped through the files, checking the labels. *There*—her name. And…Quinn Caldwell. There was no file for Marley Canton or Alana Mitchell, and there were so many names she didn't know that she couldn't guess which files would be most helpful. She paused at Tess Canton. Related to Marley? Her mother, maybe? Riley yanked the folder and added it to the other two in her hand. She wished she had time to look through the contents rather than take entire files with her, but a sense of urgency pushed at her, and she'd learned the hard way to listen to her gut.

Voices rose in the hall near the main door. *Crap*. Riley spun frantically, but there was nowhere to hide in the sparsely furnished office except under the desk, and that would be stupid. The ridiculousness of the situation bumped the fear of being caught up to hysteria, but she took a deep breath to pull herself together and dashed through a side door without even checking to see where it led.

Just in time. She heard the office door open as she pushed the side door mostly closed. She couldn't latch it without making noise, so she froze next to it, hoping they wouldn't notice the tiny crack. She slowly pressed her arms tight against her waist so the chains wouldn't rattle. They would obviously know someone had broken in, but hopefully they'd think the perpetrator had left.

The room she was in was narrow and didn't have a door to the hall, just the one she'd come through and another directly opposite it. It must have been designed as a conference room between two offices, but it was completely empty. There weren't even any marks in the beige carpet to indicate furniture had ever been there. Which hopefully meant no one would look in here.

"I don't care what his claims are," said a male voice. "He can't prove he was on company time. I'm not accepting a worker's comp claim because he can't stay on his bike." The voice sounded young and pleasant, despite his clear irritation.

"You need to talk to him," another guy said. His voice was deeper, rougher. She knew that one—Vern. She wondered why they were continuing what sounded like an ongoing conversation and not discussing the break-in.

"Why?" the first guy asked. Papers shuffled, and a chair squeaked. "He didn't do the job I sent him to do. I'm not placating anyone for bad work."

"You should placate somebody," said Vern. "Cal's gone. Refused to stay after that woman balled him up in Connecticut."

Riley covered a snicker.

"And Sharla said you're not paying enough for this shit."

"What?" The first guy sounded interested for the first time. "She quit?"

"This morning. Everyone's bailing. How am I supposed to find Kordek on my own?"

A loud, meaningful sigh. "You weren't supposed to be on your own. But you also weren't supposed to lose her in the first place, were you? Why did you let Sharla quit?"

Vern snorted. "I'm not the one paying her. But my point is, you need to change your management style. I'm all you've got left."

Interesting. But then the first guy said, "No, you're not. I have an entire team across the country."

"Theirs. Not yours."

A buzzer prevented the first guy from responding. "They're here. Go do what I told you to, and don't let them see you."

Riley listened hard, but Vern must have left the office silently. The chair squeaked again, and a drawer slid open, then closed. After a moment, rustling clothing told Riley other people had entered the room.

"Gentlemen! Thank you for coming!" He made more sounds of greeting, inviting the men to sit and offering coffee, which they declined in low murmurs.

Riley couldn't hold herself back anymore. She twisted to peer through the crack at the new arrivals. By rocking side to side, she could move one eye past the tiny opening enough to see that there were four men total. The guy with the pleasant voice stood behind his desk, wearing dress pants and a white button-down shirt. Probably a tie, too, though his back was to her, and she couldn't see.

Two men sat in the guest chairs in front of the desk, with another standing behind and between them. All three wore expensive-looking suits and held themselves like corporate bigwigs. The one standing was large, filling his suit jacket like a guy who went to the gym every day, but had a bit of a paunch. One sitting was overweight and balding—from what Riley could see, he was older, though her glimpses weren't enough to be certain. The third guy was barely visible through the crack, one long, slender arm and leg was all she could make out.

The first guy greeted the men deferentially, by names she vaguely recognized, though she couldn't say why. She grinned. The files she'd found might tell her something, but she had a feeling this meeting was going to make the entire trip worthwhile.

CHAPTER NINE

Energy is at the center of all life, of all cause and effect, whether natural or created by humanity. The form of energy that feeds our abilities is both precious and infinite, omnipresent and elusive, with the potential to be both beautiful and terrible.

— The Society for Goddess Education and Defense booklet,
"Educating Your Young Goddess"

"I don't know if I want to do this." Jennifer Hollinger wrapped her arms around herself, shifting from foot to foot. She watched Quinn and Nick with eyes that used to be dark brown but were now the color of coffee drowned in milk. They were setting up folding chaises and paperwork on the deck of Jennifer's small house, which stood on stilts about a hundred yards from a tributary of the Mississippi River. The pungent odors of mildew and mud rode the warm breeze blowing through the trees.

Sam led her to the redwood porch rail and rested his hand on her shoulder, letting her look out over the water and trying to comfort her.

"I know the unknown is scary, but you can trust Quinn."

She cast him a skeptical look. "I know why I'm first. She wants to test it on me before she uses it on her real friends."

Taken aback, Sam was too slow to protest.

"Don't worry about it." She waved him off, then tucked her hand back into her wrapped arms. "I can't blame her. I tried to get Nick fired or whatever."

"She wouldn't test on you," Sam insisted. "You were the last goddess leeched, so it stands to reason you'd be the easiest one to restore."

She shivered as the breeze picked up. "What about Beth?"

Sam didn't want to tell her that goddess had died last year, of complications from diabetes. Her abilities probably wouldn't have prevented her illness or death even if she hadn't been leeched, but the idea would be in Jennifer's head, anyway. There was already enough guilt and fear to go around, so he just said, "She wasn't available."

Jennifer nodded and watched a gull dip over the water. "Still, I don't need this. I've adapted, you know? It's been three years. I can live without it."

But Sam heard the longing in her voice and knew she wasn't going to convince herself. He murmured soothing things to her, about the ordeal she'd been through, about how being afraid was understandable, but that if she could be brave and trust for a few minutes, the reward would be worth it.

Under his hand, her muscles relaxed, and she leaned into the rail, her face lifted as if to catch the scent of the water. Sam could sense Nick and Quinn waiting behind them, but he didn't rush Jennifer. They would have a better chance of success if she were completely committed.

Finally, she turned. "I'm ready."

Quinn motioned for Jennifer to sit in one of the reclining patio chairs they'd set up on the deck. They wanted proximity to Jennifer's source. Any flowing water might do, but the Mississippi River was her favorite, like a security blanket. It would be the first thing she'd reach for when her capacity was restored, and her affinity for it might help the restoration.

"Okay, first I need to heal the crack, Jennifer. The one that occurred when Anson leeched you initially. It shouldn't hurt or anything, though you'll feel it happen like healing any injury. Okay?"

Jennifer nodded and gripped the arms of her chair, taking a deep breath and letting it out slowly.

Sam stood quietly while Quinn put one hand on Jennifer's abdomen, the other on her head. Jennifer closed her eyes. Nothing visible or audible happened, but the look of concentration on Quinn's face intensified, and something seemed to fill the air, like when a stereo was turned on but not operating. Jennifer gasped, and her eyes flew open, her whole body tensing, but then she smiled with wonder.

"I felt it close. I couldn't even tell it was open before, but now that it's not, I realize I was aware of it all along." She leaned forward. "Wow. I haven't felt this good in years." She got to her feet and hugged Quinn. "Even if the rest doesn't work, *thank you*."

Quinn laughed and hugged her back. "You're welcome."

Jennifer released her and stepped back to the rail. "I can feel the river." She turned her head and gazed into the distance. "And the creek. That's fainter, but I know it's there, ready for me." Her brow furrowed a little. "But I can't touch it. Like wearing latex gloves." She turned back to them. "Let's do the rest."

"Do you need anything first?" Nick asked. Jennifer said no, but Sam knew he'd really been asking Quinn, making sure she was okay. But healing the rift had been easy for her, Sam could tell, and she shook her head.

Jennifer sat back down, and Sam went to the other chair.

Quinn explained, "I have to move the power into Sam first, and then we'll send it into you, Jennifer. You ready?"

"Ready."

"Sam?"

"Ready." He adjusted his position on the chair and held out his hand. Quinn wrapped hers around it and closed her eyes. He didn't know what he'd expected—a slow, tingling charge, maybe, or the sensation of light entering his body—but not this. Electricity surged through his entire body almost at once. It was the closest description he could think of, but unlike an electric shock, it wasn't painful. Just the opposite. He bowed in his chair, his gaze locked on the sky, knowing he probably looked terrified but unable to convey the truth. His jaw tightened against the pleasure hitting him in waves.

"Now." Nick's voice came from very far away. As the surge from Quinn ended, Jennifer's hand laced with Sam's, and the energy drained out of him, into her. Unlike him, she didn't hide her response to the rush. Her cry was joyous, ecstatic.

In a few seconds the transfer was complete, and the women both let go of him. Sam lay limp, panting and trying to get a handle on everything.

He caught his breath and his heart rate slowed until he was able to assess where he stood. And he could feel it, too. Remnants of power. No, he knew that wasn't how it worked. Remnants of *ability*. Like Jennifer, he could sense the river. The awareness was fluid, silky, more than the usual senses. Deeper. He wanted to use the energy coming off the water, try to do something with it, but had no idea what.

Jennifer stood nearby, laughing and crying, a pebble in her hand. She held it up between two fingers, and it glowed red as she infused it with light energy, making it shine through the pigments inside it.

"It's back," she said. Tears spilled over and streamed down her face. Her eyes were darker, more naturally brown now. "I don't care if I can only ever make novelties with it, but it's here, in me. I'm whole again." She looked at all of them in turn. "Thank you. I can never thank you enough."

"We just returned what was yours," Quinn said, and the strain in her voice had Nick and Sam both jerking in her direction. She held up her hands, subtly, so Jennifer wouldn't see, and sat in a deck chair. "I'm so glad it worked."

"Me, too." Jennifer knelt at Quinn's feet and clasped her hands in her own. "I'm so sorry. For all these years, I've hated you."

Quinn looked startled, then resigned.

"I blamed you as much as I did Anson for all of this." She took a deep breath. "I thought you didn't care," she continued, "that you wanted all that power for yourself and could give it back if you tried."

Quinn's body sagged, lines deepening around her eyes and mouth. Her exhaustion was as much mental as physical, he realized. No wonder she had refused to run for Society president when they first asked her three years ago. This had been weighing on her for years.

"I'm sorry, Jennifer," Quinn murmured. "I should have kept better contact with you. I know what we did seems simple, but I've been researching it for a long time."

"I understand," Jennifer rushed to assure her, but Quinn shook her head a little.

"I didn't update you, any of you, because I didn't want to give false hope, and I didn't want to be a reminder of what you'd lost. Of course you hated me. How could you not?"

She pushed to her feet, clearly shaky. Nick walked over and slid his arm around her waist, bracing her.

"We're going to go back to the hotel," Quinn said, "but we'll check on you tomorrow, make sure everything's okay."

Jennifer sobered. "You mean, like, make sure it doesn't fade or go wild or something."

Quinn smiled a little and leaned almost imperceptibly into Nick when he tugged her toward the car. "Yeah, something like that."

"Okay." Jennifer turned to Sam. "Let me help you clean everything up." She collected Quinn's papers and shuffled them into a pocket folder, so he turned his attention to putting the furniture to rights.

As soon as Nick and Quinn were around the corner, when Nick probably thought they were out of sight, he swept her into his arms and carried her the rest of the way. Trying to preserve the façade of strength she presented, but taking care of her just the same.

Sam had a fierce throb of longing to be with Riley. She hadn't answered when he tried to call earlier, and he'd turned his phone off when they got to Jennifer's so it wouldn't interrupt the transfer. He dug it out to turn back on, and as soon as it powered up, it rang. He grinned, anticipating Riley's sweet voice, but it faded as soon as he saw *John W* on the display. For some reason, anxiety seized his chest. He tried to tell himself it was nothing, but John never called him to shoot the shit. He hoped no one had tried to attack Riley again.

"Hello?"

"Hey, Sam. Where are you?"

He hadn't told John exactly where he was going because they didn't want word to get back to Tanda and Chloe until they knew this was going to work. "I'm on the road. What's up?"

"I just talked to Marley. There's some stuff you need to know."

Sam leaned against the deck rail. With a tip of her head, Jennifer disappeared into the house. "What's going on?"

"She and Riley went home without me last night because I was stuck in traffic. Riley had a tire iron and you saw her using it, she's got some badass in her, so I didn't make them wait. Then Marley called in the security team. When they got to her apartment, she said a mugger had tried to make a move on them but hadn't succeeded. The team told me everything seemed fine when they left."

Oh, crap. "What really happened?"

"The guy tried to take Marley's bag. Riley stopped him and found a business card for Millinger in his pocket." He paused. "Marley recognized the company name. It's the same as Anson's grandmother's last name."

Sam ground his teeth. "What the hell is he up to? Is he trying to pick a new leeching victim? Or looking for someone else he can coax to give him power, this time on an ongoing basis or something?"

"Sam."

He stopped speculating immediately. That wasn't all John had to tell him.

"She's in Atlanta."

"What?" He straightened and paced across the deck. "Riley? She went down there?"

"Marley said she was tired of being jerked around. She wanted answers. She was going in smart," he admitted. "On a Sunday, with plenty of metal, according to Marley. She talked to her a little while ago, when she arrived down there. She planned to scout the offices. No reason to think she's in any trouble, but…"

"She went alone?" Sam was seething now. "Why didn't Marley stop her?"

He clenched his jaw in frustration and then sighed. He knew it wasn't fair to blame Marley. Riley had a mind of her own, and he wished he were surprised that she took it into her own hands. But he wasn't—that was Riley. "I'm sorry," he said. "Do you have any protectors in Atlanta?"

"No. I know a PI in the same building as Millinger. He's the one who was keeping tabs on our guy, but he's out of town. I didn't bother trying to reach Riley, since Marley talked to her right before she got there, and if she's smart, her phone will be off. I thought you'd want to know what was going on."

"Yeah. Thanks."

"Let me know if you talk to her."

"Will do." Sam hung up and stood in the breeze, his mind racing. He had to go to Atlanta. Getting there quickly would be a problem. The airport in Jackson was hours away, and by the time he was able to get a flight, he could probably have driven there. That would take at least six hours, and by then, who the hell knew where Riley would be?

Nick came back around the side of the house, his step faltering when he saw Sam's face. "What's wrong? Jennifer okay?"

"She's fine." He told Nick about the phone call. "I hate this."

"Yeah, impotence sucks." He laughed when Sam scowled at him. "What are you going to do?"

"I don't know." Sam reluctantly pocketed his phone and helped Nick haul the chairs around the side of the house. "How's Quinn?"

"Wiped out. It took more out of her than she expected. I think the fact that the moon's waning isn't helping." He kept his voice low as he laid the chair in the Charger's trunk, so Quinn, reclining in the front seat, wouldn't be disturbed.

"I didn't think she needed the moon anymore," Sam said before he realized it was a foolish statement. Everything had changed as of twenty minutes ago.

"It's still her main source. I think when she's done with the transfers she'll be tied to it more than ever. But she's hanging in there. So far."

They finished loading the car and went inside to find Jennifer. She was sitting on the sofa in her dim, cozy living room, her elbows on her knees, rocking with her clenched hands pressed to her mouth.

Sam hurried over to sit next to her. "What's wrong?" She'd been all right out on the deck, but they didn't know what aftereffects might hit.

"I'm fine." But her hand shook when she raised it to brush

her bangs out of her eyes. She laid the other hand on her stomach. "Physically, I feel fine. I also feel queasy, but not because I'm sick." She turned to look at Sam, her expression frightened. "I heard your phone call. I didn't mean to listen, but… God, Sam, Anson's out there, isn't he? He's doing something bad again, and if he finds out I've got my powers back…"

He caught her hand in his. "We've got Anson under surveillance," he said. "We won't leave you unprotected." It wasn't enough to tell her that, though, and Anson wasn't operating on his own right now. Sam took out his phone and called John back to arrange a protector for Jennifer. Luckily, there was one finishing an assignment nearby.

He hung up once he got everything in order. "Joe Barcelona will be here tomorrow morning, and he's been fully briefed on the Anson situation. He'll take care of you."

Jennifer finally relaxed. "I know him. He was with me right after—you know."

"Okay, good, so you can trust him."

She looked out the window toward the river, relief apparent in every line of her body. "Thank you."

Nick paused when they reached the porch and Jennifer was out of earshot. "Joe being here means we don't have to stay," he told Sam.

Sam shook his head. "I have to go to Atlanta, but you two should head to Rhode Island. We can meet you there once I find Riley."

"I don't think so." Nick's hands were shoved casually in his pockets, but Sam recognized his stance, ready to fight at any provocation. "If Tournado's on the move again, you know I'm not staying out of it."

"No. Of course not."

Nick slapped Sam on the shoulder and headed to the car. Sam hesitated despite his urgency to get on the move. The river flowing a few dozen yards away still pulled at him, the oddest sensation he'd ever felt. He was tempted to reach out, to connect, to see if he could channel the free-flowing energy he could almost taste. It scared him how visceral the need was, and the fear made him think of Riley. Had she gotten in over her head or simply failed to charge her phone's battery? She might be huddled somewhere, hiding and afraid, or captured and hurt. He couldn't let the changes from the transfer get in the way. Not now.

Not ever.

• • •

Riley stood against the wall next to the door, holding still and listening hard, but cursing whatever dampened the acoustics in this place. The men's voices rose and fell, but the snippets she got didn't make much sense to her.

She was acutely aware that Vern was out there somewhere, doing whatever he'd been told to do before Riley could hear them. He was probably looking for the person who'd broken the office's lock. To be safe, she kept a constant draw of energy through the chains so it was ready if she needed it. Her skin warmed where the chains touched, a tangible confirmation of the flow into her body.

"Mr. Tournado, we're not interested in hearing the details. We want to know the results. What is your recruitment rate?"

That was confirmation that Anson was running the company. But even if he owned it, he was obviously working for these other guys now. To recruit who? Goddesses, she assumed, based on the tactics Sam had described. But for what?

"I'm sure you'll be pleased that we've had positive response to our efforts in several quarters." Anson's voice dropped, then rose again. "Two goddess contracts should be closed by the end of the week."

"That's not as fast as targeted," said another of the suits. "Nor as many. We had higher hopes for you."

"With all due respect, sir," Anson said in a way that implied the opposite, "I'm not operating in a vacuum. These women are a tighter group, far warier and more suspicious than they were three years ago. Changing tactics is wise, but you must revise your expectations."

"If they *are* warier and more difficult to approach," one of the men said, "it's due to your high-level failure last time. There is no three strikes rule, Mr. Tournado. Instead of lecturing us on our expectations, you should be working harder to live up to them."

Riley blinked, not quite believing what she'd just heard. Anson had been working for these guys three years ago? He'd been leeching on someone else's orders? No one else seemed aware of that.

She realized that in her surprise she'd stopped drawing energy. The chains had gone cold and heavy around her arms. She quickly pulled more—too quickly, and too much. Searing pain flashed up her arms. She barely stifled a gasp and released her pull on the energy. The metal still burned, but she couldn't unwrap the chains without giving away her presence.

An odd sensation prickled in her head, distracting her. She'd never felt such a thing before. It was like sound made physical, and coming from Anson's office next door. But when she focused again, concentrating on the prickle instead of the pain in her arms, it disappeared. It was like seeing something in peripheral vision at twilight, but looking directly at it made it disappear.

They were talking about money now, the legitimacy of expenses. Riley relaxed, and the prickling reappeared immediately. What the heck was that? She closed her eyes and let her mind drift, keeping a slight awareness of the prickles in her head while trying not to let the burn in her arms distract her. After a few seconds she realized there were three distinct clusters of sensation, plus one lighter buzz, all centered in the office next door. Was she... detecting the people in there?

Focusing made the sensation immediately disappear again. The suits were making conversation-closing comments as they walked down the hall to the main entry.

Riley waited, but after a few minutes, silence reigned. Anson must have left with the suits. She didn't know where Vern was, and no matter how hard she tried, she couldn't get the prickles back. That could mean one of three things: she had been imagining things when it happened the first time, it had really happened but had stopped working, or she was *actually* detecting the presence of specific people. Part of her was disappointed, but part of her was scared, too. Maybe it was another aspect of being a goddess, but it wasn't something she'd ever heard or read about. Marley and John definitely hadn't mentioned it.

She wasn't going to think about it right now. Letting out a long, slow breath, she peeled back her sleeves. The skin under the chains was an angry red, maybe burned down into the top layer. She couldn't tell without moving the chains, and right now she had to get out before someone found her.

She peered through the crack in the door to make sure no one had snuck back into Anson's office, held the files tight against her side, and then moved quickly toward the hallway.

Which wasn't empty.

Riley froze. Anson leaned against the wall across from her, his arms folded, smiling at her. There was no reason for her to be surprised, but he was better looking than she'd imagined. Not really tall or muscular, but fit and well proportioned. He had thick, dark hair, defined cheekbones and jaw, and interesting blue eyes that were like fabric that had been saturated with color, then faded unevenly. She wondered how brilliant they'd been when he had all that power.

"Hello, Riley."

She swallowed her panic and responded, "Hello, Anson." That earned her a laugh, but anger blazed in his eyes.

"You've heard about me, then."

"Some."

"What are you doing here?"

"I wanted to know why you keep coming after me." She kept her body at an angle, wishing she'd stuffed the files into her rear waistband or something. If he took them from her, this would all be for nothing—unless she could somehow get him to talk.

She pushed her hair back so her sleeve shifted and exposed the chain around her arm. Anson followed the movement, his expression tightening. Not in fear, but in caution. He knew what metal meant to her.

"You heard my conversation, I assume."

"Some of it." Riley shrugged. "I couldn't hear much, and none of it had anything to do with me." She met his glare. "Or maybe it did. You want goddesses again, obviously. But you didn't try to recruit me. What was the plan?" All of the events of the past year added up to one possibility. "Make me vulnerable, then swoop in and save me? So I'd be so grateful I'd do anything for you?"

Any trace of amusement vanished. "Something like that. Looks like it worked perfectly."

"Except you didn't swoop in. Sam Remington beat you to it."

Anson's expression darkened. *Button pressed.* His arms dropped to his sides, and he straightened away from the wall. Riley raised her forearm and drew a little energy. It made her hiss at the renewed pain, but Anson didn't seem to notice. He shifted away from her but didn't look any less angry.

"Everything was perfect that night. You were strung tight, frightened and confused. It would have worked exactly as I'd planned."

"Until you fucked it up. You let Sam move in ahead of you."

"I had no choice. The Numina—"

Riley narrowed her eyes. That word again. Was it a group? Were those men part of it?

Anson hauled visibly on the reins of his control. "Never mind. That's in the past. You're here now." He smiled again, a clear shift in tactic, and Riley had no trouble seeing the charm that had seduced the goddesses he leeched. He wasn't giving up on her. Maybe she could pretend to be vulnerable and get him to talk.

"How did you find out about me?" she asked. "The Society didn't have any records. *I* didn't even know I was a goddess."

He didn't hesitate to answer her, perhaps thinking he could lure her in with some of the information she'd come for. Or maybe he was just a braggart. "My grandmother kept journals. She was close to your grandmother. Grams wrote about how angry Nessie was about her Society membership being revoked. She'd had a bare remnant of ability, but they didn't care. She didn't fit their definitions. Her daughter—your mother—had no power. My grandmother thought she knew why and said it would probably come back in you."

Riley wondered how much the woman had actually known and how much she'd only suspected, perhaps not even accurately. Still, Anson's take on it explained even better why her grandmother had so much hate. "So you know all this because of some old journals? Kind of creepy, if you ask me."

His smile faded. "No. We were close, me and my grandmother. The line died with my mother, so there weren't going to be any more Millinger goddesses. She talked to me a lot about it."

He sounded lonely, and Riley had to fight a surge of empathy. "So you thought you'd be my Henry Higgins?"

One side of his mouth lifted. Charm, again. "I wanted you to be my partner."

Riley scoffed, but he seemed to be…sincere. She pondered pushing a little, asking about Numina or the men in the office, but something told her if she didn't leave now, she'd lose her chance. She wanted to tell him to forget it, that she'd never consider working with him, but knew her only option was to keep him hoping.

"You've given me plenty to think about. I have your business card. I'll be in touch." She waved a hand and turned toward the exit, holding her breath and bracing for Anson to grab her arm, or worse. But he only said, "I think you're forgetting something."

She raised her eyebrows, her heart thudding against her breastbone.

"My files?" He plucked them out from under her arm. She opened her mouth to protest, but he said, "Shall I call the police about your breaking and entering and attempted theft? Or would you rather owe me one?"

Riley ground her teeth and let go of the files. She was getting damned tired of the bad guys threatening to turn the tables on her.

"That's what I thought." He waved the folders down the hall. "Don't lose that business card."

Riley had no choice but to put her back to him and walk to the exit. He knew she was armed, and he seemed to be leaving open the possibility of winning her over to his side. She couldn't help but be a little grateful for that.

Who knew what he'd be capable of if he had nothing to lose?

CHAPTER TEN

Keep your friends close. Don't have enemies.

—Numina Manifesto, revised

Riley didn't breathe again until she was back on the highway, heading north. It was a good thing traffic was light because she couldn't really remember getting in the car. Her arms burned and ached, weighed down by the heavy chains now that she wasn't drawing energy. And might never again, after this. She'd never tried to sustain a connection that long, and obviously, it wasn't a good idea. Neither was trying to unwrap the chains while she was driving, but she had to keep moving, had to get as far away as possible from Anson. He might have let her go, but only because he knew how to find her again when he wanted to.

She had to call Sam.

Her chest tightened, air feeling too thick to drag into her lungs. She had enough presence of mind to know a panic attack was approaching. She was alone, and pursued, and couldn't use her abilities for defense right now, and that put her right back where she'd started. Right where Anson had wanted her.

But you're not alone anymore, a voice in the back of her head reminded her. No one was in the car with her, or even in Atlanta, but she had people she could call. People who'd help her. Who needed to know what she'd learned.

She pulled off at the next exit and made her way to a crowded section of a Walmart parking lot. First she had to get these chains off. She left the car running while she fumbled to open the clips, unfastened the chains, and slowly unwrapped them. Oh, God, that hurt. Her eyes watered when the chain stuck before peeling away from her damaged skin. She wished healing came naturally to her like John said it did to others, but it was one thing he couldn't train her in, even if she had the ability. They'd discussed setting her up with another goddess in a few weeks, but that did her no good now.

She dropped the first chain to the floor and sat back in her seat, eyes closed, gulping air. The smart thing to do would be to go inside and buy some bandages, but she didn't have the energy to leave the car. And she still had to face removing the other chain. It took several minutes to work up to it, and then another few for recovery. She poured bottled water over the red stripes and carefully pulled her sleeves down, as if not seeing the wounds would make them hurt less.

Then she dug out her phone. She should call Marley, who had to be worried about her by now. Or John, to report what she'd learned. But she dialed Sam's number automatically, craving the connection and comfort he always provided.

"Where the hell are you?" he answered after only half a ring.

Riley burst into tears. She got herself under control quickly, but the damage was done. Sam cursed, and Riley heard keys jingle and a door slam, cutting off a shout of anger.

"Where are you?" he repeated. A car door creaked and then banged shut, and an engine turned over before Riley could clear her throat, inhale, and try to answer him.

"I'm okay," she said first, because he seemed to need to hear it. "I'm outside of Atlanta."

"Alone? If Tournado hurt you…"

"No, he didn't." She sniffled and opened her glove compartment to dig for a tissue. "He could have—he caught me with files in his office—but he let me go. Said now I owe him."

Sam cursed again, and the engine revved as if he'd pressed down on the accelerator while still in neutral. "I'm coming to you. Don't move."

That made Riley laugh. She wiped her nose and leaned against her seat again, feeling a lot better. Safer, though he was still hundreds of miles away. "Don't be silly, Sam. You don't even have your own car. You flew to Mississippi, right?"

After a few beats of silence, the engine shut off. "John called me. We were on our way to Atlanta, but Quinn got sick and we had to stop for a couple of hours." His frustration was clear, and Riley regretted making him feel that way. "I kind of lost it when I heard your voice after getting your voice mail all day."

"I'm so sorry, Sam. I didn't know."

"Anyway, I was about to take the Charger. Nick's car," he clarified. "He's gonna—yeah, there he is. He's gonna kill me."

"Not if I can help it. Listen, Sam, I have to tell you what's happening. I—"

"Not over the phone," Sam interrupted. "I need to get to you."

She shivered at the idea that someone was monitoring them, and it eliminated the slight comfort she'd gained hearing his voice. If someone knew their locations and could track them down… Then again, Anson had found her somehow, again and again, without ever having to trace a phone call.

Maybe it didn't matter what they did.

Riley listened to paper rattling, as if he'd unfolded a map. Another car door opened, and a man's voice said, "You're trying to get me locked up for homicide, right? That's your plan?"

"I need to meet up with Riley coming from Atlanta," Sam said away from the phone. "What's the best route from here?"

"What's going on? She okay?"

"I'm fine," Riley muttered.

The man—Nick, she guessed—named a route number Riley remembered passing a few minutes ago. She hit the speaker button and set the phone on the seat beside her, backing out of her parking space and speeding toward the lot exit before Sam had even told her what to do.

"We'll head your way," he said, "and you head ours. We'll meet in a couple of hours in the middle. We'll figure out a place when we get closer. Call me every thirty minutes so I know you're okay."

She blinked fast against the sting in her eyes. "I will. Thanks, Sam." She hung up without looking, her attention on the long, wide road ahead of her.

A little more than two hours later, she pulled up beside the cool, old muscle car in the parking lot of the steakhouse outside Birmingham, Alabama. Sam, who'd been pacing behind the Charger, watching nervously as she drove up, hurried around to open her door and haul her into his arms.

"Thank God you're okay."

"I told you I was," she insisted against his chest, her words muffled. She wrapped her arms awkwardly around his waist, trying not to rub or put pressure on her chain burns, and let his big, warm body swallow her up. For the first time in hours, her body stopped pumping adrenaline. She clung to him for a long moment that partially balanced the queasy shakiness as the hormone drained out of her system. She inhaled the scent of his skin and laundry soap and faded aftershave, an already familiar combination, and one that was a little arousing despite her exhaustion. His arms were so strong, his chest and abdomen hard against her body, and…

And he buzzed.

Like Anson had buzzed. Somewhere at a level of awareness

Riley didn't normally use. The uneasiness she hadn't realized she held vanished. It couldn't be a bad thing because this was Sam.

"Let's go inside." He shifted to walk beside her, his arm around her shoulders. "Nick and Quinn already got a table. She really needed to eat."

Riley had so much crowding her head, wanting out. Confusion about the buzzing and prickling, curiosity and concern about the transfer they were supposed to be doing this weekend, and speculation about everything she'd heard in Atlanta. But it all had to wait, some of it until much later.

They went inside the rustic, crowded restaurant decorated in antler chandeliers and red-and-white-checked vinyl. Sam waved off the hostess and took Riley to a corner booth, away from the bulk of the families filling the place.

"Have a seat." Sam let her slide onto the bench and followed her. "Riley Kordek, this is Quinn Caldwell and Nick Jarrett."

"Hi." Riley smiled shyly. The beautiful fortyish woman seemed to be upright only by virtue of the hot blond guy propping her. "I really appreciate that you came all this way to get me."

"Pleasure's all mine." Quinn eyed Sam as she said it, a twinkle in her eye that belied her obvious weariness, and Riley was surprised and amused to see him blush.

"Glad to meet you." Nick saluted her with his beer bottle before taking a swig. He looked like he wanted to launch into an interrogation, but the server approached to take their orders. Riley let Sam talk her into a steak, knowing she needed a real meal to help her recover from everything that had happened. She hoped it'd calm her stomach, which now roiled unpleasantly, still protesting the fight-or-flight response she'd put it through.

"All right." Nick leaned forward. "Tell us what you got in Atlanta. What's Millinger, and what's he doing with it?"

"Nothing good," Riley said. "And nothing by himself." She told them about the men in the office, and how the conversation sounded like they were trying to recruit goddesses, or maybe coerce them. "I don't know what for, though. Anson works for the men, but his plans for me seemed completely separate." She explained what he'd said about his grandmother's journal. "He wanted to rescue me. Make me grateful and stuff. But you did that." She smiled at Sam, who frowned.

"That all fits. But why didn't he move in sooner?"

"He said something about not having a choice, because of the Numina? I overheard John and Jeannine mention them, too. She wanted to keep it quiet until they knew more, but he didn't want to."

Sam's frown turned into a scowl. "This must be what John wanted to talk to me about, but he didn't get a chance because I took off to Mississippi."

Nick frowned thoughtfully. "Numina," he repeated.

"That's Latin," Sam said.

"I know." Nick nodded. "Something you can tell with your mind, but not see or hear or whatever."

The guys eyed each other, communicating in the silent manner of people who'd known each other well for a long time.

Riley glanced out at the full parking lot, the late sunlight reflecting off the cars that provided cover for anyone who wanted to be unseen. Unease crawled over her again. Nick had just described the prickling when she sensed the suits in Anson's office, and the buzzing that connected her to Sam, even now.

Sam continued, "Ancient Romans also used it to worship emperors without offending the real gods by calling *them* gods."

"Human gods," Nick said.

No one had to say "holy crap." It hung in the air between them for several seconds.

"This is bigger than leeching," Sam said.

Nick leaned back, his eyes worried. "It always was, apparently." He looked at Quinn, who hadn't said anything. "You ever heard of this?"

She shook her head. "Never. All our lore, our education, says the gods went extinct millennia ago, and no one knows why. I found some odd references in my research to men who seemed to have abilities, but I dismissed it as unrelated. There *are* people who can do extraordinary things without being descended from ancient deities. But now…"

"I can't believe, all that time, Anson wasn't working alone." Sam's hand closed into a fist on the tabletop. "Those people orchestrated the leeching?" He turned to Riley for confirmation.

"That's what it sounded like. Part of a bigger plan that went to hell when he was caught and imprisoned."

"You didn't recognize the men?" Quinn asked Riley. "Or their names?"

She pressed her lips together. "Not really. I can't tell you what Anson called them, but they sounded familiar. Like, well-known people. Businessmen, or politicians or something. But I don't pay a lot of attention to that stuff. I just don't know."

"They don't have to be gods," Sam said. "They can aspire to it. I mean, when have we ever had any hint that men with inherited power existed?"

"Never," Nick said. "Doesn't mean they don't. Secret societies are all the rage, you know. Look at *The Da Vinci Code*."

Sam ignored him. "I think it would be very difficult to hide for so many centuries, especially in modern society." He stopped talking while the wait staff delivered their food. Steaks still sizzled on cast-iron plates set into wood holders, and blobs of butter melted into baked and mashed potatoes. Riley's stomach growled, and they put the conversation on hold while they dug in, the others seeming as hungry as she was.

The residual effects of adrenaline finally dissipated, and the food soothed as well as satisfied. Since no one said much while they ate, Riley sat and absorbed Sam's nearness. His knee and part of his thigh pressed against hers, and he kept glancing her way, his body angled protectively toward her. She had to fight the urge to lean into him the way Quinn leaned into Nick, their contact both casual and possessive. Sam wasn't yet Riley's to touch—though her longing for him had only grown since she saw him standing outside waiting for her. She wanted his silky hair in her hands, to taste his mouth again. She wanted the right to want those things.

She also wanted to talk to him alone about her new awareness. That was the one thing she *could* do. But she already had an idea of what it meant, and she couldn't withhold it from the others, not when there was obviously something so much bigger than her to worry about.

"Whether or not gods exist doesn't matter," Quinn said when she was halfway done with her meal. "Not by itself. What matters is why they're suddenly trying to recruit goddesses."

"Or not so suddenly," Nick contradicted. "Anson initiated his plan way back in college, remember? We thought he learned everything he knew from Sam, but according to what he told Riley, we were wrong."

Sam paled. "You think these Numina guys set him up over a decade ago? The long-term planning for something like that…the foresight and patience…"

It was mind-boggling to Riley, but it sure seemed as if that was what had happened. Which meant their plan was likely even bigger.

"You think Numina is like the Society?" Sam asked Quinn. "Some governing body for these guys who think they're gods?"

Quinn shrugged.

"I think they actually exist," Riley said. "Not just want to be." They all looked at her.

"Why?" Nick demanded, seeming to get she wasn't simply offering an opinion.

She took a deep breath. "Something happened while I was in there, listening. I don't know what triggered it. I never noticed it before. Not when I first met—" She cast a quick glance at Sam and regretted it when Nick immediately looked at him, eyes blazing. "I mean, there was something different about the men in that room. The guys in suits created a prickle, like when your fingers go numb, but in my brain. I could sense where they were without looking, almost exactly. And there was a smaller, buzzy sensation I got from Anson. It was different."

"That's kind of how I feel when I'm at peak power and seek presences," Quinn said. "Like the showdown at Marley's when Anson attacked us? When we had to know where people were and if any of them had ability? I was trying to detect the leech and the people he'd hired," she explained to Riley. "It's not a skill I need to use often."

"Do all goddesses have it?" she asked Quinn.

"Most, to some degree. Can you sense me or Nick?"

Riley closed her eyes and relaxed her brain, made her concentration diffuse…and there it was. She'd been so worried about what Sam's buzz meant, she hadn't even tried.

For Nick, it wasn't much more than an awareness of his presence, but Quinn's was stronger, warmer. Riley spread her attention across the room. She pinpointed where she thought people would be, and when she opened her eyes, she was right.

"Wow." It seemed inappropriate to beam, but she was excited at discovering a new facet to her abilities. "That's amazing. I can sense everyone, and they're all different. People, goddesses, and—" She cleared her throat and looked down at her plate.

"Any prickles here similar to what you felt in Atlanta?" Nick asked.

Riley shook her head but avoided his gaze. She didn't know why Sam felt the same as Anson, but it didn't seem like it would be a good thing. "No one feels like the men in suits did."

But Nick seemed to recognize her evasion. "Can you sense Sammy here? Is he different from me?"

She glanced up at Sam, who was watching her. His brown eyes were darker than normal, a hint of excitement or anxiety—or both—disturbing the overall calm. It was the first time since they rescued her that he'd looked at her so directly, and desire made her tremble.

He smiled a little. "It's okay," he encouraged.

"Yes," she admitted. "The same kind of buzzy feeling I get with Anson, but not the same as the other men."

"So those three might actually be modern-day gods," Quinn said with a matter-of-factness Riley couldn't help but admire. "Watered-down descendants of the ancients like us."

"But why are Sam and Anson so different?" Riley didn't like anything connecting the two men, but Quinn didn't seem concerned.

"They're both sons of goddesses, so they're unique." She ate her last bites of asparagus and contemplated her steak, as if uncertain if she could finish it or not. "And when I drained Anson, I knew there'd be a bit of residue."

"Enough for him to sense the energy," Sam said in a low voice. "But not tap into it."

Riley gasped. "Does that mean you've done it? You returned power to one of the goddesses?"

Sam nodded. "And now there's a residue in me, from being a filter."

"I knew it." Nick stabbed an accusing finger at Sam. "When you hauled ass out of the motel earlier—you didn't just slam the door. There was energy behind it."

"I was upset!" Sam protested.

"Keep your voices down." Quinn leaned over the table. "That's more than we expected, Sam. You can actually use it? Not just feel it?"

His jaw was set, and he didn't meet anyone's gaze. "Apparently."

"What about now?" she asked.

He nodded shortly.

"There's no river near here," Nick pointed out.

"I know."

"And you still feel it?"

"Yes."

Nick's eyes narrowed on Sam. "It's a good thing Riley got herself out of Millinger, isn't it? You'd have used it on Tournado in a heartbeat."

Sam's jaw tensed even more. He held his beer bottle so tightly the label slid and wrinkled. "I'd have done what I needed to do to defend the people I care about."

Riley blushed and looked down, fussing with her napkin, but the others didn't pay any attention to the implication.

"You'd also have shown him that you have power!" Nick growled. "What do you think would stop him from coming after you if he found out?"

Sam fidgeted. He looked at Quinn's sympathetic expression, at Riley, and back at Nick. Then he let go of his beer bottle and rubbed his face with both hands. "You're right. But obviously, it's irrelevant right now." He slumped against the booth. "What are we going to do with all this?"

Quinn cut into the last bit of her filet. "If there are gods, it needs investigating. We have to find out what Jeannine and John know already."

"They won't talk over the phone," Sam said. "And neither should we. If Riley's right and these guys are powerful people in government and business, they could easily be monitoring phone lines."

Quinn sighed. "They've been watching Anson, right?"

"Right," Nick and Sam said together.

"Let's assume they know at least as much as we do. We'll talk to them when we can. But now that we've started, we have to keep going with the transfers. I can't—we can't just stop with the way things are."

Nick nodded. None of them looked happy about leaving this all up to the Society. Riley felt a lot more comfortable with the organization after spending a couple of days there, but she'd also heard enough to understand why they'd feel that way. She also suspected that if Quinn was admitting she had to keep moving with the transfers, things were way more serious than they seemed.

She suddenly remembered what else she'd heard.

"Nick, did you know John wants you to take over for him?"

The simple question had the effect of a time bomb coming to life on their table. Everyone froze.

When Nick didn't answer, Quinn turned on him. "*Did* you know?"

"No!" He snatched a french fry off his plate and tossed it in his mouth. "I didn't," he insisted at Quinn's skepticism. "I'd tell you right away if I knew for sure."

"*For sure*," she pounced. "So you knew, even if you haven't talked to him about it."

"Does it matter? I'm not taking the job."

Quinn rested her hand on her forehead. "Nick."

"Are you all right?" He scooted closer and put his arm around her. "What's wrong?"

She straightened and glared. "You're what's wrong, you idiot! They assigned you to me permanently, didn't they? And you're miserable! You want this job."

Oh, boy. Riley didn't even bother to excuse herself, just moved to slide out of the booth. Sam immediately stood, and in silent agreement, they went outside into the steamy night.

"Yikes. I opened up a can of worms, didn't I?" Riley walked along the sidewalk to a bench set out for overflow during peak hours. Once there, though, she realized she didn't want to sit and kept going. Sam kept pace with her, his long legs swinging in a slow stride.

"Looks like. Quinn's probably right about them assigning Nick to her. He's not the kind of guy to drop out of the Protectorate permanently. And Barbara, the last president, was pretty concerned about Quinn having all that power."

"So he's supposed to be protection *against* her, too?"

He grimaced. "Not exactly. Well, probably from the board's point of view. But he's been worried about her. And they were apart for fifteen years, one of those want-but-can't-have situations, so he wouldn't have left her, anyway. They'd have found some kind of compromise."

Riley nodded. "Now…about leaving this gods thing to the Society…"

"I know."

She stopped and looked up at him. "You know what?"

"Jeannine isn't the best person to deal with this. Not that we're better equipped. The repercussions are too vast. And there are way too many open questions."

"Right. Like how many are there? How widespread? How powerful? What *kind* of power do they have? The guys Anson's working for are obviously shady, to put it mildly, but are there good ones, too? Like, I don't know, Bill Gates? The President?" She stopped when she realized Sam was smiling at her almost indulgently. "I'm sorry. I shouldn't—I'm not part of this. Of the Society." Except she was. She might be new, but she belonged to the Society as much as Quinn or any other goddess now.

But Sam, Nick, and Quinn…they were a team, with a history of working together, and that made her feel like an outsider. She also knew they weren't the kind of people to stay out of something like this, especially after their history with Anson.

"You're dead right," Sam said. "I'm itching to research them— and more. I want to know how much of a threat they are, or if an alliance can be built. But honestly, Riley, the transfers have to be a priority right now. We've set it in motion and I don't know what would happen if we don't see it through quickly."

She nodded, her heart sinking. The last thing she wanted was to leave Sam again, but she couldn't get in the way of what they were doing. "I can start driving back tomorrow. Marley said she'd put me up as long—"

"Are you crazy?" Sam interrupted. "You're not going back to Boston."

"But—"

"You're staying with me. With us. Anson's still after you, and frankly..." He looked up and away, out across the parking lot. "Uh, I could use a friend right now."

Riley could tell that was a tough admission for him. She slipped her hand into his, relieved when he entwined their fingers. "Nick and Quinn are your friends."

He shook his head. "There are things I can't talk to them about."

"You mean the power residue." She walked them back to the bench and sat.

"Yeah." He blew out a breath full of relief. "What we're doing...it's similar to how a leech is made. I knew about the risks, and I don't regret taking them, but I never counted on feeling this." He pressed his fingertips to his chest. "I *crave* it. With only this tiny taste. And I'm not even near Jennifer's power source. I'm scared about what will happen with Chloe, and the ocean being right there..."

His hand tightened on hers. The angle put pressure on Riley's raw wrist, surprising her, but she managed to hold back the moan of pain. She'd moved carefully to avoid letting anyone see the damage to her skin, and especially now, she didn't want any more of the attention. It was Sam's turn.

"I know nothing about this, so I can't reassure you that everything will be fine. But one thing I do know." She shifted to look into his eyes. "You and Anson are completely different. You won't abuse this."

"I don't intend to." He sat lost in thought for several moments. Riley wasn't sure what else to say.

Noise from inside the restaurant signaled the front door opening. Riley glanced over her shoulder and saw Nick and Quinn walking toward them, holding hands.

Quinn held out a square container to Riley when they got close enough. "I had them box your leftovers. Seemed too much to leave behind."

"Thanks." That meant they'd paid for her meal. She flushed. "I'll pay you back. I have—" She stopped, acutely aware of how little she did have. "I'm sorry I walked out. I didn't mean to stick you with the bill."

"Don't worry about it." Nick moved a toothpick from one side of his mouth to the other.

"It's our treat," Quinn assured her so matter-of-factly, Riley would have felt shrewish to argue.

"Thank you."

Nick pointed with his toothpick. "There's a hotel down the road. We'll go get some rooms and drive to Chloe's tomorrow."

Riley winced as they walked to the cars. Her funds were low, but no way was she asking anyone for money. Quinn looked worn out. Nick would probably check them in and rush them up to their room. Maybe Riley could go to the restroom while Sam registered himself, then sneak back out to sleep in her Beetle.

But Sam stopped her before she unlocked her car door. "It's not a good idea for you to room alone. I can't protect you that way."

She smiled despite her embarrassment and worry. "So you're my protector now?"

"You obviously need one. So, yeah." His mouth quirked up on one side. "If I promise to behave myself, will you share a room with me? I'd normally suggest you room with Quinn, and Nick and I could share an adjoining room, but…"

"Yeah, no way he's letting her out of his sight. That's obvious."

Nick's window squeaked as he rolled it down. "Get your asses in the car!"

"We'll split the cost of the room, okay? That should help both of us, too."

It hadn't occurred to Riley that Sam might not have much money, either, despite the crappy bar he'd worked in and the fact that he drove a used Saturn against his will. But she wondered if his reasons could be excuses, and hoped they were.

Chapter Eleven

Recent surveys have indicated that sexuality may be complicated by power use, as well as connection to or distance from power sources. This is a private and personal aspect of most people's daily lives. However, the Society has made counseling available should any goddess or her partner feel a need to work through any issues that arise.

— **The Society for Goddess Education and Defense**, *monthly newsletter*

Sam stood in the middle of the tiny hotel room, listening to the shower hiss on the other side of the bathroom door. He was worn out, yet charged by the low hum of energy from the transfer. He suspected that energy was boosting his awareness of Riley, too. Dinner had been mild torture, starting with the full-body hug when she'd first gotten out of the car. Her warm-honey scent had soaked into him through dinner. Whenever he spared her a glance, all he could see was glistening lips and smooth, graceful hands.

And now she was in the shower. Naked. Tilting her head back to let the water soak her hair. Raising her arms to run her hands over it, lifting her breasts. Nipples stiff from the spray...

He jumped when a triple knock sounded on the room's gray-painted steel connecting door. His body went hot from embarrassment. Jesus. He swiped a hand down his face and hoped the lust didn't show when he opened the door a crack.

Quinn stood there, a blanket around her shoulders. "Hey. You okay?"

"Fine. Are you?"

She waved off his concern. "Yeah, just chilly. How are Riley's wrists? Does she need me to take a look at them?"

Sam frowned, not getting what she meant.

Quinn rolled her eyes. "Her wrists. She was very careful not to put pressure on her lower arms while we ate dinner. She didn't touch the table with them at all and had trouble cutting her meat. She winced a few times, too. You didn't notice?"

He hadn't. He'd been so wrapped up in everything they were talking about and his own issues.

He was such an asshole.

"She's in the shower," he told Quinn. "I'll check on her." He probably shouldn't go barging in. A full-body image popped into his head again, and he ground his teeth. Why the hell had he thought it was a good idea to share a room?

"Can I come in?" Quinn didn't wait for an answer. She pushed the door open and slipped past him. When he turned around, she'd already sat in the desk chair and propped her feet up on the foot of one of the double beds. "Not a bad place, huh?"

Besides the hideous maroon, gold, and brown pattern swirling across the polyester bedspreads and curtains, the chipped pressboard furniture, and the crack across the bottom of the bathroom mirror? Sure. The carpet didn't crunch when he walked on it, he hadn't found evidence of bedbugs, and the bathroom was free of mold.

Sam shrugged and sat on the second bed. "Better than some of the places we've stayed in. I'm sure Nick's seen much worse."

Nick used to spend all his time on the road, and whenever Sam complained about a crappy motel during the weeks they'd chased after Anson, he'd called Sam a diva.

"How are you feeling?" he asked her. "And tell the truth. I can see it's not good." She'd seemed to rally after the last stop they'd made for her to sleep a little, and the food had given her more energy. But she looked wan and pale now, and moved even more gingerly than before.

"I pulled the energy apart, and it isn't very happy." She twisted and stretched with a grimace.

"You talk like it's sentient," Sam accused. "Is it?"

But Quinn waved a dismissive hand. "I'm anthropomorphizing. It's just energy. No sentience or emotion."

"But."

"It won't stop churning. It's like when you drink too much coffee and get all hyper, but it's deeper than that. It's making me nauseous. Like I have the flu." She gave a chuckle that turned into a cough, and checked her hand not surreptitiously enough. She realized he'd caught her and shook her head. "No blood. And don't worry, Nick is watching me hard enough for all of you."

"He knows all this?" He felt a little better when she nodded.

"If we finish this," he asked, "give Tanda and Chloe their powers back, will it settle?"

"I think so."

Sam thought about Beth. Quinn couldn't give her power back, and had said she couldn't return Marley's, either. So what would happen when they were all done, and that remaining bit warred with Quinn's natural capacity?

He was too scared to ask her right now.

"So tell me about Riley." Quinn folded her arms and slid down in her seat to rest her head on the back of it. She looked tired but not as ill as she had earlier.

"You know about Riley."

Quinn snorted. "I want to know about *your* Riley. You like her."

"She's likeable." He tried not to fidget under her stare, but his fortitude crumbled in seconds. "I was trying not to."

"Why?"

He shrugged. "She's young." Of course Quinn laughed, and even he had to smile. "Younger than I was," he tried, but he couldn't keep it up. "Okay, the age doesn't matter."

"Not unless you want to be a hypocrite." She bounced her knee to rock the chair. "I talked to Marley about her. She's tough. Riley, I mean. Pretty strong considering all she's been through."

"Yeah." He told Quinn about the night they'd met and everything that had happened since. "I think she's still not sure who to trust, especially anyone tied to the Society."

Quinn grinned. "And yet she followed you there, and you're the first person she called when she was in trouble again."

"Well, I convinced her to give them a chance. That's all."

"Nick would say it's your puppy-dog eyes, but I know it's more than that." Her eyes twinkled, and she briefly looked less tired. "The attraction's not one-sided."

Hell, no, not according to the way she'd kissed him back in Boston. But things had changed with the first transfer. Sam didn't think it was fair to let things deepen with Riley when he had no idea what he was in for, but he wasn't having any luck resisting the attraction, either. Riley had been in the shower a long time now, and he didn't want her to overhear them talking about her. "Maybe. But it's complicated," he warned. "The last time I fell for someone I thought needed me was a disaster."

"That's harsh." Quinn pushed to her feet. "It's okay to take it slow. But don't lose out on something great because you're overcautious." She winked at him as she disappeared through the connecting door. The bolt clicked just as the shower turned off.

He dug a first aid kit out of his bag and laid it on the desk. A few minutes later, Riley emerged from the bathroom fully dressed.

She played with her towel as if planning to fold it, but kept it positioned so Sam couldn't see her arms.

Not that he looked that hard. The steam rolling out of the bathroom behind her caused the thin, gray tank top to cling to her upper body, while the soft, well-worn cutoff sweats hugged her hips and ass. Her nipples pressed against the fabric, her breasts so round and perfect Sam's mouth went drier than sand. A bolt of lust gave him the hard-on he'd been fighting since they'd hugged.

The lust had a hard edge to it this time. A craving hunger too close to what he'd felt during the power transfer. He swallowed and stood, his feet taking him across the room, his hands tingling.

Riley glanced at him from the corner of her eye and turned away to hang the towel on the bar. "I'm beat," she said. "I'm gonna hit the hay, if—hey!" She spun toward Sam when he grabbed her hands and twisted her arms up.

The haze of need vanished when he saw the red, raw rings on her skin. They were much worse than he'd assumed. "What the fuck? Why didn't you say something?"

Riley shrugged. "There were more important things going on. They didn't bother me much."

"Bullshit. These have to hurt like a son of a bitch. I can't believe you acted like nothing was wrong." He pulled her across the room and pushed her down to the bed while he sat in the chair. "What the hell happened?"

Riley sighed and pulled her legs up under her, resting her elbows on her knees so her forearms hung in open space. Sam looked more closely at the stripes twisting around her delicate skin. Some of it was merely red, some glistening with blood in a dashed pattern carved—no, burned through the first couple of layers of skin. "Were you *chained?*" He looked up at her, aghast. "Did Anson chain you?"

"No! I told you, he let me go without trying to stop me. I did the chaining."

Sam released her hands and unscrewed the cap on a tube of antiseptic cream. "What are you talking about?" He carefully dabbed ointment on the raw wounds while Riley explained about needing constant contact with metal to draw on while she was at Millinger.

"I've never held contact and drawn energy for that long. Not even before I knew what I was doing. I'm not sure if it was the constant draw that was the problem, or if I just pulled too much at once, or a combination of the two. Once it seared the skin, any time I tapped energy, it hurt." She rotated her arms to give him better access. "No one told me doing this could damage me." She sounded resentful, and Sam couldn't blame her.

"No one knew," he said apologetically. "Remember, we don't have a lot of goddesses who use it."

Riley winced and shifted her arms again. "So…other sources don't give this kind of backlash?"

"Not that I've heard. But any energy can generate heat, and metal is a conductor."

Riley rolled her eyes. "Especially the kind I wrapped around myself. And I thought I was being so smart."

"You were." He stroked carefully, barely touching the wounds, but his fingers brushed undamaged skin and Riley hissed in a breath. When he looked up, she was biting her lip.

"Did I hurt you?"

"No." She met his eyes, and instead of the pain he expected to find in them, he saw desire.

His lust spiked again. His cock filled, twisting uncomfortably under the fly of his jeans. He ignored it—or tried to. Somehow, he managed to operate on two levels. In his head, he kissed her and pressed her back onto the bed, covering her body with his. She wrapped her luscious legs around his hips, and he buried his face in her breasts. His nostrils filled with the scent of soap, and he could feel the pebble of her nipple on his tongue.

In reality, he wrapped gauze around her wrists, smoothing it with just the pads of his fingers so he didn't touch her skin and risk hurting her more. He peeled off strips of tape to secure the gauze and popped a couple of analgesics from a blister pack to help her with the pain.

"Quinn could heal these," he offered at one point, but Riley shook her head.

"She's probably sleeping and looked like she needed it. I'll ask her tomorrow."

Her voice had gone husky, low, and it dragged through Sam, driving his need higher. His pulse throbbed in his neck, his ears, his groin. He had to have her. *Had* to.

His hands shook as he collected wrappers and bits of trash and dropped them into the tiny can next to the desk. Heavy breathing rasped, and he was appalled to realize it was his.

"Sam," Riley whispered, and God help him, he turned to face her again instead of getting up and locking himself in the bathroom like he should have.

"What?" he managed to say, but it was thick and guttural instead of the impersonal tone he was going for. Riley tilted her head back and met his gaze, her eyes dark with need.

No, dammit, they were dark with pain. He'd irritated raw skin. *He* was the one with need blazing in his expression, judging by the way Riley… *Oh, God.*

She leaned forward, mouth open and glistening, tongue sweeping quickly over her top lip. Long lashes came down over those burning hazel eyes. Her hands tugged his knees, and the chair rolled an inch closer. The last rationally operating cell in Sam's brain said, "Dude, she wants you."

So he took her.

He slid his hands under her hair to cradle her skull and kissed the hell out of her. No gentle lead-in, no tasting or tentative moment to let her get away if she wanted to. He *devoured* her, thrusting his tongue into her mouth, moaning at the taste of her, at the smell of sex that filled the air. She wrapped her arms around him and dug her fingers into his shoulder blades, arching her body against his torso. Her tongue met his stroke for stroke, and her own breathy moans made him shudder with need.

He spread his legs wide and rolled closer, leaning forward and running his hands down Riley's back, slipping one into the shoulder opening of the tank top so he could touch her skin. He knew she wasn't wearing a bra, but *feeling* it, that she was completely unhindered, fed his hunger.

And then his fantasy became reality. He covered Riley on the bed, grunting with satisfaction when she tightened her thighs around his hips. Her body writhing under him, he sucked on her neck, nibbled her collarbone, and buried his face between her spectacular breasts. She gasped and clutched his head, arching her back. He accepted the invitation and closed his mouth over her nipple. She convulsed, and the pressure of his zipper on his cock became unbearable. He had to get free, had to take her, to fill her, to fill *himself*, to—

He didn't know what triggered it—maybe when he twisted to reach for his belt buckle, he caught sight of the moon outside the window—but sanity returned like a punch in the gut.

This wasn't right. It wasn't normal. He could *hurt* her.

The chair got in his way when he reared back and scrambled off the bed. He tripped and fell against the desk, panting, staring in shock at Riley, who looked confused and fucking delicious sprawled across the bed like that.

"I'm sorry," he ground out before she could say anything. "I'm so sorry."

And he bolted.

CHAPTER TWELVE

Today, my brother watched me heal a dove that had hit our window and broken its wing. He didn't say anything, but the look on his face made my heart ache. He no longer courts the girl who sells flowers downtown, and he stopped tutoring his students after school. I fear for what's to become of him.

*—**Meandress Chronicles,** compilation of family diaries*

Sam felt no relief when the bathroom door closed between him and Riley. Nausea washed over him, and the overly bright room spun. He gripped the sides of the sink and gagged, blinking hard, trying to get everything to settle. Parts of his body were on fire, other parts so cold the sweat beading on his skin could turn to ice.

What the hell was wrong with him?

He'd been lost in Riley, but this wasn't typical lust. At some point he'd been so far gone he wouldn't have been able to tell whether she'd been right there with him or struggling to get away.

His gorge rose at the thought of what he could've done. He whirled and got the toilet lid up in time to lose his dinner. It didn't make him feel better.

Worse, the need wasn't gone. His erection was as hard as

ever, and the craving kept getting stronger. Already, it nearly overwhelmed his revulsion. But he couldn't go back out there. Couldn't face Riley like this.

Everything in the room had a pink tinge to it, and the edges of his vision were darkening to red. He stripped off his clothes and yanked on the shower, getting under the spray without regulating the temperature. There was only one thing he could do now to ease the pressure.

Sam braced his left hand against the wall under the showerhead and let the water pound down on his head and back while he wrapped his other hand around his cock. He was harder than he'd ever been before, so fucking sensitive his first grip sent a wave of pleasure through him that abated the awful, biting hunger.

Relief gusted out in a breath, and he went to work, concentrating on his goal, focusing intently on sensation, not imagery. But control eluded him. With each stroke, he saw flashes of Riley. Tasted her skin, her nipple. Smelled her. Felt her body cradling his. Heard her cry out. Thrust into her, and—

He grunted and came violently, pleasure in a dozen concentrated bursts. He gulped in air, his muscles relaxing, tension slowly draining away. He sank onto the floor of the tub, exhausted, and held his head in his hands, his elbows against upraised knees. The water pelting him gradually cooled, and he felt more normal as the minutes ticked by.

He didn't know what to do. The power transfer had obviously triggered this in him. Why had it taken so long to manifest? He'd had the itch when it first happened, but then nothing until…well, until he stormed out of the motel when Riley called, and he let a small surge of energy burst out of him. But he'd done so little, and it triggered *this?* What if it got worse with each transfer?

But he couldn't stop. They still had Chloe and Tanda, and Sam couldn't back out. He couldn't deny them what was rightfully theirs. Especially since Quinn was sick and hurting, too. The only cure for her was finishing the job. But God, he was terrified of what would happen next time. Every transfer could affect him more strongly. Leave a greater residue. And put Riley in more danger.

He could send her back to Boston, but she wasn't some pliant, obedient flower. She wouldn't stay put now any more than she had the last time, especially with everything else they knew now, and not with Jeannine withholding information. That probably reinforced her mistrust of the Society, reversing any progress they'd made when she first arrived.

Thinking, planning, analyzing had calmed him, but then Sam thought about going out there, to Riley, and the tension returned. He could stay in here all night. Or until she went to sleep. She had to be tired, after everything that had happened. He owed her an apology, and more, but he could handle it better in the morning. Yeah, he'd wait it out.

If she'd let him.

As soon as the water shut off, Riley knocked on the bathroom door. Silence. "Sam? Are you all right?"

"I'm fine." But his voice sounded as raw as her wrists.

"Are you coming out?"

His sigh was heavy enough to hear through the door. "Yeah. Give me a minute."

Riley turned off the light and got into her bed. She had a feeling Sam would appreciate the darkness.

He'd been in the bathroom, in the shower, for more than half an hour. When he first threw himself off her she'd been in a haze of desire, and his horrified expression had pierced her to the core. But then he fled into the bathroom, where she'd heard him retching a short time later. She might have some insecurities, but she didn't think she was *that* repulsive. No, something else was going on.

She curled on her side and watched shadows flicker in the

light under the door as he moved around. The light clicked off and the door opened. Riley's eyes were adjusted enough to see he wore only a towel. Her heart skipped, but he walked quickly past the foot of her bed to the far side of his own. As far from her as he could get. With effort, Riley kept herself facing away until she'd heard him settle into bed. Then she rolled over.

"Sam."

"Riley." The low rumble was an apology all by itself.

"Talk to me." He didn't respond, so she said, "I didn't want you to stop."

Sam drew in half a breath and choked. "What?"

"I want you to know that. In case some of the problem is that you were afraid you were forcing yourself on me or something. I wanted you, too… That's all." That was so not all. Her body still hummed. She could still taste him. Her want was very much not in the past tense. But if she had any hope of desire growing into more, something lasting, she had to give Sam room.

"Thanks." His voice was soft, and then he cleared his throat. "That helps. A little. I, uh…"

"You can talk to me," Riley said. *Please talk to me.*

"Shit. I don't even know where to start."

"I can ask you questions."

He chuckled. "Okay."

"What made you stop?"

He groaned and ran a hand down his face. "I just clued in that it wasn't normal."

Yikes. What did that mean? "Not normal because…"

"It wasn't regular, uh, desire. I was driven, hungry. More than hungry. I didn't know if I could stop."

"But you did."

"Luck. I saw—" He hesitated. "It's a long story, and it's getting late."

"I can sleep in the car." So far, their relationship had been all about what she needed from him. She wanted so much to help him in return, and staying awake to listen seemed like such a small thing.

"Not all of it's mine to tell. So…don't, like—"

Riley sighed. "I would never repeat something you said to me, Sam. You can trust me."

Sheets rustled, and he cleared his throat again. "Before the whole leech thing, Quinn used to get what she called moon lust. Her body would be depleted when she channeled energy, and she needed to recharge, to balance it, with sex."

Riley stilled, a new kind of heat rising up into her face. Who did Quinn recharge with back then, before she had Nick? Probably her dedicated assistant. Her hands clenched until the burns on her arms pulled, making her wince.

Not the point. Just listen.

"I think when I filtered the power she transferred to Jennifer, I got more than the residue. I think I got something from Quinn, too. I've never felt that kind of craving before. I never understood what she was feeling, all those years."

He mused the last, and Riley forced her tense jaw to relax. Just because he was reflecting on the past didn't mean it had anything to do with the present.

"Does that mean you still need—"

"No, I, uh…I'm good."

Riley flushed with what should have been embarrassment, but understanding what he meant stoked her fire. Her mouth went dry, and she squeezed her thighs together, to no avail.

"I think that would be it if we were done with the transfers. I can't draw on additional energy and drive the, um, reaction up again."

Oh, God. She couldn't handle this! It was all she could do not to climb into his bed. She rolled to her back and swallowed hard. "So you'll be like this after you do the next transfer."

"And it may be worse."

"You don't have to do it," she said softly, though she knew he'd never say no.

"Of course I do. It's killing Quinn. She has to get rid of it. And Chloe and Tanda need their abilities back to be whole. But I was already worried about the power part, and now this. I don't want to hurt anyone." He swallowed, the sound audible from where Riley lay. "I want you to leave. To go somewhere safe. But—"

"But there is nowhere safe."

"No."

The sexual tension slid away. He sounded so lonely. Even if he didn't think of it that way, she'd been mired in it long enough to recognize it in someone else. She slid out of bed and sat on the side of his. Despite the dark, she found his hand and gripped it. "You're not alone."

His fingers wrapped around hers. "I know I'm not."

"No, I mean it. You won't talk to Quinn and Nick because you think they have enough to worry about. And you want to send me away in case you lose control. But I'm stronger than you think, and whatever I can do to get you through this, I'll do."

"You don't know what that might entail," he said half humorously.

"We'll find out together."

"Anson's still out there, and we don't know what Numina's doing."

"It's not our job to find out right now, remember? We're leaving that to the Society. If Anson messed up their decade-long plans, they're probably not close to their end game."

He sat up, and the sheet slid down to his waist. Riley forgot everything she'd been saying and stared at his torso. The little bit of light in the room gleamed across his skin, enhancing the shadows of his abs and pecs. He loomed in front of her, his size and strength rendering her offer to be his champion utterly ridiculous.

"It's usually me saying stuff like that," he said. All the tension had drained from his voice. "You make it all seem easy to handle."

She shrugged a shoulder. "One thing at a time, right?"

"Right." He raised his hand to her chin and slowly leaned forward to press a soft, warm kiss on her mouth. "Thank you."

Riley drew a deep breath and eased away to go back to her own bed. As they both settled and said goodnight, she relaxed her mind and body. As soon as she did, Sam's buzz tickled her awareness at the same intensity it had been before.

She found it surprisingly comforting.

• • •

The next morning they all piled into the Charger with bags of breakfast to go, Nick at the wheel. Riley pouted a little out the rear window when they drove away from her Beetle. It had gotten her through so much, and leaving it here, however temporarily, felt like a betrayal of the reliable little car.

After hours of hard driving, Riley talked Nick into a pit stop at the rest area on I-75 in Tennessee. She followed Quinn to the ladies room. The other woman had kept her expression overly steady and movements deliberately smooth as she got out of the car and walked up the sidewalk. Riley had a feeling it was taking Quinn a great deal of effort to hold it together and keep the guys from worrying. Nick was already almost as stressed as Quinn was sick.

She waited a couple of beats before pushing through the main bathroom door. Quinn was already in a stall, retching.

They had to do something. They weren't even halfway to Rhode Island. Nick was riding the accelerator hard and had even let Sam drive for a few hours so Nick could rest without stopping—something he clearly didn't like to do. But they still weren't moving fast enough.

Riley leaned against the wall, watching Quinn's unmoving

feet under the stall door. She shouldn't have let Quinn heal her burns this morning, dammit. Quinn had assured her it was a simple action, not enough to even make her blink. That might have been true before, but now Riley was afraid it was making her worse.

Quinn coughed and drew in an audibly deep breath. The toilet flushed, and her feet turned to face the door. Riley moved closer, ready to help when the door latch rattled. The door opened, and Riley caught Quinn before she fell flat on her face.

"Crap," Quinn said, using Riley to balance herself. "Thank you."

"Let's get you back outside," Riley said. "It smells like hell in here." She wrapped her arm around Quinn's waist and propped her up while she washed her hands and splashed her face. Figuring Quinn could use a few minutes before she had to fake strength again, Riley steered her out to the picnic area in the rear of the building. The night air was cool and carried voices and engine rumblings from the parking lot out front. The only other person in the back was an older man, smoking while he walked a Yorkie in the pet area. Floodlights cast odd shadows around them.

"The guys will worry," Quinn murmured. She leaned against a warped green picnic table, no longer bothering to hide her weakness.

"They'll be fine. We're supposed to take forever in the bathroom, right?" She helped Quinn sit. She needed food. "Be right back." She hurried back to the vending alcove and bought a cola and bag of cookies.

They sat in silence for five minutes while Quinn ate. "Thank you," she said to Riley when she'd emptied the cookie bag. "I didn't even know I needed that. But now the shakes are gone, and my stomach is settled."

Riley shrugged. "You looked like my hypoglycemic friend when her blood sugar tanked. Figured it couldn't hurt."

"You were right." Quinn sighed. "We'd better get going before I crash again."

"They'll wait a few more minutes." She didn't know how much Quinn had told the guys, but the last few hours had made clear she was hiding how bad she continued to feel. Riley had a plan, but first she had to convince Quinn, then the guys. "You want to tell me what's going on?"

Quinn sighed again and drank some of her soda. "I'm not sure I even know." She picked at a section of peeling paint on the tabletop. "When I first pulled all this energy, all this power, from Anson, I could control it. But ever since we transferred Jennifer's back to her, the rest has been…excited." She waved her hand in circles up and down her body. "It never settles, just keeps whirling and churning. Sometimes it feels like it swarms out to my fingertips and toes, tugging. Trying to get home or something."

"Whoa," Riley breathed. "No wonder you look like—" She caught herself just in time, but Quinn laughed. Even in the odd lighting, Riley saw color returning to her face.

"Like shit? Yeah."

Nothing Riley had felt in the last three years even came close to what Quinn was describing. But she could tell by the look on Quinn's face that there was more. There was energy that couldn't be returned. What would happen to Quinn when that was all that was left?

"What about the other energy? That doesn't have a place to go?"

Quinn straightened her spine. "Beth's power barely registers now. It's not a problem."

That brought it down to one that Riley knew of. "And Marley's?"

Quinn gazed across the now-empty lawn. "I'd hoped I could return it to her, but the rift there is different from the others." Her voice was low, regretful. "Not just a crack, but a hole. The part of Marley that made her a goddess is less dynamic every time I see her." A tear tracked down her cheek. "If I hadn't taken so long to find a solution, maybe things would be different."

"Hey." Riley laid a hand on Quinn's arm. "It's not your fault."

Quinn sniffed and nodded. "I know. But I hate that I can't help her. She's my sister."

There was a world of complication in the way she said that sentence. Riley closed her eyes against an answering swell of grief, of longing for her own sister. Of what could have been if she'd lived long enough to be a goddess, too.

But this wasn't about her. She opened her eyes. "What's wrong with Marley's energy exactly?"

"It's different from the others." Quinn wiped her face with a napkin. "Beth's energy is dissipating because its vessel is no longer alive. Marley's energy has a vessel, but no way to connect to it because of the permanent damage. So it's changed. It's a dark, heavy mass. Almost…toxic."

This was worse than Riley had thought. "Like poison?" she asked, aghast. "Is it poisoning you?" She didn't need Quinn to answer verbally—it was clear in her eyes. Riley stood and clenched the trash in her fist. "This is stupid. You can't handle another fourteen or more hours of driving."

"I have no choice."

"Yes, you do. You can fly."

Quinn laughed. "Nick will never leave the Charger behind."

Riley rolled her eyes. "You don't think he cares about a *car* more than he cares about you, do you?" She threw the trash in a nearby garbage can and returned to the table to sell her plan to Quinn. "We're near Knoxville. You can get a flight to Providence. That's near Chloe's, right? You can rest and then do the transfer."

Quinn raised her eyebrows. "So you want all of us to fly?"

No. But it was the only option. "You need Sam. So, you three fly up. I'll drive the car. I'll probably get there right about the time you finish the transfer."

"You think Nick will let you drive his car?" She smirked. "Or that Sam will leave you alone?"

Riley found herself fiddling with a long screw from her pocket. She'd been doing that all day, unconsciously reaching out to whatever metal was close at hand. But she never pulled any energy. The skin on her forearms stung whenever she even considered it.

"I think they'll both do anything *for you*." She glanced up to find Quinn staring at her with narrowed eyes.

"It's not like that with Sam," the older woman told Riley. "He'll do just about anything for anyone in need."

Ouch. Riley couldn't stop herself from wincing at the implication that she wasn't important.

Quinn rushed on, "No, I mean that his feelings for me are just friendship now. I promise you."

The attempt to reassure her was backfiring. She hadn't doubted that until Quinn found it necessary to say so. "That's not the problem."

Quinn took the bait. "I'd do anything for Sam, too. So if you think I'm blind to something he needs, you can tell me."

Bingo. "Let's just say Sam needs to speed this up as much as you do."

Quinn looked stricken. "I didn't realize it was affecting him that much…physically," she admitted softly.

"So, you're on board?" Riley asked.

"Yes. Let's—"

Riley shot up off the bench. "Good. Stay here." She ran back through the building to the parking lot. Nick and Sam were leaning against the hood and fender of the Charger.

Sam pushed away from the car, arms spread wide in obvious frustration. "What's taking so long? I was about to come in there after you."

Nick watched behind her. "Where's Quinn?"

"She's out back in the picnic area."

"Alone?" Nick moved to walk by her, but Riley stopped him. "She's not doing well."

Nick's jaw clenched. "We don't need you to tell us that."

Riley folded her arms, ready to do battle. A few hours confined with people told you a lot about them. Not only was Nick very proprietary about his car—something that had to be as much a symbol as a possession—as a protector, he probably hated the confined space and nonexistent escape routes on an airplane. Quinn was trying hard not to ask anything of him, nor to worry him any more than she was. And Sam had already made it clear he wouldn't leave Riley behind.

"You need to get to Chloe's faster."

Nick scoffed. Sam threw him a look and said, "We're already pushing the limit."

"Yeah, so you need faster transportation." She outlined the plan she'd already laid out for Quinn. Both guys were shaking their heads before she was halfway through.

"No way," Sam said. "I'm not leaving you. We talked about that."

"You have to," Riley argued. "Quinn can't handle the drive. She won't be able to do the transfer if you force her to travel that way."

A flicker went through Sam's eyes. "Nick said she can't fly, either. That's why they drove to Mississippi in the first place."

"This is worse," Nick admitted. "But there's stuff in that car we can't just leave, and we can't take on an airplane."

Riley stayed silent and let Nick and Sam hash out alternatives, but she knew they'd come to the same conclusions she had. She liked Quinn and hated how much she was suffering, and would want to help her because it was the right thing. But she had deeper motivations. Sam had his own suffering that he would never reveal to Quinn and Nick unless he had to, and Riley knew the only way to end that was to get through it.

She turned to Nick, who stood silently nearby. "You can trust me with your car." Riley steadily met his piercing stare and held out her hand. Half a minute went by.

"Hell." Nick bounced the keys on his palm. "I can't trust anyone with my car. But—"

"I know." She shifted her hand forward a little. Nick dropped the keys into it, then snatched them back.

"At the airport."

"No!" Sam held out his hands as if to separate the two of them. "I'm not agreeing to this. We know she's a target. She can't drive up there alone."

"How is anyone going to know where I am?" Riley argued. "There's no way for Anson to have any clue."

Nick pulled out his phone. "We'll get someone else to go with her. We need you for the transfer, man," he reminded Sam as he dialed.

"Hey, John. Nick. We need a guy." He briefly explained.

Riley listened tensely. The Protectorate had been stretched thin since she first connected with the Society, so she was surprised when John apparently offered someone to Nick.

"I don't know him," Nick said. "You're sure he's cool?" He listened skeptically, then nodded. "All right. We'll meet him at the airport."

Nick hung up as they spotted Quinn moving slowly toward them, supporting herself with one hand on the brick wall of the building. He dashed over to her, and Riley braced herself.

"This is wrong," Sam said through a tight jaw.

Riley was less certain of her plan now that she was going to be left alone with a stranger, but she couldn't let Sam see that. "I'll be okay."

He caught her shoulders and made her look at him. She tried to hide her conflicting emotions. If Sam thought she had a single moment's trepidation about this, he'd never go with them. And he was hurting almost as much as Quinn was. The sooner he got through it all, the better.

"I can stay with you," he said. "They can fly up, and she can rest. We can do the transfer when we get there."

Riley shook her head. "You need to be there and ready to do it as soon as she's able. You don't want to miss a window, and what if we hit traffic or something?" She patted the roof of the car. "This baby is pure steel. I'll be invincible. And you know John wouldn't give us someone we couldn't trust."

He smiled, the one-sided quirk of his mouth that flashed a dimple and charmed the hell out of her. Her heart thumped hard once, fluttered twice, and settled back into rhythm.

"Promise me," he said, "that you'll be careful. Keep in contact. Take some back roads—be unpredictable. There's no reason anyone should be able to track or follow you. But just in case—"

"I get it. Don't worry. I'll be there before you know it."

He hugged her and pressed a kiss to the top of her head. "I'll miss you," he murmured.

Half an hour later, she sat behind the wheel with a steely military type named Tom sitting next to her, watching them all disappear into the airport and fighting the melodramatic feeling that she'd never see any of them again.

• • •

After landing in Providence, Sam, Nick, and Quinn got a hotel room so Quinn could spend a few hours recovering. Sam called Riley just about every hour until Quinn insisted she was well enough to make the transfer. Her color was better, and she was moving more easily, though she still got out of breath quickly. But they couldn't argue when she said it was the best she was going to get, and there was no point in waiting.

Chloe fed them a late lunch while Sam and Nick set up the beach chairs and Quinn's notes. She fussed over Quinn like a grandmother, but excitement vibrated in her voice.

"You know," she told Sam when he went inside for another of her melt-in-your-mouth orange muffins. "I thought I was glad to be free of it."

"I remember." He broke the still-warm muffin in two and popped half into his mouth. When she'd been leeched, Chloe had seen only the silver lining, an opportunity to open her own bakery, which had been a raging success. "God, that's good."

She beamed. "That's exactly what I wanted. I needed to be free for a while, to concentrate on my dream. But I've missed it." She looked out the window to her source, the Atlantic Ocean. It was a perfect day outside, high sixties with the slightest of breezes, the water rolling in long, smooth swells onto the soft sand. "It belongs in me," she almost whispered, her unnaturally pale gray eyes gleaming in the reflected sunlight.

"Then let's make you whole again." Sam ate the rest of his muffin and led Chloe out onto the weathered cedar deck at the back of her little cottage, all raised eight feet off the sand with stilts. The private beach was deserted, and they were shielded from sight by scrubby bushes on either side of her property.

"Sit here," Quinn said, indicating the chair closest to the water. She nodded at Sam, and he settled into the other chair. Quinn stood next to Chloe and settled her hands on her. "Ready?"

First she healed Chloe as she had Jennifer. Sam and Nick both watched carefully, but the effort didn't seem to tax her at all. Chloe clung to the sides of her chair, and her jaw flexed as if she grit her teeth, but after a couple of minutes she loosened her grip and relaxed. When she opened her eyes, they held the same wonder Jennifer had displayed.

"How do you feel?" Quinn asked her.

Chloe rolled her shoulders and smiled. "Good. *Really* good. Full of energy. You know, like healthy." She settled back in her chair. "I'm ready for the next bit."

Quinn eyed Sam. "You ready?"

He nodded but tried to hide his trepidation. Quinn closed her eyes, but he kept his open, watching her, ready to stop her if things went bad. Her hand in his grew cold, then warmed, and something wriggled inside him. The residual power, responding to what was coming?

Quinn's hand tightened, and the conduit opened. Sam had a sense of space, of connection. He braced himself for the onslaught of pleasure.

But the power slid forward into him, cold and sluggish, jagged. It pierced, as if resisting by digging thorns or claws into him. Sam gritted his teeth against the pain. His mind tried to cringe away, to close the conduit, but he forced himself to stay open, not to resist. Quinn tensed. Her brow wrinkled, and Sam sensed her driving it through, into him.

"Quinn." Nick's voice came from far away, but his urgency was obvious. "Quinn, stop."

"I can't," she ground out, and Sam tried to open more. He wanted the slight bit of power he already had to reach out and draw in the new power, but it only churned restlessly. This was a far cry from the smooth flow of the other day.

Fear spiked. They'd screwed something up. They had to stop. He tried to pull his hand out of Quinn's, but she clutched him tighter, her hand sliding up to his wrist and her other closing over his fingers. He lay helpless while she pushed, and the power slowly filled him like a big, icy blob. The pain increased steadily, raking along his insides and coalescing in his consciousness more than any physical spot. The pain seemed disconnected from his body while wholly contained within it.

Quinn gasped and broke the connection as the last trailing tendril slid into Sam. "Chloe, grab Sam's hand," she croaked.

"No," Sam groaned. "Wrong." He couldn't communicate, couldn't explain. He felt like someone had beaten him up.

"You have to, Sam. It's okay. She'll be okay."

He closed his right hand into a fist and tried to pull it close to him. He couldn't give this to Chloe. She'd go insane. But she reached and curled her fingers around his fist, her nails scratching his palm as they pried up his fingertips.

The power went wild. In seconds the ice seemed to melt, and it whirled and spun like an excited puppy. Sam recognized Chloe's capacity, felt the affinity. He relaxed and let go, and the energy flowed out of him into her. It sliced as much going out as it had coming in, but the pain stayed behind. Chloe inhaled deep, the sound welcoming, pleased. Slowly, as the energy left Sam, the pain faded, leaving only a raw fatigue.

Chloe let go of him, but he couldn't move. He heard the rhythm of the ocean across the beach, and his blood seemed to surge and ebb along with the waves. But he felt none of the euphoria he'd felt after Jennifer's transfer. Only nausea and a pounding headache that also, unfortunately, emulated the crashing of the waves.

"Sam." A voice penetrated the pounding and surging. Not Quinn's. Another woman. His heart rate picked up, as did the nausea. "Sam, honey." The woman speaking was older than Quinn, and her voice was accompanied by a soft hand on his forehead. Chloe. He grew slowly more aware, but as the world around him solidified, his insides churned even more.

"Oh, shit." He shoved Chloe aside and scrambled to the steps off her deck, stumbling, falling down the last few and landing on his knees in time to retch in the sand. He heaved until his stomach was empty, then heaved a few more times for good measure.

"Come on, buddy. You done?" Nick half helped, half hauled Sam to his feet. "You all right?"

"Quinn," he managed, collapsing onto the steps and watching Nick kick sand over his mess.

"She's okay. Chloe's helping her."

He couldn't raise his head to see Nick's face. "Did it work?"

"Yeah. Chloe seems okay. She's not like you two, anyway. How are you feeling?"

"Like crap."

"Yeah, you look it."

Sam reached for the banister and dragged himself back up the steps to the deck. He leaned on the rail and stared at the ocean. His blood still followed the rhythm of the waves, but the sluggishness remained. He had no compulsion to test his abilities this time. Hell, he was barely compelled to keep from collapsing into a heap again.

"That didn't go so well," he told Nick.

"I noticed." He climbed the steps and settled his hand on Sam's shoulder, and for some reason, it steadied him.

"Are you sure they're okay?" He wasn't convinced Chloe hadn't been damaged the way he had.

"Yeah, you seem to have gotten the worst of it. Quinn's tired but actually better than she was before. And Chloe said it felt like she was normalizing, like she'd been sick for a long time and now she's suddenly healthy again."

"She didn't have any pain?"

"No." Nick dropped his hand and shoved them into his pockets, leaning with his back to the water so he could see Sam's face. Sam looked down at his hands braced on the rail.

"How bad was it?" Nick asked.

Sam shrugged.

"Come on, I could see it. You looked like something was slicing you up inside."

"That's how it felt. Like the power was full of needles or barbs. It resisted until I connected with Chloe. Then it flowed into her."

"Did it—was it—dammit." Nick hunched his shoulders. "Did it feel malevolent?"

Sam shook his head. "It's hard not to put human terms on it, like firefighters do with fire, but no. It's just energy. There's no intent or emotion to it. It's what we've made it." He drew a deep breath, the salt and sand scents easing into him and relaxing some of his muscles. The stomach cramping had passed, and his headache eased a little.

He heard Quinn's footsteps crossing the deck, and she came to stand between them. "How are you?" she asked Sam.

"I'm fine."

Her eyebrows lowered. "Tell the truth."

"I'm getting to fine."

"That's better." The frown eased, though she still looked concerned. "I heard what you were saying. It was Marley's power."

"What? You put the wrong power in—"

"No, no. I mean the problem was Marley's power. I had trouble separating them, and it wouldn't let go. The resistance you said you felt—I think that was it."

"Great," Nick said. "What's it going to do when you try to take Tanda's out?"

Quinn didn't answer.

"How about you?" Sam asked. "Did it hurt you?"

"No. I'm feeling much better. Honestly," she said. "Like when you throw up, everything feels better for a little while."

"Thanks, I just lived that metaphor."

She grimaced. "Sorry."

"What was it like from your end?"

She sighed. "Like a too-tight bolt on an engine block."

"Hey, I get that one!" Nick joked, making them all laugh.

"Why do you think it was so different?" Sam asked Quinn. "Jennifer's went so easily."

Quinn glanced back to the house, probably making sure Chloe wasn't in earshot. "Jennifer didn't have as much capacity as Chloe did, for one thing. She's younger, too, so she hadn't developed the same ability to draw power." She shifted toward Sam but reached back to take Nick's hand and hold it tight against her thigh.

"When Marley gave Anson some of her power, and then he leeched power from the rest of the goddesses, he created something new. Like putting milk and sugar into tea. There are methods for separating those items from each other again, but they won't separate cleanly. That's why you're so important for this."

Sam gripped the smooth, weathered wood of the rail and held in the rest of his questions. He wanted to know how much the filter was catching and holding. How much of what wound up in him was damaged and what that would mean for the next transfer. And after. But he didn't want to reveal his fears or make Quinn think she had to stop now—it was more crucial than ever that they keep going.

He focused on her. "You're suffering from the effort of separating the energy, aren't you?"

She smiled ruefully. "I think you're suffering more this time."

"Nah." He released the rail and flexed his hands to ease the cramps in his fingers. "I just lie there. Easy as pie."

Quinn rolled her eyes. "Anyway, we need to get to Tanda faster than we got to Chloe. I'm losing the moon."

Sam didn't like the sound of that. "You didn't say this was contingent on the moon."

"It's not, but I don't want to head into my weakest point at the end of this. I mean, I will anyway, but having the last quarter will help my equilibrium. I should have planned this better," she said with sudden anger. "I should have known time would be a factor and had everyone together."

Nick stroked her hair. "You didn't know it would go like this. And you wanted them to be near their main sources. Ohio wouldn't have provided any of them."

Her shoulders relaxed. "That's true."

Chloe came out of the house carrying a basket of muffins and croissants. "Anyone still hungry?" She stared down at the basket she held in both hands, levitated a muffin, and flung it through the air. Nick caught it one-handed.

Chloe beamed. "God, that feels good." Before she could pitch any others, a familiar rumble reached their ears.

"Riley's here!" Sam straightened and strode toward the front of the house. The Charger came into view, and he froze, his heart leaping into his throat.

"Son of a *bitch*!" Nick flew past him, fury in every line of his body.

The side of the car was wrecked.

Before Sam could take another step, the driver's door opened, and Riley spilled out onto the ground.

CHAPTER THIRTEEN

Success can be measured in many ways, and one is the range of partnerships made available by status and authority. Never hesitate to seek partners in unusual places, even in spheres that might seem opposed to our aims.

—*Numina manifesto,* *revised*

Driving with Tom was like driving alone. He never talked until Riley asked him a direct question, never requested a rest stop, never offered an opinion on where to get food or sleep for a few hours, even when asked. On the plus side, he didn't seem to care what kind of music she played.

She merged onto I-95 near Mystic, a few miles from the route they'd take to Chloe's, and Tom offered to drive. He hadn't offered to do that at any point along the trip, not even during a major traffic jam outside New York City or when they were almost sideswiped by a gray sedan that changed lanes too quickly. Weird.

"We're nearly there," Riley demurred. "I'm okay to make it the rest of the way."

"You must be tired, though. You can navigate."

"No, thanks. There's GPS." She motioned to the unit, which

beeped obediently and told her to drive one point four miles and then take the exit right.

Riley took inventory of the cars around them. She'd studied everything around her intently for the first hundred miles, cataloging dents and scratches and bent antennae and anything else that would help her keep track of followers. The longer they drove the harder it became to remember everything she'd seen, but she hadn't been able to stop trying.

Like that gray sedan passing them now. It didn't look any different from the dozens of similar cars on the road, except for a slight curve in the edge of the hood, like something had bent it a little. She'd swear the car that almost hit them yesterday had the same curve.

"Tom, look at that car up there. The one that just passed us. Did we see it yesterday?"

He glanced at the other lane, not even moving his head. "No."

"Are you sure? They all look similar. But that one has a dent that—"

"It's not the same. Trust me. That's what I'm here for."

Riley frowned at him, but he didn't react. That was the most he'd said at one time since he got in the car. She sped up to get near the sedan again, trying to figure out why she had this low-burning anxiety, despite Tom's dismissal of her concern. She'd missed something—she could sense it.

And then she felt it, too. The prickling, like in Anson's office.

She was cruising in a pack—I-95 was one big pack most of the time—but could still pinpoint the origin of the sensation. The gray sedan, now a couple of cars ahead of her in the left lane. *Son of a bitch.*

There was only one way they could have found her.

She stole a quick look at Tom, who crossed his arms over his chest and watched the passing landscape. She tried to keep her breathing even and quiet.

With her exit coming up, Riley didn't have much time to formulate a plan. She slowed gradually to let the sedan get far enough ahead that they wouldn't be able to get over fast enough to follow, but they must have been watching her closely. They smoothly dodged cars and switched lanes until they were two cars behind her. Riley debated her options for a few seconds. Stay on or get off? Taillights flashed ahead, so she hit the ramp to Route 234. Maybe she could lose them down there.

"Something wrong?" Tom asked, eyes now narrowed on her. He shifted so his left arm was across the back of the seat, his hand uncomfortably close to Riley's head, and rested his right hand on the dash. Good placement to grab the wheel…

A bubble of hysteria threatened to make her laugh. She needed metal and a plan. She'd tucked one of Nick's shotguns from the trunk next to her seat since she wasn't wearing any metal. She hadn't wanted anything in direct contact with her skin, afraid she'd unconsciously draw energy and burn herself again. Plus, Tom was *supposed to be on her side, dammit.*

"No," she answered his question as calmly as she could. He'd never expect to be shoved out the door, but she couldn't reach his door handle from here, and even the shotgun probably wouldn't give her enough strength to succeed, and opening the window and sticking her hand out to use the vehicle's chassis would be too obvious. He'd be able to yank her away before she could draw enough energy.

But maybe she could do something less physical. She ran through the steps in her head until she knew what to do.

She had to act quickly. Traffic had thinned considerably on this smaller road, and Riley and the sedan were already the only cars on the quiet two-lane. Towering trees dappled the road with shadow. The few houses were mostly large, on giant tracts of property and set way back from the road. There were few streets to turn onto, all residential neighborhoods lined with cars. No room to maneuver, no way to get enough speed to lose them. Besides, the Charger was too distinctive to stay lost for long.

Riley spotted a crossroads up ahead that was open enough for her plan. She reached down next to the seat to grip the shotgun while she hit the accelerator, sucking energy and concentrating hard on using it to pull the door handle on the passenger side. *Please work, please work, please work.* A *click* reverberated along the thread of energy, like the vibration of a thread on a spider's web. *Yes!*

Riley jerked the wheel left, spinning the car. The door flew open and Macho Tom, who hadn't bothered wearing a seatbelt, flew out the opening with flailing arms and a shouted curse.

Riley kept the car going in a circle. It lurched almost to a stop, facing the way she'd been going originally. She hit the gas, the vehicle's momentum slamming the passenger door closed. In the rearview mirror, she saw Tom sit up at the side of the road. The sedan sped by him without even slowing down.

No time for her to even take a breath. She'd slowed so much the sedan closed in on her tail, then suddenly whipped out into the oncoming lane and pulled up next to her. She glanced quickly over but only saw two silhouetted figures, their shapes unlike the men who'd been in Anson's office. But the prickling was a lot stronger now, with them only a few feet away, so they had to be part of Numina.

The passenger motioned her to pull over.

"Hell, no." Time to see what Nick's car was capable of.

She slammed on the accelerator and pulled ahead, letting up for the curves but picking up speed halfway through each of them. The car was heavy and the steering tight, but it handled those curves like a lover. She whooped as she rounded the third turn, the sedan so far behind now she couldn't see it. But she didn't let up. She kept going, reducing her speed to a safer level, but still flying toward the ocean and Sam.

"Recalculating route."

"What?" Riley glanced at the GPS a few times. Fuck. She'd overshot her turn.

"Recalculating route."

The Charger burned a good quarter mile of pavement before the stupid freaking GPS said "turn around when possible."

Cursing, Riley slowed and pulled to the right, preparing to make a three-point turn on the narrow road, when flashing lights appeared in her rearview mirror.

Fuck again. The cops.

She waited until they got close, making sure it was a real cop and not the sedan with a flashy light. It was real, dammit, and she pulled over as far as she could. The cop pulled in behind her, half out into the street to provide a bit of safety for the officer. Riley leaned to check the glove box for the registration, gasping when the door opened to reveal a pearl-handled pistol lying inside. She grabbed the envelope underneath it and slammed it closed again, her heart pounding.

"Calm down, Riley." She checked the mirror. The cop hadn't gotten out yet. She took a deep breath and scanned the interior of the car for anything else incriminating, and pushed the shotgun deeper under the seat, out of sight.

Driver's license. They'd want that, too. She pulled it out of her back pocket and straightened, forcing herself to sit still and breathe. By the time the officer—a female with her hair pulled up in a tight twist and her uniform without a wrinkle—reached the side of the car, Riley had managed to calm down. She didn't smile when she rolled down her window and handed over the license and registration.

The cop checked her face, eyed her hands on the wheel, and peered around the inside of the car. "Do you know how fast you were going, ma'am?"

"Not exactly," Riley answered, not even considering lying. "But I know it was too fast."

The cop's eyebrow went up, but she kept jotting information on her ticket pad. "Why were you going so fast?"

"It's going to sound insane." Riley slid her hands up to the top of the wheel, then back to ten and two. "Um…there was a gray sedan following me. Did you see it?" She hoped like hell the cop hadn't seen her dump Tom. She'd be arrested and a sitting duck in some little regional jail. Well, at least there'd be easy access to the metal bars there.

"No, ma'am. You were the only car on the road."

So the cop had been sitting around the third turn, after Riley had pulled well away from the sedan.

"Well, they followed me off the highway, pulled up next to me, and tried to get me to pull over. They scared me, so I sped up instead. This car has some muscle," she finished, sure she'd said exactly the wrong thing.

But the cop's lips quirked a bit. "Yes, it's a beefy one." She slid the license and registration card under the clip on her pad holder. "It's not yours?"

"No, it's a friend's. He had to fly east, and I offered to drive the car for him so he didn't have to leave it behind."

"Behind where?"

"We started in Atlanta."

The officer peered in at Riley. "You been resting?"

"Yes, I stayed in a hotel last night." Okay, some lying wouldn't hurt.

"Good." She tapped the holder. "I'll be right back." She returned to her car, and Riley watched in the side mirror, then the rear when the cop climbed into the cruiser. She was anxiously watching still, chewing the cuticle on her thumb, when the gray car eased around the last curve and stopped well behind them. She glared as it backed up a little, then did the three-point turn Riley had planned and zoomed away.

"Yeah, you better get your ass out of here." Speeding fine

notwithstanding, maybe getting stopped had been the best thing. The minutes ticked by. A few other cars passed, three in a row, then a truck, but no gray sedan. Finally the cop returned and handed Riley her cards.

"I'm issuing you a citation for failure to obey posted traffic signs." She scribbled something on her pad, initialed it, and ripped off the ticket to hand to Riley. "I suggest you use more caution from here on. My colleagues will be posted in various areas," she added.

Riley smiled her thanks. "Is it okay if I turn around here? I missed my turn."

The cop motioned ahead. "It's safer to drive down about a quarter mile to the Dew Drop Inn and turn there. Good coffee, too."

"Thank you." She waited until the officer was back in her car before opening the glove compartment, tossing the Nick's registration back in, and quickly shutting it. Then she put her license back and stuck the citation in her pocket. The cop hadn't moved, but Riley couldn't tell if she was watching her, talking to her dispatcher, or making notes in her log or whatever. Riley put the car in gear and pulled out, hoping the cop would follow her for a while. That would ensure the people in the sedan would keep their distance. But almost immediately, the cruiser did a U-turn, probably to go back to the speed trap.

"Safer to go forward, my ass," Riley muttered. Fine. She'd take the cop up on her suggestion and stop for coffee and crowds.

The Dew Drop Inn appeared on the left a few minutes later, a ramshackle clapboard diner with a half-full parking lot. Riley drove around to the side and behind some cars parked in the center of the lot. The Charger wasn't hidden from the street, but they might pass without seeing it. She eyed the empty road, hoping she could get inside before the sedan drove by and spotted her.

Since the building blocked her view down the road, she

climbed out, locked the door, and jogged up to the entrance, slipping quickly inside the cozy little diner, and releasing her held breath.

"Hello, sweetheart!" The man in front of her had wild white hair and sparkling blue eyes, and he wore a threadbare cardigan over baggy khakis as comfortably as his broad grin. "Early lunch today?"

"Um, just coffee, I think. And maybe—is that peach pie?" She indicated the pie safe on the counter.

The old man beamed. "It certainly is, fresh made this morning. I'd be double-dee-lighted to serve you some." He waved at the woman behind the counter and led Riley to a booth halfway back in the main dining area. The little place seemed to be a warren of rooms, and she thought about asking if she could be seated in one of the other areas, but they could take her by surprise back there. Here, at least, she could sit facing the front windows and see the road and entrance to the parking lot.

She thanked the white-haired man—who'd introduced himself as Curtis, the owner of the Dew Drop—when he set down her pie and filled her mug with coffee. He was chatty and seemed about to join her, something she normally wouldn't have minded, but right now she just wanted to lurk without distraction. Luckily someone called him over to their table and he sat with them, instead, leaving Riley to slowly eat her pie and keep an eagle eye out the window.

Half an hour later, she hadn't spotted the gray sedan, and she couldn't nurse her coffee anymore. She paid at the cash register before returning to the car. She reprogrammed the GPS, pulled out onto the empty road, and relaxed as she approached her turn.

She'd driven a scant quarter mile when her pursuers pulled up beside her again, so suddenly she didn't know where they came from. The passenger, no longer in silhouette, motioned again for her to pull over. He was younger and more refined than she'd expected. With sandy blond hair hanging over his forehead, he had the look of a trust-fund kid.

She drove faster. This time they were ready and surged up the road with her, pulling alongside quickly and veering right, bumping the Charger and pushing her toward the shoulder.

"Fuck!" She struggled with the wheel, losing speed. Metal screeched as they hit her again, the sedan scraping up the side of Nick's car before she shot ahead.

The reprieve wasn't going to last long. Time to suck it up and use the big rolling hunk of metal she had at her disposal. She unrolled her window halfway and slapped her hand on the roof. The connection was instantaneous, the energy just waiting for her to direct it, and to her relief, it was cool and exciting rather than hot and frightening.

But how could she use it? The car chasing her was bigger than anything she'd tried to move with her mind before, and she wasn't sure she could do telekinesis through the window, on the move, even with something small.

The sedan surged up beside her again. This time Riley slowed to let them get ahead of her, then took her hand off the wheel, held her palm out toward the car, and concentrated on shoving it off the road. It veered, the back end fishtailing slightly, before the driver corrected. She had to grab the wheel again when the Charger swerved. Her sweaty palm slid along the roof, but she refused to let go of her power source or change her contact to the door, where her arm could be more easily crushed between vehicles.

The road lay straight ahead for a while. She braked and tried again, pushing harder at the sedan, and this time managed to get it to skid off to the far shoulder before the driver righted them. She floored it and pulled her hand inside. The sudden ebb of power made her dizzy. She gripped the wheel and blinked hard, shaking her head to clear it.

"In…one mile…bear right…and then…turn left," the GPS told her.

Riley's heart rate sped up even more. She was so close to safety, to Sam. But she didn't want to lead these yahoos to Quinn and risk interrupting the transfer. She thought briefly of the pistol in the glove box, but she'd never used one before and had no idea if it was even loaded. If she could get far enough ahead, maybe the turn onto Route 1 would help her lose them…

She was almost out of time. She'd crossed the line into Rhode Island and was in Westerly now, the road dense with homes. The sedan was back on the road and gaining. Okay, she had to admit it. Without full concentration, the car was too heavy for her. So she needed to move something else. She scanned the side of the road ahead of her. A dead tree stood among those bursting with new leaves. Riley put her hand back on the roof, balanced the steering wheel with her knee, and aimed the other at the tree, imagining grabbing it and ripping a huge branch off. There was a satisfying *crack* as she drove under it, and she watched in the rearview mirror as a shower of dry branches clattered down behind her. Most hit the ground in front of the sedan. The biggest one bounced up onto its hood, then banged up and over the roof as the sedan bumped over the ones on the ground.

But they were still right behind her.

She squealed through the intersection of 234 and Route 1, the light flashing to yellow above her. Riley blinked as she sped. Were the trees blurring because she was going so fast, or was something wrong with her vision? It seemed harder to breathe now, too.

And the sedan had made the light.

God, what if she didn't get out of this? What if they stopped her?

"Turn right…in…one mile…and then…merge right."

That wasn't going to work. This was too residential, had too much traffic. She slammed on the brakes at the flash of taillights ahead of her and wracked her brain to remember the map of the area she'd studied last night. GPS was great, but she didn't like not knowing what she was looking for.

A sign for Route 2 flashed by, and a couple hundred feet later, she turned left. She couldn't lead these guys to the others. For all she knew, they only wanted her as bait for bigger fish. She had to find a spot where she could confront them and stop them once and for all.

The GPS stopped recalculating and flashed instructions on the screen. "In…eight hundred yards…take the exit ramp… right." That was Route 78, and meant she was only minutes away from Chloe's place. Her brain fuzzed. Thinking grew harder. She zoomed up the ramp onto the blessedly empty highway. Thank God for the off season.

The two cars hurtled down the two-lane highway bisected by a solid median and surrounded by forest on both sides. Half a mile along, she decided things weren't going to get any better than this. She held her breath and wrapped her hands tightly around the steering wheel to yank it to the left, slamming on the brakes at the same time. The car spun so its back end was perched on the edge of the ditch at the side of the road and blocking the lane with just a narrow gap between the front end and the concrete barrier.

Riley slid across the front seat and pushed out the passenger door, coughing in the swirling dust kicked up by the tires. Her feet skidded on the gravel, and she scrambled to reach the right front fender and face the sedan over the hood. Blessed strength flooded her when she pressed her left hand hard to the metal. Her vision cleared, and the dust settled enough for her to breathe.

A car raced straight at her. Sunlight glinted off it, though, so she wasn't positive it was the right vehicle. She couldn't risk injuring some innocent driver—there could even be kids in the car. She squinted, too many seconds ticking by, until she recognized the dip in the car's hood.

She pulled hard at the energy and aimed it at the back end of the sedan. It rushed through her, dry liquid surging over all her cells. She gasped, her body rocking forward behind the force of the energy as it left her.

It hit the car just right.

This time when the driver tried to correct the swerve, he sent it into a spin. It screamed across the road, the rear quarter panel heading straight for the Charger. Holy shit, it was going to hit! Riley had no time to run, no time to panic. She closed her eyes and pushed, the sound of squealing tires filling her ears, her arm shaking as the car resisted. It smacked into the side of the Charger. The vehicle rocked, knocking Riley to the gravel. Her head bounced off the stones and sent the bright sky above her into an explosion of stars.

She didn't hear car doors opening, but when the stars cleared two figures loomed over her. The prickling increased, as uncomfortable as a hand or foot that had fallen asleep. Riley tried to shut it off, but it only prickled faster.

Trust-Fund Guy reached down with a bloody hand. Riley swatted it away, but the other guy—this one bigger, brawnier, with a purpling goose egg already rising on his forehead—grabbed her upper arm and hauled her to her feet. Pain burst in her low back, her neck, her head. Her feet shuffled. She was too weak to pick them up and walk properly.

If the guys said anything to her, she couldn't hear it, the ringing in her ears still sounding like the sedan's tires.

They halted her at the front of the Charger, both men cursing. She blinked and fought for clarity, and the ringing in her ears faded, fog clearing from her skull. She tilted toward the car, desperate for the metal, but the guy holding her arm yanked her back a few feet, well away from both vehicles. He cursed again and pressed his free hand against his side, hunching as if to protect injured ribs.

"What are we gonna do now?" Trust-Fund Guy limped over to further block her access to the Charger.

"Change the friggin' tire, you idiot."

"How? We're blocking the road. Someone's gonna call the cops if we take the time to fix it. And we've got to get her out of here."

"Figure it out, asshole!" The fingers around Riley's arm tightened. Strength trickled into her biceps and shoulder, and she realized he wore two rings on that hand, the metal making contact with her skin. She scanned the rest of him for any additional metal that might feed her body.

"Move the fucking car across the street!" he yelled at the other guy, who stood scratching his head. "We'll take her car."

Oh, hell, no. Nick was going to be pissed enough at the damage. He'd go berserk if she let them steal his car. She stumbled, the motion swinging her around to the front of her captor, and she clutched him for balance. Her fingers closed over his belt buckle. A slight bit of energy filled her, and when his partner turned to see what was happening, she lashed out with a rear kick to the side of his knee.

He shouted and fell. Riley dropped, pulling the other guy down with her by his belt. He flailed, letting go of her and removing contact with the rings, but she had momentum on her side and a few of the tricks John had taught her. She swung her legs up and back, pushing him over her head. He landed in a heap on the ground, unhurt but vulnerable when she scrambled to her feet and spun to kick him. The glancing blow to his skull only had her normal strength behind it, but he curled onto his side and didn't move.

Riley hurried to the passenger door of the Charger and clambered in, throwing herself over the gearshift to the driver's seat. The damaged car was still running but groaned when she put it in gear and tried to pull away from the sedan that had T-boned it. She had to steer right, along the shoulder, and then swing left to go around the wreck and the man shouting at her. He limped after her as she fled while his friend still lay on the ground.

Riley forced the tension out of her hands and shoulders, loosening her grip on the wheel and shifting to get more comfortable in her seat. She was okay. She was only ten minutes from help, and those guys couldn't follow her now.

But her energy level drained rapidly. She could barely see the white line on the shoulder. The sun reflecting off the barrier between lanes bleached out everything around her. The GPS instructions came from far away, and she risked letting go of the wheel to bump up the volume dial on the side. Twice she took a left instead of a right and had to backtrack. Her mouth was so dry her tongue stuck to the roof, and her lips burned as if chapped raw. She could feel herself fading toward unconsciousness and had to force herself to concentrate.

And then there it was ahead of her, at the end of a sandy lane, a cottage on stilts right on the beach. She pulled into the driveway, idling up along the side of the house. *Brake to a stop. Put it in park. Shut off the engine. Open the door.* She put one leg out and fell the rest of the way onto the ground.

The last thing she saw before it all went black was Sam. She was safe.

Chapter Fourteen

Our centuries-old purpose is funded by and founded on trust.
The men who dedicated their lives to forming the Protectorate
ensured our mission would never be compromised due to a lack
of sufficient income. It is our duty to ensure the integrity of the
Protectorate remains as strong.

— ***The Protectorate,*** *Mission Manual*

Riley woke, lying on her side, in a dark room. Awareness came slowly, her brain sluggish and sore. Her last memory was falling out of the car after the near-abduction on the highway. She looked around, moving just her eyes. The dark room was a bedroom. Soft bed, velvety quilt under her, light and homey scent in the room. Like vanilla and icing, not perfume. No place she'd ever been before.

The closed door muffled loud voices. Riley couldn't hear any words but recognized Sam, Quinn, and Nick yelling at each other. She must be at Chloe's. A switch clicked behind her. The room dimmed, and Riley rolled onto her back to see an older woman emerge from an en suite bathroom. She smiled at Riley and raised the window shade next to the bed. Sunshine didn't pour directly in but filled the room with light.

"What's going on?" Riley croaked as she sat up. Her head throbbed, and clusters of muscles in her neck and back spasmed. She moaned and put her hand to the back of her head.

"To convey the obvious, Nick's in the stratosphere over his car. Sam thinks the way you arrived means someone's after you, and he wants everyone out of here ten minutes ago. He alternates that with threatening Nick if he threatens you. Quinn's a little riled after the transfer, so she's irritated at both of them and yelling at them to chill. And I'm Chloe. It's nice to meet you." She smiled and held out a hand.

Riley shook it, wincing both at what she'd been told and at the pain of moving. "How long was I out?"

"Just a few minutes. I did a diagnostic, but I didn't try to heal you yet. That's another thing they're fighting over. Quinn wanted to do it, but Nick refuses to let her, and Sam says Quinn can make her own decisions. Which," she added, leaning forward conspiratorially, "is being contrary, because Quinn's definitely not up to it yet, but Sam's in a right state about your condition."

"Okay. Um…" Riley wasn't sure where to start. The transfer seemed a good place. "It worked, then? You're whole?"

Fine lines in the corners of Chloe's eyes crinkled, and they shone with enthusiasm. "Oh, yeah. I'm ready to take on the world. I'm fresh, and basic healing was always one of my abilities." Her expression turned earnest. "But all I've had time to do so far is toss a few muffins." She mimed throwing a baseball. "I feel normal, but I have no idea what will happen when I try to use it. So I wasn't going to do anything without your permission."

Riley needed to assess her own condition first. She swung her legs around, bending her knees to avoid kicking Chloe where she squatted next to the bed, and gasped at the pain stabbing through her low back and right hip. She'd never hurt so much in so many places. "You said you did a diagnostic. How bad am I?"

"Slight concussion. Muscle strain in the neck, thoracic spine, and right hip," Chloe catalogued. "A few scrapes—elbows, one hand. The wrist injuries that are a couple of days old seem mostly healed, but there are newer, similar-looking burns on the heel of one hand."

Riley glanced down at it, now registering the sting. She hadn't channeled energy for as long as she had with the chains, but the massive amount on that final push against the car had done its damage, too.

"I'd send you to a chiropractor," Chloe finished, "but I can slide the spine into alignment, too, and ease those muscles faster."

Riley nodded, as curious about the process as she was eager to get rid of the pain. This was a bigger task than when Quinn healed her forearm burns, the majority of her injuries untreatable except by time. "Go ahead. And thank you."

Chloe closed her eyes and put her hand on top of Riley's head. After a few seconds, the throbbing slowed, then eased, and her brain stopped crowding the inside of her skull. Chloe moved her hand to the back of Riley's neck, then slid it slowly down her spine. As she did, the aches and sharp pains disappeared, and Riley would have sworn she even felt her vertebrae clicking into place. The skin at her elbows, wrists, and palm tickled, and when Riley checked, the flesh there was smooth and undamaged. There were still faint marks from the chains, but the healing was far more complete than what Quinn did the other day.

"Wow." Riley stood. The only remnant of the "incident" was a dragging fatigue. She reached for the iron scrollwork of the headboard but froze, having to push past the instinctive fear before she touched it. It wasn't hot—it wouldn't hurt her unless she let it. Sure enough, when she made contact, the metal was cool and comforting. She closed her eyes and tipped her head back, drinking in the refreshing energy. When she released the scrollwork, the energy settled into her. The fatigue wasn't gone, but her body had absorbed enough to keep her going for a little while.

"Thank you." She sank back down onto the bed. The fight still raged in the other room, and she wanted to talk to Chloe before she joined it. "How are Quinn and Sam doing after the transfer?" She deliberately named Quinn first, but Chloe gave her a knowing look.

"Not so good. Quinn's suffering, you can tell, though she claims she felt better after it was over than she had before. She's doing okay. Sam…" Her gray eyes darkened with concern.

Riley twisted her fingers together and tried to smooth her expression. "What happened?"

Chloe shook her head. "It made him really sick. I think he's still a mess, but he won't let either of us get near him, especially since he's so worried about you."

She'd better get out there. "Those guys who were after me—I don't know what they want, and they might find me again. They weren't too far away. Sam's right, we need to leave."

Chloe stood. "Any idea who they were?"

Riley wasn't sure how much they should tell others about Numina, at least not until they knew more themselves. Especially since at least one of the protectors had been compromised somehow. But she also didn't know what Chloe knew already. She'd play it coy.

"Not really." She moved past Chloe and opened the bedroom door into a cozy living room filled with rattan furniture. The airy, pastel décor flowed into the dining room and a kitchen separated by a breakfast bar. Sam, Quinn, and Nick stood in a triangle at the junction where all the rooms came together.

Riley might as well have fired Nick's pearl-handled pistol, the shouting cut off that abruptly when she opened the door. All three turned to stare at her. A heartbeat later, Sam had her in a hug.

Riley hadn't realized how much she'd needed that. He surrounded her, and a completely different kind of warmth and strength suffused her. She closed her eyes and inhaled, pressing her head to his firm chest covered in a soft, long-sleeved T-shirt, and pressing her hands against his back so she could touch as much of him as possible. This had become her go-to move when she needed comfort.

"Are you okay?" His voice rumbled through her. She suppressed a shiver of desire, faint but threatening to grow.

"I'm fine. Chloe took care of me." She pulled back and looked up at him. "Oh, Sam," she whispered, raising her hands to the sides of his face. He looked so haggard. Red rimmed his eyes. The hollows of his cheeks were deep, sharpening his cheekbones, and under his dark hair, his pallor had a definite sickly element. "How bad is it?" She kept her voice low so the others couldn't hear, as close as they were.

He didn't answer, but shook his head slightly. Riley wished she knew how to heal, or at least to see what was going on inside him. She reluctantly turned back to Chloe. "Are you up to—"

"We need to get out of here," Sam cut her off. He stepped back to include Nick and Quinn but held onto Riley's hand. "Where's Tom? What happened? Was it Vern again?"

"No. Not this time." She cut her eyes toward Chloe, and Sam understood.

"Do you have somewhere you can go?" he asked her. "I don't think they'll be after you, but it's better if you're not here if they figure out where Riley went."

Chloe shrugged. "I'll go shopping for a couple of hours. Then I'm meeting someone for dinner." She blushed.

"What?" Sam gaped at her. "After we planned this for today? You didn't know if it would work, or what the aftereffects would be! Who is this guy?"

The pink rose higher on her cheeks. "Who says it's a guy?"

Quinn rolled her eyes and stepped closer. "It's a guy. Anyone we know?"

"No." She met Quinn's gaze steadily, her embarrassment already gone. "He's the first guy I've dated since I was leeched. I've thoroughly vetted him. We only meet in public places, and he knows what I am and what I've been through. I'm comfortable seeing him tonight, and we can set up some kind of system so I know if it's safe to come home, with or without him."

Nick nodded. "Yeah, I've got some stuff in the trunk." He glared at Riley, but it didn't have much heat. "Assuming it's not smashed."

"I'm sorry—" she started, but he held up a hand.

"Not your fault. It's just a car." But he half choked on the last part.

"Let's get it set up." Sam went out the front door with Nick.

Quinn motioned to Chloe. "Let's pack you a bag in case it's not safe for you to come back right away." The other woman nodded, and they disappeared into the back room.

Riley hurried after the guys down the back steps to the overgrown driveway. "Nick!" she called after him.

He looked up from the trunk where he was handing what looked like a camera bag to Sam. "What?"

"Tom was part of it. I think." She folded her arms tightly around her middle. "I'm second-guessing myself now, but I don't know how they could have found us otherwise." She briefly described what had made her suspicious.

"Son of a bitch." Nick hefted equipment out of the trunk and headed for the house again. "We need to get these cameras set up. Tell us everything. I mean every detail."

After Chloe left the house, Riley explained everything that had happened when they reached Rhode Island and what she'd done to Tom.

"The car didn't stop for him?" Quinn asked from her spot on the wicker loveseat. She watched Sam hand tools to Nick, who stood on a chair installing a camera in a fake plant on top of a pine hutch. "And the guys who tried to take you didn't mention him?"

"No. You think I was wrong?" Riley asked miserably. "That I panicked?"

"Don't know." Nick dropped to the floor and put the chair back under the dining room table. "We'll find out. Did you tell Tom where you were going? I mean, the address?"

"I don't think so. But John could have."

Rage roiled off Sam. "I want to know who the hell Numina is and how they've infiltrated us. And then—"

"Whoa, slow your roll, cupcake." Nick took Quinn's leather duffel from the sofa and helped her to her feet. "We're not assuming anything yet. Let's get moving before they find us here."

They all headed outside and down the stairs.

"Where are we going?" Sam pulled open the car door to get in.

"I know a place up the road a few miles, a summer unit my dad's family shares. No one should know about it." Nick helped Quinn into the front seat, though to Riley's eyes, his fiancée was in much better shape than the last time she'd seen her and was only letting him help because it made him feel better.

"Wait." Riley dug her heels into the gravel a few feet away. She needed to be with Sam, to make sure he wasn't alone if the aftereffects of the transfer worsened again as they had the other night. But her conscience wouldn't let her go with them without at least trying to do the right thing. The *other* right thing.

"I shouldn't go with you. I shouldn't have even come here, but I wasn't thinking clearly." Nothing beyond getting to people who made her feel safe.

Sam spun on her. "Fuck that."

"Listen." She held up a hand. "If Tom didn't call them, they're tracking me some other way. I should lead them away so you aren't in danger."

"Because we're so weak and vulnerable," Nick snarked, and Quinn laughed. When Riley and the guys looked at her, she rolled her eyes.

"Oh, please. I know this whole thing has cut me down some, but I'm not helpless. You're not leaving," she told Riley. "Except to come with us."

"We'll watch Chloe's place tonight and deal with anyone who shows up. Then we'll head to Tanda's." Nick made an impatient motion. "Get in the car."

Well, at least she'd tried. Their reactions made her feel less guilty. She got into the back seat with Sam and sat sideways, watching through the rear window as they drove up the shoreline road.

Nick and Quinn talked quietly, personal murmurs Riley couldn't hear without concentrating, which would be rude. Beside her in the back seat, Sam jittered his left leg up and down and beat his thumb and fingers against his thigh in an agitated rhythm.

She tilted closer until his ear was only a couple of inches away. "You okay?"

"Fine." His head fell back against the seat, his eyes closed. His Adam's apple bobbed with the kind of swallow you make when you're trying not to throw up. Riley stroked her hand through his hair, fingers rubbing over his scalp. His expression eased, and he leaned into her palm. She laid her other hand on his, and he threaded their fingers, holding tight. She kept half her attention on him and the other half on the road.

A few minutes later, Nick asked, "Spot any tails?"

Riley whipped her head around. She half-expected Nick to be picking on her, but his eyes in the rearview mirror were serious.

"No," she told him. "The few cars I saw turned off already. I checked the side streets, too," she added. "I'm pretty sure no one is watching us. Not unless it's from a distance."

"Cool." He spun the wheel to make a sudden left turn,

following it with enough lefts and rights to make Riley carsick. After a couple of minutes, they roared up a long, open driveway to a humungous house on a bluff overlooking the sea.

Nick jumped out of the car to punch a code into a box next to one of the three-bay garage doors. Quinn climbed over to drive the car in next to a—Riley's eyes bugged at the Rolls Royce beside them.

"This is your *father's* place?" she asked as they climbed out of the car.

Nick lowered the overhead door. "His family's. The Rolls is my great-grandfather's. They show it in parades and stuff."

Sam helped Nick unload the trunk. "Lucky this was so close."

Nick shot him a look. "Don't sound so suspicious. He grew up in Connecticut, and six cousins co-own this place now. Some of them were here for a long weekend, just left yesterday, or we would have stayed here while Quinn rested." He used a key on the door into the house, and they all followed him into the biggest kitchen Riley had ever seen.

A beeping behind her grew louder and faster. She turned to watch Nick tap the keypad of an alarm system until the beeping stopped and a light flashed green.

Quinn looked around, smiling. "I think I could be comfortable here."

They fanned out into the house's open, airy floor plan. Riley couldn't close her mouth as she passed through the wide arch between the marble-rich kitchen and the pine-floored, combination living and dining area. Two walls of windows gave an incredible view of the ocean. The furniture, arranged to maximize that view, was mostly rattan, with microfiber cushions in sage greens, ocean blues, and satiny white. High ceilings were bordered with crown molding and bisected by skylights that let the sunshine pour in.

Past the front door and a wide staircase to the left, Riley found a den or office and a short hall to a bathroom and a small bedroom that she imagined must be for a housekeeper or something.

She bumped into Quinn when she backed out of the small bedroom. They grinned at each other.

"I could live here," Riley said.

"Me, too."

They walked side by side down the hall, Quinn pausing to study a picture of a bunch of kids wearing shit-eating grins. She touched one, and her expression was sad, proud, and loving all at the same time.

Riley assumed the kid was Nick and decided to give Quinn a moment to herself. She returned to the main room, where the guys had already set up a laptop on the massive pine table in the dining area. Cables snaked out of it, connecting equipment Riley didn't recognize.

Sam flipped a switch. The laptop blinked to a full-screen video feed of Chloe's driveway.

Riley moved closer. Sam sat in front of the computer and tapped at buttons, moving from shot to shot. The front steps and entry, the main deck, below the house, out on the sand, and in the living room.

"Didn't have enough cameras." Nick braced one hand on the back of Sam's chair, the other knocking Sam off the keyboard to page through the shots himself. "More important to cover the approaches than inside."

Quinn joined them. "Nice job." She touched Nick's back. "John?"

"Yeah." Nick pulled out his phone and hit several more buttons than necessary to make a call. "Disabled the GPS," he said as he hit the speaker button and ringing filled the room.

"Yeah, Nick," John answered.

"We think Tom's dirty."

John inhaled. "The hell he is!"

"Riley was ambushed on the road. He's the only one who could have told anyone where she was."

"No way in hell. Hold on." The phone went silent for several minutes. Nick set it on the table and bickered with Sam over the best order to display the angles. Sam set up a main page with all six camera views but got more agitated as he worked, far worse than he'd been in the car.

Quinn sank onto a chaise and rested her head, but Riley couldn't settle, and she wanted to stay close to Sam. She tried resting her hand on his shoulder, and his muscles relaxed. But this time when her fingers brushed the skin of his neck, he leaped out of the chair and crossed the room, all the way to the front windows. His eyes were wild, and his hands clenched and unclenched. He shook his head at her when she started to go to him, so she stayed near the phone, worrying.

"Nick." The phone came to life again.

"Yeah."

"Riley there? She okay?"

"Nice of you to ask, but yeah. She's safe."

"I talked to Tom. He claims he got a text from me asking for their location and destination. He only knew the route, not the address, but texted back. He told me Riley spotted a car he didn't think was a threat, and she was getting upset enough to cause an accident. He was trying to calm her down."

It sounded plausible, but… "Why didn't he report in when I dumped him out of the car?" Riley asked.

"Phone smashed. He had to hitch to town and find a store to replace it. Says he'd finished up when my call came through."

"Is he okay?" If he was telling the truth, Riley didn't want him to be hurt. She didn't feel bad for her decision, though. She'd done what she had to do to keep everyone safe. *If* he was telling the truth.

"Few scrapes, nothing major."

"So what's the deal with the text messages?" Nick demanded. "You get hacked or something?"

"Something." John hesitated. "More than ever, I don't want to talk about this on the phone."

"It's all right," Nick said. "I think we can figure it out. Keep checking out Tom," he ordered. "I'm not buying his story. Seems pretty coincidental that he was nearby when we needed a protector. He could have been tracking Riley for someone."

John didn't argue, nor did he take issue with being bossed around by his employee. "You all be careful. Things are splintered." He put emphasis on the last word.

"We will." Nick disconnected and kept pacing. "So, Numina could have mimicked John's number to make Tom think the text messages were coming from him."

"Or they could have planted Tom," Sam suggested. "Like they planted Anson in college."

"What did John mean when he said they're splintered?" Quinn pulled her knees up and wrapped her arms around them.

"He said *things* are splintered," Riley corrected before she thought about it. "But I guess that's an odd way to say it, isn't it?"

Quinn propped her chin on her knees. "Maybe the ones who've been after Riley and approaching the other goddesses are a splinter of the main organization."

Riley was only partly listening to Quinn. She watched Sam go deeper into himself, his skin growing paler, his eyes more haunted and desperate. He glanced at the computer, then at Nick, obviously avoiding looking at her.

"Call me if you see anything," he told Nick suddenly. In a few strides he was across the room, bounding up the stairs three at a time.

"Sam," Nick called after him. A door upstairs slammed closed.

"Dammit!" Nick stormed across the room but stopped at the base of the stairs, his hand on the newel post. He turned to look at Quinn and Riley. "I can't leave you two, but no one should be alone, even in the house." The alarm pad on the wall next to the front door beeped. Nick checked it and cursed. "Balcony door opened. He went outside." He tapped on the keypad for a few seconds. The beeping stopped.

"I'll go to him." Riley didn't hesitate. Sam needed her, even if he was struggling to keep his distance. She wasn't afraid of him, but *for* him.

Nick caught her arm when she reached him. "Wait."

"What?" Riley moved up a couple of steps, anxious about leaving Sam alone too long.

"He's not handling things well."

She bit back the urge to defend him. It wasn't his fault, but Nick didn't sound like he was blaming him. "I know."

"He'll probably lash out. He won't mean it, but he could hurt you."

Her fingers tightened around the banister. She didn't like that his words echoed her own thoughts but not in a reassuring way. "You don't trust him?"

"I trust him with my life. And Quinn's." He shook his head. "That doesn't mean anything."

She nodded. "It's okay. I understand what's going on."

"Do you?" He tucked his fingers into his jeans pockets and leaned against the front door. "Being a protector, you learn to look at the long-term consequences of something, not just the immediate situation. Dealing with stuff like this" —he tilted his head to indicate where Quinn and the surveillance were— "it's easy to react in the moment. Especially when everything's new."

"What are you trying to say?" Riley shoved her hair behind her ear. "Are you giving me the 'relationships based on intense experiences never work' speech? Seriously?"

Nick laughed. "No. That might apply, too, but it's none of my business."

Except the glint in his eye told her it was very much his business. He and Sam might bicker like brothers, but they apparently loved each other like brothers, too.

"Then what?"

Nick glanced upstairs. "I'm saying take care of him. But be careful."

He walked away, and Riley dashed upstairs.

The airiness downstairs was echoed up on the second floor. Skylights lined the slanted ceiling over the wide hallway that ran above the garage. Windows looked out on the driveway and the lawns sloping down to the road below. A cozy nook had been set up at one end, and a plush chair draped with a chenille throw sat next to a tall lamp on a side table. To the left of the stairs the hall was dimmer, narrower, and lined with twice as many doors as the bright side.

"Sam?"

Only the rolling surf answered her. She shouldn't have been able to hear it from here. The *roll-crash-hiss* of the waves grew louder when she approached the open door of the last bedroom. The sun was on its way down on the opposite side of the house, so the room was dim, but French doors opened onto a balcony. Sam wasn't visible through the glass, and Riley didn't see him when she stepped out onto the cedar deck.

The sea breeze whipped her hair back, carrying laughter and squeals. Out on the sand, an old man wearing gigantic headphones waved a metal detector over two-foot patches of beach. Down the beach a little ways, a young couple watched two small boys running from the surf. But Sam was nowhere in sight.

The deck spanned this section of the house and turned the corner at both sides. Holding her hair back in the blustering wind, Riley tried to decide which way Sam would have gone. Before she guessed wrong, she closed her eyes and tried to sense him.

Trying turned out to be unnecessary. Instead of the buzz she usually associated with him, her awareness flared with a burning, golden light. When she opened her eyes, it was still there, though unseen.

She knew exactly where he was.

CHAPTER FIFTEEN

If there is one thing we have learned from the events of the last several months, it is that complacency, a belief that we understand all we need to about our gifts and the world around us, is a mistake. There is always more to discover.

— Goddess Society for Education and Defense, *"New Focus" Educational Initiative*

Twilight closed in as Riley walked to the right. The sun cast long shadows toward the surf before being obscured by a cloud, dimming everything around her. It would have been a peaceful moment if she hadn't been so anxious about Sam.

She paused at the corner of the balcony, which dead-ended halfway along the side of the house. Below them was an entire one-story wing she hadn't realized was there. A pair of folded beach chairs leaned against the wall. Sam sat on the floor next to them, knees raised and feet flat on the floor. His forearms rested on his knees, one hand wrapped around the other wrist. His body rocked slightly, and the wild look hadn't left his eyes.

Riley knelt on the boards in front of him. They'd already chilled in the shade, and the cold seeped through the knees of her jeans.

"Tell me." She shifted forward so she could rest her hands on his legs. At the simple touch, his eyes closed and his body stilled. Riley wasn't sure if he was soothed or holding tighter to control. His gaze flicked out over the water, down to the beach, then back, but he didn't look at her.

"Nick said you got sick this time. During the transfer."

He nodded slightly and barely moved his lips when he admitted, "Yeah, pretty bad."

"Not the same as the first time?"

"Opposite."

"And how do you feel now?"

He took a deep breath, his body moving with a conscious effort to relax. "Jittery. Tense. Like hopped up on too much caffeine, but not exactly."

"Can you feel the power?"

A wry laugh escaped. "Yeah."

"How?"

He lifted a shoulder.

"I mean, is it like a ball of energy, or more diffuse, or—"

"It's just there. All through me." He jerked his chin toward the water. "I want to swallow the ocean."

"What else? Do you still feel sick?"

"Nauseous, yeah."

Riley wasn't sure where she was going with this. She wanted so much to help him, but only knew one possible way, based on the other night. And today seemed totally different. She should ask him straight out if he needed sex, but God, the very thought of saying those words tied her tongue.

"Have you tried using it?" she asked. "You know, drawing on the energy from the ocean and doing something, uh, goddess-like?"

He smirked and finally met her eyes. "Are you calling me a girl?"

"You should be so lucky." She patted the side of his leg. "So try something."

But he didn't move, just studied her for a few moments. "What do I feel like?"

She understood what he was asking, even if he hadn't phrased it exactly right. "You're brighter. It's not a buzz anymore. I can see you, though it's not really visual." She shook her head, frustrated. "I can't really explain it. What matters is that whatever I'm sensing in you is stronger than before."

He nodded. "That's why I haven't tried to use it." He let go of his wrist and pressed his hands to the floor next to him. "It shouldn't be like this. All desperate and crazed."

His leg practically vibrated under her hand. "No, but maybe it's like this because you're fighting it."

"Maybe. But what if I use it and crave more? What if I become addicted? After I filter Tanda's, that's it. When someone who doesn't naturally have capacity is given access to power, using it drains them. They can't just tap a source and keep using it unless they get more from another goddess. That's how leeches are made."

She thought about her great-grandfather, about the possibility that he drained her great-grandmother so much that she couldn't pass the legacy on to her daughters. Maybe she and Marley had interpreted that all wrong. Maybe they hadn't known what would happen when Henrietta bestowed power on Earl, and she'd willingly given him whatever he needed. It was possible she'd been too ashamed to explain to her daughters what had happened, and deflected blame on the Society.

Would Riley be willing to make that sacrifice for Sam, if it was the only way to keep him sane and healthy? The answer came quickly enough to disturb her, but understanding her family a little better gave her strength.

She swiveled to sit next to him and looped her arm through

his. "I know you're afraid, but I think you need to try. Something small. It might settle down all that excess energy." She dug into her pocket and pulled out a long, slender screw. "Move this."

Sam rolled his eyes. "Riley."

"Come on." She bounced her hand at him. "See if you can knock it off my palm."

Sam swept his hand up under hers, a light smack that sent the screw bouncing in the air.

"Hey!" She half-laughed, but on its way down it changed trajectory and shot sideways, clattering across the floor.

Riley gaped at it, then at Sam. "You did it!"

Sam gasped and blinked hard. Shock slowly turned to elation. "I controlled it."

Riley leaned and snatched up the screw. Sam took it in both hands and tested its strength with his thumbs. Then his brow puckered with concentration. A few seconds later, it curved under pressure. He formed a loop and held it out to Riley.

"There, now you can wear it as a ring."

She didn't want to. She rubbed her thumb over the palm of her hand, where the car had burned her a couple of hours ago. Sam still wore a proud, lighter expression, and Riley couldn't take that away from him. She held out her thumb and let Sam slip the unwieldy "jewelry" over it before settling down next to him, against the wall.

Casually, Sam threaded his fingers through hers and looked out over the water. The sun had finished setting, and it was difficult to see much along the beach.

"How do you feel now?" Riley asked softly, though she hardly needed to. Sam was more relaxed, the jitters gone, with just the one small burst of power.

"Better." He closed his eyes again and reached his free hand out to the ocean. "I can feel it. The tide, the current. Even tiny points of living energy, like you did in the restaurant." He flinched slightly in Riley's direction. With his eyes still closed, he turned more fully toward her. "Yeah. I can…" He caressed her cheek. His lips curved, and he murmured, "Beautiful."

Riley's cheeks warmed. She cleared her throat. "Uh, how about the queasiness? Gone?"

When Sam opened his eyes, they were nearly opaque in the growing darkness. "Yeah. All the pain where it was slicing into me is gone, too. That didn't fade much on its own, but now it all seems to be…" He frowned. "Equalizing, I guess."

"Good." Riley pulled her feet under her and stood. "Let's stop here, then. Quit while the quitting's good." She tugged Sam's hand and helped him to his feet. "We should go inside. I wonder—*oof.*"

Sam pulled her against his chest. "Thank you, Riley. I'd never get through this without you." He bent his head and kissed her, much like he had the other night. With tender gratitude.

Riley wanted so much more from him, but she didn't want to trigger the desperate lust he'd had that night and send him running again. He wrapped his hands around her waist, and she let herself snuggle closer. She pressed one hand to his chest, curved the other around his neck. Her lips parted and he accepted the invitation, sliding in gently, but with a little more hunger.

Then he gave a low moan, and the desire Riley had kept banked relit. She arched and rubbed against him, sucking his tongue deeper.

Sam groaned. His hands went to her back and held her tightly while he lowered them to the floor. Riley wriggled on the hard surface, and Sam broke the kiss with a gasp.

"You're killing me, Riley."

She immediately stilled. "I'm sorry."

"No, I am. I didn't mean like—I meant in a normal, God-I've-got-to-have-you kind of way." He smiled against her mouth. "If that's any better."

"It's perfect." She kissed him again, letting her hands map

every muscle. His shoulders were so *broad*. Someone looking down at them wouldn't even know she was here.

Sam swept his hand down her side and under the hem of her shirt. His skin against hers was electric, and when his palm settled on her hip, the fire flared even higher. She arched again, wanting him to touch every inch of her, but he moved so *slowly*. He could span half her torso with that hand, but instead kept it on her waist, gradually spreading his fingers across her ribcage. Riley's heart pounded, and she ached for him.

"Sam," she whispered, arching her neck so he could nuzzle her.

"Mmmhmm." He sucked a little on her neck. She gasped and rose up, and he went with the move and slid his hand up to cup her breast. Riley had to bite back a cry of pleasure.

Sam hung his head. His breath panted against her collarbone. "We should stop. Someone could see." His voice was thick and urgent.

"No." Riley didn't want to, and wouldn't no matter the circumstances. "No one's around. I want you, Sam." She reached down and touched him through his jeans, and oh, God, he was so freaking hard. She went completely wet and shuddered, cupping her fingers around him.

"Jesus." Sam shoved her shirt up and her bra down so he could cover her nipple with his mouth. He tongued it, and this time Riley couldn't hold back the cry. She thrust her hands into his hair and rocked under his body, her brain and vision blurring. Sam flicked open her jeans and pushed his hand inside. His long, strong fingers glided over her swollen clit and into her. She had to clamp down to keep from coming right then, and Sam cursed into her shoulder.

"Sam, please. I want—" And then his fingers moved inside her, even confined by her jeans, and she went off, a quick, blinding orgasm that was a shower of golden light.

• • •

Sam had some faint belief, buried under the mindless need to devour Riley, that giving her pleasure was going to keep him from melting down. His own lust was under control. Barely. But the hard edge from the other night was gone. He wanted to keep the focus on her...and this time, he didn't have to question whether or not she really wanted it. Her hands yanked at his buckle, and she wrapped one leg up around his hip. Her pelvis lifted against him, the smallest pressure making him throb.

Then her hand was on his cock, skin to skin, and Sam's brain completely fuzzed. His breath hissed out between his teeth, the only sound he could hear. He held himself up off Riley, fine sand on the deck grinding into his palms, his entire body taut while she stroked and squeezed.

"*Uhn.* Stop. I'm gonna—" She froze just in time. Sam cursed again and reached for his back pocket with one hand before his brain recovered enough to realize there was nothing there. "Shit. I don't have anything."

"I do." It had grown too dark to see, but Sam heard the crinkle of a familiar packet, then a tearing noise, and a couple of seconds later, he shuddered as she slid the condom over him.

"Where did you get that?" he managed through gritted teeth, holding on with all his power. He was going to be inside her when he came. Fuck, the *anticipation* of her wet heat was almost enough to make him come. He needed distraction.

"Are you kidding?" Riley shimmied away enough to shuck her jeans, then slid back under him and curved her hands over his shoulders. "I've carried condoms since they handed them out in health class. It's 'part of being a responsible adult.'" She sounded like she was quoting someone, but Sam could barely hear what she was saying. Her bare thighs glided up his and cradled his hips.

His body cramped, but a tiny warning went off and he held himself still. "You've had this since health class?"

Her laugh purred through him. "No. I've had *a* condom since health class. This one is within expiration date." She dug into his shoulders, her voice deepening, going huskier. "Come on, Sam. I want you inside me."

God. He couldn't hold back anymore. He rolled them over so she was on top, and Riley threw her head back and arched her body. Her skin glowed in the faint light of the rising moon, her nipples dark and hard. She shifted to position herself over him, and he slid right in, a long, slow stroke that took him deeper than he thought he could go on the first thrust. It was incredible, so hot and wet and close and *good*.

Energy thrummed in his body, as if doing this made the power happy. Sam thrust as slowly as he could, out, in, then a deeper, upward press that made Riley gasp. Sam absorbed everything— every moan of pleasure, each shift of her body, the silken heat of her skin where they touched, her softness, her tight wetness, the unbearably gorgeous smell of her. He coaxed her down to his chest, cradling her head and holding her tight.

She closed her mouth on his neck and bit. His eyes rolled back, and he lost all sense of rhythm, pumped into her harder and harder, as pleasure coalesced, sharpened. It built, built, and burst, punching a shout out of him accompanied by a brilliant burst of light, a flash of intensity that seemed to draw him deeper into her. Her heartbeat was his heartbeat, the blood rushed through her veins at the same speed as his, her heaving lungs expanded his own chest.

Riley shuddered, her body convulsing, closing around him as she came again. His orgasm continued, pulsing downward and drawing out every ounce of tension until he was a giant, boneless mass.

Riley's fingers stroked through his hair, soft, sweet, soothing. He inhaled her, registering the silky tickle of her hair against his cheek, her gentle pants past his ear, the slowing thump of her heartbeat and occasional spasm around him.

Words crowded into Sam's head. Words he'd only ever considered saying to one person in his entire life. He swallowed them back with considerable effort. Riley deserved better than heat of the moment. She deserved better than him, actually, but Sam wasn't going to make decisions for her. He'd been on her side of that, and it sucked.

When had anyone ever taken care of him like this? It was supposed to be his job to watch over everyone else. He'd made it his job, back when he enrolled in college and again when meeting Riley forced him out of limbo. But everything had gotten twisted around, and it was…nice. It felt good to share a burden, instead of taking on someone else's. To have a person care about him so much she'd make sacrifices for him.

Like sex on a scratchy, hard balcony.

With that thought, reality restored itself. Sam had been so lost in Riley he'd stopped hearing the waves and feeling the floor. Sound and sensation rushed back now, along with the chill breeze. She had to be freezing. And they'd been gone a while. Nick might come looking for them.

"Thank you," he murmured.

"Mmm."

Purely male pride made him smirk at the satisfaction in her hum. "Are you okay? I hope I didn't crush you."

"No, but…" She leaned upward, and their bodies separated. "Sorry, I—" She froze, like a bunny on a lawn or a deer at the edge of the road.

"Wha—"

"Wait."

Sam waited. Riley stared into the dark, down toward the beach.

"Someone's here." She barely whispered it, but a sharp edge came through anyway.

Sam jerked as a buzz split the air. He didn't clue in that it was his phone in his pocket, halfway down his thigh, until it buzzed again. He cursed and sat up, helping Riley to her feet. Her movements were frantic as she dragged her clothes back on.

"Where?" Sam asked as he automatically checked the text.

Where the hell are you guys? Nick.

"Close," she whispered back.

Sam shoved the phone in his pocket and fastened his jeans. He grabbed her hand and they dashed around the corner to the back of the house. Sam headed for the bedroom he'd come out through, but something about the rail at the far end of the balcony caught his eye. He halted and stiffened his arm, keeping Riley behind him.

"What is it?"

Sam pointed at the odd shape in the darkness and eased them closer. He strained to hear any movement or other sounds, but the ocean surge was too loud.

When they were several feet away, he saw that the shape was a grappling hook caught around the top of the rail. A rope dangled down the side. He stiffened and let go of Riley, urging her back. But she stuck close, her fist with the screw-ring upraised.

All the doors were closed and the rest of the balcony empty, so Sam knew if someone had climbed up here, they must be around the far side of the house. He braced himself as he reached the corner, but even prepared, he couldn't stop the blow. The heel of a hand whacked him under his chin—the move of a smaller attacker on a bigger target. Sam's teeth snapped together. He tasted blood, saw stars, and then pain radiated through his jaw and up over the top of his skull.

But the attacker was an amateur. He'd only landed the blow because it was a sucker punch in the dark. Sam sent two quick punches where he estimated the other guy's head to be. The first missed, but the second cut off the guy's laugh. Something crunched under Sam's knuckles, and a howl filled the air.

Sam's vision cleared, and despite the faintness of the moonlight, he recognized Anson on his knees, clutching his nose.

"You son of a bitch!" Sam hauled him up by his collar. "What the hell do you think you're doing?"

But Anson was in no shape to answer. Dark blood stained half his face and trickled over his fingers. He'd stopped howling but hung in Sam's grip, clearly dazed.

"Crap. Let's go." Sam motioned Riley to walk in front of him while he dragged Anson's stumbling form. He couldn't believe this guy used to be so fearsome.

"Do you sense anyone else?" he asked Riley.

"No, just him. But I don't know my range." She hurried ahead to pull the hall door open all the way.

"Wait." He shoved Anson into the hall and peered out past him, double checking. Light filtering up the stairs pushed back most of the shadows. The hallway was clear. He shoved Anson down, and the loser crumpled into a heap on the floor.

Riley moved to his side. "What do we do?" she whispered.

He turned to put his mouth against her ear for maximum silence and hesitated. Her shampoo was different, he noticed. But buried beneath the surface floweriness was Riley and, more importantly, Riley and him. His hand tightened possessively around her upper arm, and he had to close his eyes against the emotions rushing through him. He swallowed and remembered what was happening. They couldn't assume Anson was alone.

"Find some metal," he whispered. She disappeared back into the bedroom and came back clutching a pair of silver candlesticks. Sam used hand motions to convey that she should stay up here with Anson. He didn't want to leave them alone, but the guy hadn't moved, and Riley loomed over him, gripping her fancy weapons. She nodded.

Sam crept to the top of the stairs and paused, listening to intense silence. He had no sense of anyone downstairs. But he also had no weapons except for his fists, and a position that fully exposed him if he tried to get a line of sight into the living room.

He had no choice. He inhaled slow and deep. He had to be a moving target. He barreled down the stairs and prepared to swing left, behind the wall. But nothing happened. The room was empty.

Sam hurried toward the laptop, whose screen still showed Chloe's place, all images still. Anson or Numina or whoever was supposed to have gone to her house. How the hell had Anson known to come here? And where were Nick and Quinn?

The alarm was still armed and showing no breaches, so he hurried back upstairs to get Riley and the bastard. She stood over the weasel, a fierce-looking warrior with her tousled hair tumbling around her face and the candlesticks that, in the dim light, could almost have been short swords. Sam wanted to haul her up against him and kiss her, but even though Anson's bloody face was still buried in his hands, Sam refused to give the man any ammunition, including revealing the extent of his relationship with Riley. Assuming the jerk hadn't heard or seen them outside, but he thought that was a safe assumption, given Riley's ability to detect his presence.

"What's going on?" she asked.

"I don't know." He dragged the dirtbag to the stairs and forced him down into the great room. Quinn and Nick were just coming in through the door to the garage. Quinn held a couple bags of frozen vegetables, Nick a big package wrapped in white butcher paper. They stared, open-mouthed, as Sam dumped Anson in a dining room chair.

"Should I tie him up?" Riley glared down at Anson and hefted one of her candlesticks. He huddled, still holding his face.

"I don't think that will be necessary." Sam clenched his fists and tried not to break Anson's face. Again.

"What the hell?" Nick's package thunked when he dropped it on the marble counter and walked out of the kitchen section. He stopped, hands on his hips, in front of Anson. "Where did this shit come from?"

Sam explained how they'd discovered him. "Riley doesn't detect anyone else around."

"Neither do I." Quinn came to stand next to Nick and gazed coolly at the leech. "How did you find us? What are you doing here?"

"Bleeding," Anson said nasally. "I could use some ice."

Sam would have given him another injury to take his mind off the first, but Riley went into the kitchen, put ice in a baggie, wrapped it in a hand towel, and gave it to Anson.

"Thank you." He laid it gingerly against his face, wincing, and flashed Riley what he probably thought was his usual charming smile but looked rather gruesome. Riley's expression didn't change, but since Sam was watching closely, he saw revulsion in her eyes. That made him feel better about her giving comfort to the enemy. She was just playing the good cop side of things.

"What are you doing here?" Sam demanded, looming over Anson, willing to use every ounce of intimidation he could get from his size and position. Nick folded his arms and silently backed him up.

"Spring break," Anson muttered from behind the towel-wrapped ice. He shook his head and studied the blood on the towel. "You broke my nose, you big ox."

"You deserved it. What did you think I'd do when you sucker-punched me?"

Anson put the ice back and sat sullenly. Quinn leaned against the half wall behind her, and Nick grabbed a second chair, spun it around in front of Anson, and straddled it with his arms crossed over the top. He leaned forward slowly until it tilted, and Sam realized he'd set one leg on the toe of Anson's shoe. Not directly on top of his foot, but the pressure still had to send an uncomfortable message.

"You'll answer all our questions," Sam warned, "and maybe we won't call the cops." Riley made a slight, jerky movement that Sam noticed because his body still hummed for her, and she still held half his attention. He also felt Nick's disapproval, but he held his ground. The tactic wouldn't work if Anson didn't believe it was possible.

"What are you gonna tell the cops?" Anson challenged. "Look at me, and look at you!"

Sam assumed he didn't show any evidence of Anson's smack on his chin, while the leech's nose had swollen into a misshapen hunk, still oozing blood. That might work against him, but… "I have the witness on my side. A witness," he continued when Anson opened his mouth, "you've been chasing all over the eastern seaboard. But hey, if that's not enough for you." He leaned forward. "Tell us, and maybe I won't *kill* you."

Anson sighed and folded the towel to a clean spot, rewrapped the ice, and held it to his face again. "What do you want to know?"

"Everything," Sam and Nick said at the same time.

CHAPTER SIXTEEN

Strength is vital to success, and partnerships are essential to strength. Merging the talents of one party with the complementary skills of another can create mutual benefit. Join us, and gain access to better partnerships and greater success than you have ever thought possible.

—Millinger.com

Anson leaned back in the chair, faded-denim eyes narrowing with resentment. "Can I at least have a drink of water or something?"

This time, Riley didn't move. "Not until you start talking." She kept her tone smooth and encouraging despite the tough words, and was gratified to see Sam's mouth twitch. She retrieved one of the candlesticks she'd set down and waited.

Anson heaved a great sigh and tossed the towel-wrapped ice on the table. "Fine. Ask away." He folded his arms and stretched out his free leg, trying to look like he didn't care about his situation. But Riley noticed he leaned away from Sam, and his eyes kept darting between him and Nick. He was more afraid than he let on.

She wasn't surprised when Sam started his questions all the way back at the beginning. He'd hinted at his guilt for the connection to the leech. "Back in college," Sam said. "Were you working for Numina then?"

Anson's eyebrows went up, making him wince and grimace. He tentatively touched the bridge of his nose. "Uh, no. Not then. You've probably figured out the whole leeching thing, right?" He glanced around at them. "Why it works?" When they nodded, he continued. "I was adopted, but my grandmother stuck around. She wanted me to know about my mother and my heritage, but she wasn't that powerful and could only teach me so much. I figured I could 'bond' with another son of a goddess and pick his brain, get an in to the community. I hacked the Society's database, found other male descendants my age, and picked you." He shrugged and rubbed at some dried blood on his hand. "Bad choice, as it turned out. You were too noble to be of much use after that."

It wasn't hard to read between the lines. Jealous boy, resentful that he didn't have the power he'd have had if he were a girl, seeking a way to take it instead of living a normal life and trying to be successful on his own merits. His methods made Riley's skin crawl.

"So you were always planning to leech a goddess," Sam said with disgust.

"Not from the beginning. But once I found out it could be done, I started planning."

"Why Marley?" Quinn asked. Riley glanced at her, relieved to find she didn't seem to need the wall to hold her up. At least, not yet.

Anson shrugged. "I liked her. That made it easier. You know she had to bestow power willingly, and that was going to be a challenge." He gave Quinn a steady look that almost seemed sincere. "I didn't intend to hurt her. She'd have been fine if you had left her alone."

Quinn snorted. "You can't lay any guilt on me. You get full the responsibility for the damage."

Riley wondered if Quinn would tell her sister what he'd said, and if that would make her feel better, or worse.

Nick leaned on the chair again, pressing harder until Anson yelped. "When did you hook up with Numina?"

"I don't know exactly. They must have tapped into my research somehow. They never told me how I came on their radar."

"You didn't ask?"

He raised his eyebrows. "Guys like that come to your door, offer you a job like this, for that kind of money—you don't ask a lot of questions."

"Guys like what?" Nick demanded.

Anson looked as delighted as someone with a broken nose and blood all over his face could look. "Seriously, you don't know who Numina is?"

"We know," Sam fibbed. "Who are you working with specifically?"

He shifted on his chair and pretended Sam hadn't said anything, addressing his answers toward Quinn and Riley, as if he was gifting them with a history lesson. "Numina's core leadership is made up of guys like William Yates, Benjamin Odrama, Darren Breffet."

Somehow, Riley wasn't surprised that he'd just named the world's biggest computer magnate, a former U.S. president, and the most respected investment guru in history. How many more of the world's leaders were part of that legacy?

"Gods," Nick said, half scoffing.

Anson sneered back. "Yeah. Descended just like the goddesses. Only instead of having physical powers, they got power based off influence."

"Influence," Sam repeated.

Anson gestured. "You know how people say a guy has charisma? Seems charmed, no matter what he does. Everything he touches turns to gold. All those clichés? Influence."

Riley wondered if he even saw the irony in his dismissal, calling the traits clichés. He obviously recognized his own charisma and used it whenever possible. Even when it didn't work.

"I assume their use of it isn't all the same," Sam said. "Goddess abilities vary, as does the amount of power they have."

Riley thought about John's reference to splintering and said, "The men you named wouldn't have a need to go after the power of goddesses. They have a high level of respect and success they wouldn't want to risk."

Anson winked at her and gave a little nod.

"How many Numina are there?" Nick asked.

Anson shrugged. "No idea. My best guess is about as many as there are goddesses."

"Imagine that…men having the more subtle skills," Riley snarked.

Anson ignored that, too. "Numina is a secret organization, even from within. You're a member from birth, and all male descendants are included, no matter how much influence they have, but only certain ones are part of the inner circle. So there's a wide range of success. And as you can imagine, some abuse it, get greedy, and fall off their peaks."

"People like Broginvicci, Danner, Lilling." Sam named some of the biggest recent falls from grace, CEOs and politicians who fit Anson's description.

Riley gasped in recognition. Anson nodded at her. "Exactly. One of those guys was in my office a couple of days ago. They all want their power back, and influence isn't doing it fast enough. So they came up with a bigger plan."

The pieces were coming together now. Sam relaxed his threatening stance and paced at Anson's side. "They found out you planned to leech goddesses—"

"A goddess," Anson interrupted, one finger in the air. His self-righteousness was so ridiculous, Quinn laughed. "I only intended to leech one goddess. They came to me and offered me everything I'd ever wanted if I leeched more and used the power to help them get theirs back."

Sam didn't buy it. "They couldn't offer you everything you'd ever wanted. You wanted to be a goddess."

Anson made an annoyed face. "Yeah, well, their offer was still hard to turn down. I promised I'd work for them, and once Marley did the initial bestowment, it wasn't hard to go after the others."

"Because you were addicted." Riley was sure she was the only one who heard the crack Sam barely kept out of his voice, the statement driven by his own fears.

Anson nodded but didn't look chagrined or rueful.

"I would have been unstoppable." He gazed into the distance, as if considering what could have been. "If I'd leeched Quinn—"

"Except she stopped you." Nick's hard tone stripped Anson's wistfulness off his face. "So, then what? Numina didn't cast you off?"

"I don't work for Numina. These guys are members, but they're working outside the organization." He winced. "And no, they weren't too happy. You notice they didn't keep me out of jail. Too risky. They didn't want a traceable connection to me."

His tone gave Riley an inkling of why Anson had suddenly become so cooperative. Maybe he wasn't thrilled with his treatment at his employers' hands and was looking to change sides? She glanced at Sam, who didn't seem to be thinking along the same lines. In fact, he looked suspicious, and that made Riley wonder if Anson was talking as a stall tactic. But for what? She tuned out for a second to check for prickles but still only sensed the people in the room.

"They came up with this other plan when they found out that I could track—" Anson broke off, his eyes widening and his face going red. He glanced at Riley out of the corner of his eye but kept his face forward.

Her mind raced. The Numina had found out that Anson could track…goddesses. It had to be goddesses. Quinn had said he could sense them with the residue from his leechings.

Suddenly she knew how Vern and Sharla and all the other shadow stalkers kept finding her, even when she traveled with no plan, no destination in mind. How they'd followed her on the way up here when the only people who knew where she was were people they should have been able to trust.

"How?" She stepped forward and raised a candlestick over his head. "How do you track goddesses? How did you track me?" Sam came around the back of the chair and nudged Riley out of Anson's reach. But just let the bastard try to get a jump on her. So far tonight, all she'd felt for Anson was disgust and pity. But now fury lit, fueled by all those months of confusion and anxiety.

Anson's smile was smug this time. "Once I tag a goddess, I always know where she is."

"Why me?" It didn't make any sense for Anson to have "tagged" her, even if their grandmothers were friends. "I didn't even know I was a goddess. What did you think you could get from me when I shouldn't have had any power?"

Sam tugged her back again. She hadn't even realized she'd stepped nearer. She *really* wanted to brain Anson.

But this time Sam spoke, his voice hard, his arm tight around Riley's shoulders. "Think about it. He's patient. Look how long his first plan took. He knew you weren't part of the Society, that you didn't know goddesses, because of his grandmother's journals. He probably had you in reserve from day one. If you didn't know anything about yourself, he could teach you. You'd be grateful."

Anson's expression had darkened while Sam spoke, losing any hint of charm, but he was smart. He must know that arguing would have made Sam's assessment sound more true, so he just glared at them all, mouth pressed tight and hands clenched on his thighs.

"He was hedging his bets. If you didn't come into your power when you turned twenty-one, there was no loss for him. But if you did, and if things didn't work out the way he planned with Marley and the others—which it didn't—you were his backup. You wouldn't know anything about him. Unlike all the other goddesses, you weren't warned about him."

Pain stabbed through Riley, a shockingly intense stab of loss and nausea. "Did you...did you kill my family?"

Anson had the grace to look appalled. "No! I would never do something like that. It was a horrible accident."

That he'd capitalized on. She pressed a hand to her burning stomach.

"What were you going to do with her?" Sam sounded as sick as she felt. "Leech her?"

"No. I don't think I can do that anymore." He sounded sad. "Quinn broke me." He tipped an imaginary hat in her direction. She didn't move.

"Good," Nick barked. Anson ignored him.

"I wanted her to be mine. To care about me the way Marley did. I underestimated that kind of power," he admitted, and Riley caught a glimpse behind all his pretense, to the lonely boy underneath.

In any other circumstances, she might have felt sorry for him.

"What's their plan now?" Quinn asked in such a soft voice Riley spun toward her, alarmed. She was sagging against the wall now, but her gaze was steady on Anson. "It sounds like they're moving on from you."

Anson didn't like that. He straightened in the chair and yanked his foot out from under the leg of Nick's, which he'd eased up on just enough. "The Numina losers wanted me to identify goddesses so they could send recruiters to them. They'd feel them out for weaknesses or ambition. See who might be willing or susceptible to working for them."

"Leeching them?" Riley asked, though they didn't meet the

criteria. Maybe their heritage made it possible for them, just like sons of goddesses.

But Anson shook his head. "Just employees with really unique skills. They want to set up a network and use the goddesses to help them get back on top."

"I've heard enough." Nick hauled Anson up by the collar and dragged him toward the garage door. "We thank you for your cooperation. Sam, call the security team in. They can decide what to—"

The prickles burst into Riley's brain, and she gasped. "Nick, no!" Too late. Before she could tell him someone was out there, he twisted the handle on the garage door. It slammed inward, knocking both Nick and Anson back, and three men barreled in. Nick recovered immediately, tossing Anson at the first guy and kicking the door into the face of the third. The second guy made it inside and swung a fist at Nick's head. He missed, and Nick didn't hesitate to fight back.

Riley caught Quinn and pulled her away from the fight, into the living room. Sam put himself in front of them, but then the front door blasted open, too, splinters flying, the alarm blaring into life. Bodies seemed to pour in from every direction, though Riley flash-counted only half a dozen. Still, too many. Nick had his guy down, but the first one was on his back, struggling to pull Nick's arms behind him and yank him upright and vulnerable. Sam moved forward to meet the second bunch, looking like an action movie hero as his fists connected with heads and guts, but there were too many.

Riley squeezed her candlestick and drew harder than she ever had, shoving two attackers off Sam in quick succession but not doing enough damage to keep them down. She watched Quinn for a second. The woman was weak and didn't go for blunt force like Riley had. She pulled a rug and sent two guys tumbling to the ground, then dropped crystal vases and knick-knacks off a shelf onto their heads.

Sam landed a fist deep in someone's abdomen, not just doubling him over but sending him staggering halfway across the room, where he tripped and crashed into an end table. There was no way Sam, as big and strong as he was, could have done that without putting power behind it. But the effort took its toll. He swayed on the spot and shook his head as if to toss off dizziness.

Another attacker ran in to tackle him around the waist. Riley wound up with her candlestick, threw power behind her swing, and swung for the cheap seats. The metal connected with his chin, flattening him before he reached his target.

Sam appeared to have recovered. He bounced on the balls of his feet, hands held loosely in front of his face, a small sneer forming as the remaining guys backed off. And then Riley heard a hollow *pop*.

Quinn yelled and made a pushing motion with both hands but fell to her knees, obviously tapped out. Riley spun, drew, aimed, but she was again too late. A thud vibrated the floor under her feet. Nick had been felled like a tree by a tranquilizer dart just like the one heading straight for Sam's neck. She lashed out again, and again, until the candlestick seared her hand and she was forced to drop it.

"No!" she screamed as someone thrust a hood over Quinn's head and dragged her upright, hauling her toward the open door. She struggled against hands and arms, tried to draw on Sam's screw-ring, but it wasn't enough. The more desperate she grew, the less the energy came. And then there was a sting in her arm, her head went fuzzy, and everything faded away.

CHAPTER SEVENTEEN

*One discovery that has stemmed from our new focus on education
and understanding is the range of limitation for each goddess.
Years of practice and training can make us believe we know our
limits, but circumstances can always push our boundaries and give
us new knowledge about each other and ourselves.*

— **Goddess Society for Education and Defense,** *"New Focus"*
Educational Initiative

Riley blinked in a sudden burst of light when the hood was pulled
off her face. She barely had time to register a basic beige hallway
before they shoved her into darkness and slammed a door behind
her. She landed on her hands and knees on a shaggy rug.

"Fuck!"

A feeble glow lit and moved across the space toward her.
"Riley?"

"Quinn?" Riley rose to her knees. Quinn huddled on a bed
against the wall. She knee-walked across the floor. "Are you all
right?"

"Relatively speaking." The phone dimmed, and Quinn hit a
button with her thumb. "Are you?"

"Mostly. Assholes." Stupid ones. They hadn't searched her or taken anything away. She dug in her inside jacket pocket for her keychain. It had a small flashlight attached. She twisted it on and waved it around the room.

Colors were hard to distinguish, but the walls were bare, painted drywall. The bed was the only furniture, and the light fixture in the center of the ceiling had no bulbs. No windows in the room, either, not even covered. "This looks like Millinger."

"We haven't been gone long enough to be in Georgia," Quinn said. "I don't think."

"I know, but I mean, it's just as empty and cold." Riley set the light on the floor and crossed her legs. "Do you have any idea where we are?"

"Not at all. I passed out. Were you able to pick up any clues coming in?"

"They drugged me, so I was foggy but conscious. I heard city sounds, but nothing specific."

"You didn't overhear conversations or anything?"

"No." Riley fumed, replaying the whole attack in her head. "Who the hell were those guys?"

"I don't know." Quinn cleared her throat and shifted again. "They all seemed young. In their twenties."

Riley had noticed that, too. "And they weren't dressed like Anson's thugs. Their clothes were more expensive. Speaking of Anson." She thought harder, but couldn't remember seeing him after he'd been knocked to the ground. Had he just run, or were their attackers working for him? "That had to be the reason he was stalling, right?"

"That's my guess. Riley…they tranqed the guys, didn't they? What did you see? Is Nick—" Her voice quavered and stuck, as if she didn't want to know the answer.

"I think he's okay. I don't know if they took them, but I don't think so. When we got here I heard them carry you out, and then they made me walk. I couldn't hear anything that sounded like they were hauling a few hundred pounds of muscle. And you know Nick and Sam would have been fighting if they were awake. Or at least cursing."

"You're right." Quinn sighed.

They sat in tension-thick silence for a few minutes. Riley prayed Sam was okay. Maybe Anson wouldn't have reason to harm them. He'd been genuinely shocked by the idea that he might have hurt her family. He'd let Riley go, back in Atlanta, and he didn't seem to like getting his hands dirty. He sure as hell hadn't fought after Sam broke his nose.

But things had escalated with this abduction. He was working with other people now, men whose greed might far outweigh their squeamishness, and he had plenty of reasons to lash out at Sam. Riley stifled a sob. If he was hurt, it was her fault. She should never have let him go with her to Boston. Or never even have gone into his bar in the first place. He'd been her champion from beginning to end. How much was he going to suffer for that, because of her?

But she couldn't honestly say she wished she had never gone to him for help. He was the most amazing man she'd ever met, and every moment she'd spent with him, even over distance, had made her fall harder. When they'd made love on the balcony, they'd been so close, so entwined in each other, that Riley couldn't tell them apart. Not only in the romance novel sense but also in a power-centric one. His golden light and whatever made up her own essence had merged into a mentally blinding flash of not just ecstasy, but joy.

She didn't know if Sam had felt it too. What if she fell in love with him, and all he needed from her was a way to balance himself with the power?

Quinn moaned and bent forward, her arms across her stomach.

"What's wrong?" Riley got up and leaned closer. "What can I do?"

"Nothing," Quinn whispered. After a moment she eased back against the wall again. "It's the power."

Riley tried not to panic. "What's it doing?"

"Since I separated the strands, it doesn't stop moving. It's like Tanda's is trying to get back to her—that's the best way to describe it. Beth's feels lost and sad, like grief, but it's fading."

Riley tried not to think of what the remnants were doing to Sam right now. And that wasn't even the worst of what Quinn was dealing with. "And Marley's?"

"Sick," Quinn groaned before taking a deep breath.

"What's it going to—"

Quinn cut her off. "I'll deal with that when the time comes. When it's all that's left, I'll figure out what needs to be done. I just need to get Tanda's transferred."

Before she was literally torn to pieces from the inside out.

Riley couldn't fathom what it would do to Nick if they didn't get out of here and Quinn died from this. And where would that leave Sam?

They *had* to get out of here.

The first step was to try to let the guys know where they were. Quinn wouldn't be able to get very far without help, and Riley was afraid she wasn't enough. "We need to figure out a way to talk to the guys." She patted the pocket where her phone usually was, but it was flat and empty. Dammit, it must have fallen out somewhere. "Can I see your phone?"

"Of course." Quinn passed it over, her hand shaking at its slight weight. "We don't have a signal in here, though. I've tried."

Riley didn't know if her idea would work. Energy was energy, so she should be able to use what she tapped through metal to feed the phone, and if she did it right, maybe she could even increase its receiving ability.

She needed more metal than the ring on her thumb or the small things in her pocket. She turned and felt the bed, hoping to find some metal pieces, and to her surprise, she found that the whole frame was metal. Like something from a barracks. Were these guys stupid, or just hired guns who knew nothing about the women they'd kidnapped?

She closed her eyes and concentrated, her free hand curled around the metal bed frame. The faint hum in the phone increased after a minute or two, and it grew warm in her hand. She opened her eyes and checked the symbol. Four bars. "Awesome!"

"What?" Quinn asked.

"I boosted the signal."

"Wow. Nicely done."

"Thanks." Riley held out the phone. "Do you want to call Nick?"

Quinn didn't move. "As much as I want to hear his voice, no. If he hears mine, he'll know how bad off I am."

Riley tried speed-dial number one, smiling when Nick's name flashed on the screen. But the four bars dropped to three, then two before bouncing back to three. *Please let him answer. Please let them be okay.*

The first ring cut off halfway through. "Hello," Nick said warily, as if he didn't trust the caller.

"Nick! It's Riley, on Quinn's phone. We're okay, but we're being held somewhere. Get Sam to trace this." She rushed on when he started to ask a question. "Do it fast! I had to boost the signal magically, and it's already fading."

Nick's orders to Sam were muffled, as if he'd moved the phone away. Sam argued, his voice sounding sweet to her despite the edge of desperation and anger in it. She drew in a relieved breath. He was okay, too.

Their voices cut in and out for a few seconds. "No no no no!" She pulled the phone from her ear and scowled at the single bar that remained. She tried to focus on it again, but it heated so fast against her palm she stopped, afraid it would stop working. "The signal's fading already. They might not have time."

"Got it!" shouted Nick, loud and clear before the phone beeped the dropped call.

"Can you boost it again?" Quinn asked, but Riley shook her head.

"I'm afraid the heat will damage the circuits or something. Hopefully they got the location. But unless they had already guessed what direction we were taken, they'll still be a couple hours away." She shifted into a more comfortable position and sighed. "You okay?"

Quinn didn't answer.

• • •

Red and blue lights fuzzed into a flashing mess in Sam's vision. He squeezed his eyes shut and pressed his fingers to them. "Cop ahead."

"I don't care," Nick growled back.

"Getting pulled over will slow us down."

"I won't get pulled over."

"You can't be reckless. They need us."

Nick ignored him, his glare practically burning a hole through the windshield, his hands uncompromising on the steering wheel, and when Sam checked, the gas pedal was mashed under his foot. But he drove smoothly, his reaction time keeping up with their speed. Sam knew he wouldn't be reckless, per se, but he wondered what was going on in his friend's head.

Fucking Anson Tournado. When he got his hands on him again...

None of what he'd fed them had sounded like bullshit. Sam suspected he was running multiple games, playing different groups off each other. He never would have pegged his old roommate as someone happy to work for someone else, but pretending to, if it would further his own goals? Totally.

He wished he'd been able to talk to Riley. Nick said she sounded okay, but he wanted to hear it for himself. He'd pinpointed their location in Boston right before the call dropped, but they got voice mail when they tried to call back. By the time they got up there, who knew what they'd have done to her? The car flew over a bad patch of highway, bouncing and sending Sam into the ceiling despite his seatbelt. "Ow! Come on!" He glared at Nick.

"Sorry." He motioned to the glove box. "Get the map out, will you? I want the address marked on hard copy. We can't carry your laptop around while we search."

"Yeah, okay." He dug around Nick's family photos, a pistol, the plastic envelope with the car's papers, and a dozen maps from all over the country. "You really need to organize this, man." He found the map of the Northeast and pulled it out, but the print blurred when he opened it. He squinched his eyes shut again and then blinked hard, trying to make out the route.

Nick glanced over and frowned. "You all right? What's the matter with you?"

"I don't know. It's this…the transfer stuff. Don't worry about it." He unfolded and refolded the map with the target area facing up.

"Great," Nick grumbled. "That means it's something to worry about. I need you at your best if we're going to—well, shit. We're going to Boston. We don't have to do this alone."

Sam watched him pull out his phone and hit a number to speed dial. John's name flashed in the display. "Come on, come on, come on. Pick up. Crap." He tapped the steering wheel while the voice mail message played over the speaker.

"Hey, John. Nick. Got a situation here." He gave a rundown and the address Sam had identified. "Those people you don't want to talk about on the phone have Quinn and Riley. We need your help. Meet us there or call me back." He flipped the phone closed and stepped on the gas again.

"You think it was a good idea to give him that over a possibly compromised phone?" Sam murmured.

Nick shook his head. "I don't know, man. Anson's got to know we'd try to come after them. He'll be ready. Can it make it any worse for them to have heard me say it? Even if they intercept John on his way over, the situation can't get much worse."

Sam wasn't sure he fully agreed with Nick's logic, but he was sure that Anson either thought he had Quinn and Riley somewhere they couldn't get to them, or he'd have a trap waiting.

An hour later—four hours after the women were taken, two after Riley's phone call—they sat in the Charger in a dark parking garage, waiting. Nick had driven around the brick apartment building a couple of times before settling into a spot where two lights were out. John was on his way, but he hadn't been able to reach any local goddesses capable of fighting, and there were still no protectors close enough to join them.

All Sam's symptoms had worsened during the drive, too. Nausea, jitteriness, jagged intensity. He wasn't sure if there was any useable power left in him, or if he'd burned it all off in the fight. He was too much of a mess to tell. None of the ill effects had resurfaced until they drove inland and away from the ocean. The power in him was totally unlike anyone's understanding of the goddess/energy connection. When he'd pushed the screw in mid-air and then bent it into a ring, he used what was already in him, rather than drawing on the energy of the ocean. The act had normalized him, and he'd felt even better making love with Riley.

Immediately afterward, he'd been completely absorbed by her. But with everything that happened after that, he hadn't noticed when he started to feel fucked up again. Maybe while Anson talked, but it was hard to tell what was physical and what was emotional.

The apartment building where Quinn and Riley were apparently being held was in Brookline, far enough inland that

Sam couldn't even sense the sea, never mind hope to be calmed by it. The Charles River was a little closer, but he couldn't sense that, either. Using whatever power remained might make him feel better, but he hated to waste it and was afraid of what would happen when it was gone. He was functional right now—that had to be good enough.

Sam took a deep breath and concentrated on the building specs on his laptop screen. "Okay, looks like six floors, ten apartments on a floor, with four layout variations." He flipped a page. "Top floor has the luxury units, only four up there."

"Can you access ownership records?" Nick leaned forward and peered across the parking level. He'd backed into the space so they could keep watch and get away faster when the time came.

"Yeah, but these names mean nothing to me." He angled the laptop for Nick to scan the list. The protector shook his head and went back to watching for John.

"We don't have time to research them. Even if the abductors are rich, they might be smart enough to have rented one of the lower units. Put a layer between their names and anyone looking for them."

"Too bad we can't count on them not being smart," Nick grumped.

"Yeah." Sam shook his head with a humorless chuckle. "They did get us, after all. How's your head, by the way?" Nick had insisted he was okay to drive despite the nasty headache the tranq gave him.

"Pounding. But it'll be fine."

For a fleeting second, Sam considered trying to heal Nick. At the immediate image of his hand on the back of Nick's head, while Nick screamed and his brains scrambled, Sam stopped considering.

"There's John." Nick climbed out of the car and closed his door quietly. The small thud still echoed in the dark silence, and the figure walking up the entry ramp turned, hesitated, and walked in their direction.

Sam dumped the laptop into its case and opened his door, moving slowly and willing his body to cooperate. Every muscle had stiffened and most ached. He forced himself upright and closed the car door to join Nick and John.

"They could be anywhere." Nick gestured at the building connected to the garage by a stairwell/elevator combo. "We'll have to search the whole place."

"How are we gonna have any clue which unit they're in?"

"I have an idea about that—" Nick broke off at the scrape of a shoe down the aisle. He and Sam both looked, but John didn't turn.

Sam understood why a moment later, as Marley walked under the closest light.

"What's she doing here?" he asked.

"She wanted to help." John gave him an implacable look. "Quinn's her sister, and Riley's her friend."

She reached John's side and nodded a greeting. "Have you heard from them again?"

"No." Sam told himself that didn't mean anything.

"You still buzzing?" Nick asked Sam.

Sam frowned. "Can you be more specific?" He was buzzing in four different ways.

"From the transfer. The power thing?"

"Some, yeah. I guess."

"Think you could use it like Riley does, to sense where she and Quinn are? Or the Numina people?"

John grunted at the word but didn't say anything.

Sam lifted a shoulder. "I don't know. I can try. If I have any power left I can probably detect Riley." He'd gotten a pulse of her energy at the beach, and something deeper than endorphins had surged when they made love. He could identify that energy if he sensed it again, but he didn't know how far the range extended or how to seek it, and he doubted he could do it with anyone but her right now.

"So what's the plan?" John asked. "Just walk around?"

"That's what it's going to have to be," Nick said. "Once Sam identifies their location—"

"*If* I can identify their location."

Nick didn't even look at him. "We'll scope it out and decide how to go in."

"I'll go with Sam." Marley said. When the men all stared at her, she leaned as if to back up, then straightened and squared her shoulders. "It would look suspicious for you three to walk the halls together. Sam and I can blend in better."

"You don't have any defenses," Nick pointed out.

Marley flinched and didn't respond directly. "If anyone realizes we're wandering, we can claim we don't know which apartment we're looking for. A dinner party or something."

Sam was skeptical. "It's almost midnight."

"Some people have late parties."

It was better than nothing, and they didn't have time to argue. "All right, fine."

"Hang on." Nick opened the Charger's door and pulled the pistol out of the glove box. He checked it, then held it out to Sam, who held up his hands and backed away. There was no way he was steady enough to carry that safely.

Nick swiveled to offer it to Marley. She hesitated, then shook her head. "Where am I going to hide that?"

Nick swore and went around to the trunk. He rummaged in it a minute, then came back and gave Marley a switchblade that she slid into her front jeans pocket. He tried to hand Sam a combat knife that would probably be more dangerous to himself than anyone he came up against.

"They haven't used weapons yet," Sam told him. "We're just scoping out an apartment building right now. I'll be fine."

He and Marley left a very disgruntled Nick and walked together toward the stairwell.

"Keep us posted," Nick called. Sam waved acknowledgment and pushed through the fire door. They went down one flight and into a long, narrow extension of the lobby that ran along the side of the building, an access hall connecting the garage and main entrance. It was very white, freshly painted with a gleaming floor.

Sam cleared his throat as they walked toward the front of the building. So much had happened, the few days since he last talked to Marley felt like a lot longer than the year before it. What he wanted to ask her was full of awkward references and emotional minefields.

"Did you, um, back when you still…you know…could you tell the difference between regular people and goddesses?" He braced himself, but Marley only nodded, watching her feet as she walked.

Maybe he could actually do this. "What's it like? To sense someone? I thought I could feel the life in the ocean, but it was like pulses. I had no idea *what* each pulse was."

"That part is different for everyone. It was almost like lights for me. Glittery, like the crystals."

Crystals had been her power source. Since the ocean was the dominant source for the power in Sam right now, and the other part—if there was any left—was the river, he'd guess there was something watery about identifying goddesses. But without having one nearby, he had no guide. And he was no longer close to the power source, so whatever he'd seen in Riley before, he wasn't sure it would be there now.

He blew out a breath as they neared the end of the hall. "I have no idea how to do this."

"Try it on me."

Sam frowned at her and held up a hand as they reached the corner. He listened and heard nothing, so he leaned to check the lobby. Empty. Not even a security desk. The front door had a keycard slide to unlock it, but they hadn't needed one from the garage.

"Something's off here," he murmured.

"What?" Marley stepped up next to him and looked around at the nondescript lobby and glass front door. "Looks normal to me."

Sam huffed a laugh. "Of course it does. But these guys have money. I knew the building didn't have much security, but…"

"How do you know they have money?"

He looked down at her. "What do you mean?"

"John told me about Numina, and your theory that this is a splinter group. He and Jeannine have been meeting with a few members of the leadership. It's been slow going, since Numina haven't revealed themselves to us in centuries, but he thinks they reached out now because of that splintering. So maybe these are the kids of those disgraced men, and they *don't* have money."

"Maybe. Puts a new spin on the 'luxury' of those top-floor apartments, too." He took a deep breath and closed his eyes. Marley didn't have the abilities of a goddess anymore, but maybe she still had a signature. It was worth trying.

He focused on each of his senses in turn. He smelled floor wax, a hint of car exhaust, and something sweet that was probably Marley's perfume or lotion or something. He heard traffic outside, a distant horn, and in here…humming in the walls. Wiring, AC and heating equipment maybe. Metallic clanking in the nearby elevator shaft. He stretched his arm out to press a hand to the wall, and the hum vibrated into his fingers. The wall itself was smooth, glossy enough for his fingers to stick when he tried to slide them along the surface.

Normal senses catalogued, he tried to expand his mind, to "see" something extra. The power in his body surged. He mentally caught on to it, as if grabbing a tendril of smoke, and everything suddenly heightened. He focused outward, and there she was.

But instead of a buzz or golden light like Riley described, or even the shimmery, illusion-type thing he'd imagined, Marley was more of a smudge on his subconscious. Something dark and heavy.

Not malevolent, but absent of life or purpose. Null.

He blinked and found Marley smiling sadly at him. "Don't tell me what you saw."

He nodded and turned away to hide the expression he knew would only show sadness and pity. He took a deep breath and as they entered the first-floor hallway lined with apartment doors, tried not to think of all the ways this could fail.

CHAPTER EIGHTEEN

Uncle Martin came for a visit yesterday. He brought friends, which always upsets Mama. She made them sleep in the barn, but they still look at me at mealtimes. I know what they want. It's not what other girls are afraid of from boys. But those men won't get it. My power is mine, and I won't give it to anyone.

—*Meandress Chronicles, compilation of family diaries*

Riley and Quinn had powered down the phone and flashlight, so Riley had no idea how long they sat in the dark, planning in whispers in case the room was being monitored. They could hear noise from outside, occasional horns and sirens, so it wasn't soundproof.

"Can you sense anyone nearby?" Quinn asked. Her voice was weaker than it had been when Riley first got here.

"No, but I still haven't determined my range." So they might be alone in the apartment, or there might be a dozen hired goons waiting somewhere close. "How are you doing?" she asked Quinn.

"Not good." A moan escaped when she shifted position.

"You won't be able to fight."

Quinn sighed. "No. The power that's left, as little as it is relative to the mass I originally held, is draining me. Fighting would be an epic fail."

Riley got to her knees and ran her hands along the bed frame. "I need metal. I want to be prepared when they come in here." The room was empty except for the bed, so she found what pieces she could detach from the frame and worked them loose, stuffing curled-up springs, screws, and nuts into her pockets. Digging under the mattress, she jerked on the support posts. One of them rattled.

"Yes! Can you shift down the bed a little so I can work this free?"

Quinn complied, and Riley shoved the mattress up to work at the bolts attaching the post with L-braces. "Ow, fuck," she muttered. The edge of the bolt hole was jagged, and a couple of nails caught and ripped at the quick, but she kept going until she held a three-foot-long metal club. She hefted it, drawing a little energy, slowly increasing it until the metal warmed under her hand. By shifting her grip to a cooler spot, she could avoid the burns she'd suffered with the chains.

"I'm going to try breaking down the door," she told Quinn, walking over. "The hinges and deadbolt have got to be metal, so maybe I can—" She touched the doorknob and yelped, yanking her hand away as a shock ran up her arm. "Crap. They've got it wired somehow." She reached again, trying to imagine a shield of energy over her hand. It worked, to an extent. When she neared the doorknob there was resistance—which meant she couldn't get close enough to touch it.

"Please be careful," Quinn said from the bed. "Don't—"

Riley let out a string of curses as her groping fingers found the hinges, and the jolt went through her entire body this time. Furious, she kicked at the door, near the lock, then near the center, thinking she could kick a hole through it at least. But the thing was solid. Probably reinforced. She barely cracked the center, even after kicking several times, and it didn't even rattle in the jamb.

She limped back to Quinn and dropped onto the mattress. "I need to try to unlock it telekinetically, but I don't know how."

"Maybe I can talk you through it. You opened the car door that way, right?"

"Yeah." But Riley was skeptical. "I know how to pull a handle. It wasn't easy though, because my abilities are more punch than pull. This is finesse, and I have no idea what the inside of a lock looks like."

"Rest a minute, and then we'll try."

But as she'd expected, Riley was unable to make it work. She thought about melting the metal but needed contact for that, and she still couldn't push through the pain of the electricity to touch anything near the door, even the latch plate that curled slightly around the jamb.

She paced the dark, empty room, frustrated. "Boosting the phone signal was finesse. Why can't I do something else that's finesse-y?"

"It's different," Quinn placated. "The phone signal is energy. You just fed it with the energy you pulled through the metal. Don't be so hard on yourself."

That didn't make Riley feel better. Despite the new things she'd tried since meeting Sam and John's training, it still seemed as haphazard as when she first realized she was a freak.

Suck it up, Riley. Whatever you can do, you do. You're the only one here who can.

"Okay, new strategy. We'll wait for whoever comes for us first. If it's Sam and Nick, yay. If it's not, I have this." She brandished the metal tubing she'd detached from the bed. "We'll fight our way out."

Quinn didn't comment on her optimistic *we*.

They sat in silence, Riley working to build her strength and the amount of energy she held without doing damage. Quinn's breathing, beside her, was slow and even, and Riley knew she was gathering her own strength.

Riley waited, alert. Eyes closed, listening. Voices. *People*—a presence she felt an instant before the latch clicked. She had a brief throb of disappointment that the signature wasn't Sam's before she jumped to her feet and braced against the wall next to the door, strong and ready, just before it opened. Her breathing was steady, her heart rate normal. Sweat didn't slick her palms or bead on her forehead. She'd do whatever she needed to protect them both.

She whacked the first guy through the door on top of the head. Not hard enough to kill him, but enough to drive him to his knees.

"Wha the fuh?" He swayed and lifted his hand. Riley kicked him between the shoulder blades and followed him to the carpet.

Everything seemed to happen at a normal speed, though Riley knew it was moving faster. The guy groaned and tried to get up. "Stay down," she ordered, and pushed him flat with her foot.

Now she faced the doorway and the next guy coming in. He rushed Riley, growling. She swung the pipe like a baseball bat and connected with the side of his head. He fell into the door, knocking it against the wall, and tumbled to the floor.

"Ground rule double," Riley muttered, and Quinn laughed behind her.

The hall outside was empty, but Riley stood at the ready, waiting, all her senses tuned to high. She got a very light prickle from the two goons on the floor, but still sensed nothing beyond this room.

"Go," Quinn croaked. "Get out, and get help."

"No way." Riley flipped over the first guy, who seemed slightly more coherent than his partner, and yanked him up by his Polo shirt. "What do you want with us? Who's in charge?"

His mouth stretched in a wobbly grimace that she assumed was supposed to be a grin. "Not telling."

"Yes, you are." She raised the metal tube again, gratified to see fear flicker through his eyes, but the feeling was short-lived. She didn't want to be that person. The bully. Someone who got off on intimidating other people or even hurting them. Was it her power or the circumstances that were making her this way?

Her strength ebbed, and their jailer sagged in her grip. Pain seared through the muscles in the underside of her forearm. Okay, she wanted to be that person, at least until they got out of here. She'd go to counseling later.

She pulled more energy and got right in the guy's face. "Tell me."

He tried to shrug and only succeeded in flopping his arms. His speech was clearer, though. "Tournado told us to leech you two. Just enough to get us started. Then we'd have the power to get more."

"Oh, for God's sake." She dropped him in disgust but didn't bother to correct his understanding of how leeching worked. "How many of you are here?"

"Too many for you," he mumbled, and she took that to mean none.

"Come on." She hustled over to Quinn and tried to help her off the bed.

"No, you need to scout the place. I'll slow you down, and if he's not lying about having backup, we're cooked."

Riley hated that Quinn was right. Leaving her here felt completely wrong, but dragging her blind wasn't going to get them far. "Okay, but…" She hesitated, then handed Quinn the pipe.

"You need that." Quinn tried to give it back.

"No, I'm good. I have other stuff. You need something to defend yourself with. It's hard, and at the very least, maybe you can clang it against the bed frame to call me back if you need help."

"All right. Thanks." Quinn wrapped her hand around the pipe and balanced it in the crook of her elbow. Riley was afraid she wouldn't have the strength to swing it, but…

"Hey, wait a second." Metal gave *her* strength. Could she

channel that? Not just the raw energy as a concussive burst, but the strength itself? Feed Quinn, kind of like feeding the cell signal. She wrapped her hands around Quinn's, making sure to contact the metal, and closed her eyes to concentrate on infusing Quinn with the energy Riley had already internalized. It was all instinct, maybe applied with a little bit of logic, but unaffected by doubt. Slowly, her body seemed to deflate as Quinn's skin warmed.

Quinn drew in an audible breath. "Riley," she breathed. "Wow."

Riley opened her eyes and smiled. Quinn blinked at her in the light from the hall. "It worked?"

"Yes. Thank you. But you—"

"I'm good." She got off the bed and dug into her pockets, coming out with fistfuls of small metal parts. The strength she'd lost returned. She pushed it all into her arms and fists and grinned. "Now I just need someone to punch."

"Be careful. Don't burn yourself."

"I won't." She couldn't draw constantly on the energy, especially since she couldn't let go of the metal and there was no cool spot to shift to. She'd have to perfect quick draws and bursts on the fly until she found something better.

She stopped wasting time and spun away, dashing to the door and peering up and down the hall. It was a standard apartment hallway, though longer than she'd anticipated. There were three other typical flat-panel doors, neutral, high-grade carpet, and off-white painted walls. No art. The ceiling light fixture was ornate, though. A smoke detector sat next to it. Maybe she could set that off, but if it wasn't wired to the fire department, it would call attention to them without getting help.

She stepped over the second guy's legs into the hall. Neither punk tried to stop her. They hadn't provided much of a challenge. Maybe sniveling, greedy weasels didn't have as much of their ancestors' influence, and that was why they registered so low to her Numina senses. She didn't want to refer to them as gods. Before it was a little scary to consider. Now it seemed to be giving them too much credit.

The hall dead-ended to her left, but she went that way first to hurriedly check the other rooms. Having both hands full wasn't going to work, so she shoved the nuts and springs in her left hand into her pocket again and tried the door handles. All were locked except the one opening into a basic, all-tan bathroom. The gleaming fixtures and new-paint smell made her think this apartment hadn't been occupied in a while. The vanity was bare, the glass door to the step-in shower very clean.

Riley backed up and listened at the locked doors, trying to feel the interiors of the rooms. She heard no sounds and felt no prickles. She couldn't assume the rooms were empty, though. She tapped the first doorknob. When it didn't shock her, she twisted it hard enough to break the lock and pushed open the door. The light from the hall showed it to be as empty as everything else. Ditto the other room.

The lack of...*anything* gave her a chill. Were they planning to abduct other goddesses and trap them here? These doors had been easy to break into, but maybe the reinforced door of the other room was stage one and they hadn't gotten this far yet.

The two guys staggered into the hallway from the room Quinn was in, blocking Riley's access to the open end. One of them pointed at Riley. "Get her!"

She couldn't get enough energy from the metal she held to knock them back from here, so she charged down the hall, braced to plow through them. She pushed the energy out in front of her, hoping to knock them out of her way.

Except they'd gotten smart, or stopped underestimating her, or decided they weren't scared of her after all. Maybe getting hit in the head had pissed them off, or fear of what Anson would do to them if she got away galvanized them. Also, she apparently sucked at creating a shield. They didn't budge when the energy she thought she pushed ahead of her hit them. Then, despite her speed and strength, they stood firm and grabbed her, working together to hold on when she immediately kicked and flailed.

"No! Let me go!" She wrenched one arm free, but the metal in her fist wasn't enough. She couldn't draw enough power to get away, not with four arms and hands alternately wrapping around her and grabbing her wrists and legs.

"Hold her, goddammit!" one of them growled.

The other cursed and dodged her skull when she tried a reverse head-butt. Her hand stung, the metal heating. She had to change strategies.

She went limp so abruptly it took them by surprise, and her body slid through their hands. Once on the floor, she scrambled away, digging into her pocket for the other metal pieces. This time, she made sure the sharp ends of the springs poked between her fingers, and when they chased after her down the hall toward the main area of the apartment, she spun and scratched one in the face.

"Shit!" He skidded to a halt, his hands pressed to the bloody marks. "Get her!"

The other guy got a determined look on his face and charged. Riley reached the kitchen and dodged around the center island, trying to keep an eye on him and find alternate metal at the same time. The appliances were stainless steel, but it would be too easy to drag her away from them. Unless…

No, crazy idea. Too heavy, too slow if it didn't work. She stared around, her vision blurring as she tried to take in her surroundings all at once. She wasn't calm and steady anymore. Her lungs hurt from panting, and her heart pounded, pulse throbbing in her neck and arms. Her palms were burned and scratched. But she had to neutralize these two long enough to get Quinn out. Maybe then they could hide somewhere until Nick and Sam got here.

The kitchen shared an open floor plan with the dining room, separated from the living room by a half wall on the other side. More neutral colors. Brown, boring furniture matched the brown marble countertops, and the same plush carpeting flowed all the way to the front door, save where speckled tan ceramic tile lined the kitchen floor. The rooms were all large, and besides the doors leading to closets and a powder room, that was it. The entire apartment. Like in the bathroom, it smelled of new paint and cleaning products, and Riley assumed it was staged for sale. Or maybe a new purchase, since there was absolutely nothing on the countertops. No cute canisters, no fancy toaster or coffeepot. Nothing that would help her.

No time to search drawers. Both guys approached her again, one from either side of the island. The one she'd scratched still held his cheek, blood seeping through his fingers, and looked very pissed. The other was cautious, moving more slowly than his partner.

"You guys know how to drain me?" she taunted. "You wanna become leeches like your pal Anson? You have to start with a willing goddess, morons. You can't just steal it the way you are. If it were that easy, everyone would be doing it."

"Don't listen to her," the unscratched guy told his friend. "Anson said we'll have all the power we want. He knows how to do it."

"Why would you believe him?" They'd stopped moving, and she caught her breath. If she could distract them long enough, maybe she could find a way to knock them out completely this time. There was no one else here, so she had time…

She'd barely thought the words before the jinx went into effect. The front door opened, and four more dudes with rich-kid clothes and lightened, carefully tousled, or just-a-bit-too-long hair came in. They stared at the group in front of them, and unfortunately for Riley, easily grasped what was going on. There was only one thing left to do.

She opened her hands and let the metal pieces clatter to the floor.

• • •

"This is taking too long." Sam stopped halfway down the first second-floor corridor and stuck his hands on his hips. Way too many apartments stretched ahead of them. At every door he stopped, concentrated, registered Marley as a kind of marker, and tried to sense anyone in the apartment. Sometimes they heard TVs, people talking or yelling or laughing, music, or odd noises he couldn't identify. Regular sounds of regular people living regular lives. He never got anything like the seventh sense that identified Marley as non-regular, and every stop took a couple of minutes. At this rate, it could be hours before they found Riley and Quinn.

"We should go upstairs. Start at the top."

"We could. But you said you thought it was equally likely they'd use a smaller apartment to throw you off, in case you knew they were rich. Or used to be."

Sam moved to the next door and closed his eyes, leaning close. Silence. Darkness. Nothing. "I don't know. This just seems fruitless. But if we go upstairs and no one is up there, it'll be just as much a waste of time." He tried the next door. More TV murmuring, nothing else. "I don't even know if I'm doing this right." He fisted his hand and brought it up like he'd hit the wall, but landed it in a light tap, instead.

"Are you okay?" Marley stepped closer and looked up at him with concern. "You don't seem right."

"I'm fine." He shoved away from the wall and kept going. The mess of hunger and illness and nerves was nothing compared to what might be happening to his...to Riley and Quinn. A ticking clock at the back of his head told him they might already be too late. "Let's go upstairs. There's nothing down here."

Marley didn't answer, but speed-thumbed the buttons on her phone as they waited for the elevator. Sam assumed she was texting Nick to tell him what they were doing.

He closed his eyes and let his mind go, feeling for Riley. His anxiety could be messing everything up. Or maybe some of the power had drained, and he didn't have enough to find her. He could have bypassed her location already.

He swallowed down the renewed rise of nausea and swayed, lightheaded. With a tight grip on the wall rail, he righted himself before Marley glanced up from her phone. She didn't notice his weakness, luckily, or she might have tried to make him stop.

Another wave of dizziness brought blackness and sharp, tiny lights around the edges of his vision. Fuck. Even if he managed to find Riley, how the hell would he rescue her without falling on his face?

• • •

The four newcomers grinned at what they clearly thought was cornered prey.

"What's this?" the tallest asked Gashface. "I thought Anson said to keep them locked up until he got here."

Gashface shifted his gaze, and Riley knew they'd been acting against orders when they first came into the bedroom. "She was trying to get out."

"Looks like she succeeded." Another one raked her body with his gaze, so slimy and disgusting she couldn't believe he wasn't riddled with pustules. He took a few steps closer. "You get a sample?"

"No one's getting a sample," the other guy Riley had hit in the head ordered. He'd abandoned caution and moved up on her left, boxing her in fully but holding a halting hand out toward his friends. Riley wasn't fooled. He wasn't helping her. He just didn't want to face Anson if these guys got carried away. Eying the various looks of avarice and excitement, she thought he was the only one here halfway in his right mind.

Okay, then. She was down to the crazy idea. She had to time it right, though. The little bit of power she'd held onto faded completely. Twisting her body, she gripped the handle of the top oven door, which was half the size of the main oven. The action looked frightened, and she tried to sell it with wide eyes and faster, shorter breaths. It worked, and the semicircle around her shrank, closing in.

She only had one shot at this. Ignoring the heated pain in her hands, Riley drew hard on the energy flowing through the stainless steel, harder even than she'd drawn to lift the forklift.

"Come on, babe, we—" Slimy dude laid his hand on Riley's shoulder.

With a shout, she ripped the oven door off its hinges and spun, swinging it around as hard as she could. The motion itself knocked the slimeball off her. The guy behind him yelped and scrambled back, knocking over a third guy.

Riley kept going, hitting guy number two in the head again and leaping over him as he dropped, this time eyes rolled back, body completely limp. With her momentum exhausted, the oven door sagged toward the floor and bumped her legs. Someone wrapped his arms around her from behind, shouting orders to his friends. Riley couldn't get free to swing the door. Panic closed her throat and loosened her grip, but that stupid door was her only weapon. The only thing keeping Quinn safe.

She held on and concentrated on her own strength. She let go with her right hand and jabbed her hugger in the side with her thumb. Despite her lack of leverage, he jerked sideways, his grip loosening. Riley closed her fist around the fabric at the back of his shoulder, bent, and flipped him on top of his unconscious buddy.

"Who's next?" she demanded. Yikes. That hadn't come out quite as warrior-like as she'd intended. Kind of high and squeaky instead.

Gashface now stood sentinel at the end of the hall, as if keeping Riley from getting back to Quinn. But she knew he didn't want to go up against her again. Unlike the others, he had a healthy fear in his eyes. He also, she realized, had the weakest prickle of all of them.

Two were down, one probably for the duration of the fight, the other with enough wind knocked out of him to be no threat for a few minutes, at least. That left three.

Their confident glee had given way to furious determination of the "no girl will beat *me* up" variety. Riley shifted her grip on the oven door handle so she could hold it up by her shoulder, almost like a shield, and pressed her other palm out toward the boys. Power zoomed through her from the metal to her free hand and blew outward in a shockwave. Two of the guys flew backward, one hitting a jutting corner of the wall with a sickening *crack*. The other landed on his back in the middle of the empty floor between the kitchen and living room. His breath whooshed out of him.

The third guy leaped lightly onto the island countertop and crouched, ready to spring on top of her. Riley didn't have time to draw more energy and barely got the oven door up between them when he leapt. His weight bore her to the floor. She cried out at the crushing combination and let go of the handle, scrabbling in her pocket for the remaining smaller, sharper pieces.

He grabbed at her wrists and after a few seconds of tussling, he had the upper hand. He straddled Riley, who lay twisted on the floor on her left hip, with her right wrist held down above her head. She panted and tried not to yell again with the pain stretching her muscles.

"Get…*off*…me!" She didn't stop struggling, even as he laughed and pinned her harder.

"Looks like I won this round. Anson has to let me go first now." He leaned closer to her face. Sour breath made her gag, and she turned toward the floor trying to avoid it. "You're lucky I didn't learn how to suck you dry yet. But just wait. It's coming." He made a slurping, tongue-flipping sound.

"Oh, God, I'm gonna throw up." Riley heaved in his direction. He jerked back but didn't move far enough away. When nothing happened, he immediately pinned her again.

"Help me!" he called over his shoulder. "We need to get her into the room with the other one."

Unseen hands clamped around Riley's ankles, and her pinner swiveled to pick her up by the wrists. She bucked and arched and twisted, but with no metal, she couldn't get the strength to break free. In fact, she didn't even seem to make it hard for them. She'd crashed, weaker after all the power she'd drawn.

They hauled her down the hall and dropped her on the floor in the original room. But instead of locking her in alone with Quinn, who didn't seem to have moved at all, they closed the door behind them. The one who'd pinned Riley flicked on a flashlight and shone it directly at the bed.

Riley's heart stopped when she saw Quinn, so pale and still, her eyes closed, listing sideways under the weight of the steel bar in her lap.

"What's with her?" one of the guys said *sotto voce*, as if not wanting his friends outside to hear what they were doing. And he probably didn't, if these two were here for first dibs.

"Dunno. But she's ripe. Can you feel it?" Excitement lit the guy's voice. The beam of light brightened around Quinn as he moved closer to the bed. "All that power, completely unstable. It'd be easy to take." He inhaled deeply through his nose.

Holy crap, he was insane. Riley got up on her hands and knees, but the other guy kicked her in the side. Pain exploded around her ribcage, and she fell sideways, unable to draw breath. Sam's image flashed in her head, his fury if he saw what they were doing to her, the retribution he'd exact on them. She imagined his gentle hands lifting her, supporting her, and rolled onto her hands and knees.

"What are you doing?" the kicker asked. Riley heard him from a long way away. She had to get up, to stop them somehow, but couldn't move any farther.

"I'm taking it. It's right *there*." Now he sounded like an addict.

Riley blinked hard. Her vision focused on his feet right in front of her, his shins up against the bed. She craned her neck and saw him leaning, reaching slowly for Quinn. She just had to grab his legs. Tackle him, pull him down. Away from Quinn.

Riley's arms shook, barely keeping her off the carpet, and lifting even one hand from the floor seemed beyond her capability. *Okay, then, reach for the bed.* Talk about addiction. If she could touch the metal, she should be able to fill her lungs and gain enough strength to keep fighting.

Guy number two stepped closer to the bed and leaned toward his friend. But before he even opened his mouth, Quinn exploded into motion, swinging the metal pipe in a quick backhand to the crazy guy's head, and even quicker forehand to the other one. *Boom. Boom.* They were down.

The blaze of red pain along Riley's side subsided, her lungs expanded, and blessed air filled them. "Quinn," she croaked.

Quinn shoved herself off the bed, but as soon as her feet hit the floor she overbalanced and landed next to Riley. "Crap. That didn't work."

"Come on." Riley struggled to her knees and reached for Quinn, who waved her off.

"I'm okay. Just overestimated. I can do it." And she pulled herself up with a lot less grunting and moaning than Riley.

"I was afraid they'd hurt you before." She braced her hands on her knees, panting.

"They were too panicked about losing you." Quinn held out the pipe.

Riley took it gratefully, closing her eyes with relief and joy at the immediate infusion. "How did you do that?" She mimicked Quinn's one-two swings with the pipe.

"The strength you gave me. I was able to hold on to it, save it for the right moment."

"Yeah, but…"

Quinn smiled. "I wasn't always an old lady, Riley."

She felt herself blush and hoped the flashlight, now on the bed, was dim enough to hide it. "That's not what I meant. I thought you were dead."

"Sorry. Had to lull them. I wasn't going to be flying around the room or anything. Shot my wad on that one move, too." She lurched toward the door. "There are others out there, right? I heard the commotion."

"Yeah, four of them. They're probably recovered by now." Riley let Quinn go out the door before her, but squeezed past her in the hall to take the lead. She had more versatility with the pipe, and she was not letting those assholes take *anything*. Not magically, not physically.

The hallway was clear, and no bodies—prone or standing— were visible. Riley dashed down into the main room.

And came face to face with Anson and his three Numina bosses.

CHAPTER NINETEEN

In all our centuries of existence, we have dealt internally with factions who did not fall in line with Numina's greater purpose and intent. The time has come, we fear, when internal sanction will no longer suffice. As such, we must reach out to our counterparts to seek mutually beneficial outcomes.

*—**Numina**, board of directors e-mail*

As soon as Sam stepped off the elevator, he felt them.

All of them.

"Get Nick and John up here," he ordered. "Now."

Marley dialed and put the phone to her ear. "What is it?"

Sam looked from one end of the corridor to the other. The elevator was in the middle of one long hall. Unlike downstairs, which had both interior and exterior apartments built in the building's square layout, this floor only had the one hallway. Two apartment entries were on either side, with a fire door directly across from the elevator. A set of stairs led down to the next level, where the main fire stairs were in the four corners of the building.

"Sam?" Marley had finished telling Nick to come up to the

top floor and moved to stand in front of him, looking worried. "What is it?" she repeated.

"That way." He strode down the hall to the right. Stupid, he knew, but he couldn't wait for the others. Something was happening. "A whole mess of them. I don't know. Five? More? Some of the signatures are hard to read. Almost like they're merging and splitting. But Quinn and Riley are definitely in there. They're bright. Hot." He stopped before anything else came out of his mouth. Like how he could tell Quinn's because of the poison slicked through her blue and green light, and Riley's had the smell of honeysuckle, which was so stupid because he couldn't *smell* anything. But they were very different from the Numina morons.

Sam thought he saw them differently from how Riley did. She felt their location, the prickle a physical expression of something mental. For Sam, it was more of a shimmer, like the mirage hovering above hot pavement in the summer. So light he could barely detect it, and that was why he wasn't sure how many.

He faced the apartment door and prepared to kick it in.

"No!" Marley jumped forward and blocked his leg. "You have to wait for Nick and John!"

"There's no time!" Sam pointed back to the elevator. "Go wait for them. Show them which apartment. I have to go in there *now*. Don't argue, Marley, please. I have no choice."

Sam couldn't explain how he knew this. When he'd made love with Riley, that brilliant flash of light, that sense of sinking into her, joining with her…it hadn't been metaphorical. Now that he was near her again, he understood. His illness hadn't been because he wasn't close enough to the ocean. It was because he wasn't close enough to *her*. His body knew her, knew she was near, and thirsted for what she could give him.

Which terrified him almost as much as her abduction, and on a whole different level.

The nausea, headache, and raking pain faded as he moved closer to the bodies he sensed, though the movement of the power inside him sped up. It was eager and tired of being pent up.

Well, he was about to give it something to do.

As soon as Marley was far enough away, Sam lifted his foot again and slammed it against the door, following it into the bland apartment. He held his fists loose and ready, and balanced on the balls of his feet as he swiftly took in what he was up against.

A bunch of guys in their young twenties gaped at him from their sullen group in the kitchen area. One bled from cuts on his cheek. He and some others had nasty facial bruises, too. A couple looked dazed, one kept an arm wrapped around his waist, and one stood as if he had unbearable back pain.

Flanking them were three older, obvious father figures, if not actual fathers of some of the guys. Sam recognized Danner, the financial wizard who'd swindled half his clients yet still managed to avoid jail despite being partly responsible for the economy's collapse. Another was a man named Lilling, a former senator who'd stepped down after pictures of him with prostitutes were spread around the Internet, time-stamped and confirmed to have been taken while his wife was in the hospital recovering from the stillbirth of their third child. Sam didn't recognize the third guy but had no doubt he was as much of a scumbag as the first two.

"What are you doing?" Danner demanded. They'd shifted to face Sam, puffing themselves up with indignant self-importance but presenting no immediate physical threat.

What chilled Sam's blood, the reason he'd known it was so urgent to get in here, was the rest of the scene.

Riley lay on the floor, blood trickling from her temple. She was limp, apparently unconscious—please, just unconscious. Anson ignored Sam as he shoved a scuffed, painted square metal tube under Quinn's chin and pinned her to the wall with it. Quinn got her hands up behind it but clearly didn't have the strength, or any goddess-based ability, to budge it from her neck. Still, her expression was unfazed, almost bored.

Anson was only a couple of inches taller than Quinn. He leaned in close to her face and hissed, "It's mine. All of that awful, dark, angry power churning inside you? It was mine first, and it's mine now, and you'll give it to me. Or I'll kill her." He gave a head jerk toward Riley. "And Sammy gets to watch. If we're lucky, your precious protector will join him. Now *that* would be a dream come true. Draining you, painfully and slowly, while he's impotent."

Quinn's eyes darted to Sam, and now she showed real fear. She shook her head at him, and Sam knew she meant for him to leave. Not to give Anson incentive or another victim. But she knew better.

Sam readied to engage his old college buddy, but he'd been too quick to dismiss the suits.

"Don't move." Lilling raised a semiautomatic pistol, aimed at Sam's heart. Sam lifted his hands to his sides, willing to stall and give Nick and John time to arrive. Even the odds. Or reverse them.

His heart raced anxiously as he eyed Riley. She hadn't moved at all. He couldn't even tell if she was breathing. His throat tightened, cutting off his air. *Think, you moron.* Nick's voice as his subconscious was back. *You're not normal anymore.*

Sam swallowed and closed his eyes, but his mind darted around in panic. He couldn't settle on anything, couldn't calm himself enough to tap the ability. Moments ago he'd been alight with awareness, but now he couldn't separate anything.

Deep breath. Pull it inward. Ignore everyone here except yourself. Feel what's inside you.

That was Riley's voice, not Nick's. Sam followed the words instinctively and imagined a dome around him, protecting him from outside interference. Another deep breath, and the anxiety faded. There was a *snap* of energy, and the power in Sam seemed to identify the energy in Quinn. He could "see" it, and gasped at the darkness dominating it. Three distinct swirls intertwined but didn't combine. One silvery-green, cool and clear, like sheets of rain. That had to be Tanda's, and to Sam's relief, it didn't seem damaged by the poison around it. A faint, barely there strand would be Beth's. It was pure grief, fading even as he examined it. The last was exactly like the smudge that was Marley, only this was live, and demanding. It had nowhere to go and battered at Quinn like a crazed, caged animal.

Sam shifted his focus to Riley and had to lock his knees when her power sparked to life in his awareness. He recognized it immediately, though he'd only glimpsed it before. It was more solid than the others, with less fluidity and swirl. The shine was metallic, hard, and contained every color in the universe.

All Sam cared about was that it was there. She was alive.

He opened his eyes, wondering what had happened while his eyes were closed. No one had moved, and he realized it had been only seconds, not the long minutes it had seemed.

Anson didn't back off Quinn but gave orders despite his bosses standing right there.

"Danner, get her." He indicated Riley again. Instead of the older Danner, though, one of the young guys—the one with the scratched cheek—separated from his friends and walked warily to Riley. "Take her back in the other room. Strip her down. I don't want to risk leaving a single sliver of metal on her."

Sam growled and shifted forward, but Lilling went, "Ah-ah!" and cocked the pistol. Sam's jaw clenched until it ached, and he wanted to flatten them all. But even if he had enough power for that, which he wasn't sure he did, he definitely wouldn't have the control to avoid hitting Riley and Quinn with it, too.

"Tie her up. Then you guys—" Anson glared over his shoulder. Sam felt a spike of alarm at the brightness of Anson's eyes. They'd been dimmer than that earlier tonight. More normal. Was he leeching Quinn right now? *How?* Sam closed his eyes again and couldn't detect any flow of power between Anson and Quinn. Maybe it was a trick of the light.

"The rest of you, go with him. Keep her quiet until I get there. You can handle that when she's unconscious, can't you?"

Anson's scathing tone cut through Sam's fear. The implication was that they couldn't handle Riley when she was awake. Sam held back a smirk of pride. She must be responsible for all of their injuries.

That's not a good thing. The smirk dropped. She was helpless now, and they'd want revenge. They were going to do their worst if Sam didn't stop them.

Anson's next words froze his blood. "If she wakes up, let her know she's next."

Sam didn't move, but his expression must have changed because Lilling cleared his throat and shifted his body to block Sam from the group gathering Riley up and carrying her down the hallway.

Godammit, he couldn't let them do this. Impotent fury warred with the knowledge that he couldn't help her with a bullet in his chest, either. He braced himself to act, to lash out at Lilling and his gun in three…two…

But then, right in front of him, Anson tipped his head back and wrapped his hand around Quinn's throat. The sudden surge of energy raised all the hairs on Sam's body. Anson was doing the impossible. Somehow, some connection between them made him capable of taking power back from Quinn. Sam wanted the poison out of her, too, but not like that. And Anson wouldn't stop there. He'd leech whatever natural ability Quinn had left, leaving her empty. Maybe killing her. Finishing the job the transfers had started.

And then he'd go for Riley.

Sam leaned forward scant inches. A sharp report echoed around the room, and he jerked back a few steps. He stared at

Lilling, then at the bullet hole in the wall to his right. His reaction had been instinctive, but he couldn't move fast enough to avoid a bullet. Not even when enhanced with residual power.

"Don't. Move." Lilling re-aimed at Sam's chest. "Next time will be fatal."

Fuck! Nick, where the hell are you?

Sam had no other options. This time, he didn't bother closing his eyes. He gathered all the power inside him and fired a spear of it across the room. It sliced between Anson and Quinn, knocking the leech back. Everyone else froze at the motion. Gasping and choking, Anson bent with his hands at his neck. Sam closed his fist, imagining the energy closing around Anson, forcing itself down his throat. *You want it? Eat it!*

Lilling's attention was off Sam for a few seconds in the ruckus. Long enough. In two big strides, Sam gripped Lilling's wrist and shoved upward, twisting the gun out of his hand by the barrel. Thank God for protector training. He ejected the clip and the round in the chamber, stripped the weapon, and tossed the pieces in different directions.

He never stopped moving. All he could think about was getting to Riley. Danner Senior, apparently wiser than the others when it came to self-preservation, didn't get in his way.

"Son of a *bitch*!"

Nick had arrived. Finally.

Sam didn't look back. Nick and John knew what they were doing. They'd take care of Quinn. "I'm coming, Riley!" he bellowed, wanting her to hold on, to fight. But it was a tactical error because at his shout the hall filled with Anson's minions. They weren't any better at fighting than their bosses—fathers?—in the outer room, but they were far better at getting in the way.

Sam punched, jabbed, dodged, but each Numina loser he took down blocked his path, tripped him up. He hauled some behind him and plowed through the melee. If he'd had any power left, he could have gotten through much more easily, but the little bit still glowing in him wouldn't obey him.

His last opponent stood in front of the door to the room where Riley was, a knife in his right hand. Sam lurched to a stop, eyes flicking from the blade to the guy's arm across the doorway to the dark room beyond. He strained for any sound and thought he heard a sob.

"If you hurt her," Sam growled.

"Yeah, you can't do anything about it." The guy handled the knife well, unlike most thugs. Sam might have a foot on him in height, greater reach, and superior strength, but none of that would stop him from being gutted if the guy knew what he was doing.

"What do you think you're getting out of all this?" Sam asked. "You got daddy issues you're trying to resolve? You think if you help him get back on top, he'll be proud of you or something?"

Knife Boy sneered. "Don't bother with the amateur psychology crap. My father has nothing to do with this. He died a long time ago. All I'm in this for is power. They have it, I want it. So I'll take it. That's the way it's been for thousands of years."

Sam nodded. "Sure. I get it. Much easier to steal something from someone else than to work hard to achieve your own goals. Lazier, but easier."

"If you say so."

"So how are you going to steal it? Anson tell you the secret yet?"

He didn't answer, but the sudden lack of expression told Sam that Anson hadn't let them in on anything. He'd probably strung them all along with promises he couldn't—or simply wouldn't—fulfill.

"You are one dumb fuck," Sam said amiably. He relaxed his stance and grinned as if they shared a joke. The kid's face darkened, and his hand tightened on the knife. Sam eased onto the balls of his feet and watched the kid's eyes, because they'd telegraph his movement.

And then those eyes rolled up into the guy's head, and he slumped to the floor. Riley stood behind him, her hand still raised where she'd done…*something* to the kid. Her lower lip was split, and a three-inch bruise bloomed above her left eye. Her chest showed scratches where the bastards had torn at her shirt.

"You were taking too long," she said. "I got bored."

Sam engulfed her, unable to get her close enough even though his arms could have wrapped around her twice. "You scared me," he murmured against her hair. His turmoil eased further with each moment of contact. Craving replaced it, a need to bury himself in her—physically, emotionally, forever. The terror he'd felt outside the apartment spiked for a second and then slid away, no match for the richer, stronger emotion that welled up after it.

"Are you okay?" he managed to ask.

She pulled out of the embrace and gave a half-hearted nod. "Okay enough."

Sam pulled himself together and concentrated on the here and now. "What the hell did you do to him, the Vulcan nerve pinch?"

That got a smile out of her, though it immediately became a frown when she spotted the crowd on the floor. A couple of the boys were trying to extricate themselves.

"Something like that, I guess. I just applied energy to a particular spot and willed him unconscious."

Sam stared at her. "You are incredible." She didn't look at him, and he was afraid she read the wrong thing in his voice. "Seriously, Riley. Look at me." He pinched her chin and tilted it until she had to look at him. "I'm sorry I didn't get there sooner. But you are amazing."

It didn't help. Darkness clouded her eyes. Guilt, maybe, or an echo of his earlier fear.

A shout came from the front room. Sam tried to hold Riley back, but she shook him off. Whatever had knocked her out before didn't seem to be affecting her now. She leaped across the pile of

Numina kids—landing on some of them as she went—and dashed down the hall. Sam followed but froze when he reached her side at the end of the hall.

The room was almost completely empty. The three Numina men and the protégées who hadn't been in the hall were gone, and so was John, if he'd ever arrived after Nick did. Marley crouched next to where Nick was on one knee, supporting her sister. Quinn opened her eyes, and Sam went icy cold at how pale they'd become. She'd been leeched—not completely, but anything was too much.

"God, no."

Nick looked up. "Anson. The shit got away."

"*No*," Sam repeated, louder. He whirled toward the front door, hands in fists, fury pulsing in every muscle. As long as Anson was out there, free, he could do this. Not just to Quinn, with whom he had a unique connection, but now that he'd gotten some power back, he could do this to anyone. To Riley.

Nick's voice stopped him. "Sam. It's too late. And we have to take care of Quinn."

Sam hauled back on his rage, his driving need to chase down the enemy and stop him for good. "What do we do?"

"I don't know." Nick's voice shook. "I've never seen her so weak."

"Water," Quinn croaked.

Marley jumped up. "I've got it."

Riley limped over to them. "I think I can help." She knelt to put her hand on Quinn's and raised her eyebrows in question. Quinn nodded and closed her eyes.

Sam couldn't tell what happened, but a few moments later, he caught Riley as she swayed back. Quinn sat up.

"That's better." She sounded a little stronger. "Thank you, Riley, and I'm sorry."

"Don't be stupid." Riley tried to stand, but Sam held her down. "Give yourself a minute."

Cupboard doors banged in the kitchen several feet away. "There's nothing here!" Marley cried.

"In my pack." Nick indicated his bag on the floor inside the door. "There's a flask in there. Empty." He helped Quinn sit up and, when she shifted to stand, locked his hand around her wrist to gently pull her upright. "What do you think?"

She nodded. "I can get to the car."

"Downstairs. I'll bring the car to you."

"No time." She took the flask Marley handed her and drank deeply, nodding her thanks. "We have to get out of here before John comes back with the cops."

Sam and Riley stood. He kept his arm around her as they all moved toward the door. "That's where he went?"

"He called the cops from the elevator when Marley told us what was going on," Nick explained. "If we're lucky, they intercepted the Numina fuckers on their way out. They hauled ass when John and I came in here. We'll deal with all of that later." He lifted Quinn into his arms. "This is faster," he bit out to cut off her attempt to argue. Marley grabbed Nick's bag and followed them out the door, Sam and Riley taking up the rear.

"Where are we going to go?" Riley asked once they were in the elevator. She pressed the button for the lobby while Sam positioned himself in front of the doors. "Portland," Quinn said without lifting her head from Nick's shoulder. "Tanda's next." She coughed and closed her eyes.

Sam checked behind him in the reflection on the elevator's highly polished doors. Nick stared at the numbers flashing above, as if willing them to move faster. Sam thought he might shatter if he loosened up even a fraction. Marley had moved close to her sister and kept making reassuring touches to her hair, her shoulder, her hand. Quinn rested her head on Nick's shoulder and smiled at Marley.

Still without looking, Sam reached over and threaded his

fingers through Riley's. He shouldn't give in to the clawing need. Shouldn't take them closer to something that could devastate them both in the end. But the comfort and stability that came with touching her was worth it. For now.

No matter what happened next, he'd do everything in his power to make it all right.

For everyone.

CHAPTER TWENTY

Failure is never defeat, but simply a reminder to see alternate paths to your destination. Sometimes, failure actually indicates that you are on the wrong path altogether. Recognition of this can lead to enlightenment, and even peace.

— Millinger.com

Rain clattered against the apartment window. Normally a comforting sound, today it grated on Sam's nerves. He shifted on the hard wooden chair and sighed before plugging another database into the browser. His finger came down harder on the "enter" button than he'd intended.

"Nothing yet, huh?" Riley dug her thumbs and fingers into Sam's shoulders.

"No sign of him." He closed his eyes and rubbed his forehead. She was trying to soothe him, to help ease his tension, but need seeped into him with every stroke of her hands. He'd tried everything he knew to track Anson, to no avail. "Nick call?"

"Not yet."

"Fuck." He scoured both hands over his face and left them there, for a few seconds not fighting the comfort and pleasure she gave him. Not giving over to the guilt that permeated everything. Riley felt him give in and sighed, digging deeper, leaning into him so her body pressed against his. And Sam let her, for far longer than he should have.

Every time he closed his eyes, his senses ignited—with the power residue inside him, making itself at home instead of making him sick. With Riley's power, a beauty that made him ache with longing and more. And with the awful mess of Quinn, asleep in Tanda's guest room, where she'd been for most of the last three days.

Tanda's elegant living room told the tale of those days. The cushions of the plum-colored love seat and plush chairs were all askew, half of them covered with old papers and books. The cherry wood coffee table was barely visible under dirty dishes and their pizza box left over from lunch. More books and papers littered the card table where Sam worked, surrounding the laptop that now beeped in annoyance when he tried to enter information into the database search box. The table was set up next to the wide windows and sliding doors that opened to her concrete balcony, which was now saturated with the rain that hadn't stopped since they arrived.

With rain, Tanda's source, the conditions for transferring her power back to her couldn't be more perfect.

Tanda had taken them in without question, and without caring that they couldn't make her whole again. Yet, Quinn had said. Many times. Except the more time that passed, the more it looked like "yet" meant "never."

John turning the Numina gang over to the police had been a bold, confusing move. The police had held everyone except Danner and Lilling, experts at self-preservation. They'd thrown the kids under the bus and disappeared. John's story and the condition of the apartment had meshed, so they'd held the kids while they tried to figure out what had happened. But since Riley and Quinn hadn't stayed, the stall tactic expired about a day and a half ago.

Quinn hadn't been fully leeched. In fact, Anson hadn't taken much at all—Sam and Riley had both confirmed that. But it was enough to leave Quinn too weak to initiate the transfer. Marley had spent the previous three days caring for her sister, and Riley infused Quinn with strength several times a day. Otherwise, Sam was afraid she'd have died under the strain…and taken Nick with her. Sam had never seen the guy like this. He'd always been one to hold everything inside, to keep his most personal emotions locked in a lead box. Now, Sam wasn't sure at any given moment if Nick would snap at them, blow up, or burst into tears.

Okay, probably not the tears.

But the worst part was Anson. Sam had heeded Nick's plea not to go after him, and it turned out they needed the asshole anyway. The power he'd taken had included Quinn's and Marley's and Tanda's in one entangled mass. Even though he hadn't gotten it all, Quinn wouldn't be able to do a clean transfer until it was all restored. And they couldn't find him. He'd gone completely off the grid. The Society had their entire security team looking for him, too, and John had shuffled protectors to the closest and most vulnerable goddesses in case Anson went straight for a new source.

Riley stayed by Sam's side as she'd promised she would, her very presence maintaining his equilibrium, even without much physical contact. But the limbo applied to them, too. His feelings for Riley had become relentless. Everything he'd worried about when he first met her, first started to fall for her, had been rendered insignificant. His real feelings entwined with his energy need until he clung to control with his fingertips. Every night he lay on the floor in the living room, staring at the ceiling, dying to go into the guest room she shared with the other women and lie with her, propriety be damned. But he didn't want to hurt her, and there were so many ways he could.

"Sam, take a break." Her soft hands pried his gently off his face, and she sat in the folding chair next to the table. "You haven't slept in days."

"No one has." He pulled his hands away and blinked hard, staring at the computer screen. With a few keystrokes, he set the site back to the initial entry and got it working. *Searching...* flashed on the monitor. "It's all right. I just need more coffee."

"We're out. Tanda went to get some—and groceries—so we can have a real meal. Marley went with her." Riley frowned at Sam. "I talked to Quinn about the transfer this morning."

"Yeah?" The search results filled the screen. Sam skimmed over them. *Here's a promising one.* A credit card charge in California. He highlighted, copied, and pasted the data into another search engine.

"Giving Tanda back her ability isn't going to be enough," Riley said.

"Yeah, I know... Crap." Dead end. "I think Anson might have been in Sacramento yesterday, but I can't find anything to back it up."

"Beth's power is almost gone. So she thinks that won't be a problem."

"Right," Sam agreed. "And whatever tiny bit is left can stay in me until it fades naturally, like it has since she died."

"But Marley's power can't stay in Quinn. It's strangling her."

He pulled up a folder of bookmarks to see what resources he hadn't tried yet. Medical care, but Anson hadn't been hurt in the confrontation. Though... Sam thought about how sick Quinn was. There was a slim possibility the power Anson stole was making him sick, too. He shrugged and clicked a bookmark for a site that he knew was completely illegal.

"Sam!"

He jumped a little at her near shout and turned his attention away from the computer. "What?"

"I don't want you to do it." Her hazel eyes were as dark as he'd ever seen them, tired and filled with worry. And something else that set his heart pounding.

"Do what?"

"Take Marley's power. It can't go anywhere, and it's poison. That's the word *you* used."

Sam stretched his arms over his head and winced as his back cracked. "We don't know how it will affect me."

"We know how it's affecting Quinn. Why would you be any different?"

"I can't leave—" He stopped. He didn't want to talk about this. He *had* to take that power from Quinn. He was the only one who could. There were no other options. No point in debating it.

That was the problem. He knew it might leave him completely debilitated. He was willing to accept that, to make that choice. The uncertainty of what would happen kept him from telling Riley how he felt. The last thing he wanted was for her to think she had some obligation to keep taking care of him afterward, even when he had nothing to give her.

"I know, Sam." She put her hand over his, her voice soft and hurt. "But you can't keep it. Transfer it to me."

"What? No!" He lurched to his feet and moved away a couple of paces. "What's the difference between leaving it in Quinn or putting it in you?" Wow, that hadn't come out right. "I won't do that to you, Riley. I won't deliberately do something to hurt you." He said it significantly, not looking away from her eyes, hoping she understood.

"But—"

The apartment door slammed open. Riley jumped up and Sam spun, half expecting a battered Marley or Tanda to fall through.

Never in a million years would he have expected Anson.

He looked horrible, like patient zero in an epidemic movie. His face was pasty, with shadows around his eyes so dark they were almost black, the eyelids red, the blue glow of his eyes almost visible turmoil. His lips were cracked and dry, his clothes rumpled and stained, his hair standing on end—and, Sam was pretty sure, missing tufts.

"Sam," he croaked. "I'm sorry."

And then he passed out on the carpet.

Nick appeared in the doorway. "Where the hell did he come from?"

"I don't know." Sam leaped the two steps up to the foyer area and stood next to Nick, looking down at Anson. "What a mess."

"This had better not be another fucking ambush." Nick checked the hall, then closed and locked all six locks. "Where are Tanda and Marley?"

"Store," Riley said. She'd stayed right where she was, on the far side of the room. Her expression bore no sympathy for Anson. "He's sick like Quinn."

"What?" Sam focused to view his energy, and sure enough, the power he'd taken looked like Quinn's…with Tanda's silvery tendrils gliding around the furious, thrashing power that had been Marley's. "Good," he stated with grim satisfaction. "Serves him right."

"Maybe." Riley took a few steps closer. "But he's here. We can take it back. Complete the transfers, so Quinn can get better."

"Yes." Sam suddenly felt lighter than he had for days. Weeks, even. "Nick—"

"I'll get her. Call Tanda," he ordered Riley, but she already had her phone out.

Sam bent to slap Anson on the face. "Wake up."

It took a few more slaps, but he blinked awake. When he saw Sam looming over him, he lunged upward, clutching his flannel shirt in both hands. "I'm sorry. I know you won't believe me, and I know you'll think it's because it's killing me, but I am sorry. I promise, if you help get this out of me, you'll never see me again."

"Don't worry. We're way ahead of you."

In a short time, Sam had Anson strapped down on a cot next to Quinn's bed. They weren't taking any chances. Quinn lay on her side, a hungry look on her hollowed face as she watched them get everything ready. Riley stood behind her, one hand on a tall brass lamp, the other on Quinn's shoulder, feeding her strength again.

"All right. What do you need?" Nick asked Quinn.

"Nothing. This part I can do myself." But she didn't reach for Anson. "Why didn't you take more?" she asked him.

His mouth pressed into a line. Sam assumed the answer would piss them all off.

"I couldn't. I mean, I *could*. I always wondered if I could get it from you, even though I couldn't get it from anyone else, because I'd had it last. I could have taken it all. I just…knew that was a very bad idea."

"But instead of sending it back, you took off like a coward," Sam accused.

Anson nodded. "That's about it, yeah."

Sam rocked on his heels, unable to think of anything else to say.

Quinn set her hand in the center of Anson's chest. Neither one moved. There was no surge like Sam felt in the Numina apartment, no crackle of electricity in the air. And no evidence, thank God, of pain or sickness. After a moment, Quinn rolled up to sit, then stand.

"Where's Tanda?" Her voice was strained, but her body straight, her manner calm and determined.

"She should be here any minute," said Riley. "She and Marley were already on their way back." She'd barely finished speaking when they heard the front door locks snapping open. Those who weren't cot-bound moved to the living room, and Tanda burst in, super-pale eyes bright and face flushed.

"I'm ready," she said breathlessly. She handed a paper bag to Marley, who'd come in quietly behind her. Marley took it and slipped into the kitchen while Tanda met the rest of them in the sitting area.

"We don't have time to set everything up right," Nick said. "We're doing this the down-and-dirty way." He dragged the side chair closer to the sofa while Sam and Riley lifted the coffee table and moved it across the room. At Nick and Quinn's direction, Tanda lay on the couch. After Quinn healed her damaged vessel, eliciting the same reaction Jennifer and Chloe had both had, Sam settled into the chair next to her, his stomach churning.

Relax. You'll fuck it all up if you're not relaxed. This had to work. It was so close to being over. But what came after? He tipped his head back, and Riley, standing behind him, smiled encouragingly while she brushed his hair off his forehead.

"We'll talk," she said. "After."

The tender promise in her eyes, deepened by conviction, gave him hope. He nodded at Quinn, who stood next to him and took his hand. She closed her eyes, and Sam tried not to tense.

The surge came so fast and hard he didn't have time to react. Pure, silvery energy gushed into him as if being chased. Quinn yanked her hand back with a gasp as Sam flinched away from the burning touch of the rest of the power. Marley's power.

"Now!" she yelled, and Sam grabbed onto Tanda. There was no ecstatic rush, no clawing pain, just a smooth glide of power into the other goddess.

"Quinn!" Nick shouted.

Sam turned back in time to see Nick catch his collapsing fiancée. She shuddered with suppressed convulsions.

"What the hell?" Nick's voice was high with panic. "What do I do?"

Sam lurched out of the chair and crouched over Quinn. "Give it to me, Quinn." He used the soothing, implacable voice of her old assistant, the voice he'd used to get her to rest, to stall clients who'd take everything she could give and more. "I can handle it."

Liar.

He ignored the voice in his head that was now strictly his own, and captured Quinn's hand in both of his. He reached for the power but had no ability to take it. Quinn had to give it to him.

"I won't do that to you," Quinn groaned, her jaw clenched so tight they could barely understand the words. She tried to pull her hand away, but Sam held on.

"You have to. You'll die." His voice broke. An echo of the sound made him look up, and his gaze locked with Riley's. The longing and despair there took his breath away, but he didn't know how to fix it. "Riley," he whispered.

She shook her head and backed away. He didn't know if she was withdrawing or giving him permission, but he had no time to weigh his options. He bent back over his former boss, his first love, his friend.

Kind of ironic that he was the only one who could save her.

"Quinn." He had to connect with her, convince her, but saying her name over and over wasn't going to do it. "It's my turn. You know I've been wandering. Displaced. This is what I need. It's my purpose. Don't take that from me."

She actually laughed and opened her eyes with a wince. "You are so full of shit."

"No, he's not." Marley appeared and sat cross-legged next to her sister, taking her free hand. "I'm so sorry, Quinn," she whispered. "All of this is my fault."

"No, it's his." They all turned at Tanda's hard tone.

She stood behind the sofa, staring at Anson, who had managed to get free of the cot and had obviously planned to sneak out. He was only a few feet from the door. Sam didn't understand why he didn't keep going, and then realized why Tanda stood so awkwardly. She held a nine-millimeter in a ready stance, the barrel aimed halfway between the floor and Anson.

"What's she doing with a gun?" Riley asked in a low voice.

"She's a PI," Nick responded, watching Tanda closely. "Which is why she won't shoot him."

"You don't want her to shoot him?" Sam was surprised.

Nick shrugged one shoulder. "I don't care about him. I don't think she needs the consequences, after everything that's happened."

Tanda ignored all of them, her eyes never leaving their enemy. "You took everything from me. From her." She jerked her head sideways. Sam didn't know if she meant Marley or Quinn.

Riley moved closer to Sam, her eyes on Anson. "Look at him. He's dying."

Outwardly, Anson looked no better than when he arrived. He tried to stand straight, but his body shook with the effort. His face was paler than the moon, and his eyes were no longer the color of faded denim, but the pale blue of an early-morning sky. The yellow that tinged the edges wasn't sunshine, but sickness. Anson's own ambition turning on him.

"Really look," Riley whispered, and Sam looked deeper. Anson still had the residue of stolen power, but now it was black and oily. All Marley's, poisoned by the damage Anson had done years ago, by its lost connection to its original vessel. It ate at Anson's soul. He *was* going to die, and it wouldn't be the merciful death of Tanda's bullet.

"Let him go," Sam said. "Riley's right. It's more punishment to turn him loose than hold him."

Tanda's hands tightened on her pistol, her finger sliding to the trigger for a second. Then the click of the safety echoed in the tense silence, and she dropped her arms.

Anson turned and left, closing the door gently behind him.

Quinn cried out, her body bowing, her hand twisting out of Sam's. He cursed and bent over her, begging. Nick added his pleas, and Sam was shocked to see tears on the man's face.

"I promise you," Sam murmured in Quinn's ear, bent low so

no one else could hear. "I'll be okay. You don't have to carry this burden anymore. Let it go, Quinn. Don't be selfish."

The hint of humor on the tail of sincerity did the trick. She relaxed and turned her head to meet his eyes. "You have to swear to one more thing." She waited for his nod, then amended, "Two more, actually."

Sam chuckled and gripped her hand more tightly. "Now who's the greedy one?"

"Promise you won't lie about what it does to you. We'll find a way to fix whatever happens, but you have to be honest. Don't try to carry it alone."

Since he'd seen what carrying the burden had done to Quinn, he nodded without hesitation. He wouldn't ever transfer it to someone else, but he'd let others help him deal with it, if they could. Unless it killed him right off the bat. But if that happened, she couldn't hold him to his promise, anyway.

The possibility gave him pause. "I promise. But give me a minute. There's something I need to do."

She nodded. Sam rose, throwing his fear aside, the weight of all of their watchful gazes on him while he took Riley's arm and moved her away.

"There's no time for a long speech," he said softly. "I don't know what this is going to do to me."

She nodded and sniffed, lifting her chin as if to belie the moment of weakness. "I know."

"I don't know what to say to you." His throat tightened and he swallowed, frowning. "Except I'm sorry. I l—" He couldn't say it. He wanted it to be a promise, a comfort, but it might just be pain. "There's so much between us…and the transfers, what they do to me, have confused everything. I don't know what I'll have to off—"

She smiled and pressed her fingers to his mouth. "You don't owe me anything. You've given me so much already. My promise holds, Sam. I'm here for you, no matter what." Her eyes crinkled, the smile going deeper, tempered by sadness and worry. "We'll deal with the rest later."

"I don't deserve you." He had so much more to say, and there might not be a later. There definitely wasn't time now. He slid his hand under her hair, along the side of her neck, and bent to kiss her. She tasted unbearably sweet and soft. Their mouths clung. Hers trembled, and her hand fisted in his shirt. Sam pulled her closer and deepened the kiss but pulled back before the emotion swelling in him could take over. He rested his forehead on hers for a few long seconds and then abruptly backed away, leaving her alone at the side of the room. Pain sliced into his chest, but he forced himself back to Quinn and took her hand.

"I'm ready." Then he remembered. "Oh, what was the other promise?"

Quinn laughed up at him, looking almost happy despite the way her body contorted in pain. "Never mind."

He grinned and shook his head. "Still trying to run my life."

"You seem to be doing okay on your own." She sobered and tightened her hand around his. "Are you sure about this?"

Sam braced himself and nodded once.

"Get ready."

But there was no way he could have gotten ready for this. Pure pain, pure *hell*, invaded his body. His vision went dark, not like unconsciousness or lack of light, but churning, boiling clouds of black. The acidic burning that touched him during the transfer to Tanda filled every cell in his body. Sam thought he screamed, felt the rawness in his throat, but could hear nothing but a roar. How the hell had Quinn endured this? How had the natural ability Marley inherited turned to such awful contamination?

As more and more poured into him, Sam lost the ability to think. He couldn't feel Quinn's hand anymore, had no idea where he was. Who he was. His only existence was pain.

And then everything stopped.

CHAPTER TWENTY-ONE

The idea that when two people are meant to be together, nothing can tear them apart is a fallacy. What we must recognize is that some obstacles are impossible to overcome. This does not devalue feelings but enhances them.

—**Society Annual Meeting,** *Special Session on Relationships*

Riley stood in the doorway to Tanda's guest bedroom, unable to leave Sam and wondering if anything would ever feel okay again.

Her life had changed twice in an unbelievably short time. A week ago, she'd been alone and frightened, certain she was crazy or a freak. Then she'd found a community that denied both possibilities. Somewhere she belonged, could have a life. There'd been hope—despite the bitter truth of her family's history—and a hot guy who liked her. Then it all fell apart. But in trying to hold it together, she'd found something much deeper and more meaningful than belonging and attraction.

Nothing anyone had said in the last few hours could convince her she wasn't about to lose it all again. Sam's screams still echoed in her skull, the most horrible sound she'd ever heard. Helplessness had held her immobile, held them all immobile, during the few seconds, the eternity that Sam had been in more obvious pain than any person could endure. Then it all just…stopped. Sam had gone limp and unresponsive, and still was.

"How is he?" Nick handed her a mug of coffee. Riley took it gratefully, but in the few seconds she tore her eyes from Sam, she saw how haggard Nick looked. Maybe even worse than her.

"No change. Quinn?"

Nick drew in a long breath. "She's okay. I mean, we keep saying that, but I think she's finally telling the truth. Except being physically okay won't matter if this doesn't get better." He motioned to Sam with his own mug, then took a long swallow.

"It's not her fault." Riley meant it, but her voice rasped as if her throat didn't want to give up the words. "What about Tanda?"

"Fine. Just like Jennifer and Chloe. No ill effects. They're pretty much back to normal." Bitterness sharpened his tone, but Riley couldn't blame him.

"What if he doesn't wake up?" she whispered.

Nick didn't answer. He watched Sam lying there unmoving for another moment, then turned and walked away.

Riley went into the bedroom and set her mug on the nightstand. Sam's forehead was a normal temperature, dry and smooth. His chest rose and fell in an even rhythm, and when she pressed her fingers to the inside of his wrist, his pulse tapped steadily beneath them. Quinn had said she needed time to acclimate to her new state, especially with the moon waning to nothing, but she'd coached Riley through checking Sam for injuries. Everything had seemed fine. There was no physical reason for him to be in this…coma.

Riley lifted his hand to her mouth and pressed her lips to his knuckles. What if, in her inexperience, she'd missed something, and his brain was swelling or bleeding? What if his electrical system was all messed up, or he had permanent psychological damage? Worse, what if the power he'd taken in had overwhelmed him, and he was lost forever?

Except Riley couldn't find Marley's power in him. Not a trace of it. And even more, not a trace of anything else. No residue from Tanda or Chloe, or even remnants from Beth. When Sam used his power back in the Numina apartment, he'd reduced it to a nearly unusable level. But Riley had still been able to see the residue, to know where Sam was at any given moment. Now, there was nothing. She could barely detect him at all.

The only thing keeping her from going off the deep end was that his signature was the same as Nick's, the only other fully non-powerful human in the apartment.

"Riley, dinner's ready." Tanda hovered in the doorway. "We're going to have a meeting. John's here."

She sighed. She didn't want to leave Sam, but whatever they decided they were doing next, she would be part of. After everything that had happened, she had to be.

"I'm coming." She stood and laid Sam's arm across his abdomen. Tears pricked behind her eyelids and she blinked them back, suddenly angry. Sam could have told her he loved her, dammit. Instead of laying his guilt on her, apologizing for whatever he thought he'd done wrong. But she could have done the same. Could have put herself out there instead of protecting her heart, a stupid, immature hesitation that might have cost her what little comfort that sharing could have brought her.

She kissed him on the forehead and joined the others in the kitchen. They were already seated around the table, an oak rectangle inlaid with painted ceramic tiles that matched the ivy tiles on the backsplash and the pale green walls. She sat next to Marley and accepted the bowl of pasta Nick handed her.

"How is he?" Quinn asked.

"Same," Riley managed.

"He'll be okay," Tanda tried to assure her, but the words were hollow. Riley nodded anyway. Marley passed a basket of garlic bread to Riley, her eyes lowered. She took it hesitantly, wondering what was wrong but not wanting to ask in front of everyone. Not that it was her place, anyway. Marley had been with Quinn all afternoon, and if she had any problems, she'd tell her sister, not Riley.

"We need to talk about Numina," John said once all the food had been passed. "I had a pow-wow with Jeannine." He ignored Nick's snort of derision. "Her term is almost up, which has made her…reluctant to initiate any real action, even with the possibility that Numina, or Tournado's snot-nosed group of them, anyway, might have infiltrated us."

Riley watched Tanda's hand tighten on her fork, her knuckles going white. Marley kept her head down while she toyed with her pasta, and Riley wasn't sure she was even listening. Quinn carefully didn't look at anyone, but Nick had stopped eating and stared at her.

"Um, what about the president elect?" Riley asked. "What's her take?"

"We kind of don't have one," Tanda said. "But it'll be Quinn."

Quinn dropped her fork. Riley jumped, alarmed, but understood immediately that Quinn had done it on purpose. She stared back at Nick. Riley could almost see the words zipping back and forth between them.

"Aren't you going to tell me I'm too weak?" Quinn asked him.

"Are you?" Nick smirked and glanced at Riley. "She's stuck. She can't use the excuse of being too sick, and then tell me to back off because she's fine."

"I wouldn't tell you to back off. I'd tell you to take his job." Quinn jerked her head at John, who grinned.

"Dinner *and* a show. How lucky are we?" He nudged Tanda, who laughed.

Marley stood and walked out of the room, a swirl of blackness following her that confused Riley. She automatically checked her as she had everyone else over the past several days. There was only Marley's signature emptiness.

The bathroom door closed, and everyone sat awkwardly for a moment before continuing without comment.

"I'll take his job if you take the one you were elected to," Nick shot at Quinn.

"Wait, what?" Riley looked around the table. "You said there was no president elect."

"Quinn refused to run," Tanda told her. "We elected her anyway. Jeannine wouldn't hold a special election or appoint anyone because we were all hoping she'd give in."

"I was off politics," Quinn said.

"Was?" Nick asked, his voice low, his gaze steady.

Quinn sighed. "I guess. It's better timing now. Maybe." She raised an eyebrow at Tanda. "How are you feeling?"

"Fine. Normal. The *real* normal."

"I called Jennifer an hour ago," Nick said. "Still fine."

"And Chloe sent me an e-mail that she's got another date with the new guy." Tanda smiled. "Looks like everything's fine there too. Like we keep telling you."

"Yeah, well," Quinn said wryly, "people—including me—have been saying that for three years without it being true. You can understand my skepticism."

"So there you go," Nick told John. "So what's the plan?"

"We've met with a few of Numina's legitimate leadership. We've proceeded cautiously, not knowing what they were up to, but after all this we need to formalize and expand."

"We need to do research first," Quinn cut in. "I want to know more before we launch a task force." She went quiet suddenly and picked up her fork again. Nick's eyes flicked to the hall, and Riley realized they were thinking about Sam. Their resident research geek.

The distraction the conversation had provided disappeared, and Riley tried to wash down the dry bread lodged in her throat.

John cleared his. "We know the faction going after goddesses has had another setback, with Anson disappearing."

"Do we really know that though?" Riley asked. She wasn't afraid of Anson anymore, not after seeing what he'd become. What the poison had done to him. What it was doing to Sam. She couldn't sit here anymore. As important as all this stuff was, she wasn't. They didn't need her for planning.

"Where are you going?" John asked when she stood without paying attention. She'd probably interrupted someone mid-sentence.

"Sorry. I was going to check on Sam."

"So does that mean you don't want to be part of the task force?" Quinn asked.

Riley flushed. "No. I mean, well, sure. But why would you want me?"

"Well, let's see," Nick said sarcastically. "Why *would* we want a brave, smart, independent goddess who already knows more about Numina than anyone else in the goddess world, and oh, yeah, can *physically detect them*?"

She felt herself go a deeper red. "None of that really means anything. I have no idea what a task force does."

"We're not asking you to lead it," Quinn said, not unkindly. "Just work with us."

"Of course." Riley shoved aside her insecurities and saw the value in what she could bring. "Thank you."

"Planning without me, huh?"

Riley spun at the raspy, tired, but gorgeously deep voice behind her. Sam stood in the kitchen doorway, one hand on his stomach, a sheepish look on his face, and his hair a tousled mess.

"Sam!" Sweet, cathartic relief took Riley's tension and despair so completely she could barely hold herself upright. Her heart thudded with joy.

"You okay, buddy?" Nick rose and took a few steps to stand, feet wide, close enough to Sam to help him if he needed it, but far enough away not to insult him.

"Yeah, actually, I feel surprisingly good." His brows came together, a perplexed expression. "I don't know why. But…it's gone."

"What is?" Quinn turned in her chair but didn't get up. Riley had heard a soft hiss when she moved and knew her recovery was going to be much slower than Sam's had apparently been.

"Everything." Sam waved his hand out and slapped it back to his abdomen. "There's no power left. No residue, no abilities. I'm back the way I was."

Quinn and Nick looked to Riley, and she did a quick check. He was the same awake as he'd been unconscious. "Still no trace," she confirmed. Tanda murmured her agreement.

"H-how?" Quinn reached out a hand, as if having to touch Sam to make sure he was as okay as he claimed.

"I don't know."

"What happened?" Nick ushered Sam over to his chair and made him sit, then gathered the food toward his end of the table. "You hungry?"

"Yeah, starved, actually."

"I'll get you a plate."

Sam watched Nick quizzically as he collected a plate, glass, and flatware, and raised one eyebrow at Quinn, who shrugged. But Riley could have told him why Nick was being so solicitous. He might hold a lot inside, but Nick cared deeply for his friends. He'd been as afraid for Sam as he'd been for Quinn, though he'd probably threaten to shoot Riley to keep her from telling Sam.

She returned to her seat, letting her knee press against Sam's under the table. He squeezed her leg for a second. His hand was warm and possessive, and the impression of it lingered even after he removed it.

"So?" she asked him. "What happened when Quinn sent you Marley's power?"

Sam looked up. "Where is Marley?"

"Down the hall." Quinn frowned, then smoothed her expression. "You were screaming so horribly, when you stopped, I thought it had killed you."

He shook his head. "I have no idea. One minute it was invading me, taking over, and the next it was gone."

"Gone *where?*" Quinn leaned forward. "It can't just disappear. Energy changes or moves; it can't be destroyed."

"I don't know," Sam insisted, "but it's gone. No trace. You know it. You can feel it."

"Well, not right now I can't." Quinn gestured outside. "Moon's off. But Riley and Tanda say you're right, so what the hell?"

Sam shrugged and loaded pasta onto his plate, covering it with a healthy serving of meat sauce. "I'm not complaining." He definitely wasn't acting like a guy who'd just come out of a coma. Maybe he really was going to be okay.

"No." Quinn shook her head. "Let's hope it doesn't come back to haunt us."

They spent the next half hour discussing approaches to the Numina problem. Sam had enthusiastically agreed to join the task force, alongside Riley. When they finished eating and cleaning up, Sam took Riley's hand.

"Would you come outside with me?"

Her heart began pounding the moment he looked at her and only picked up speed as they stepped out onto the balcony and he carefully closed the door behind them. He leaned against the concrete wall, facing her, but crossed his arms and legs. Defensive, closed posture. She tried not to assign reasons for it, but folded her own arms, pretending the breeze was chilly.

"How are you really?" Riley asked him. "I don't mean physically. But with the power all gone?"

Sam studied her, his mouth curling up on one side. "Of course you'd ask me that."

"Well, nobody else did."

"Exactly." He drew in a deep breath and looked out over Portland for a few seconds. "I'm okay. I don't think there's an addiction issue. I'm just…normal."

"Good. But you know that's not what I meant. Do you miss it?" A person didn't have to be addicted to something to become obsessive about it when it was gone.

"Maybe." His brow puckered. "I mostly miss seeing you."

Riley blushed.

"Your power, I mean. All the other stuff…I didn't have it long enough to get acclimated to it. And, yeah, it felt good to have a weapon against Anson when I needed it, but…" His mouth turned down, and he shook his head. "Nah. I don't need that. I have other weapons at my disposal."

"Good," she said again. The lengthening silence shifted toward awkwardness.

Sam sighed. "I have so much to say," he said, "and no idea where to begin."

Riley took a deep breath. "Then let me start." Encouraged by Sam's smile, she decided to just go for it. Lay it all out. Self-protection meant nothing compared to everything that had happened even today.

"I know we've only known each other for a week."

Sam blew out a breath. "Seriously? That's all?" He stared at the wall above Riley's head while he counted. She waited impatiently until he said, "Wow. You're right."

"Can I continue?"

He smiled again, wide enough to show the dimples that sent a zing through her entire body.

"You just made my point," she said. "A psychologist would probably say my feelings are intense because of the intense circumstances, but my mother would say these circumstances meant we showed each other our true selves. And Sam…" She swallowed hard. Okay, this wasn't so easy. What if he didn't feel the same way? Didn't need more than the woman who'd balanced him against power he wasn't supposed to have?

He didn't move, and his eyes never left her face. Their golden brown had deepened, despite the watery evening sunlight that followed the rain. He didn't look wary or dismayed, but anticipatory. Riley's anxiety faded.

"I'm falling in love with you." She tempered it at the last second—it sounded more believable this way than *I love you*. More of an acknowledgment of the extreme circumstances. More realistic considering it might not last in a normal, mundane life.

Except she didn't know what normal and mundane were anymore.

"I don't want you to settle," he said.

Riley's heart stopped racing. It stopped completely at his first words, and even with the qualifier it didn't seem to resume— though it had to or she wouldn't be enduring this tearing pain in her chest. This was the goddess-world version of *it's not you, it's me*.

"Settle for what?" she demanded.

Sam sighed, long and painfully. "I thought when this was all over, when Quinn finished the transfers and she and Nick could focus on themselves, that we could do the same. Get to know each other. See what can happen between us."

"And now you don't want that," she guessed miserably.

"No, I'm saying we can't have that. Numina's splinter group is still out there, still desperate to take goddess power to augment their own. I want to say I can walk away from that and just be with you, but I can't. I could never do that."

Angry, Riley dropped her arms and stepped toward him. "Of course you couldn't. Neither could I, not if I believed I could really help." That sounded like she still didn't believe… "I *can* help. So I can't walk away." She forced herself to face her deepest fear about his feelings. "Do… do you not want me anymore now that we're not connected by the energy? Now that moon lust doesn't drive you, you don't—"

"No!" He lurched off the wall. Since the balcony was only about two feet deep, that put them toe-to-toe, practically face-to-face. "I'm saying the opposite! But I don't know why you'd believe me."

"Believe *what?*" Riley spread her arms. Her heart pounded again, throbbed in her neck and ears, muffling his voice and narrowing her vision. "Stop beating around the bush and tell me what you feel!"

"I love you, dammit!" He shoved his hand through his hair and shook his head at the sky. "I started to fall in love with you, God, I don't know. That first day, when you charged out there and confronted Vern and Sharla."

It seemed a decade ago. Riley's joy at his confession couldn't get past her confusion. "So what's the problem? I don't understand why you're holding back now. Quinn is fine, the power is all transferred, and you're *you*. The guy I started falling for when I saw that video on the Society website."

"That's the problem. You needed help, and I was able to provide it. I brought you to the Society, where—"

"Where I learned my family lied to me my whole life, and your vaunted Society kicked us out. They never bothered to find out why my grandmother and aunt had no power, or to determine if their descendants did. They just forgot about us."

Sam dropped his head. "I know. I'm sorry. I wanted it to be—"

"That's not the point!" she yelled at him. "What I feel for you is not fucking gratitude!"

Movement beyond the glass caught her eye. Nick watched them from the living room. His feet were braced wide, one hand in his pocket, the other holding a beer, but his expression told Riley he'd be through that door like a shot if he thought either one of them needed his protection. She was surprised to realize it didn't matter which one.

She blinked back warm tears, overwhelmed, and nodded at Nick to reassure him they were okay. She turned back to Sam in time to see him give a dismissive, placating hand movement. Nick moved back, out of their view, but Riley would bet he was still watching. She hadn't had friends like that, ever.

"I'm not grateful," she said again in a much lower voice. "I don't care that we don't have a magical connection anymore. I can't prove to you that things wouldn't be different if we went on to live quiet, boring lives together, but it doesn't really matter, does it? We can live exciting, dangerous lives together and be happy. Can't we?"

"Oh, Riley." He finally pulled her into his arms. She laid her head on his chest and hugged him hard, squeezing her eyes closed. He sighed and held her for a few long moments before she leaned back to look up at him.

"What do you want?" she asked.

One side of his mouth quirked. "I want you to be happy."

She shook her head hard, annoyed. "No, what do you want for *you?* The truth."

He sobered and moved back so they could see each other better. "Okay. Full, blunt honesty. No more searching for the words that will work. Just the right ones."

She nodded and held her breath.

"I've fallen in love with someone strong and brave. Someone willing to stick her neck out for people she doesn't really know because she thinks she can help them. She's beautiful and has a rockin' body, and our chemistry is through the roof—with or without energy influence."

Riley's hands tightened on his sleeves, the need to kiss him practically killing her. But he hadn't said what he wanted. So she waited, standing still.

"But what I really love is how she loves me. With so much going on, she was the only one who cared more about my well being than about anyone else. I don't know if she knew I saw it, and I never thanked her."

"Of course you did!"

He pressed a finger to her mouth. She held still again, not wanting him to move it away, and knowing she'd derail everything if she gave in to the impulse to lick it.

"I want you." He shrugged. "That's what it comes down to. The reasons don't matter, and everything around us doesn't touch that truth. The first thought in my head when I woke up tonight was that you weren't there, and I needed you next to me. I want you to be mine, Riley."

She leaned forward until their bodies touched. "I am yours, Sam. I have been since the moment you set that disgusting Pepsi on the table."

He chuckled on his way down to her mouth. Halfway there, the amusement fell away, taking everything but the intensity of their need. His hands molded her body against him, and despite his ridiculous height, they fit together perfectly. Their lips were warm when they met, their tongues gliding into each other's mouths. It was a kiss of promise, of exploration, of hope.

Riley knew that in a few minutes they'd have to go inside and face a million decisions, a hundred challenges that would both test and strengthen their relationship. But that could wait. Right now, all she needed was right here.

EPILOGUE

Marley slipped out of the apartment after everyone had wound down and gone to bed. She'd have done it sooner—right after she left the dinner table—except she didn't want to risk anyone trying to stop her. It was obvious no one knew what to say after she left the table, and she was glad. The responsibility for everything that had happened today—for the last three years, actually—fell completely on her.

None of them seemed to know what had happened to Sam, and she was glad. Because she knew. She'd felt it happen. Hadn't believed it, except it had marked her as surely as the transfers had marked Sam. Tanda and Riley said there was no trace of the power left in him, but they weren't quite right. There was a scar, but Marley suspected only she could see it. If anyone had asked her to describe it, she'd have compared it to surgery to remove something diseased or destructive, like a tumor. It marked him by its absence rather than by a lingering presence.

Null. The word echoed in her head, knocking around until it should have been meaningless. But it was just the opposite. It was the rest of her life.

Quinn and Nick went to bed first, and Marley stayed locked

in the bathroom until Sam and Riley left to get a hotel room. No secret why, though they claimed it was to relieve the burden on Tanda and free up some space. John left with them, heading back to D.C. to prepare for Nick to take over as head of the Protectorate. He'd been gleeful about telling Jeannine that Quinn would accept the Society presidency in a couple of months, when the current term was up.

Marley tried to be happy for her sister and Nick, and for Sam and Riley, but she couldn't feel it. Couldn't feel much of anything, actually. She silently gathered the few things she'd brought with her, snuck through the still apartment, and went out to the street to catch a cab to the airport. She'd go back to her inn first. She missed Maine, longed to be home at least until she could sell it. Luckily, a developer had poked at her a couple of times a year, feeling her out. He'd probably snap it up if she said she was ready.

After that…

A few days ago, she'd obeyed Sam when he told her to stand back. Pointed the way for Nick and John, and stood in the hall crying while she listened to her sister scream and people fight, knowing she'd only be another liability if she went in there. When the Numina men and boys had streamed out of the apartment, not a single one of them had looked at her, never mind considered her a threat.

Well, she was done with that. Done with being helpless. Done with being a victim. Done with struggling to make up to everyone else for a mistake she'd already paid for. Things had changed, and somehow, she'd been given a gift. Or a curse. Probably both.

When Sam had flailed around on that floor, screaming in the depths of hell, Marley had reached to touch him, knowing she couldn't soothe or heal any more than the others could. But the instant her hand brushed his face, everything stopped. The power doing so much damage disappeared. One second it was there, the next it was gone. And not just hers. Beth's power, the little bit remaining, had gone with it.

Quinn said it was impossible, but Marley knew it wasn't. She'd felt it happen.

She'd *caused* it.

Giving Anson power had damaged her vessel, her ability to channel energy through crystals. Maybe the damage would have been barely noticeable if Anson hadn't later leeched her. But when he sucked all the capacity out of her, he'd created something new. He'd carved an emptiness into her that wasn't static, as she'd always thought. It had a purpose. Or at least, she could give it one.

She'd have to research it, but she suspected she'd find no one else had ever been what she now was. A null. A black hole. She could remove power, energy, ability from someone who wasn't supposed to have it.

Goddesses were safe, she was sure of it. She'd been around them nonstop for two years, running the educational and tracking programs. It was only once she touched Sam, struggling against the barbs of her orphaned power, that her ability had gone active. She'd saved him.

And in doing so had saved herself.

ACKNOWLEDGMENTS

The Dew Drop Inn, featured briefly in chapter thirteen, was a real place in North Stonington, Connecticut. I took some artistic license, moving it to suit my heroine's travel route and ignoring the fact that ownership and name had changed. My family often stopped at the Dew Drop on our trips to the beach in Misquamicut every summer, and my mother developed a friendship with Curtis Moussie. These memories are touchstones to the things that were most important in my childhood, and even before I learned that Curtis had passed away and the Dew Drop was demolished, I wanted to pay tribute to them in this book—and by extension, pay tribute to my mother.

Heavy Metal would not be the book it is without Kerri-Leigh Grady, Liz Pelletier, and especially Danielle Poiesz, who somehow drew out of me the story I was trying to tell in the way it really needed to be told. Huge thanks to Liz Pelletier for the amazing cover, and to all the behind the scenes folks along the production line, making sure we come as close to perfection as possible. Finally, thanks to Crystal, Jaime, and Dani—my Entangled publicity team—for their support and hard work in what is, for some of us, the most challenging aspect of being an author.

Megan Hart deserves a massive thanks for taking time out of her own insane schedule to read a draft of this book and provide the cover quote. Smith, Simon, and Bix, thank you for listening to my rants and giddiness and making this journey so much fun, even when it's frustrating. And thank you, Lisa Mondello, for slapping me upside the head with genuine affection whenever I start spiraling.

Every book I write also owes a great deal to my family. Jim, Dakota, and McKenna, thank you so much for your unwavering support and understanding when I'm lost in my fictional worlds or crazy on deadline. Thank you for celebrating every silly little victory with me, for telling everyone with pride that I'm an author, and for helping me live my dream. I love you.

Turn the page for a flashback to

the first book in the Goddesses Rising series

Under the Moon

by

Natalie J. Damschroder

CHAPTER ONE

*Society views goddesses the same way they view psychics—
most people don't believe in us, and since there are only about a
hundred goddesses in the United States, skeptics rarely have
occasion to be proven wrong. Some people have open minds but
still no reason to seek to use a goddess's talents. If you choose a
public career as a goddess, you join in the responsibility for image
maintenance.*
Help us keep public opinion positive.

—The Society for Goddess Education and Defense,
Public Relations Handbook

When Quinn Caldwell's cell phone rang, she assumed one of
her clients needed an appointment or a Society member had a
question about next week's annual meeting. It took her a second
to pull her attention from the paperwork on her desk, another
three to register the name on the screen.

Nick Jarrett.

Her spark of joy at seeing his name quickly changed to
concern. He wouldn't be calling for anything good. Quinn plugged
her ear against the noise from the bar outside her office door, held
her breath, and flipped open the phone. "Nick?"

"Quinn." The rumble of his vintage Charger's engine

harmonized with Nick's voice. "Service isn't good out here so just listen."

She knew it. "What's wrong?"

"We have a problem. I'm coming early. I'll explain when I get there. I won't have a very good cell signal most of the time. I'm at least a day away, so stay close to Sam, and don't…" His voice cut in and out before disappearing altogether.

Quinn's skin prickled. She closed the phone, frowning. Nick never came until at least the week before new moon, when she was most vulnerable. In the fifteen years of their relationship, he'd never come a whole week early.

Something big had to be happening.

Quinn was the only goddess whose power source was the full moon, which meant she was only fully able to use her abilities for the seven days around it. As the month waned, she grew more "normal" until the new-moon period, when she had no ability to tap the power. That was when Nick appeared. Never now.

"Who was that?" Sam's solid, warm hand landed on her shoulder, and he dropped a pile of papers on the desk in front of her. Quinn blinked at the shift from the surreal nature of the phone call to the mundane clutter of her narrow office at the back of Under the Moon, the central-Ohio bar she'd inherited from her father. It was her main business, a connection to the parents who died within months of each other twelve years ago, leaving her without any real family. It also kept her connected to the public between power cycles. The goddesses who made a living with their abilities mostly relied on word of mouth to find clients, and Quinn's bar, centrally located for locals and travelers, had enough people channeling through it to give her customers for both businesses.

"Nobody," she said, still lost in thought. She shook off the fog. "I mean, Nick."

Sam's eyebrows disappeared under his dark, shaggy bangs. He crossed to his smaller but far more organized desk near the office door. His chair squeaked when he dropped into it. "Nick called you?"

"Yeah. He's coming early."

"Great." Sam glowered and mumbled something under his breath. "Why? The moon is barely waning gibbous."

"I don't know. The signal dropped." She worried her lower lip. *Stay close to Sam*. Why? The order was protective—and after all, Nick was her protector, so that was his default mode—but what did she need protection from? She rubbed her right forearm, the phantom ache a reminder of the first time Nick had been assigned to her, that "goddess" wasn't a synonym for "invincible."

Sam sighed. "When is he getting here?"

"I don't know that, either." She rested her head on her hand, her elbow on a pile of folders on her worn oak desktop. The full moon would completely wane by tomorrow, taking most of her power with it, so she'd worked steadily for the last week, using mostly telekinesis and her healing ability to help her clients. She hadn't slept enough to balance the depletion of her normal energy, and her sluggish brain resisted the apprehension buzzing in her now.

"We'll have to wait until he shows up, I guess." She shook off the mental fuzzies and focused on Sam. He watched her, longing mixing with concern in his light brown eyes.

"How long did you sleep?" he asked.

She stifled a yawn. "Seven hours, six minutes."

He shook his head. "That's not enough."

"Gonna have to be. It sounds like we have a full house tonight."

"It's busy for a Tuesday," he acknowledged. Murmurs and laughter mixed with the jukebox music filtering in from the main room. It was still early, too.

"Bets and Katie are both sick, so they probably need us out there." She stood and stretched, closing her eyes briefly and arching with her arms high. He didn't answer. "Sam?" She caught him staring at the stretch of skin bared by her sweatshirt and tugged it over the waistband of her jeans. Heat seeped through her, dragging tingles in its wake. Did he notice her skin flush?

He gave himself a little shake and pulled his gaze away. "Yeah. Yeah, I guess." But he scowled.

Quinn propped her hands on her hips. "What's wrong?"

"Nothing." He sat up and shifted papers on his desk, but she knew it wasn't "nothing."

"Sam."

He sighed. "We need to talk. You've put me off all week, and now we've got Nick…"

Shit. She had hoped Nick coming early would put an end to this debate. She dragged her cotton apron off the back of her chair and busied herself tying it. "I'd better get to work."

But Sam didn't get up. His voice was low and deep when he said, "Why didn't you come to me?"

Her hands stilled, and she avoided his steady gaze by checking for her order pad and pen. "You know why."

"I'm still here." He stood and came around the desk, and she couldn't help but look at him now. He dwarfed her, filling her vision, his scent flooding her senses, feeding the grinding need she'd battled for weeks. She kept her lids shuttered so he couldn't see the inevitable dilation of her pupils and take the reaction the wrong way. Her moon lust knew what Sam could give her, her body giving a Pavlovian response to his nearness.

Tapping her power source had a price. As energy flowed through her, it depleted her resources like exercise depleted an athlete. Instead of needing water and vitamins to balance her body, Quinn needed sex. She'd never understood why, but her body had always been recharged by that primal connection to another human being. She hadn't had that for three months now, and the longer she resisted, the more difficult it got.

So Sam's long legs, ridged stomach, and broad chest all called to her. Quinn's hands flexed, anticipating the silk of his shaggy hair bunched in them. *Only a few minutes*, a voice whispered in her head. *That's all it will take. For balance.* A moment of thought, of remembering the heat between them, was enough to make her crave it again. Her mouth watered as she watched Sam's long-fingered hand track up his chest and around the back of his neck, a move she knew was calculated.

That didn't matter. She took a step toward him, then forced herself to stop. She'd told Sam three months ago that she wouldn't use him anymore and had held fast to the decision no matter how willing he was. It had been six years since she'd first had sex with him, and she'd only recently understood the damage they were doing to each other. Sam didn't believe she could stop, but she *had* fought the moon lust for nearly twelve weeks. Tomorrow would end this full-moon cycle; she'd have it completely under control, and it would get easier next month. It had to. *Yeah, because it's been a cakewalk so far.* But she didn't have to convince herself—she had to convince Sam.

"I've told you. What we're doing isn't fair. You've stopped dating, stopped even looking for—" She hesitated, uncertain how to phrase it.

"I don't need to look for it." His tone was hard with conviction, and Quinn closed her eyes, despairing.

"That's my point," she said. "I'm tying you up, and you deserve better."

"That's a matter of debate, and you don't have to suffer because of it."

Her laugh didn't need to be forced. "Not having sex isn't suffering."

"For you it is."

He'd closed the distance between them, and though Quinn knew she didn't move, her body seemed to surge toward him in agreement. She breathed in the remains of the aftershave he'd used this morning and wavered. He smelled so *good*.

A shout came from the other side of the paneled door, jerking Quinn out of her trance and replacing it with guilt. She couldn't give in. Sam cared too much. And so did she, but not in the way he wanted.

"We'll talk about this later," she said as the racket outside the door escalated.

"You bet we will." He set his jaw and opened the door, striding out ahead of her.

Quinn followed, her heart and body aching. She immersed herself in taking drink and snack orders from the bikers crowding around four-tops and stroking cues around the two pool tables, but being busy didn't distract her mind. When she wasn't detouring every trip around the room to peer out the front door to see if Nick had arrived, she was fretting over Sam.

He was her best friend and more. The son of a goddess, he'd been fresh out of college when he came to her six years ago looking for a job. He'd designed his education around becoming his mother's assistant, but she'd died soon after graduation. Sam believed she'd put too much wear and tear on her body using her power to help others. Since he couldn't save her, he'd found Quinn.

She poured a pitcher of light beer for a group of Tuesday regulars and watched Sam help Katie deliver a full tray to a celebrating bowling team. He'd become indispensable within three months of her hiring him. He did research for the full-moon jobs on topics as wide-ranging as agriculture, medicine, geometry, and psychology. He also managed the bar and her schedule—managed *her* so she didn't deplete her resources too fast or take on jobs she shouldn't.

He caught her watching as he carried the tray back behind the bar and flashed a dimple. She couldn't help smiling back, but then quickly bent to wipe down an empty table.

When she needed to recharge during the full moon, he

volunteered. He joked that it was the best perk of the job, but they never discussed a long-term plan, assuming they'd take things as they came. Like Sam would meet someone he wanted to be with, and they'd stop.

But it hadn't happened. Quinn realized that Sam didn't flirt with any of the women who came through the bar, and he kept his relations with her staff professional. He never pushed her when it wasn't full moon. There was only one reason a guy would settle for that, and she couldn't give him what he needed.

She considered and discarded a dozen speeches as she drew ale, poured whiskey, and brushed up against Sam whenever she had to get to the register. She was acutely aware of the tightness of her nipples, the sensitivity between her legs that grew whenever their bodies were near. As the moon rose, even as weak as it was, it tugged on her like the tides. Desire surged and ebbed, but it took concentration on her lingering guilt to force the latter.

The bikers, transients who'd been well behaved and heavy tippers, waved as they left at twelve thirty. To Quinn's relief, the place was empty of customers within fifteen minutes. For a moment, she watched the waitresses and busboy wiping down tables and flipping chairs while Sam counted cash at the old-fashioned register.

Resigned to the coming confrontation and wanting to get it over with, she said, "Why don't you guys go home? We can handle the rest of this." No one argued. As they filed out, chorusing their good nights, Quinn braced herself for Sam's first salvo.

"Did you talk to Nick again?" he asked, surprising her.

"No." She ducked under the bar pass-through and crossed to the door to lock it, peering out the small pane of glass onto the gravel lot for the millionth time. "I tried to call, but I still can't get through."

"He's never come this early before." Sam flipped one of the heavy oak chairs up onto a hewn and polished tabletop. "What do you think is going on?"

"There's no point speculating." She went to the other side of the room to help him. "Let's not start listing all the possible reasons. That's too stressful." She didn't want to tell Sam that Nick had told her to stay close to him. That would increase his worry and maybe keep him from going home. She desperately needed some space to get through the next few hours without giving in to the moon lust.

"Okay. So we'll talk about us." Sam pulled down a chair and sat in front of her.

"Can I say no?"

He just looked at her.

"Fine." She sighed and half sat on a nearby table. Sam waited, his eyebrows raised, his mouth cocked, as if he already knew what she was going to say and found it absurd.

"You're twenty-eight, Sam."

"I know how old I am."

Quinn folded her arms. "I'm ten years older than you."

"I know how old you are, too."

"I don't want to keep you from fulfilling your destiny."

He chuckled, shaking his head. "And what's my destiny?"

"It doesn't matter." She steeled herself, ignoring the slow roll of need in her gut. "It's not me."

He sobered. "Quinn…"

"No, Sam." She made an effort to keep her voice steady. "You deserve a chance to find someone right for you. But that's not the main issue." She sighed. "It's time."

She didn't want to talk about the way he'd been watching her. She recognized something in him that she'd buried deep inside herself, didn't even acknowledge anymore. The belief that there was nothing else out there that could give him what he was missing. She'd tried to fill a hole in herself with Sam, using the moon lust as an excuse, not realizing it or seeing that she was creating a matching hole in him. And now she couldn't believe she'd been so blind and selfish.

"I don't get it." He spread his arms wide. "I'm not looking for someone else!"

"That's the problem!" she shot back. "I'm holding you back from finding something real and lasting. A relationship with a woman who won't relegate you to one week every month, for one thing."

A muscle in his jaw twitched. "You need me."

He meant it in a general sense, but it resonated physically. Need of the more carnal variety pulsed in half a dozen places. Quinn clenched her thighs, shifted her folded arms, and fought the impulse to reassure him. She'd told him the first week he worked for her that she would never lie to him. If she said she didn't need him, he'd recognize the deception, and that would hurt him more than not being needed would.

"I'm not going to die if I don't have sex," she said instead. "I've managed three months already."

"Yeah, and it took its toll. You had to work harder to do the same things this month, didn't you?"

"No." That wasn't a lie, but it wasn't completely true, either. When Sam raised his eyebrows, she said, "I got tired faster. But I need more sleep, that's all. I should be able to manage this another way." Frustrated, she pulled the bar towel off her shoulder and slapped it on the tabletop behind her.

"You've tried," Sam said. "You told me so, back when you first hired me. It never worked, and the need grew. So why do you think it will be different now?"

"Because I'm older."

"And more powerful. Wouldn't that make the need worse?"

Damn him, he had an answer for everything. "I'll find someone else." Her gut twisted. The consequence of her heritage would be much easier to deal with if she didn't care whom she slept with, but she always had. As much as it balanced her physically, sex with strangers or acquaintances left her more emotionally bereft, especially after her parents died.

Then came Sam. He'd filled so many holes in her life. Business manager, friend, family. Quinn knew that if she let him, he'd take that even further, marry her and raise children with her, and as blissful as the fantasy was, it would never be as perfect as he wanted it to be. She couldn't love him the way he deserved to be loved.

"Who else?" He spread his hands and looked around. "Where are you going to find a guy like me? Available whenever you need him, able to take what you give—and give what you demand—and be safe? Not in here, I'll tell you that much."

Quinn didn't respond. He was right. She'd tried before. She'd figured one-night stands were every guy's dream, so it would be easy. But too much got in the way. Locals wanted her to do it on their schedule. Basic standards, like avoiding disease and not having sex with attached men, were impossible if she targeted travelers. Most of all, though, was the compulsion that grew as she got older and used more power. The sexual need for mental and physical balance wasn't something she could rein in once unleashed. Sam was the only man who had managed to withstand the intensity long-term. The only one who hadn't called her a freak.

Sam sprawled in his chair in front of her, his long legs so close, the frayed cuff of his jeans brushed her ankle. To keep from moving away, she gripped the edge of the table until her knuckles cracked. Retreat would be an admission that she couldn't handle it. "I've managed fine so far."

"Have you?" He held out a hand, a knowing in his eyes that she couldn't refute. The moon had risen hours ago, close enough to last quarter that she could do only the smallest tasks, but it fed her passion.

I have. The words caught in her throat. Her palms itched,

wanting her to reach out and touch him. Take in the smoothness of his hot skin, get her close enough to breathe him in again. She'd climb onto his lap with the friction of denim on denim, his hard thighs between her legs, the rails of the chair digging into her knees. For an instant, the image was so real she thought she'd done it, given in. She blinked and found herself still standing, the involuntary ache almost unbearable. She curled her fists harder around the table edge until her knuckles ached, determined not to make the hallucination reality. She finally managed a nod to answer his question.

"Really." He pushed out of the chair and slowly unfolded his body to stand inches away, deliberately testing her. She held herself still, hoping he couldn't see the pounding of her heart beneath her white button-down shirt. She closed her eyes as he gathered her in to him, his arms loose around her back.

Her hands rose to rest against his chest. Her fingertips dug in to the resistant muscle, and her breath came out almost as a groan. Tension eased out of him as her body gave in, relief sending tingles head to toe as it curved toward him. "Dammit, Sam." Her thoughts blurred under the intensity of Sam's body heat. She couldn't fight it anymore. Fight him.

"Tell me what you want, Quinn." His voice rumbled through the swishing, thumping pulse in her ears. She dragged her focus back from the soft fabric beneath her palms, the delicious pressure of his hardness against her belly.

"What?" she managed to gasp.

"I'll do what you want. Whatever you want." His lips brushed her ear. Tingles erupted and danced across her skin, but what he'd said, what he was doing, penetrated. The offer wasn't just for wild sex. Though he could take advantage of the lust raging through her, he respected her decision. Which brought home all the reasons he didn't deserve the wrong choice.

She leaned back, unable to look at him, her arms trembling with the effort of denying them both. The guilt almost overwhelmed the need. "I'm sorry, Sam."

He eased away, his hands sliding from her back to her upper arms, making sure she was steady, and then dropping when he'd put a foot of space between their bodies. "You're sure." Not a question.

Quinn nodded and finally met his eyes, regretting the sorrow she'd put there. "I have to do this. Please, please understand."

He sighed and twisted to replace his chair on the tabletop. He stood with his back to her for a long moment, one hand still on the leg of the chair, before facing her again. "I won't push anymore. Just…promise me you won't…" He waved a hand. "You know. Get yourself into trouble."

Her voice squeezed past the burning thickness in her throat. "I promise."

They worked in silence to finish closing, their usual easy tandem punctuating the finality of her decision.

When they were done, Sam nodded and looked around, hands on his hips, clearly at a loss. "Okay. I guess I'm going home, then. You're all right?"

Nick had told her to stick close to Sam, but there was no way she could ask him to stay now. She wished she knew how much longer Nick would be.

"I'm fine," she lied. "Thanks." She nudged him toward the door, turning him away from her so he couldn't see the tears filling her eyes. "I'll see you tomorrow."

"Lock up after I leave."

She closed the door hard behind him and twisted the lock so he'd hear it, then pulled down the blind. Sobs pushed upward from deep within her and she sank to the floor, covering her mouth to keep the sound from reaching Sam, whose presence she still felt on the other side of the wood. Finally, his boots crunched on the gravel, growing fainter with each step. When the familiar hum of his Camaro faded, she allowed herself to break down.

• • •

Quinn slept late the next morning. Her night had been full of erotic dreams, interrupted by abrupt waking to check the clock and try to call Nick, to no avail. Hoping some combination of rest, nutrition, and physical exertion would purge her system of the moon lust, she followed a workout with oatmeal and a shower. She was relieved, when she was done, to find herself less *hungry*. It wasn't gone, but she could distract herself with work and by this time next week, maybe she'd be back to normal.

She took a deep breath before heading down the rickety staircase hugging the side of the building. Sam's schedule had him there by ten or eleven most mornings, but she wasn't sure what to expect after last night. Maybe he'd call in sick, or have cleaned out his things and left a letter of resignation on her desk. Maybe, in trying to preserve the most valuable thing in her life, she'd destroyed it.

Bracing one hand on the rough wood planks of the outer wall, Quinn yanked on the warped back door, taking a moment to prop it wide and let in the sunlight and crisp October breeze. Not stalling. Just…setting up.

She paused on the threshold to let her eyes adjust to the dim office. Her desk was how she'd left it the night before, with piles of invoices and orders to approve, checks to sign, and client files to review. Dust floated in the beam of sunlight that hit the floor in front of her feet. Quinn forced herself to look deeper into the room to Sam's desk, usually as full as hers, if more neatly organized. She held her breath as her vision sharpened, and movement turned into Sam's hand making sharp notations on a printed spreadsheet. He flipped open a file and tapped a few keys on his keyboard without looking up at her.

"How long did you sleep?" he asked.

Breathing was suddenly easier than anything she'd done so far today. Sam asked her that every damned morning. "Eight hours, thirty-three minutes." Her perfect internal clock had amused and delighted him at first, then became nagging when he used it to manage her, whether over how long she'd slept, gone without eating, or focused on a client. But that was what he was paid for, after all, and she welcomed the symbol of normalcy. He nodded his approval and kept working. Quinn went to her desk and booted up her computer.

Sam said, "You hear from Nick?"

"No." The ongoing lack of contact after the urgency of his call scared her. "Sam, I—"

He shoved to his feet and headed out front. "We're low on vodka. I'll pull some up."

Quinn sighed and slumped. So much for normalcy.

It didn't get better. Sam worked out front while she stayed in the office. When she went into the bar, he retreated to the back. She stopped trying to talk to him, hoping the space would be a buffer both for their personal and professional relationships, and for her fading moon lust.

There was still no word from Nick.

Finally, Quinn settled herself in a corner of the bar with her laptop to handle stuff that had piled up over the week, hoping her full e-mail in-box and the routine work, the easy decisions, would keep her eyes off the clock. Requests for appointments and vendor info she forwarded to Sam. Most of the rest was related to the Society. Quinn served as the board's secretary, and many of her personal e-mails were about the annual Society meeting next week. Those she moved into a folder to address later. The official Society list e-mail was full of political posts, with elections coming up in November, but she skimmed and deleted most of them.

She'd gotten into such a rhythm that when Nick's name appeared, it was a moment before her reaction caught up. The words were innocuous at first, so she didn't understand the fear filling her until it merged with her ongoing low-level anxiety over last night's phone call.

I plan to ask Quinn to put this on the agenda for the meeting, but I thought you should all know ahead of time, so you can be careful.

Nick Jarrett's gone rogue.

Quinn pulled her cell phone out of her pocket to try to reach Nick yet again. This had to be why he was coming here—but what the hell did it mean and what did it have to do with her?

A crash on the other side of the room redirected her alarm. She was on her feet before she'd even spotted the source of the disruption.

"I'll goddamn keep drinking if I wanna keep drinking!" An old man, greasy gray hair hanging below a dingy trucker cap, wobbled in front of his overturned chair, arms flailing. Despite his obvious intoxication, his aim was good enough to hit Katie's tray and send glasses flying. Quinn stormed across the room, glaring at anyone who looked like they might want to join the fight. None of her regulars moved. Most had seen her in action, and they didn't want to get involved. A few strangers half rose but subsided when they saw her striding to the rescue.

Not that Katie needed rescuing. Nearly as tall as Quinn's five feet ten, the young woman had honed her manner and strength in New York City. By the time Quinn reached them, Katie was quietly telling the drunk how he was expected to behave in Under the Moon.

Quinn's heart rate and footsteps slowed, ready to back up her waitress but also willing to let her handle it. Then the drunk fumbled a switchblade out of his pocket and flicked it open.

Shit. She lurched forward, but she was still too far away to do anything, and Katie hadn't noticed the knife. Reacting on instinct rather than thought, Quinn snapped her fingers and opened her hand as the knife soared to it. Relief flooded her. *Concentrate. This isn't over yet.* She squeezed the handle of the knife so no one could see her shaking.

The drunk waved his hand, then frowned when he realized it was empty. "What the—" He looked up and blinked at Quinn. "How'd you do that?"

Quinn signaled a white-faced Katie to step away. She glanced around to be sure everyone was out of reach and then faced the drunk.

"You want to leave my establishment," she told him with forced calm.

He scowled. "T'hell I do. I ordered a beer! And I'm not leavin' till I get it!"

"Yes you are." She jerked back as the man lunged at her, flicking her fingers at him. He slammed into an invisible wall but only grew angrier. Quinn swallowed hard. She didn't have the power for more than this, and she couldn't risk her staff getting hurt. Summoning the knife and stopping the drunk's movement required only a little access to the waning moon. But because it had already passed the zenith of its arc, even this drained her.

She had enough for one more act. *Please let it be enough.* She thought *heat* and pointed at the sleeve of the man's denim jacket. A second later it caught fire. He yelled and slapped at it, extinguishing the flame almost immediately, but it had done its job.

His eyes wide, he tried to back away. The overturned chair tripped him up and he stopped. "What are you?" His voice quavered.

Electric awareness alerted Quinn to the presence of the man two feet behind her before she heard his voice, a slight Texas drawl mellowing the deep rumble that always made her think of his perfectly tuned muscle car.

"She's a goddess."

"Goddess," the drunk scoffed. "Them's just a myth."

Nick Jarrett stepped past Quinn, standing between her and the drunk without making it look like he was getting in her way. The hunger that had been easing all day flared, but because she'd never recharged with Nick, she was able to stamp it down more easily than she had last night.

"You don't believe your own eyes?" Nick said to the drunk.

The drunk scowled at them, then at the tiny wisp of smoke rising from his sleeve. He blinked blearily and stumbled toward the door, grumbling under his breath.

"That's what I thought." Nick swung around to look at her, a hint of a smile on his full lips and welcome in his green eyes. "Nice parlor tricks."

Quinn snorted, covering how happy and relieved she was to see him, and turned to her busboy. "Catch that guy and call Charlie to pick him up in his cab, will you?"

"Sure." He pulled out his cell phone and hit speed dial on his way out. Everyone else dispersed, leaving Quinn relatively alone with Nick. Adrenaline drained out of her, and she would have sat, if showing weakness in front of him wasn't so unappealing.

"So what's going on?" She tucked her fingertips into her jeans pockets. The anxiety buzzing in her all day disappeared, allowing the alarm triggered by the e-mail to resurge. "You're never early."

"We've got a problem."

Quinn watched him scan the room, cataloging her customers and staff, lingering on her computer in the far corner and the closed door to her office. His face tightened, and he moved a step closer.

"I know we do," she said.

He whipped his head around, his eyes sharp. "You do?"

"I just found out. Come here." She led him to the table where her computer slept, its screen dark. "I read this e-mail not five minutes ago." They sat down, and she tapped a key to wake the computer while Nick signaled for a beer.

They waited for the wireless connection to reestablish. "You getting a lot of trouble like that guy?" he asked.

"No more than usual." She glanced at him. "Why? Is someone else?"

"Nah." He stood to pull off his battered, hip-length brown leather coat and hang it over the back of the chair, then rolled the sleeves of his flannel shirt up strong forearms. A waitress sashayed over to set an amber bottle on their table. She looked at Quinn, who shook her head, but Nick made a face and dropped the money on her tray. "Don't listen to her."

Quinn didn't bother to argue. They had the same argument every time he came. Sometimes she won, sometimes he did. It balanced in the end.

Nick sat back down and took a pull of the beer, his strong throat working with the swallow. Light from a nearby candle picked up glints of gold in his short-cropped, dark blond hair. "Where's Sam?"

Quinn cleared her throat. "In the office." She diverted her eyes to the computer screen but heard his small snort of derision. "I had it under control, Nick."

"The moon's waning, Quinn. I don't care how powerful you are at peak, you're tapped out by this time—"

"Not completely. And protecting me isn't Sam's job." She winced, realizing too late it might sound like criticism of Nick, and she hadn't meant it to be.

He froze, the bottle halfway to his mouth, then set it down. "I told you to stick close. He should be out here. Or you shouldn't. And I'm not listening to you argue with me. What have you got?" He turned the computer toward him, ignoring her exasperation.

She twisted to read the e-mail with him, now more confused by the words on the screen than anything else. "Well?"

Seconds passed while his eyes tracked over the words. "Fuck

me," he said softly. "That's not the problem I was talking about at all."